PENGUIN BOOKS

THE
BRIDGE
KINGDOM

Danielle L. Jensen is the *USA Today* bestselling author of The Malediction Novels, the Dark Shores series, and The Bridge Kingdom series. She lives in Calgary, Alberta with her family and guinea pigs.

Follow her on the web at:
https://danielleljensen.com
TikTok: https://www.tiktok.com/@daniellelynnjensen
Facebook: https://www.facebook.com/authordanielleljensen
Instagram: https://www.instagram.com/danielleljensen

30108 035844492

THE
BRIDGE
KINGDOM

BY *USA TODAY* BESTSELLING AUTHOR

DANIELLE L. JENSEN

PENGUIN BOOKS

PENGUIN BOOKS

UK | USA | Canada | Ireland | Australia
India | New Zealand | South Africa

Penguin Books is part of the Penguin Random House group of companies
whose addresses can be found at global.penguinrandomhouse.com

First published in the United States of America by
Context Literary Agency, LLC 2018
First published in Great Britain by Penguin Books 2022
002

Copyright © Danielle L. Jensen, 2018

Cover Artwork Illustration by Richard Anderson
Cover Design by Silver Wing Press, LLC
Interior Formatting by Silver Wing Press, LLC
Cover produced in association with Audible Originals, LLC
Printed and bound in Great Britain by Clays Ltd, Elcograf S.p.A.

The authorized representative in the EEA is Penguin Random House Ireland,
Morrison Chambers, 32 Nassau Street, Dublin D02 YH68

A CIP catalogue record for this book is available from the British Library

ISBN: 978-1-405-95585-0

www.greenpenguin.co.uk

Also by

USA TODAY BESTSELLING AUTHOR

DANIELLE L. JENSEN

THE MALEDICTION TRILOGY
Stolen Songbird
Hidden Huntress
Warrior Witch
The Broken Ones (Prequel)

THE DARK SHORES SERIES
Dark Shores
Dark Skies
Gilded Serpent
Tarnished Empire (Prequel)

THE BRIDGE KINGDOM SERIES
The Bridge Kingdom
The Traitor Queen
The Inadequate Heir

https://danielleljensen.com/

HARENDELL
AMARID
NORTHWATCH
THE TEMPEST SEAS
GAMIRE
ERANAHL
MIDWATCH
KESTARK
SOUTHWATCH
VENCIA
MARIDRINA
RED DESERT
NERASTIS
PYRINAT
VALCOTTA

L ARA RESTED HER elbows on the low sandstone wall, her eyes fixed on the glowing sun descending over the distant mountain peaks, nothing between here and there but scorching sand dunes, scorpions, and the occasional lizard. Impassable for anyone without a good camel, the correct provisions, and a healthy dose of luck.

Not that she hadn't been tempted to try more than once.

A gong was struck, the reverberations echoing over the compound. It had called her to dinner every night for the last fifteen years, but tonight, it rattled through her like a war drum. Lara took a deep breath to steady her nerves, then turned, striding across the training yard in the direction of the towering palms, her rose-colored skirts whispering against her legs. All eleven of her half sisters were converging on the same place, each dressed in a different gown, the color carefully selected by their Mistress of Aesthetics to complement their features.

Lara detested pink, but no one had asked for her opinion.

After fifteen years caged within the compound, tonight would be the sisters' last here together, and their Master of Meditation had ordered them to spend the hour before dinner in a favored location, contemplating all they had learned and all they would accomplish with the tools they'd been given.

Or at least, what *one* of them would accomplish.

The scent of the oasis drifted over Lara on the faintest of breezes. The smell of fruits and leafy things, the char of cooking meat, and, above all, water. Precious, precious water. The compound was located on one of the few springs in the midst of the Red Desert, but far off caravan routes. Isolated. Secret.

Just the way their father, the King of Maridrina, liked it. And from what she'd been told about him, he was a man who always got what he wanted, one way or another.

Pausing at the edge of the training yard, Lara brushed the bottoms of her feet against her calves, dusting off the sand before sliding on delicate, high-heeled sandals, her balance as steady as though she wore combat boots.

Click, click, click. Her heels echoed the frantic beat of her heart as she walked down the pathway of mosaic tile and crossed the small bridge, the gentle sound of stringed instruments rising above the gurgle of water. The musicians had arrived with her father's entourage to provide the entertainment for tonight's festivities.

She doubted they'd be making the return journey.

A bead of sweat trickled down her back, the strap holding a knife against her inner thigh already damp. *You will not die tonight*, she silently chanted. *Not tonight*.

Lara and her sisters converged on the center of the oasis, a courtyard encircled by the spring, which turned it into an island of greenery. They walked toward the enormous table draped with silk and heavy with the silverware required for the dozen or more courses waiting in the wings. Servants, all of them mute, stood behind the thirteen chairs, eyes fixed on their feet. As the women approached, they drew the chairs back, and Lara sat without looking, knowing the rose-colored cushion would be beneath her.

None of the sisters spoke.

Underneath the table, Lara felt a hand grip hers. She allowed her eyes to flick to her left, briefly meeting Sarhina's gaze, before returning to her plate. All twelve of them were the King's daughters, now twenty years of age, each born by a different one of his wives. Lara and her half sisters had been brought to this secret place to undergo training that no Maridrinian girl had ever before received. Training that was now complete.

Lara's stomach twisted sour, and she dropped Sarhina's hand, the feel of her closest sister's skin, cool and dry relative to her own, making her want to be sick.

The gong sounded again, and the musicians went silent as the girls rose to their feet. A heartbeat later, their father appeared, his silver hair gleaming in the lamplight as he traversed the path toward them, his azure eyes identical to those of every girl present. Sweat ran in rivulets down Lara's legs even as her training had her take in every detail. The indigo of his coat. The worn leather of his boots. The sword belted at his waist. And, as he turned to walk around the table, the faintest outline of the blade hidden along his spine.

When he sat, Lara and her sisters followed suit, none of them making a sound.

"Daughters." Leaning back in his chair, Silas Veliant, the King of Maridrina, smiled, waited for his taster to nod, then took a long mouthful of wine. All of them mirrored the motion, but Lara barely tasted the crimson liquid as it crossed her tongue.

"You are my most prized of possessions," he said, waving his glass to encompass them all. "Of the twenty of my progeny who were brought here, you are all that survive. That you do, that you *thrive*, is an achievement, for the training you've received would've been a test for the best of men. And you are not men."

It was only that very training that kept Lara from narrowing her eyes. From showing any emotion at all.

"All of you were brought here so that I might determine which of you is best. Which of you will be my knife in the dark. Which of you will become Queen of Ithicana." His eyes had all the compassion of one of the scorpions in the desert. "Which of you will fracture Ithicana's defenses, and, in doing so, allow Maridrina to return to its former glory."

Lara nodded once, all of her sisters doing the same. There was no anticipation. At least, not for their father's choice. It had been made days ago, and Marylyn sat at the opposite end of the table, her golden hair braided like a crown at her brow, her dress lamé to match. Marylyn had been the obvious choice, brilliant, gracious, beautiful as the sunrise—and as alluring as the sunset.

No, the anticipation was for what would come next. The choice had been made as to who would be offered to the crown prince—king, now—of the Kingdom of Ithicana. What remained unknown was what would become of the rest of them. They were of royal blood, and that made them worth something.

All the sisters, Marylyn included, had gathered close on a pile of pillows the last two nights, each of them speculating as to their fates. To whom of the King's viziers might they be wed. To which other realms might they be offered as brides. Neither the man nor the kingdom mattered. What every girl cared about was that it would be freedom from this place.

But all those long nights, Lara had rested on the outskirts, offering nothing, using the time to watch her sisters. To love them. To remember how she had fought each of them as often as she had hugged them tight. Their smiles. Their eyes. The way, even past childhood, they nestled together like a pile of puppies newly away from their mother.

Because Lara knew what the others did not: that their father intended for only *one* sister to leave the compound. And that would be the future Queen of Ithicana.

A salad garnished with cheese and vibrant fruit was placed before her, and Lara ate mechanically. *You will live, you will live, you will live*, she chanted to herself.

"For as long as memory, Ithicana has placed a stranglehold on trade, making kingdoms and breaking them like it were some dark god." Her father addressed them, his eyes flaring bright. "My father, and his father, and his father before him all sought to break the Bridge Kingdom. With assassins, with war, with blockades, with every tool at their disposal. But not one of them thought to use a woman."

He smiled slyly. "Maridrinian women are soft. They are weak. They are good for nothing more than keeping house and raising children. Except for you twelve."

Lara didn't blink. None of her sisters did, and she wondered for a breath whether he realized that every one of them was considering stabbing him in the heart over the insult of his words. He should know well that every one of them was capable of doing it.

Her father continued, "Fifteen years ago, the King of Ithicana demanded a bride for his son and heir as tribute. As *payment*." His lip curled up in a sneer. "The bastard is a year dead, but his son has called in his due. And Maridrina is ready." His eyes went to Marylyn, then to the servants moving to clear the salad plates.

In the shadows of the growing night, Lara sensed movement. Felt the presence of the mass of soldiers her father had brought with him. The servants reappeared with steaming bowls of soup, the scent of cinnamon and leeks drifting ahead of them.

"Ithicana's greed, its hubris, its contempt for *you*, will be its downfall."

Lara allowed her eyes to leave her father's face, taking in each one of her sisters. With all their training, all their knowledge of his plans, he never intended for any of them, save his chosen one, to live an hour past this dinner.

The soups were placed before them, and every one of her sisters waited for their father's taster to take the first mouthful and nod. Then they picked up their spoons and dutifully began to eat.

Lara did the same.

Their father believed that brilliance and beauty were the most important attributes in the daughter he'd select. That she be the girl who'd shown the most acumen for combat and strategy. The girl who'd shown the most talent in the arts of the bedroom. He'd thought he'd known which traits mattered most—but he'd forgotten one.

Sarhina stiffened next to her.

I'm sorry, Lara silently whispered to her sisters.

Then Sarhina's body began to spasm.

I pray that you'll all find the freedom you deserve.

The soupspoon in Sarhina's hand went flying across the table, but none of the other girls noticed. None of them cared. Because all of them were choking, foam rising to their lips as they twitched and gasped, one by one falling forward or backward or to the side. Then all of them were resting motionless.

Lara set her spoon next to her empty bowl, looking once to Marylyn, who was facedown in her dish. Rising, she rounded the table, lifting her sister's head from the bowl and carefully cleaning away the soup before resting Marylyn's cheek against the table. When Lara looked up again, her father was pale and on his feet, sword half drawn. The soldiers who'd been lurking in the wings rushed forward, corralling the panicked servants into place. But everyone, *everyone*, was staring at her.

"You were mistaken in your choice, Father." Lara stood tall as she addressed her king. She stared him down, allowing the dark, grasping, and selfish part of her soul to climb to the surface and stare out at him. "*I* will be the next Queen of Ithicana. And I will bring the Bridge Kingdom to its knees."

L ARA HAD KNOWN what would come next, but it seemed to happen so very quickly. And yet she was certain every detail would be burned into her mind until the day she died. Her father slammed his sword back into its sheath, then reached down to press his fingers against the throat of the nearest girl, holding them there for several moments while Lara watched impassively. Then he nodded once at the soldiers surrounding them.

The men who'd been intended to dispatch Lara and her sisters turned their swords instead on the servants, whose tongueless mouths uttered wordless screams as they tried to flee the massacre. The musicians were cut down, as were the cooks in the distant kitchens and the maids turning down sheets on beds that would never be slept in again. Soon, all who remained were the king's loyal cadre of soldiers, their hands coated with the blood of their victims.

Through this, Lara remained still. Only the knowledge that she was the sole remaining daughter—that she was the last horse *left* to bet on—kept her from fighting her way free of the carnage and fleeing into the desert beyond.

Erik, the Master of Arms, approached through the palms, blade glistening in his hand. His eyes went from Lara to her sisters' still forms, and he gave her a sad smile. "I'm not surprised to find you still standing, little cockroach."

It was the endearment he'd bestowed upon her when she'd arrived, five years old and barely alive, thanks to a sandstorm that had befallen her party on their trek to the compound. "Ice and fire might ravage the world, but still the cockroach survives," he'd said. "Just like you."

Cockroach she might be, but that she still breathed was thanks to him. Erik had dispatched her to the training yard as punishment for a minor transgression two nights prior, and she'd overheard members of her father's cadre plotting the deaths of her and her sisters. A conversation led by Erik himself. Her eyes burned as she regarded him—the man who'd been more a father to her than the silver-haired monarch to her right—but she said nothing, gave him not so much as a smile in return.

"Is it done?" her father asked.

Erik nodded. "All have been silenced, Your Majesty. Save myself." Then his eyes flicked to the shadows not touched by the table's lamps. "And the *Magpie*."

From those shadows stepped her Master of Intrigue, and Lara coolly regarded the wisp of a man who had orchestrated every aspect of the evening.

And in the nasal voice she'd always loathed, the Magpie said, "The girl did most of the dirty work for you."

"Lara should have been your choice all along." Erik's voice was toneless, but grief filled his eyes as they passed over the fallen girls before returning to Lara's face.

Lara wanted to reach for her knife—how *dare* he grieve them when he'd done nothing to save them—but a thousand hours of training commanded her not to move. He bowed low to his king. "For Maridrina." Then he pulled his knife across his own throat.

Lara clenched her teeth, the contents of her stomach rising, bitter and foul and full of the same poison she'd given her sisters. Yet she didn't look away, forcing herself to watch as Erik slumped to the ground, blood pulsing from his throat in great gouts until his heart went still.

The Magpie stepped around the pool of blood and coming fully into the light. "Such dramatics."

Magpie wasn't his real name, of course. It was Serin, and of all the men and women who'd trained the sisters over the years, he was the only one who'd come and gone from the compound at his leisure, managing the king's network of spies and plots.

"He was a good man. A loyal subject." There was no inflection in her father's voice, and Lara wondered if he meant the words, or if they were for the benefit of the soldiers watching the proceedings. Even the most stalwart loyalty had its limits, and her father was no fool.

The Magpie's narrow eyes turned on her. "Lara, as you know, Majesty, was not my first choice. She scored close to the bottom in nearly all things, with the lone exception of combat. Her temper continually gets the better of her. Marylyn"—he gestured to her sister—"was the obvious choice. Brilliant and beautiful. Masterfully in control of her emotions, as she *clearly* demonstrated over the past several days." He made a noise of disgust.

Everything he said about Marylyn was true, but it wasn't the sum of her. Unbidden, memories flooded through Lara's mind. Visions of her sister carefully caring for a runt kitten, which was now the fattest cat in the compound. Of how she'd listen quietly to any of her sisters' troubles, then offer the most perfect advice. Of how, as a child, she'd given names to all the servants, because she'd thought it cruel that they should have none. Then the visions cleared, leaving only a still body before her, golden hair crusted with soup.

"My sister was too kind." Lara turned her head back to her father, her heart skittering in her chest even as she challenged him. "The future Queen of Ithicana must seduce its ruler. Make him believe she is guileless and sincere. She must make him trust her even as she uses her position to learn his every weakness right up to the moment she betrays him. Marylyn was not that woman."

Her father's eyes were unblinking as he studied her, and he gave the faintest nod of approval. "But you are?"

"I am." Her pulse roared in her ears, her skin clammy despite the heat.

"You are not often wrong, Serin," her father said. "But in this, I believe you were mistaken and fate has intervened in order to rectify that mistake."

The Master of Intrigue stiffened, and Lara wondered if he was now realizing that his own life hung in the balance. "As you say, Majesty. It seems Lara possesses a quality that I'd not considered in my testing."

"The most important quality of all: ruthlessness." The king studied her for a moment before turning back to the Magpie. "Ready the caravan. We ride for Ithicana tonight." Then he smiled at her as though she were the most precious of things. "It's time for my daughter to meet her future husband."

FLAMES LICKED THE night sky as the group departed, but Lara only risked one backward glance at the burning compound that had been her home, the blood-spattered floors and walls blackening as the fire consumed all evidence of a plot fifteen years in the making. Only the heart of the oasis, where the dinner table sat encircled by the spring, would remain untouched.

It was still almost more than she could bear to leave her slumbering sisters surrounded by a ring of fire, unconscious and helpless until the concoction of narcotics she'd given them wore off. Already their pulses, which had been slowed to near death for a dangerous length of time, should be quickening, their breathing obvious to anyone who looked closely. If Lara found excuses to linger to ensure their safety, she would only risk discovery, and then all of this would be for naught.

"Don't burn them. Leave them for the scavengers to pick their bones clean," she'd told her father, her stomach twisting into knots until he'd laughed and acceded to her macabre request, leaving her sisters slumped over the table, the slaughtered servants forming a gory perimeter around them.

That was what her sisters would wake to: fire and death. For only if their father believed them silenced did they have any chance at a future. She would carry their mission forward while her sisters made their own lives, now free to be masters of their own fates. She'd explained all of it in the note she'd slipped into Sarhina's pocket while her father ordered the compound swept for survivors. For no one must be left alive who might whisper a word about the deception that now journeyed toward a wedding in Ithicana.

Their journey across the Red Desert would be fraught with hardship and peril. But at that precise moment, Lara was convinced the worst part would be listening to the *Magpie's* chatter the entire way. Lara's mare was laden with Marylyn's trousseau, while she was forced to ride pillion behind the Master of Intrigue.

"From this moment forward, you must be the perfect Maridrinian lady," he instructed, his voice grinding on her nerves. "We cannot risk anyone seeing you behave otherwise, not even those His Majesty believes loyal." He cast a meaningful glance toward her father's guards, who'd formed the caravan with practiced ease.

Not a single one looked at her.

They did not know what she was. What she'd been trained to do. What her purpose was beyond the fulfillment of a contract with the enemy kingdom. But every one of them believed she'd murdered her sisters in cold blood. Which made her wonder how long her father would let them live.

"How did you do it?"

Hours into their journey, the Magpie's question pulled Lara from her thoughts, and she tightened her white silk scarf across her face, despite the fact his back was to her. "Poison." She allowed a hint of tartness to enter her voice.

He snorted. "Aren't we bold now that we believe we are untouchable."

She ran her tongue over her dry lips, feeling the heat of the sun rising behind them. Then she allowed herself to slip into the pool of calm her Master of Meditation had taught her to employ when strategizing, among other things. "I poisoned the soupspoons."

"How? You didn't know where you'd be seated."

"I poisoned all, save those set at the head of the table."

The Magpie was silent.

Lara continued, "I've been taking small doses of several poisons for years to build up my tolerance." Even still, she had purged herself the moment she'd had a chance, vomiting again and again until her stomach was dry, then taking the antidote, the dizzying malaise the only lingering sign she'd ingested a narcotic at all.

The Master of Intrigue's tiny frame tensed. "What if the settings had been altered? You might have killed the king."

"She clearly believed it worth the risk."

Lara tilted her head, having noted the jingle of bells on the horse's bridle as her father had ridden up behind, the creature festooned with silver rather than the tin the guards' mounts wore.

"You guessed that I intended to kill the girls I didn't need," he said. "But instead of warning your sisters or attempting to escape, you murdered them to take the chosen's place. Why?"

Because for the girls to fight their way out would've meant a lifetime on the run. Faking their deaths had been the only way. "I may have spent my life in isolation, Father, but the tutors you selected educated me well. I know the hardship that our people endure beneath Ithicana's yoke on trade. Our enemy needs to be brought low, and of my sisters, I was the only one capable of doing it."

"You murdered your sisters for the good of our country?" His voice was amused.

Lara forced a dry chuckle from her lips. "Hardly. I murdered them because I wished to live."

"You gambled with the king's life in order to save your own skin?" Serin turned to look at her, his expression green. He'd trained her, which meant it was within the king's right to blame him for all that she had done. And her father was known to be merciless.

But the King of Maridrina only laughed with delight. "Gambled and *won*." Reaching over, he pushed aside Lara's scarf to cup her cheek. "King Aren won't see you coming until it's far too late. A black widow in his bed."

King Aren of Ithicana. Aren, her soon-to-be husband.

Lara only vaguely heard her father give the order to his guards to make camp, the group intending to sleep through the heat of the day.

One of the guards lifted her off the back of Serin's camel, and she sat on a blanket while the men set up the camp, using the time to think of what was to come.

Lara knew as much as—probably more than—most Maridrinians did about Ithicana. It was a kingdom as shrouded in mystery as it was in mist: a series of islands stretching between two continents, the land masses guarded by violent seas made more treacherous by defenses the Ithicanians had placed in the waters to ward off infiltrators. But that was not what made Ithicana so powerful. It was the bridge stretching above and between those islands—the only safe way to travel between the continents ten months out of the year. And Ithicana used its asset to keep the kingdoms who depended on trade hungry. Desperate. And most of all, willing to pay any price the Bridge Kingdom demanded for its services.

Seeing her tent was erected, Lara waited until the men had placed her bags inside before slipping into the welcome shade, curbing the urge to thank them as she passed.

She was alone for barely the length of time it took to remove her scarf before her father ducked inside, Serin on his heels. "I'll have to begin training you on the codes now," the Master of Intrigue said, waiting until the king was sitting before ensconcing himself in front of Lara. "Marylyn created this code, and I daresay that teaching it to *you* in such a short time will be a challenge."

"Marylyn is dead," she replied, taking a mouthful of tepid water from her canteen before carefully closing it again.

"Don't remind me," he snapped.

Her smile was filled with a confidence she didn't feel. "Come to terms with the fact that *I* am all who remains of the girls you trained, and then I will not need to refresh your memory."

"Begin," her father commanded, and then he closed his eyes, his presence in her tent for propriety's sake, only.

Serin began his instruction on the code. It needed to be entirely committed to memory, as she couldn't bring notes into Ithicana. It was a code she might never even use, its usefulness entirely predicated on the King of Ithicana allowing her the kindness of corresponding with her family. And kindness, she'd been told, was not an attribute the man was known for.

"As you know, the Ithicanians are exemplary codebreakers, and anything you manage to send out will be subject to intense scrutiny. There's every chance they'll break this one."

Lara held up her hand, ticking off her fingers as she spoke. "I should expect to be completely isolated, from both the Ithicanians and from the outside world. I may or may not be allowed to correspond, and even if I am, there is every chance our code will be broken. There is no way for you to reach me to retrieve a message. No way for me to send something through their people, because you've yet to swing the loyalties of a single one." She balled her hand into a fist. "Other than escaping, which means an end to my ability to spy, just how do you expect me to convey the information to you?"

"If this were an easy task, we'd have accomplished it already." Serin extracted a heavy piece of parchment from his satchel. "There is only one Ithicanian who corresponds with the outside world, and that is King Aren himself."

Taking the parchment, which was embossed with Ithicana's crest of the curving bridge, the edges trimmed with gilt, she examined the precise script, which requested that Maridrina deliver a princess to be his bride in accordance of the terms of the Fifteen Year Treaty, as well as an invitation to negotiate new terms of trade between the kingdoms. "You want me to hide a message within one of his?"

He nodded, handing her a jar of clear liquid. *Invisible ink.* "We'll attempt to entice messages from him to give you the opportunity, but he's not prone to frequent correspondence. For that reason, we should return to studying your sister's code."

The lesson was tedious work and Lara was exhausted. It took all her self-control not to sigh with relief when Serin finally departed to his own tent.

Her father rose, yawning.

"Might I ask a question, Your Majesty?" she asked before he could depart.

At his nod, she licked her lips. "Have you seen him? The new

King of Ithicana?"

"No one has seen him. They wear masks, always, when meeting with outsiders." Then her father shook his head. "But I have met him, once. Years ago, when he was only a child."

Lara waited, her palms soaking the silk of her skirts beneath them.

"He is rumored to be even more ruthless than his father before him. A harsh man, who shows no mercy to outsiders." His gaze met hers, and the uncharacteristic pity in his eyes made her hands turn to ice. "I feel he will treat you cruelly, Lara."

"I have been trained to endure pain." Pain and starvation and solitude. Everything that she could possibly face in Ithicana. Taught to endure it and remain true to her mission.

"It may not come in the form of pain, as you understand it." Her father took her hand and turned it over to reveal her palm, studying it. "Be wary most of all of their kindness, Lara. For above all, the Ithicanians are cunning. And their king will give up nothing without demanding his due."

Her heart skipped.

"The heart of our kingdom is caught between the Red Desert and the Tempest Seas, with Ithicana's bridge the only safe route beyond," he continued. "Neither desert nor sea bends to any master, and Ithicana . . . They'd see our people impoverished, starved, and broken before they'd ever allow trade to flow freely." He dropped her hand. "For generations, we've tried everything to make them see reason. To make them see the harm their greed causes the innocent people of our lands. But the Ithicanians are not men, Lara. They are demons hiding in human form. Which I'm afraid you'll find out soon enough."

Watching her father depart the tent, Lara flexed her hands, wanting to wrap them around weapons. To strike out. To maim. To kill.

Not because of his words.

Dire as her father's warning was, it was one she'd heard countless times before. No, it was the slump of his shoulders. The resignation in his tone. The hopelessness that briefly showed itself in his eyes. All signs that despite everything her father had put into this gambit, he didn't truly believe she'd succeed in her mission. As much as Lara detested being underestimated, she hated those who mattered to her being harmed even more. And with her sisters now free of their shackles, nothing mattered to her more than Maridrina.

Ithicana would pay for its crimes against her people, and by the time she was through with its king, he'd do more than *bend*.

He'd bleed.

Another four nights of travel north saw the red sand dunes giving way to rolling hills covered with dry brush and stubby trees, then craggy mountains that seemed to touch the sky. They followed narrow ravines, and slowly, the climate began to shift, the endless brown dirt broken by patches of green and the occasional brilliant bloom of flowers. The dried creek bed they followed turned muddy, and several hours later, the caravan was splashing through sluggish water, but beyond that, the earth was bone dry. Harsh and seemingly unlivable.

Men, women, and children stopped working in their fields to shield their eyes, watching the group pass. They were all skinny, wearing threadbare homespun clothes and wide-brimmed straw hats that shielded them from the ceaseless sun. They survived on the sparse crops and boney cattle they raised; there was no other choice for them. While, in prior generations, families were able to earn enough at their trades to purchase meat and grain imported from Harendell through the bridge, Ithicana's rising taxes and tolls had changed that. Now only the wealthy could afford the goods, and the working class of Maridrina had been forced to abandon their trades for these dry fields in order to feed their children.

Barely feed them, Lara amended, her chest clenched tight as the children ran to line the caravan route, their ribs visibly protruding from beneath their tattered clothes.

"God bless His Majesty," they shouted. "God bless the Princess!" Little girls ran alongside Serin's camel, reaching up to hand her braids of wildflowers, which Lara draped across her shoulders, then across the saddle when they grew too many.

Serin gave her a sack of silver coins to disperse, and it was a struggle to keep her fingers steady as she pressed them into tiny hands.

They learned her name soon enough, and as the muddy creek turned to crystal rapids racing down the slopes toward the sea, they shouted, "Bless Princess Lara! Watch over our beautiful princess!" But it was a growing chant of "Bless Lara, Maridrina's Martyr" that turned her hands cold. That kept her awake long after Serin had finished his lessons each evening, then filled her head with nightmares when sleep finally took her. Dreams where she was trapped by taunting demons, where all her skills had failed her, where no matter what she did, she could not get free. Dreams where Maridrina burned.

And every day, they traveled closer.

As the earth turned lush and moist, the caravan was joined by a larger contingent of soldiers, and Lara was moved from the camel to a blue carriage pulled by a team of white horses, their trappings decorated with the same silver coins as her father's horse. And with the soldiers came a whole retinue of servants tending to Lara's every need, washing and scrubbing and polishing her as they traveled to Maridrina's capital city of Vencia.

Their whispers filtered through her tent walls: that her father had kept the future bride of Ithicana hidden in the desert all these long years for her own safety. That she was a treasured daughter, born of a favored wife, hand-selected by him to unite the two kingdoms in peace, her charm and grace destined to see Ithicana grant Maridrina all the benefits an ally should have, which would allow the kingdom to thrive once more.

The very idea that Ithicana would concede so much was laughable, but Lara felt no amusement at their naiveté. Not as she took in the desperate hope in their eyes. Instead, she carefully stoked her fury, hiding it beneath gentle smiles and graceful waves from the open window of the carriage. It was a strength she needed, given that she'd heard the other whispers, too. "Pity the poor gentle princess," the servants said with sorrow in their eyes. "What will become of her amongst those demons? How will she survive their brutality?"

"Are you afraid?" Her father pulled the carriage curtains closed as they approached the outskirts of Vencia, much to Lara's dismay. It was the city of her birth, and she hadn't seen it since she'd been taken from the confines of the harem and brought to the compound to begin her training at the age of five.

She turned to him. "I'd be a fool not to be afraid. If they discover I'm a spy, they'll kill me and then cancel the trade concessions for spite."

Her father made a noise of agreement, then pulled two knives encrusted with Maridrinian rubies from beneath his coat, handing them to her. Lara recognized them as the ceremonial weapons that Maridrinian women wore to indicate they were wed. They were supposed to be used by a husband in the defense of his wife's honor, but typically they were kept dull. Decorative. Useless.

"They're lovely. Thank you."

He chuckled. "Look more closely."

Pulling them from their sheaths, Lara tested the edges and found them keen, but the balance was off. Then her father reached over and pressed one of the jewels, and the gold casement fell away to reveal a throwing knife.

Lara smiled.

"If they won't allow you to communicate with the outside world, you'll need to bide your time while you learn their secrets, then escape. Perhaps even fight your way free and return to us with what you've learned."

She nodded, flipping the blades back and forth to get the feel of them. There was no chance of her willingly returning to hand-deliver her invasion strategy. To do so would be a death wish.

After learning her father's intention to kill her and her sisters at the dinner, Lara had had time to consider why her father wanted the daughters not destined to be queen dead. It was more than a desire to keep his plot a secret until he'd succeeded in taking the bridge. Her father wanted this plot kept secret *forever*, for if anyone learned of it, his ability to use his other living children as negotiating tools would be negated. No one would ever trust him. Just like he'd never trust her. Which meant if Lara ever returned, successful or not, she too would be silenced.

Her father interrupted her thoughts. "I was there when you girls had your first kills," he said. "Did you know?"

The blades stilled in her hands as Lara remembered. She and her sisters had been sixteen when the line of chained men had been brought to the compound under Serin's watchful eye. They were raiders from Valcotta who'd been captured and brought to test the mettle of Maridrina's warrior princesses. *Kill or be killed*, Master Erik had told them as they were pushed one by one into the fighting yard. Some of her sisters had hesitated and fallen beneath the raider's desperate blows. Lara had not. She would never forget the meaty *thunk* her blade made as it sank into her opponent's throat from across the yard. The way he stared at her in astonishment before slowly collapsing onto the sand, his lifeblood pooling around him.

"I didn't know," she said.

"Knives, as I recall, are your specialty."

Killing was her specialty.

The carriage was rumbling over cobbled streets, the horses' hooves making sharp little sounds against the stone. Outside, Lara heard intermittent cheers, and flicking aside the curtain, she tried to smile at the filthy men and women lining the streets, their faces pale from hunger and illness. Worse were the children among them, eyes dull and hopeless, flies buzzing near their eyes and mouths.

"Why don't you do something for them?" she demanded of her father, whose face was expressionless as he stared out the window.

He turned his azure eyes on her. "Why else do you think I created you?" Then he reached into his pocket and gave her a handful of silver to toss from the window, which she did. She closed her eyes as her impoverished people fought each other for the gleaming metal. She would save them. She would wrest the bridge from Ithicana's control, and no Maridrinian would go hungry again.

The horses slowed, making their way down the steep switchbacking streets to the harbor below. Where the ship waited to take her to Ithicana.

She tugged aside the curtain to get her first look at the sea, the scent of fish and brine on the air. There were whitecaps on the water, the rise and fall of the waves stealing her attention as her father plucked the knives from her hands to be returned when the time was right.

The carriage pulled through a market that appeared nearly devoid of life, the stalls empty. "Where is everyone?" she asked.

Her father's face was dark and unreadable. "Waiting for you to open the gates to Ithicana."

The carriage rolled into the harbor, then came to a stop. There was no ceremony as her father helped her out. The ship awaiting them flew a flag of azure and silver. Maridrina's colors.

He led her swiftly down the dock and up a gangplank onto the ship. "The crossing to Southwatch takes less than an hour. There are servants waiting to prepare you below."

Lara cast one backward glance at Vencia, at the sun burning hot and bright above it, then turned her sights on the clouds and mist and darkness that lay across the narrow strait before her. One kingdom to save. One kingdom to destroy.

L ARA STOOD ON the ship's deck, which lurched and bucked like a wild horse, digging her fingernails into the railing, fighting to keep the contents of her stomach from spilling out into the sea. To make matters worse, raised in the desert, she had never learned to swim—a weakness that had already begun to haunt her. Every time the ship heeled over in the heavy wind, her breath caught with the certainty they'd capsize and drown. The only things that distracted her from visions of waves closing over her head were the more certain dangers facing her.

By tonight, she'd be married. She'd be alone in a foreign kingdom with a reputation for the worst sort of cruelty. The wife of a young man who was lord over it all. *This* was the life she'd been protecting her sisters from, at the sacrifice of her own, and all of it for the sake of her people. But now the consequences of that choice were terrifyingly imminent. Clouds hung low over the white-capped sea, shifting and moving like sentient beasts, but through them, ever so faintly, she could make out the shadow of an island. *Ithicana.*

Her father joined her at the railing. "Southwatch."

His travel-stained clothing had been replaced with a pristine white shirt and black coat, his polished sword hanging from a belt decorated with silver and turquoise disks. "Aren keeps a full garrison of soldiers there at all times, and they have catapults and other war machines trained on the ocean, ready to sink any who'd attempt to take the island. There are spikes set into the seafloor to spear any ship that manages to approach any point other than the pier, which is itself rigged with explosives should they feel it has been compromised. The bridge cannot be taken at its mouth." His jaw tightened. "It's been tried and tried."

Countless ships and thousands of men lost for every attempt. Lara knew the history of the war that had ended fifteen years ago with Ithicana triumphant, but the specifics rose and fell in her mind like the waves on which the ship rode. Her knees were shaky, her whole body weak with seasickness.

"You are the hope of our people, Lara. We need that bridge."

She was afraid if she opened her mouth, she'd spill whatever remained in her stomach overboard, so she only nodded once. The island was in full view now, twin peaks of stone festooned with lush vegetation rising out of the sea. At their base was a lone pier crusted with armaments, a cluster of unadorned stone buildings, and beyond, a single road leading up to the yawning mouth of the bridge itself.

Her father's sleeve brushed her wrist. "Don't for a heartbeat believe that I trust you," he murmured, stealing back her attention. "I saw what you did to your sisters, and while you might claim to have Maridrina foremost in your heart, I know you were motivated by the desire to save your own life."

If saving her own life had been what she'd cared about, she would have faked her own death. But Lara said nothing.

"While your ruthlessness makes you desirable for this role, your lack of honor makes me question whether you'll put our people's lives above your own." Grabbing her arms, he twisted her toward him, nothing on his face betraying that this was anything more than a conversation between a loving father and his daughter. "If you betray me, I will hunt you down. And what I will do to you will make you wish that you'd died alongside your sisters."

The sound of steel drums danced across the sea and into her ears, punctuated by the distant grumble of thunder.

"And what if I succeed?" Her mouth tasted sour, and she turned her head away, taking in the hundreds of figures on the island waiting for the ship. Waiting for her.

"You'll be the savior of Maridrina. You'll be rewarded beyond your wildest dreams."

"I want my freedom." Her tongue felt strangely thick as she spoke. "I want to be left alone, to my devices. Free to go wherever I choose, to do as I will."

One silver eyebrow rose. "How different you and Marylyn are."

"*Were.*"

He inclined his head. "Even so."

"Do we have an agreement then? The bridge in exchange for my freedom?"

His nod was punctuated by a loud boom of thunder. It was a lie, and she knew it. But she could live with his lies because their goals were aligned.

"Drop sails," the captain of the ship bellowed, and Lara gripped the rail as they lost momentum, the sailors running about to make ready to land. The drums continued their beat, pace escalating along with Lara's heart as the ship drifted against the empty pier, sailors leaping the gap to tie off the ship.

The gangplank was lowered, and her father took her arm, leading her toward it. The drumming intensified.

"You have one year." He stepped onto the solid stone of the pier. "Do not falter. Do not fail."

Lara hesitated, dizzy, and, for the first time since the night she'd freed her sisters from their dark fate, desperately afraid. Then she took her first step into the world that was now her new home.

The drums let out a thundering beat, then went still. Holding tight to her father's arm, Lara walked up the pier, biting back a gasp as she took in the masked Ithicanians for the first time.

Their steel helmets were sculpted like raging beasts with mouths full of snarling teeth and brows bearing curved horns. She could see nothing of the men beneath except their eyes, which seemed to glitter with malice as they watched her pass, hands on swords and pikes. No one spoke; the only sounds were the whistle of the wind between the two towers of rock and the call of the storm beyond.

Tearing her eyes from the soldiers, Lara's gaze went down the paved road rising up to the gaping mouth of Ithicana's bridge. It was enclosed like a tunnel, maybe a dozen feet wide and equally as tall, made of a grey stone gone green with exposure to the damp air. A great steel portcullis was raised, the entirety of the bridge's mouth framed by a guardhouse.

A figure stepped out of the dark opening, the steel spikes of the portcullis hanging above him like fangs, and Lara felt her stomach lurch.

The King of Ithicana.

Dressed in trousers, heavy boots, and a tunic of drab greenish gray, he was tall and broad of shoulder. Her training told her that he was as much a soldier as any of those lining the road. But those details were lost, her heart beating staccato, as she took in the helmet that concealed his face. It had a snout like a lion's, open to reveal glittering canines, and horns like a bull sprouting from both temples.

Not a man, a demon.

The lingering dizziness from the voyage passed over her in waves, and with it came fear that possessed her like an angry spirit. The heel of her sandal slid on the stone, and Lara stumbled against her father, the ground feeling as though it were moving beneath her like the rocking ship.

This had been a mistake. A terrible, horrible mistake.

When only a handful of paces stood between them, her father stopped and turned to her. In his free hand was a jeweled belt with her camouflaged throwing knives hooked on either side. He wrapped it around the waist of her sodden gown, fastening the buckle. Then he kissed both her cheeks before turning back to Ithicana's king. "As was agreed upon, I stand here to offer my most precious daughter, Lara, as a symbol of Maridrina's commitment to its continued alliance with Ithicana. May there ever be peace between our kingdoms."

The King of Ithicana nodded once, and her father gave Lara a gentle shove between the shoulders. With halting steps, she walked toward the king, and as she did, a bolt of lightning lanced through the air, the flash making the visage of his helmet seem to move, like it wasn't metal, but flesh.

The drums resumed, a steady and harsh beat: Ithicana incarnate. The king reached out one hand, and though every instinct told her to turn and run, Lara took it.

For reasons she couldn't articulate, she'd expected it to be cold like metal, and equally unyielding—but it was warm. Long fingers curved around hers, the nails cut short. His palm was calloused, the skin, like hers, covered with tiny white scars. The nicks and cuts that couldn't be avoided when combat was one's way of life. She stared at that hand. It offered some strange comfort; what stood before her was nothing more than a man.

And men could be defeated.

A priestess approached on her left and tied an azure ribbon around their hands, binding them together before belting out the Maridrinian marriage vows so that all could hear over the growing storm. Vows of obedience on her part. Vows to create a hundred sons on his. Lara could've sworn she heard a soft snort of amusement from behind the king's helmet.

But as the priestess raised her hands to proclaim them man and wife, he spoke for the first time. "Not yet."

Waving away the startled priestess, he shook loose the ribbon that Lara was supposed to have worn braided into her hair for the first year of their marriage. The silk flew off toward the sea. One of his helmeted soldiers stepped out of the ranks, coming up to stand before them.

He shouted, "Do you, Aren Kertell, King of Ithicana, swear to fight by this woman's side, to defend her to your dying breath, to cherish her body and none other, and to be loyal to her as long as you both live?"

"I do." The king's words were punctuated by the hammer of a hundred swords and spears against shields, and Lara twitched.

But the shock of the noise was nothing compared to what she felt when the soldier turned to her and said, "Do you, Lara Veliant, Princess of Maridrina, swear to fight by this man's side, to defend him to your dying breath, to cherish his body and none other, and to be loyal to him as long as you both live?"

She blinked. And because there was nothing else for her to say, she whispered, "I do."

Nodding, the soldier pulled out a knife. "Now don't be a baby about this, Majesty," he muttered, and the king answered with a tense chuckle before holding out his hand.

The soldier sliced the knife across the king's palm, then before Lara could pull away, he grabbed her arm and ran the knife across her hand as well. She saw the blood well up before she felt the sting. The soldier pressed their palms together, the King of Ithicana's hot blood mixing with hers before running down their entwined fingers.

The soldier jerked their hands up, almost lifting Lara off her feet. "Behold, the King and Queen of Ithicana."

As if to punctuate his words, the storm finally fell upon them with a resounding clap of thunder that made the ground shudder. The drums took up their frenzied pace, and the King of Ithicana pulled their hands out of the soldier's grip, lowering his arm so Lara wasn't on her tiptoes. "I suggest you board your ship, Your Grace," he said to Lara's father. "This storm will chase you home as it is."

"You could always offer your hospitality," her father responded, and Lara's attention flicked from him to Serin, who stood with the rest of the Maridrinians beyond. "We are, after all, family now."

The King of Ithicana laughed. "One step at a time, Silas. One step at time." He turned and gently tugged Lara into the depths of the bridge, the portcullis rattling its way down behind them. She had only the opportunity for a brief glance back over her shoulder at her father, his expression blank and unreadable. But beyond, Serin met her gaze, inclining his head once in a slow nod before she was pulled out of sight.

It was dark inside, smelling faintly of animal dung and sweat. None of the Ithicanians removed their helmets, but even with their faces concealed, Lara felt their scrutiny.

"Welcome to Ithicana," the king—her husband—said. "I'm sorry to have to do this."

Danielle L. Jensen

Lara saw him lift a hand holding a vial. She could've dodged it. She could have taken him down with a single blow, fought her way free of his soldiers. But she couldn't let him know that. Instead, she gave him a doe-eyed look of shock as he held it up to her nose, the world spinning around her, darkness rushing in. Her knees buckled and she felt strong arms catch her before she hit the ground. The last thing she heard before she faded from consciousness was the king's resigned voice: "What have I gotten myself into with you?"

AREN, THE THIRTY-SEVENTH ruler of Ithicana, lay on his back, staring up at the soot stains on the roof of the barracks. His helmet rested next to his left hand and, as he turned his head to regard the monstrous steel thing he'd inherited along with his title, he decided that whichever one of his ancestors had come up with the idea of the helmets had been both a genius and a sadist. Genius, because the things put fear in the hearts of Ithicana's enemies. Sadist, because wearing it was like having his head stuffed in a cooking pot that smelled of sweaty socks.

His twin sister's face appeared in his line of sight, her expression amused. "Nana has examined her. Says she's shockingly fit, most certainly healthy, and, barring tragedy, likely to live a goodly long while."

Aren blinked once.

"Disappointed?" Ahnna asked.

Rolling onto one elbow, Aren sat upright on the bench. "Contrary to the opinions of our neighboring kingdoms, I'm not actually so depraved as to wish death upon an innocent girl."

"Are you so sure she's innocent?"

"Are you arguing that she's not?"

Ahnna scrunched up her face, then shook her head. "In true Maridrinian fashion, they've given you a beautiful and sheltered shrinking violet. Good to look at and not much else."

Remembering how the young woman had shaken as she'd walked up the pier, holding tightly to her father's arm, her enormous blue eyes filled with terror, Aren was inclined to agree with his sister's assessment. Yet even so, he fully intended to keep Lara isolated until he could get a grasp on her true nature. And learn exactly where her loyalties lay.

"Have our spies learned anything more about her?"

Ahnna shook her head. "Nothing. He appears to have kept her hidden away in the desert, and until she rode out of the red sands, not even the Maridrinians knew her name."

"Why all the secrecy?"

"They say it was for her protection. Not everyone is pleased about our alliance with Maridrina, Valcotta most of all."

Aren frowned, dissatisfied with the answer, though he could not say why. Maridrina and Valcotta were continually at war over the fertile stretch of land running down the western coast of the southern continent, the border contested by both kingdoms. It was possible the Valcottan Empress might have attempted to disrupt the alliance by assassinating the princess, but he thought it unlikely. For one, Silas Veliant had more daughters than he knew what to do with, and the treaty had not been specific about which girl would be sent. Two, every kingdom north and south knew that Aren's marriage to a Maridrinian princess was nothing more than a symbolic act, all parties involved more interested in the trade terms underpinning the agreement and the peace they purchased. The treaty would have endured even if the princess had not.

But third, and what troubled him most of all, was that it wasn't Maridrinian nature to *hide* from anyone. If anything, Silas would have relished the assassination of a daughter or two because it would renew the flagging support of his people for the war against Valcotta.

"She awake yet?"

"No. I came down as soon as Nana deemed her a fit and healthy wife for you, because I wanted to be the one to share the wonderful news."

His twin's voice dripped with sarcasm, and Aren shot her a warning look. "*Lara* is your queen now. Perhaps try showing her a little respect."

Ahnna responded by flipping him her middle finger. "What are you going to *do* with Queen Lara?"

"With tits like that, I'd suggest bedding her," a gravelly voice interjected.

Aren turned to glare at Jor, the captain of his honor guard, who sat on the far side of the fire pit. "Thank you for the suggestion."

"What were they thinking, dressing her in silk in the pouring rain? Might as well have paraded her naked in front of us all."

Aren *had*, in fact, noticed. Even bedraggled by the rain, she'd been stunning, her form curved, her exquisite face framed by hair the color of honey. Not that he'd expected anything else. Despite being past his prime, the King of Maridrina remained a vital man, and it was known he chose the majority of his wives for beauty and nothing else.

The thought of the other king made Aren's stomach sour. He recalled the smug expression on Silas's face as he handed his *precious* daughter over.

It was an expression the Rat King was entitled to.

While Ithicana was now bound to new and undesirable trade terms, all the King of Maridrina had given up was one of his innumerable children and a promise to continue the peace that had stood between the two kingdoms for the past fifteen years. And not for the first time, Aren cursed his parents for making his marriage to Maridrina part of the agreement.

"A piece of paper with three signatures will do little to unite our kingdoms," his mother had always replied when he complained. "Your marriage will be the first step toward creating a true alliance between peoples. You will lead by example and, in doing so, you will ensure Ithicana does more than just survive by the skin of its teeth. And if that means nothing to you, then remember that your father gave his word on my behalf."

And an Ithicanian always kept his word. Which was why, on the fifteenth anniversary of the agreement, despite his parents being a year dead, Aren had sent word to Maridrina to bring their princess to be wed.

"Can't argue that she's easy on the eyes. I can only hope I'll be so lucky." Though Ahnna's voice was light, Aren didn't miss how her hazel eyes turned dull at the mention of her half of the bargain. The King of Harendell, their neighbor to the north, had yet to send for his son's Ithicanian bride, but with Aren now wed to Lara, it was only a matter of time. Harendell would know by now the terms Maridrina had negotiated, and they'd be keen to extract their own pound of flesh. Both deals would incite retaliation from Amarid. The other northern kingdom's relationship with Ithicana was already fraught with conflict, given that their merchant ships competed for business with the bridge.

Giving Jor a meaningful look, Aren waited until his honor guard made themselves scarce before saying to his sister in a low voice, "I won't make you marry the prince, if you don't wish to. I'll compensate them some other way. Harendell is more pragmatic than Maridrina; they can be bought." Because it was one thing for Aren to take a girl he hadn't chosen and never met as a bride for the sake of peace. Quite another to give his sister to a foreign kingdom, where she'd be alone in a strange place to be used however they willed.

"Don't be an idiot, Aren. You know I'll put the good of our kingdom first," Ahnna muttered, but she leaned against his left shoulder, where she'd stood with him and fought for him all of their lives. "And you didn't answer my question."

That was because he didn't know *what* he was going to do with Lara.

"We can't let our guard down," Ahnna said. "Silas might have promised peace, but don't for a second believe he intends to honor that for the sake of *her*. The bastard would probably sacrifice a dozen daughters if it saw us lowering our defenses."

"I'm aware."

"She might be beautiful," his sister continued, "but never believe for a heartbeat that isn't by design. She's the daughter of our enemy. He *wants* you to be distracted by her. She's probably been instructed to seduce you, to find out what she can about Ithicana's secrets on the hope she'll be able to pass them back to her father. We don't need him holding that kind of bargaining chip."

"How, exactly, would she manage that? It isn't as though we'll be sending her home for visits. She'll have no contact with *anyone* outside of Ithicana. He has to know that."

"Better to be safe. Better that she be kept in the dark."

"So I should keep her locked up in our parents' home on this empty island for the rest of her days?" Aren stared at the glowing embers of the fire. A gust of wind drove rain into the hole in the roof above, the droplets hissing as they struck the charred wood. "And if"—he swallowed hard, knowing he had obligations to his kingdom—"*when* we have a child, should I keep him or her locked up here as well?"

"I never said it would be easy." His sister took his hand, twisting it upright to regard the cut across his palm, bleeding where he'd picked at the scab. "But our duty is to protect our people. To keep Eranahl a secret. To keep it safe."

"I know." But that didn't mean he didn't feel an obligation to his new bride. Whom he'd brought through the dark stretches of the bridge, knowing that when she woke, it would be in a place entirely different than any she'd known. Not the life she'd chosen, but one that had been forced upon her.

"You should go up to the house," Ahnna said. "The sedative will wear off soon enough."

"You go." Aren lay back down on the bench, listening to the thunder rolling over the island, the storm nearly passed, though it would soon be replaced by another. "She's been through enough without waking up in a room with a strange man."

Ahnna looked for a moment like she might argue, then nodded. "I'll send word when she wakes." Rising, she left the barracks on silent feet, leaving him alone.

You're a coward, he thought to himself. Because it had only been an excuse to avoid seeing the girl. His mother had believed that this princess was the key to achieving greatness for Ithicana, but Aren wasn't convinced.

Ithicana needed a queen who was a warrior. A woman who'd fight to the death for her people. A woman who was cunning and ruthless, not because she wanted to be, but because her country needed her to be. A woman who'd challenge him every day for the rest of his life. A woman Ithicana would respect.

And there was one thing he was certain: Lara Veliant was *not* that woman.

L ARA WOKE WITH a start, her head aching and her mouth tasting sour.

Without moving, she opened her eyes, taking in what she could of the bedroom. She spotted an open window, through which poured a humid breeze filled with the scents of flowers and lush greenery she possessed no names for, having spent her life surrounded by sand. The view was of a verdant garden, the light flat and silvery, as though it were filtered through thick clouds. The only sound was the faint pitter-patter of rain.

And that of a female humming.

She relaxed the hand that had instantly balled into a fist, primed to attack, and slowly turned her head.

An extraordinarily striking woman, perhaps five years older than Lara, with long, curling dark hair, stood in the center of the room wearing one of Lara's dresses. *One of Marylyn's dresses*, she realized with a pang.

Seeing the way she'd cocked her head, Lara knew the other woman had heard her move, but she carried on as though she had not, swishing the too-short silken skirts from side to side, continuing with her humming.

Lara said nothing, taking in the carved fruitwood furniture that was polished to a shine and vases of brilliant flowers sat on nearly every flat surface. The floors were made of tiny pieces of wood laid out in elaborate designs; the walls were plastered white and decorated with vibrant artwork. A door led to what appeared to be a bathing chamber and another, shut, which she assumed led to a hallway beyond. Satisfied that she had the lay of her surroundings, Lara asked, "Where am I?"

"Oh, you're awake!" the woman said with feigned surprise. "You're in the king's home on Midwatch Island."

"I see." If Midwatch was, as the name suggested, in the middle of Ithicana, she'd been unconscious for longer than she'd realized. They'd drugged her, which meant they did not trust her. No surprise there. "How did I get here?"

"You arrived at Midwatch by sea."

"How long was I asleep?"

"You weren't precisely asleep. Just not . . . present." The woman gave her an apologetic shrug. "Forgive us. It's in every Ithicanian's nature to be secretive, and we are still coming to terms with having an outsider in our midst."

"So it would seem," Lara murmured, noticing that the woman hadn't answered her question, though she knew *exactly* what they'd dosed her with and why. Keeping a person unconscious for days had consequences—often of the fatal variety. Drugging her to wipe her memory was safer.

But fallible. Especially when the individual being dosed had been exposed in the past. Already, shadows of memory were creeping around the edges of Lara's thoughts. Memories of walking. Walking in ill-fitting footwear on a hard surface. She'd been in the bridge, and at some point along its length, they'd brought her out.

Refocusing her gaze on the woman, she asked, "Why are you wearing my dress?"

"You have a whole chest of them. I was hanging them up for you, and I thought I'd try one on to see if I liked it."

Lara cocked one eyebrow. "And do you?"

"Oh, yes." The stranger arched her back, smiling at her reflection in the mirror. "Entirely impractical, but appealing nonetheless. I could use one or two in my own closet." Reaching up one hand, she pushed the dress's straps off her shoulders, allowing it to slide down her body and pool on the floor at her feet.

She wore not a scrap underneath, her body all curved muscle, her breasts small and pert.

"Gorgeous gown you wore for your wedding, by the way." She pulled a short-sleeved tunic over her head, then tugged a pair of snug trousers on beneath. There were a set of vambraces sitting on the floor, and she buckled those on as though she'd done so a thousand times. "I'd ask to borrow it for my own part in the Fifteen Year Treaty, but I'm afraid it took a bit of wear on your journey."

Lara blinked, realization dawning on her. "You're the Ithicanian Princess?"

"Among other things." The woman grinned. "But I don't want to give away all our secrets. My brother would never forgive me."

"Your brother?"

"Your husband." Picking up a bow and quiver, the woman—the princess—strode across the floor. "I'm Ahnna." She bent down to kiss Lara's cheek. "And I, for one, am so looking forward to getting to know you, sister."

There was a knock at the door, and a servant carrying a platter of sliced fruits entered, setting the food on a table before announcing that dinner would be at the seventh hour.

"I'll leave you alone," Ahnna said. "Give you a chance to get settled. I'm sure waking up here was quite the shock."

After years of Serin's aggressive tutelage, it would take a great deal more than waking in a feather bed to shock Lara, but she allowed a faint tremor into her voice as she said, "The king . . . Is he . . . Will he . . ."

Ahnna shrugged. "Aren is not horribly predictable in his comings and goings, I'm afraid. Better that you make yourself comfortable rather than wait for him to come home. Have a bath. Eat some fruit. Have a drink. Or ten."

A flash of disappointment surged through Lara, but she gave Ahnna a smile before shutting the door and flipping the latch. She stared at the bit of metal for a long moment, surprised the Ithicanians would allow her privacy, then she set aside the thought. Everything she knew about them was more speculation than fact. Better to approach her circumstances as though she knew nothing at all.

After donning the gown Ahnna had discarded and belting on her knives, which she was surprised to find sitting on top of her trunk, Lara circled the room looking for signs she was being spied on, but there were no holes in the walls or the ceiling, no cracks in the floorboards. Picking up her tray of fruit, she wandered into what she'd presumed to be the bathing chamber, only to discover it devoid of anything resembling a bath, despite the wooden shelves laden with soft towels, scrubs, soaps, and whole collection of brushes and combs. However, there was another door.

Lara pushed the solid slab of wood open, revealing a sloped courtyard resplendent with a lushness she had never seen before. The walls of the building were concealed by climbing vines laden with brilliant flowers of pink and purple and orange, and two trees with enormous split leaves climbed toward the sky, several colorful birds sitting on their branches. A pathway made of square cut stones framed by tiny white rocks meandered through the courtyard, but what took her breath away was the stream flowing through the center of everything.

The building, she realized as she stepped into the courtyard, had been constructed almost like a bridge over a small waterfall. The water cascaded over slabs of rock into a pool below, which flowed through a channel to another pool, and then yet another, before running under the far side of the home to whatever lay beyond.

At the base of the waterfall, by the pool, she noted the curved stone benches beneath the water. *This* was where one was intended to bathe. Steam rose faintly from its surface and a quick dip of her toe turned her skin pink with heat. There was only one other entrance to the courtyard, and that was a door opposite to the one leading to her rooms.

Crossing the stream using a small footbridge, Lara walked up to the door and silently tested the handle. *Locked.* The rooms beyond also had a window that mirrored hers, but it was closed and curtained.

Tilting her head skyward revealed nothing but swirling clouds, and a quick test of the vines on the walls revealed them strong enough to bear her weight, should she choose to climb out. Countless ways to escape, which meant this home was not intended to be a prison.

A voice caught her attention.

"She's awake then?"

Aren.

"About a half hour ago."

"And?"

Lara hurried down the path next to the spring, dropping to her knees where the water flowed under the building.

"She was calmer than I anticipated. Mostly she wanted to know why I was wearing one of her dresses. I suppose we all have our priorities."

Silence. Then, "Why *were* you wearing one of her dresses?"

"Because they were pretty and I was bored."

The king snorted, and Lara crawled forward a few feet under the building until she could see their legs. He had a bow held loosely in one hand, which he swung back and forth. She wanted to go farther, to attempt to see his face, but she couldn't risk being heard.

"She say anything of note?"

"I've had more exciting conversations with your cat. Your dinners together are destined to be lively affairs."

"Shocking." The king kicked a rock, sending it bouncing into the stream, splashing Lara in the face. "*Most precious daughter*, my ass. I'd bet he has boots that are more precious to him than that girl."

I'll take that bet, you self-righteous bastard, Lara thought.

He added, "These concessions weren't what I wanted out of this treaty, Ahnna. I don't like them, and I don't want to sign the order."

"You have to. Maridrina fulfilled their end of the deal. If we break faith, there will be consequences, the loss of peace being the first of them."

They both started walking, then there was a scrape of boots, the measured thuds of two people walking up stairs, and Ahnna's voice was faint as she said, "Giving the Maridrinian King what he wants will make him depend on us all the more. It might pay off."

And just barely, Lara heard his response: "Maridrina will starve before it ever sees the benefit of this treaty."

The embers of Lara's fury burned hot on the heels of his words, memories of the gaunt children she'd seen on the streets of her kingdom filling her eyes. Straightening, she stormed up the path to her room, intent on finding that asshole of a king and plunging one of her knives into his wicked, Ithicanian guts.

But that would accomplish nothing.

Stopping on the path, she stared up at the sky and took a series of breaths, finding calm in the sea of fire that was her soul. As delightful as gutting her *husband* would be, it wouldn't solve Maridrina's problems. Otherwise, her father would've sent an assassin a long time ago to do that very deed. It was not a matter of bringing down a man, but bringing down a kingdom, and to do that, she needed to play the long game. To delay her strike for when it would be most effective. To remember what she'd been trained for and why. To *be* the woman that her father had created to save their homeland.

A door slammed behind her, and Lara whirled around, expecting one of the servant women had come to offer her services.

She could not have been more mistaken.

The man was naked, save for the towel wrapped around his waist that kept him from being exposed to her entirely. But what she could see was more than enough. Tall and broad-shouldered, his muscled body was as defined as if it were carved from stone, his arms marked with old scars that were white against tanned flesh. And his face . . . Dark hair framed high cheekbones and a strong jaw, which were tempered by full lips. His eyes roved over her, making color rise to her cheeks.

"Of course of all the rooms she could've put you in, she chose *that* one," he said, and the familiarity of his voice was like a pail of icy water being dumped over her head as she realized *who* was standing before her. All she saw now was that wicked mask, and all she heard was *Maridrina will starve*.

Lara's hands twitched to the knives at her waist, but she covered the motion by adjusting the waist of her dress.

He wasn't fooled. "Do you even know how to use those?"

The thought that she could kill this arrogant, condescending man where he stood danced through her head, but Lara only gave him a sweet smile. "I've cut my fair share of meat."

His eyes brightened with interest. "So the little princess has a backbone after all." Gesturing to her knives, he said, "I meant, do you know how to fight with them?"

To say no meant she could *never* be caught using them in any capacity without outing herself as a liar, so instead Lara cocked one bemused eyebrow. "I was raised to be your queen, not a common soldier."

The interest in his eyes flickered out. Which would not do. She was supposed to seduce him and, in doing so, make him trust her. But for that to happen, he had to want her. The misting rain had made the silk of her dress damp, and she could feel it clinging to her breasts. She'd been trained for this. Had sat through countless lessons where she'd been taught precisely what she needed to do to catch a man's interest. And to keep it. Arching her back, she said, "Are you here to claim what is your due?"

His expression didn't shift. If anything, he appeared bored with her. "The only thing I'm due for is a bath before dinner. Dragging your ass back from Southwatch was sweaty business. You're heavier than you look."

Lara's cheeks flamed.

"That said, if you are inclined to do the same, you are welcome to go first. Given you haven't seen a wash in three days, you probably need it more than I do."

She stared at him, at a loss for words.

"But, if you're only out here to admire the . . . *foliage*, perhaps you might grant me a modicum of privacy." He gave her a lazy smile. "Or not. I'm not shy."

That was what he expected. For her to be dutiful little Maridrinian wife and attend to his needs, whether she wanted to or not.

It was what he expected, she thought, watching him watch her, *but it wasn't what he wanted.* Thoughts flicked through her mind one after another. Of the clothes he wore, the colors intended to blend into jungle around them. The scars, which had clearly come from battle. The bow he'd held in his hand, ready to use at a heartbeat's notice. *This man is a hunter*, she decided. *And what he wants is a chase.*

She was more than happy to give him one. Especially if it meant delaying a certain inevitability that she was desperate to avoid.

"Then you can wait." She smiled inwardly at the surprise that lit up his eyes. Unbuckling her belt, she dropped the weapons next to the edge of the pool, then turned her back on the king, pushing the straps of her dress off as she did. Peeling the damp silk from her body, Lara kicked the garment aside, feeling his eyes on her as she stepped into the pool, with only her hair hanging to the small of her back to conceal her naked flesh.

It was scorching hot. A temperature that one needed to ease into, slowly, but Lara gritted her teeth and waded down the steps, only turning when the swirling water covered her breasts.

The king stared at her. She gave him a serene smile. "I'll let you know when I'm finished."

He opened his mouth as though to argue, then shook his head once and turned. Lara allowed him to take three steps before calling out, "Your Majesty."

The King of Ithicana turned to regard her, not quite hiding the anticipation in his expression.

Lara let her head fall back so that the waterfall poured over her hair. "Please leave me the soap. I'm afraid I forgot to bring any out with me." She hesitated, then added, "The towel, too."

The bar landed in the water next to her with a splash. Lara opened her eyes in time to watch him remove the towel from his waist and toss it on a rock, his feet smacking against the path as he strode naked back to his room.

Biting the insides of her cheeks, Lara struggled to contain her grin. This man might be a hunter. But he was mistaken if he believed she was prey.

LARA

L ARA STAYED IN the hot springs until her skin was pink and wrinkled, half to annoy the King of Ithicana and half because the sensation of being wholly immersed in warm water was an unfamiliar delight. In the oasis, bathing had been limited to a basin, a cloth, and lots of vigorous scrubbing.

Back in her rooms, she took care with her appearance, selecting a sky-blue gown that left her arms and most of her cleavage bare, braiding her wet hair into a coronet that revealed her neck and shoulders. In her trunk was a chest of cosmetics, the false bottom concealing tiny jars of poisons and drugs, from which she tucked a vial into her cleverly designed bracelet. She darkened her lashes and swept gold dust across her skin, staining her lips a rosy pink right as the clock on the desk struck the seventh hour. Then, taking a deep breath, she stepped out into the hallway and followed the smell of food.

The polished floor of the hall reflected the light from beautiful sconces made of Valcottan glass. The walls were covered with a latticework of thin pieces of amber-colored wood, on which several bright paintings framed with bronze were hung. The end of the hallway led to a kitchen, so she took the door leading left, and found herself in a foyer tiled with marble, a heavy exterior door framed with windows revealing nothing in the growing darkness.

"Lara."

Turning her head at the sound of her name, she looked through the open doors into a large dining room, which was dominated by a beautiful table made of wood inset with squares of enamel, around which a dozen chairs were placed. Ahnna sat with her chair pushed back and a glass balanced on one trousered knee.

"How was your bath?" The amusement in Ahnna's eyes suggested she was not unaware of Lara's conversation with her brother.

"Delightful, thank—" She broke off with a surprised gasp. Sitting on a chair across from the princess was the largest cat she'd ever seen, at least the size of a dog. Regarding her with golden eyes, it lifted one paw and licked it, proceeding to groom itself at the dinner table. "Good god," she muttered. "What is that?"

"That's Vitex. He's Aren's pet."

"Pet?"

The other woman shrugged. "Aren found him abandoned when he was just a kitten. Took him into the house and then couldn't get the damned creature to leave. He does keep the snakes out, I'll give him that."

Lara watched the animal warily. It was big enough to take down a human, if it got the jump. "Is he friendly?"

"Sometimes. Best to let him come to you, though. Now shoo, Vitex. Shoo!" The enormous creature gave her a look of disdain, then hopped off the chair and disappeared from the room.

Lara sat down across from the princess, taking in the full wall of windows, which she expected showcased an impressive view in the light of day. "Where is everyone?"

Ahnna took a long mouthful of wine, then picked up the bottle on the center of the table and filled Lara's glass and her own, the act making Lara blink. In Maridrina, only servants handled a bottle. One did not pour for oneself. She rather thought that her countrymen might perish from thirst before ever breaking with the custom.

"This is my parents'"—Ahnna broke off with a wince, then

corrected herself—"*my brother's* private residence, so there isn't anyone here right now but us three, plus the cook and two servants. And I'll be gone tomorrow once my hangover wears off." She lifted her glass. "Cheers."

Lara dutifully lifted her own and took a swallow, noting the stemware was also from Valcotta, the wine from Amarid, and unless she missed her mark, the silverware from her homeland. She catalogued the details away for later consideration. Ithicana made the market for most goods, buying at Northwatch, transporting the products through their bridge, then selling them at a premium at Southwatch, only to reverse the process with the southern kingdoms' exports. Merchants who traveled the length of the bridge paid stiff tolls for the privilege, and they were always kept under guard by Ithicanian soldiers. Ithicana itself exported nothing, but it appeared they had no compunction against importing products from other places.

"Is the entirety of this island the king's private domain, then?" Lara asked, wondering when or if the man in question would make an appearance.

"No. My father built this home for my mother so that she would be comfortable during the times of the year they were here."

"Where were they the rest of the time?"

Ahnna smiled. "Elsewhere."

Secrets.

"Are there others living on this island whom I should be aware of?"

"Aren's honor guard is here. You'll meet them at some point, I imagine."

Frustration bit at Lara, and she took another sip of wine to soothe the sensation away. She'd only been here a matter of hours. No one—not even Serin and her father—could expect her to find a way through Ithicana's defenses in the space of a day. "I look forward to meeting them, I'm sure."

Ahnna snorted. "I doubt that. They're a little rough around the edges compared to what you're used to, I expect. Though you are something of a mystery."

The princess was doing her own digging. Lara smiled. "What of you? You say that you will be leaving tomorrow? Is this island not your home?"

"I'm the commander at Southwatch."

Lara choked on her mouthful of wine. "But you're a—"

"Woman?" Ahnna supplied. "You'll find we hold to a different way of life in Ithicana. What's between your legs doesn't determine the path you'll walk in life. Half the garrison at Southwatch is made up of women."

"How liberating." Lara managed to get the words out between coughs even as she envisioned the horror on her father's face should he discover the island he'd failed time and again to beat in battle was defended by women.

"It can be for you, too, should you want it to be."

"Don't make promises we can't keep, Ahnna," a male voice said.

The King of Ithicana strode into the dining room, his dark hair damp from bathing, though she noted his face was still rough with stubble. It gave him a roguish appeal, but she stamped the thought down the moment it rose.

"What's wrong with her learning how to wield a weapon? Ithicana's dangerous. It would be for her own safety."

He eyed the table, then sat at the end of it. "It's not her safety that I'm concerned about."

Lara shot him a look of disdain. "You'd fit in well in Maridrina, Your Grace, if the thought of your wife knowing how to wield a knife puts such fear in your heart."

"Oh my." Ahnna filled her glass up to the brim and leaned back in her chair. "I misjudged your wit, Lara."

"You're wasting your breath, Ahnna," Aren said, ignoring the comment. "Lara believes weapons are the domain of *common* soldiers and not worthy of her time."

"I said no such thing. I said I was trained to be a wife and a queen, not a common soldier."

"And just what *did* that training entail?"

"Perhaps fate will favor you and one day you'll find out, Your Majesty. Although as it stands, you'll need to content yourself with my flawless needlework."

Howling with laughter, Ahnna poured herself yet another glass of wine and then filled one up for her brother. "This might help."

Aren disregarded them both in favor of the servants who appeared bearing trays of food, which they set down on the table, disappearing only to return again with more. There were fresh fruits and vegetables, all brilliantly colored, as well as large fish still in possession of their heads. One fish sat on a bed of steaming rice, which Lara eyed and then dismissed, her attention snapping to the herb-crusted roast beef, the question of its origins tamping down her anger at the excess of food. Food that could've gone to Maridrina.

She waited for one of the servants to serve her, but they all departed. Then the royal siblings began helping themselves, loading their plates with salad and fish and beef all at the same time with no regard to the order of things. "This is more diverse fare than I'm used to," she said. "I've never had fish before, although I suppose it's a staple here."

Aren lifted his head, eyeing the offerings, and Lara saw the corner of his eye tick. "There are some islands with wild boar. Goat. Chicken. Snake is often on the menu. Everything else is an import—usually from Harendell via the market at Northwatch."

Serin's spies reported that not all the goods that entered the bridge at Northwatch exited at Southwatch, indicating that the Ithicanians used the structure to transport products within their own kingdom. *There are ways in and out of the bridge beyond the openings at Northwatch and Southwatch*, Serin had shouted continually at Lara and her sisters. *Those are the weak points. Find your way in.*

Taking healthy servings of everything, Lara cut into her slice of beef, watching the juices pool beneath. Then she took a bite. Smiling at one of the servants who'd reappeared with more wine, she said, "This is delicious."

None of them spoke for a long time, and for her part, Lara's silence was a result of her mouth being full of food. It was better than anything she'd ever had, fresh and seasoned with spices she couldn't even name. *This is what possessing the bridge meant*, she thought, imagining all this food arriving in Maridrina.

"Why did your father keep you in the middle of the Red Desert?" Aren finally asked.

"For our safety."

"Our?"

Give the truth, when you can, Serin's voice instructed from her thoughts.

She swallowed a bit of fish that was drenched with a citrus-butter. "Mine and my sisters'. Well, half-sisters."

Both siblings stopped chewing.

"How many children was . . . *is* he hiding out there?" Aren asked.

"Twelve, including myself." Lara took a sip of wine, then refilled her plate. "My father selected from amongst us the girl he believed would be most fitting as your queen."

Aren was staring at her with a blank expression while his twin nodded sagely before asking, "The most beautiful, you mean?"

"No, I'm afraid not."

"The most intelligent?"

Lara shook her head, thinking of how swiftly Sarhina and Marylyn could crack codes. And build them.

"Why you, then?" Aren interjected.

"It wasn't my place to question the reasons behind his decision."

"Surely you have an opinion on the matter?"

"Certainly: that my opinion doesn't matter."

"What if I asked you for it?" He frowned. "I *am* asking for it."

"My father is the longest ruling monarch in Maridrina's history. His wisdom and understanding of the relationship between our two kingdoms is what guided him to choose me to be your wife."

Ahnna abruptly jerked toward her brother, her voice urgent as she said, "Aren, we've been infiltrated. There's a spy amongst us."

Lara felt her stomach drop as Aren's eyes turned on her. Her fingers twitched toward the knives at her waist, ready to fight her way out if she needed to.

"There's no other explanation for it," Ahnna said. "How else could that deceitful prick of a king have known which daughter would make the absolute *worst* wife for you?"

Snorting, Aren shook his head. Lara hid her relief behind another mouthful of fish, which now held the same appeal as swallowing sawdust.

"No wonder he looked so damn smug at the wedding," the princess continued. "He probably figured you'd send her back after a week."

"Ahnna." The King of Ithicana's voice was full of warning.

"It's amazing, really. It's *almost* as though she were *created* to drive you into an early grave."

More accurate than you know, Lara thought.

"Ahnna, if you don't shut your mouth, I'm going to drown you in your wine."

Ahnna held up her glass in toast. "You're welcome to try, brother dearest."

Lara chose that moment to interrupt, while at the same time, refilling both the siblings' glasses. Pouring the wine herself made it an easy thing to deposit several drops from the tiny vial hidden in her hand into each, ensuring they'd both sleep heavily tonight. "Speaking of my father, will you allow me to correspond with him?"

They stared at her, their displeasure at her request clear as they both drained their glasses, seemingly unaware of how they mirrored each other. Lara smiled internally, knowing the narcotic mixed with the alcohol would do its duty well.

Finally, Aren asked, "Why would you want to? And please don't tell me it's to sustain what is so obviously *not* a close father-daughter relationship."

A dozen nasty retorts formed in her mind, and Lara bit down on every last one of them. She *did* need the cursed man to fall for her. "It has been made clear to me that to protect the interests of Ithicana, I will never be allowed to see my family, my home, or even my people again. That this house, as lovely as it may be, is to be my prison for as long as you see fit. Pen and paper are all I have left to maintain my connection with all that I have left behind. That is, if you allow it."

He looked away, his jaw working as though he were waging some great internal debate. Then his eyes flicked to his sister, the woman giving him the very faintest shake of her head. Which was interesting.

Ahnna portrayed herself as the lighthearted and compassionate of the pair, but perhaps that was not an accurate assessment of her character.

Yet whatever warning had passed between brother and sister, Aren chose to ignore it. "You are welcome to correspond with your father. But your letters will be read, and if they contain information that jeopardizes Ithicana, you will be asked to remove it. If you're caught using a code, your privileges will be revoked."

What he might ask her to remove would reveal a great deal, a concept that was not lost on the Commander of Southwatch. Ahnna's eyes flashed with irritation, and she opened her mouth before shutting it again, unwilling to compromise her performance. Though Lara had no doubt she'd argue against the correspondence once Lara was out of earshot.

"I don't care for having my private letters read," Lara argued, only because he'd expect it.

"And I don't overly care to read them," Aren snapped. "But we must all do things we don't care to do, so I suggest you get used to it." And without another word, he shoved back his chair and exited the room with a slight sway to his step.

Ahnna let loose a world-weary sigh. Pulling the cork from another bottle of wine, she filled Lara's glass to the brim. "At Southwatch, this is what we call an Ahnna pour."

Despite knowing that the woman's behavior was an act to earn her trust, Lara smiled, taking a mouthful of the liquid. "Is he always this quick to temper?" she asked, even as she thought, *Is he always this much of a prick?*

The smile on the other woman's face fell away. "No." There was a slight slur to her voice, and she frowned at her glass. "God, how much of this did I drink?"

"Amarid makes the finest wines in the world—hard not to indulge."

Moments later, Ahnna's chin hit the table with a heavy thud. One of the servants entered at that precise moment, his jaw dropping at the sight of his princess snoring at the dinner table.

"Overindulged," Lara said with a grimace. "Will you help me get her to her room?"

Ahnna was deadweight between the two of them as they half dragged, half carried her down the hallway and into her room, which was as lovely as Lara's own.

"If you hold her, Majesty, I'll check the sheets for snakes."

Snakes? The thought distracted Lara enough that she nearly fell sideways under Ahnna's weight when the boy let go. He walked over to the bed and gave it a solid kick before flipping down the bedding, which was thankfully devoid of serpents.

Easing Ahnna onto the bed, Lara dodged a near kick to the face as the taller woman rolled onto her stomach with a muffled grumble. Jerking off her boot, which had a wicked-sharp blade concealed within it, Lara tossed it next to the bed, followed by the other, then dusted off her hands. "Thank you for your assistance," she said to the boy, exiting the room and waiting for him to follow. "What's your name?"

"It's Eli, my lady. I should say, this isn't normal for Ah . . . Her Highness." He bit at his lower lip. "Perhaps I should let His Grace—"

"Let it be." Lara closed the door. "No need to embarrass her further."

The servant looked ready to argue, then Ahnna let out a loud snore, audible through the thick door, and seemed to think better of it. "Do you require anything else this evening, Your Grace?"

Lara shook her head, wanting him gone. "Goodnight, Eli."

Bowing, he said, "Very good. Please check your bed for—"

"Snakes?" She gave him a smile that turned his cheeks pink against the soft brown curls of his chaotic hair. He bowed again before fleeing down the hallway. Lara listened for the clatter of dishes being removed from the dining room, then silently let herself back into Ahnna's room, flipping the latch shut behind her.

The princess did not so much as twitch as Lara methodically searched for any information of use, sighing covetously at the woman's arsenal of weapons, which were all of the finest make. But else of interest, there was nothing beyond a few keepsakes, a jewelry box with some worthless items, and a music box with a false bottom filled with poetry. A childhood bedroom now seldom used.

After turning down the lamp, Lara eased open the door to ensure the hall was empty before striding to her own room. There had been noise of activity at both ends of the hallway; no chance of her making it to the other side of the house without one of the servants noticing. Chewing on her thumbnail, Lara eyed the clock. The narcotic wasn't intended to last long, and the king hadn't indulged in wine to the extent his sister had. Which meant she was running short of time.

Slipping off her dress, Lara retrieved some toweling, along with soaps and scrubs and, lamp in hand, she stepped out into the courtyard. The night air was cool, a light mist of rain dampening her shift as she walked barefoot down the stone path toward the hot spring. Setting her bathing supplies next to the pool, Lara slid off her shift and slipped into the steaming water, taking one of her knives in with her. Then she turned down the lamp to a bare glow and allowed her eyes to adjust to the darkness.

The noise of the jungle managed to be both deafening and soothing, a ceaseless cacophony that settled the rapid patter of her heart as she rested her elbows on the edge of the pool, perusing her surroundings. The chittering of birds merged with the rustle of leaves, the sharp shrieks of monkeys called back and forth through the trees. A creature, perhaps a frog of sorts, made a repetitive rattling noise, insects droned, and mixed with it all was the gurgle of the waterfall behind her.

Watch. Listen. Feel.

The latter had always served her best. Master Erik had called it the sixth sense—the unconscious part of the mind that took what all the other senses provided, then added something *more*. An intuition that could be tuned and honed into the most valuable sense of all.

So whether she heard a sound or saw a motion, Lara could not have said, but her attention snapped from the roofline to the opening under the house through which the stream flowed.

Guard.

Sure enough, as she stared into the darkness, her eyes eventually picked out the shape of a foot resting against a rock. A flash of irritation that they'd *dare* to watch her while she bathed was erased by the obvious necessity. Aren was the King of Ithicana, and she was the daughter of an enemy kingdom. Of course any avenue between them would be guarded.

After ensuring there were no other guards, she marked the sightlines. Searched for places that would give her cover. She glanced at her white shift resting in clear sight and eased into the stream that drained the pool, crawling on her elbows to keep her body beneath the bank. Warm water caressed her naked body as she crept down to the decorative bridge, which she used as cover to ease out, moving silently behind a bush with wide leaves.

From there, she made quick work of crossing the courtyard, coming up beneath the king's window, which was slightly ajar.

Adjusting a frond to cover her arm, she stretched upward and pulled the window open wider.

Breathe.

Reaching up with both arms, she heaved herself through the small gap, the frame scraping over her naked ass as she flipped, landing silently on her feet inside the dimly lit room, knife blade clenched between her teeth.

She was met by Aren's cursed enormous cat staring at her with golden eyes. Lara held her breath, but the animal only leapt onto the windowsill and slipped out into the courtyard.

Her gaze went immediately to the man sprawled across the large, canopied bed. Aren lay on his back, wearing only a pair of undershorts, the sheets tangled around his lower legs.

Knife gripped in her hand, Lara stepped carefully toward the bed, using one of the rugs to clean her feet. No need to leave her tiny footprints.

There'd been no doubt in her mind after seeing him naked earlier that he was an impressive specimen of a man, but this time, she had no fear of being caught staring. Twice her breadth in the shoulders, he was muscled in the way of an individual who pushed his body to the limits on a regular basis. Combat, judging from the scars, but his leanness spoke of an active life, not a man who sat back and ruled from a throne.

Circling the bed, she examined his face: high cheekbones, strong jaw, full lips, and black lashes that a harem wife would die for. Scruff marked the line of his chiseled jaw, and she had to curb the urge to reach out and run her finger along it.

Maridrina will starve before they ever see the benefit of this treaty.

His words echoed through her mind, and of its own volition, Lara's hand snaked up, resting the edge of her blade against the steady pulse at his throat. It would be easy. One slice, and he'd bleed out in a matter of moments. He might not even wake long enough to sound the alarm. She'd be gone by the time they even realized he was dead.

And she would have accomplished nothing besides destroying the only chance Maridrina had for a better future.

Lara lowered her knife and made her way to the desk. Her heart skipped as she took in a polished wooden box of heavy parchment embossed with Ithicana's bridge, edges gleaming with gilt. The very same stationery Serin had shown her that Aren used for official correspondence. She immediately searched for anything written on it that was directed to Maridrina. All she found were stacks of short notes on cheap paper, and she flipped through, taking in the reports from spies from every kingdom north and south. More reports from Northwatch and Southwatch islands, revenues, requirements for arms and soldiers and supplies.

Provisions for Eranahl . . .

Frowning, she eased the sheet of paper out from under a stack when the bed creaked behind her.

Twisting, her stomach plummeted as her gaze locked with Aren's. He was propped up on one arm, shoulder muscles straining against the sleek golden brown of his skin.

"Lara?" His voice was rough, eyes blurry from narcotics, sleep, and . . . lust. His gaze roved over her naked body, then he rubbed his eyes as though not quite certain whether she was real or an apparition.

Do something!

Her training, drilled into her by her masters, finally kicked in. Either she followed through with what her standing there naked promised, or she found a way to get him back to sleep. The former was the safer strategy, but . . . But that wasn't a card she was yet willing to play.

"How did you get in here?" His gaze was sharpening. If she didn't act soon, he'd remember seeing her when he woke, and that was not part of her plan.

Believe that you are something to be desired, and he will believe it, too, the voice of Mezat, the sisters' Mistress of the Bedroom, said, invading Lara's thoughts. *Desire is your weapon to wield as wickedly as any sword.*

That had seemed so simple back on the compound. Much less so, now. But she had no other choice.

Slipping the vial from her bracelet, Lara covered her finger with the drug before lifting it to her mouth to coat her lips.

"Shh, Your Grace. Now is not the time for conversation."

"A shame. You have such a pleasant way with words."

"I've other talents."

A slow smirk rose to his face. "Prove it."

A droplet of the narcotic beaded on Lara's bottom lip as she strolled with false confidence toward the bed, feeling Aren drink her in. Watching his arousal take hold. Perhaps there was something to Mezat's teachings after all.

Climbing onto the bed, she straddled him, her pulse roaring in her ears as he reached up one hand to cup her ass. His lips parted as though he'd say something, but she silenced him with a kiss.

The first kiss of her life, and she was giving it to her enemy.

The thought danced away as he groaned into her, his tongue chasing over her drug-laced lips, then delving deeper into her mouth, the sensation opening an unexpected floodgate of heat between her legs.

She silently willed the drugs to work as she kissed him again, hard and demanding, feeling his other hand graze the bottom of her breast until she caught hold of it and pinned it to the mattress. He chuckled softly, but she marked the way his eyelids fluttered, barely conscious, even as his other hand trailed down her bottom, down the back of her leg and then up the inside of her thigh. Up and down. Lara felt the drugs starting to take effect on her even as she felt something else building in her core.

He rolled, catching her other hand and pinning them both to the mattress, his teeth nipping at her earlobe and pulling a gasp from her lips. The room spun above her even as her skin burned hot, his lips kissing her throat. Between her breasts. A singular kiss, just below her navel, turning her breathing to ragged gasps.

Then Aren sighed once, slumped, and went still.

Lara stared unblinking at the ceiling, her heart in her throat. But every beat seemed to grow more sluggish, sleep tugging at her, welcoming her into its warm embrace.

Move, she ordered herself, worming her way out from under his weight.

Knowing she had only a matter of minutes before the drug knocked her out, Lara stumbled toward the window, giving the room only a passing glance to ensure it was as she had found it. Her arms shuddered as she eased outside, numb feet finding the cold ground, mud oozing between her toes as she backtracked through the courtyard. Back in the stream, the water danced over her skin, which, despite the narcotic, felt so sensitive that the touch hurt.

The water was warm. Strangely soothing as it pulled her under, welcoming her into its depths.

Soon she was choking. Gasping. Fighting to keep conscious as she reached for the edge and dragged herself out of the pool.

Her body swayed as she pulled the shift over her head. She stumbled up the path, praying the guard would only think her drunk. Her hands hit the solid wood of the door, pushing it in. Shutting it. Turning the bolt.

Get to the bed. Don't give them a reason to suspect.

Get to the bed.

Get to the . . .

AREN PUT AWAY the whetstone he'd been running across the blade of a knife, staring off into the depths of the jungle surrounding his home. Though a hundred sounds emanated from the trees—the trickle of water, the calls of animals, the hum of insects—the island felt quiet. Serene. Peaceful.

A warm furry body rubbed against his arm, and Aren reached up to rub Vitex's ears, the big cat purring contentedly until something in the bushes caught his attention. There'd been a female running about, and even now, Aren spotted her yellow eyes watching them from beneath a large leaf.

"Want to go get her?" he asked his cat.

Vitex only sat on his haunches and yawned. "Good plan. Let her come to you." Aren chuckled. "Let me know how that works out for you."

Behind them, there was the sound of boots against marble and the door swinging open. His sister blinked as she stepped outside.

"You're in better form than I thought you'd be," he said dryly.

Ahnna frowned at him, using one foot to shove the cat inside so she could shut the door. "Why's that?"

"Because the amount of wine you must have consumed to have passed out at the table probably means my cellar's looking lean."

"Good god, did I?"

"If the chatter I heard coming from the kitchen is to be believed." Picking up his bow, Aren stood from where he'd been sitting on the front step, tapping the end of the weapon against his booted toe. "Eli and Lara dragged you back to your room."

Passing a hand over her eyes, Ahnna shook her head as if to clear it. "I remember talking to her and then . . ." She shook her head again. "Sorry. And sorry I'm late. I slept like the dead."

So had he, which was strange, given it had been a clear night. Without a storm to guard Ithicana's shores, Aren normally tossed and turned half the night. He would've been late to rise himself if the damn cat hadn't woken him.

"Good morning, children."

Aren turned to see Jor appear through the mist, a bread roll he'd clearly filched from the kitchen in one hand.

The older man gave Aren a once-over. "You're looking awfully well rested for a man who's just been married."

Ahnna cackled. "I don't think he had much company last night. Or any."

"Pissed the new wife off already?"

Aren ignored the question, a vision of Lara standing at the foot of his bed swimming across his thoughts, her naked body so damnably perfect that it had to have been a dream. The taste of her lips, the feel of her silken skin beneath his hands, the sound of her breath, ragged with desire. It had all been so vivid, but his memory stopped there.

Definitely a dream.

Pulling a folded sheet of paper out of his pocket, Aren handed it to Ahnna. "Your marching orders for Southwatch."

She unfolded it, eyes running over the revised trade terms with Maridrina, brows furrowing with renewed annoyance.

"I'll walk down with you to the barracks," he said. "I need a runner to take Northwatch their copy. Maridrina's already sent buyers through the bridge with gold. They'll be wanting to get underway." To Jor, he said, "Who's on watch?"

"Lia."

"Good. Keep her here. I don't expect Lara to cause any trouble, but . . ."

Jor coughed. "About Lara. Aster's here. He wants a word."

"He's at the barracks?"

"On the water."

"Of course he is." The commander of the Kestark garrison—south of Midwatch —was a member of the old guard. He was appointed near the end of Aren's grandfather's life, and Aren's mother had spent nearly her entire reign looking for a legitimate reason to have him replaced, with no success. The old bastard clung to Ithicanian tradition like a barnacle to a boat, and Aren had not failed to notice that of all the Watch Commanders, Aster had been the only one who hadn't been at his wedding. "I suppose we shouldn't keep him waiting."

The mist hung in the air like a great grey blanket, reducing the sun to a silver orb and making it impossible to see more than a few dozen paces in either direction. Down at the cove, Ahnna's bodyguard awaited her, as did his own, the men and women silently pushing their craft out into the water. Ahnna joined him in one of the Midwatch vessels.

The air was still, not a breeze to fill a sail, and the rattling of the chain rising from where it blocked the cove's entrance felt like a vulgar violation of the silence. Paddles dipped in and out of the water as the group eased around hazards lurking only a few feet beneath the surface, moving out into the open and toward the hulking shadow of the bridge.

"Aren."

Turning to look at his twin, Aren tracked her gaze to the water, where he caught sight of an enormous shape moving beneath them. The shark was longer than the boat he sat in—and more than capable of destroying it, should it feel inclined—but that wasn't why Ahnna had pointed out the predator. Its arrival heralded a calming of the Tempest Seas, and it wouldn't be long before Ithicana's waters were red with blood.

His spine prickled and Aren reached for a spyglass, panning their surroundings, his efforts yielding nothing but grey. A fine thing for hiding the comings and goings of his people, but it served their enemy just as well.

"It's weeks early. Nana hasn't called the end of the season yet." But for all Ahnna's words, he noticed her hand had drifted to the weapon belted at her waist, her eyes watchful. "I need to get back to Southwatch."

Through the mist a pair of vessels appeared. Aster—always one for overt symbolism—having chosen to wait directly beneath the bridge.

"Your Grace." The older man reached out to pull the two boats together. "I'm relieved to see you well."

"Were you expecting otherwise?" The vessels rocked as his guards switched places with the commander, giving the three of them some semblance of privacy.

"Given what you've brought into your house, yes."

"She's little more than a girl, alone, and at our mercy. I think I can handle myself."

"Even a child can slip poison into a cup. And the Maridrinians are known for it."

"Rest easy, Aster, my life is in no danger from Lara. Silas Veliant is no fool—he knows that having his daughter assassinate me would only cost him his new trade deal with Ithicana."

"Lara." Aster spat into the water. "I can hear in your voice that she's already digging in her claws. You must know there's a reason they sent a woman as beautiful as her."

"How would you know what she looks like, Commander?" Ahnna interrupted. "I didn't see you at the wedding, though I suppose it's possible you were hiding in the back."

Aren bit down on his tongue. The Kestark commander was short for an Ithicanian, and he did not like to be reminded of it.

"I've heard what she looks like." Aster's gaze was as dead-eyed as the shark's swimming beneath as he regarded them. "I did not attend, because I did not support your choice in taking her as your wife."

He wasn't alone in that. There were a great many, especially the older generation, who'd protested the union vehemently. "Then why are you here now?"

"To give you some advice, Your Grace. Take the Maridrinian girl down to the water and drown her. Hold her under until you're well and sure she's dead, then feed her corpse to the sea."

For a moment, no one spoke.

"I'm not in the habit of murdering innocent women," Aren finally said.

"Innocent. There's a word." Aster scowled, casting his gaze up at the bridge above them before turning it back on Aren. "I forget how young you are, Your Grace. You were only a boy kept safe in Eranahl the last time we went to war with Maridrina. You didn't fight in those battles where they threw their entire navy against us, blockading Southwatch and stymying trade, all while our people starved. You weren't there when Silas Veliant realized that he couldn't win by force and took his vengeance on the outlying islands, his soldiers slaughtering families and stringing their bodies up for the birds to feast on."

Aren hadn't been old enough to fight, but that didn't mean he didn't remember how desperate his parents had been when they proposed the treaty to Maridrina and Harendell. "We've had fifteen years of peace with them, Aster. Fifteen years of Silas not lifting a hand against Ithicana."

"He's still the same man!" Aster roared. "And you've taken one of his progeny into your bed! I've taken you for many things, Aren Kertell, but not until now did I take you to be a fool."

Ahnna had a knife in her hand, but Aren gave her a warning shake of the head. He'd spent the past year being pushed and questioned by his Watch Commanders and it would take more than a few insults to crack his temper. "I know as well as anyone what sort of man Silas Veliant is, Commander. But this treaty has bought us peace and stability with Maridrina, and I will do nothing to jeopardize that."

Aren waited for the other man to settle, then continued. "While the rest of the world moves forward, Ithicana languishes. Our only industry is the bridge and the fight to keep the bridge. We grow nothing. We create nothing. We know nothing but war and survival. Our children grow up learning a hundred ways to kill a man, but are barely literate enough to write their own names. And that's not good enough."

Aster stared him down, having heard this speech before. But Aren would repeat it a thousand times if that was what it took for men like Aster to accept the change that Ithicana needed.

"We need alliances—true alliances. Alliances that go beyond pieces of paper signed by kings. Alliances that will allow our people opportunities beyond the sword."

"You're a dreamer, just like your mother was." Aster lifted a hand, signaling to the other boats to return. "And it's a beautiful future you envision, I'll give you that, Your Grace. But it's not Ithicana's future."

The boats bumped together, and the commander jumped between them, settling himself among his guards. "And lest your dream turn into our nightmare, do us all a favor, Your Grace, and keep that woman locked up."

L ARA SLEPT BETTER than she had in some time, in part due to the
narcotics, and in part due to the silence. Her sleep during the
journey through Maridrina had been constantly interrupted by
ambient noise. Soldiers, servants, horses, camels . . . But here, there
were only the faint sounds of birds chirping in the courtyard trees.

It was peaceful.

But that sense of peacefulness was a cloak that hid the violent
truth of this place. And the violent truth of herself.

Dressing quietly, Lara ventured out in the direction of the dining
room. She braced herself for the possibility that Aren would remember
what happened in his room last night. That he'd realize she'd drugged
him and her mission would be over before it had even started.

The table was loaded with trays of sliced fruits and meats, creamy
yogurt, and tiny little pastries sprinkled with cinnamon and nutmeg.
But her eyes were all for the view out the enormous windows. Though
it was late morning, the sunlight was dimmed by a filter of clouds,
making it no brighter than twilight. Yet it revealed what the darkness
last night had hidden: the wild jungle, the trees soaring high, the foliage

beneath so dense as to be impenetrable, all of it coated with mist.

"Where is His Majesty?" she asked Eli, hoping he didn't notice the color that had risen on her cheeks. Circumstances had wrested free from her control last night. In more ways than one.

The older servant woman gave Eli a sharp glance. "His Majesty is early to rise. He has gone with the commander to ensure the new trade terms with Maridrina have been conveyed to Northwatch and Southwatch markets."

Thank god. She wasn't sure if she was ready to be face-to-face with him. Not after the things they'd done, whether he remembered them or not. Lara gave the woman a grave nod, hoping it hid her discomfort. "The new trade terms will be a godsend for my homeland. Only good can come from it."

A shadow seemed to pass over the older servant's gaze, but she only inclined her head. "As you say, my lady."

"What is your name? I've met Eli, and I should like to know the rest of you better."

"It's Clara, my lady. Eli is my nephew, and my sister, Moryn, is the cook."

"Only you three?" Lara asked, recalling the legion of servants that had accompanied her party from the outskirts of the Red Desert to Ithicana.

A slow smiled worked its way onto Clara's face. "His Majesty was in the habit of staying in the company of his soldiers rather than this house. Though I expect your presence will change that, my lady."

There was a faint glint in the servant's eyes that made Lara's cheeks warm. "Do you know when he will return?"

"He did not say, my lady."

"I see." Lara allowed a hint of disappointment to enter her voice.

Satisfaction filled her as the woman's face softened. "He is kept busy during most days, but his stomach will drive him home for dinner, if nothing else."

"Am I restricted in where I might go?"

"The house is yours, my lady. His Majesty requested that you make yourself comfortable."

"Thank you." Lara then left them to clear the table as she began her tour of the house.

Besides her rooms and Aren's there were four other bedrooms, the dining room, kitchen, and servants' quarters. The entire rear side of the home was filled with overstuffed chairs, a variety of games set on the tables, and walls lined with books. She longed to pick them up, but only trailed a finger along the spines before moving on. Every room was filled with windows, but the view was the same from them all: jungle. Beautiful, but utterly devoid of civilization. *Maybe this is what Ithicana is like*, Lara thought. *The bridge, the jungle, and little else.*

Or maybe that's just what they wanted her to think.

Retreating to her rooms, she examined the selection of Ithicanian clothes in the closet, selecting a pair of trousers and a tunic that left her arms bare, as well as a pair of stiff leather boots, and then walked down the hall and out the front door of the house.

Test your limits in a way that won't make them suspect your capabilities, Serin silently instructed. *They expect you to be ignorant, helpless, and indulged. Capitalize upon their mistakes.*

Anticipating that she might be followed, Lara started walking. There was a path that lead upward, but instead she chose to follow the spring, knowing that it would eventually deliver her to the sea.

It was only a matter of minutes until she heard the faint tread of someone walking behind her. The crack of a branch. A soft splash of water. Whoever it was had a hunter's stealth, but she'd learned to tell the difference between sand shifting on the wind and that moving beneath a man's weight, so catching the errant sounds of pursuit in this jungle was nothing to her.

Noting the signs of several booby traps in the jungle, Lara continued to follow the stream, soon finding herself drenched with rain and sweat, the humidity of the air making her feel like she was breathing water, but still, she had caught sight of neither bridge nor beach. Nor had her follower made any move to interfere.

She rested a hand against a tree trunk and feigned weariness as she stared up, trying and failing to penetrate the canopy and the mist.

Serin had explained in detail what they knew about the bridge. That the majority of the piers were natural towers of rock jutting out of the sea, holding the spans often a hundred or two hundred feet above the water. There were only a few islands onto which the bridge landed, and those were defended by all manner of hazards designed to sink ships. The most central of her goals was to find out how the Ithicanians accessed the bridge along its length, but she needed to find the thing first.

The stream was flowing down an increasingly steep slope, the now cool water pouring over ledges in tiny waterfalls, filling the air with a gentle roar. Holding onto vines and bracing herself on rocks, Lara picked her way down, already dreading the pain of the climb back up.

Then her boot slipped.

The world turned sideways, a blur of green as she tumbled, her elbow knocking painfully against a rock. Then she was falling.

Lara shrieked once, flailing her arms as she struggled to catch hold of a vine. She slammed into a pool of water, the force driving the wind out of her. Water closed over her head, bubbles streaming from her mouth as she kicked and thrashed her arms. Her boots knocked against the bottom, and she bent her knees to kick off . . .

To find herself only waist deep.

"Bloody hell," Lara snarled, wading to the water's edge. But before she reached shore, a hiss caught her attention.

Freezing where she stood, Lara scanned her surroundings, eyes landing on the brown and black snake shifting angrily in the underbrush. The creature was longer than she was tall, and it was caught between her and the cliff wall. She took a tentative step back into the water, but her motion only seemed to agitate the creature. This is what she got for not heeding Eli's warning.

It took a great deal of self-control not to reach for one of the knives belted to her waist, her ears picking up the scuff of boots and a faintly muttered oath. Throwing knives were her specialty, but her follower was at the top of the cliff and the last thing she needed was to be seen using one of her weapons.

The snake reared up, its head eye level with her. Hissing. Angry. Ready to strike. Lara breathed steadily. In and out. *Come on, whoever you are*, she silently grumbled. *Deal with this creature already.*

The snake swayed from side to side, and Lara's nerve began to fray. Her hand closed over her knife, her finger clicking open the case around the hilt.

The snake lunged.

A bow twanged, a black-fletched arrow spiking the creature's head to the ground. Its body thrashed about violently, then went still. Lara turned.

Aren knelt on the edge of the waterfall she'd so gracelessly toppled off, bow in hand, a quiver full of arrows peeking over his broad shoulders. He straightened. "We have something of a snake problem in Ithicana. Not so bad on this island in particular, but"—he leapt off the edge, landing almost silently next to her—"if she'd sunk her teeth into you, you wouldn't have been long for this world."

Lara glanced at the dead snake and its body twitched. Despite herself, she flinched, and she attempted to conceal the motion with a question. "How can you tell it's female?"

"Size. The males don't get this big." Crouching, he jerked the arrow out of the animal's skull. Wiping blood and bits of scale from the arrowhead, which was three-edged, unlike the barbed broadheads Maridrinians favored, he turned his dark gaze on Lara. "You were supposed to stay in the house."

She opened her mouth, about to tell him that she'd been given no such instruction, when he added, "Don't play the fool. You knew what Clara meant."

She chewed the inside of her cheek. "I don't care for being confined."

He snorted, then jammed the clean arrow back in his quiver. "I would've thought you'd be used to it."

"I am used to it. But that doesn't mean I have to like it."

"You were kept locked up in that desert compound for your own safety. Consider my motivations for keeping you confined here the same. Ithicana is dangerous. For one, the entire island is booby-trapped. And two, you won't walk two paces without passing by some manner of creature capable of putting you in your grave. And three, a coddled little princess like you doesn't know the first thing about taking care of herself."

Lara ground her teeth together. It took every ounce of control in her body to keep from telling him just how wrong he was on that account.

"That said, you did make it farther than I expected you would," Aren mused, his eyes raked over her body, her soaking wet clothes clinging to her skin. "What did they have you and your sisters *doing* on that compound? Running laps and shoveling sand?"

It was an inevitable question. While her frame was small, she was also corded with lean muscle from endless hours of training—hers was not the body of most Maridrinian noblewomen. "Desert living is hard. And my father wanted me prepared for the . . . *vigor* of life in Ithicana."

"Ah." He smiled. "How unfortunate that he didn't also prepare you for the wildlife." Reaching up with his bow, he flicked the tip of it across her shoulder, and out of the corner of her eye, Lara watched a black shape sail through the air.

A spider the size of her palm landed in the dirt before scuttling off into the shadows. She watched it with interest, wondering if it was poisonous. "No worse than the Red Desert's scorpions."

"Perhaps not. But I suspect the Red Desert isn't littered with these." Picking up a rock, he tossed it a dozen paces to the left.

There was a loud crack, and a board covered in wooden spikes snapped up from the ground. Anyone who triggered the device would find themselves sporting half a dozen holes in their body from the waist down. She'd seen the dew clinging to the tripwire a dozen paces back, but in fairness, it would've caught her in the dark. "You've won the pissing contest," she said in a way that implied he really hadn't. "Shall we carry on?"

Instead of snapping back with a witty rejoinder, Aren stepped closer, his hand closing on her wrist. Lara should've recoiled, but instead she froze, remembering the feel of that hand on her naked body, the soft strokes up and down her thigh.

She started to pull away, but he rotated her arm, frowning at the shallow cut on her elbow. Reaching into the pouch on his belt, he extracted a small tin of salve and a roll of bandage and proceeded to tend to the injury with practiced hands. The muscles of his forearms flexed beneath the steel and leather of the vambraces buckled around them. This close, she gained a new appreciation for how much larger he was than her, head and shoulders taller and easily double her weight. All of it lean muscle.

But Erik, her Master of Arms, had been just as big, and he'd trained Lara and her sisters how to fight against those who were larger and stronger. As Aren finished bandaging her arm, she imagined where she would strike. To the arch of his foot or his knee. Knife to open his guts. Another to the throat before he had the chance to get a grip on her.

He tied off the bandage. "I gave up a great deal in this exchange with your father, and all I got in return beyond the promise of continued peace was you. So you'll excuse me for not wanting to see you dead within the first days of your arrival."

"And yet you obviously were content to allow me to wander your dangerous jungles."

"I wanted to see where you'd go." Motioning for her to follow, Aren moved through the deadfall covering the jungle floor, making minimal use of the glittering machete he held in one hand. "Were you trying to escape?"

"Escape to where?" She forced herself to accept his arm as he guided her over a fallen tree. "My father would have me killed for dishonoring him if I returned to Maridrina, and I possess no skills that would allow me to survive elsewhere on my own. Whether I will it or not, Ithicana is where I must remain."

He laughed softly. "At least you're honest."

Lara contained her own laughter. She was many things, but *honest* wasn't one of them.

"Then what were you doing out here?"

Save the lies for necessity. "I wanted to see the bridge."

Aren stopped in his tracks, turning to give her a sharp look. "Why?"

She met his gaze unflinchingly. "I wanted to see the bit of architecture that was worth the rights to my body. My loyalty. My life."

He recoiled as though she'd slapped him. "The rights to those things are yours to give, not your father's."

It wasn't what she'd expected him to say. But rather than easing her trepidation about that particular aspect of her mission, it made her skin burn hot with an anger that she couldn't quite explain, so she only gave a curt nod. "So you say."

Smacking a vine out of his way with the machete, Aren strode up a steep incline, not waiting to see if she followed. "You were going the wrong direction, by the way. Now try to keep up. There's only a brief window in which you'll be able to see the bridge through the mist."

They climbed upward, mostly on a narrow trail, during which they said not a word to one another. There was nothing to be seen but endless jungle, and Lara was beginning to believe Aren was toying with her when he walked into a clearing containing a stone tower.

Tilting her face to the sky, she let the endless rain wash the sweat from her face, watching the clouds twist and swirl on winds that didn't breach the tree canopy.

Aren gestured at the tower. "The break in the cloud cover will be brief at this time of year."

The tower smelled of earth and mildew, the stone stairs circling upward worn in the center from countless footsteps. They reached the top—a small empty space open on all sides, revealing misty jungle in every direction. The lookout was at the apex of a small mountain, she realized, and she could only barely make out the grey sea below. There was no beach. No pier. And most importantly, no damned bridge.

"Where is it?"

"Patience." Aren leaned his elbows on the stone wall framing the space.

More curious than annoyed, Lara went to stand next to him, taking in the trees and clouds and sea, but her attention was drawn to him. He smelled of damp leather and steel, of earth and leafy things, but beneath that, her nose picked up the smell of soap and something distinctly, and not unpleasantly, male. Then a blast of wind roared through the tower, chasing away all scents but that of sky and rain.

The clouds parted with incredible speed, the sun burning down upon them with an intensity she hadn't felt since she'd left the desert, turning the swaths of faded green into an emerald so vibrant, it almost hurt her eyes. The mist raced away on the wind, leaving behind sapphire skies. Gone was the mysterious island, and what was left in its place was all brilliant color and light. But no matter how she searched, she could not see anything remotely resembling a bridge.

An amused laugh filled her ears just as fingertips caught her chin, gently lifting her face. "Look further," Aren said, and Lara's eyes went to the now-turquoise seas.

What she saw took her breath away.

ALL THE DESCRIPTIONS given to her during her training paled in comparison to reality. It was not *a* bridge. It was *The Bridge*, for there was nothing that compared with it in the world.

Like a great grey serpent, the bridge meandered as far as the eye could see, joining the continents. It rested on top of naturally formed tower karsts that seemed to have been placed by the hand of God for just such a purpose, defying the Tempest Seas that crashed against their feet. Occasionally, its grey length drifted over the larger islands, resting on thick stone columns built by ancient hands. The bridge was a feat of architecture that defied reason. That defied logic. That should, by all rights, not even exist.

Which was exactly why everyone wanted it.

Tearing her eyes from the bridge, Lara glanced up at Aren whose own gaze was fixed on the stone structure. Though he must have seen it every day of his life, he still exuded a sense of wonder, as though he, too, could hardly fathom its existence.

Before she could look away, he turned his head, and their eyes met. In the sunlight, she saw that his eyes were not black, but hazel, the brown flecked with emerald green that mirrored his kingdom. "Does seeing it bolster your sense of self-worth?"

Her skin burned hot, and she turned away, needing to move. "I am not a commodity."

He huffed out a breath. "That's not what I meant. The bridge, it's . . . For Ithicana, it's everything. And Ithicana is everything to me."

Just as Maridrina was everything to her.

"It's . . . impressive." A weak word for the ancient structure.

"Lara." Out of the corner of her eye, she saw him reach for her, then withdraw his hand as though he thought better of touching her. "I know that you didn't choose to be here."

He scrubbed a hand through his hair, his cheeks clenched as though he were struggling for words, and her heart began to pound anticipating what he would say. "I want you to know that you don't have to do anything you don't want to. That this . . . this is whatever you want it to be. Or don't want it to be."

"What is it to you?"

"The treaty means peace between Ithicana and Maridrina. It means lives saved. Maybe one day it will mean the end to violence on our shores."

"I didn't think we were talking about the treaty." She was intent on understanding what motivated this man, which included his desires.

Aren hesitated. "I hope our marriage will be the first step toward a future where my people's lives aren't tied to this ancient piece of stone."

The statement was so contradictory to what he'd said about the bridge being everything that Lara opened her mouth to ask for him to explain, but she was cut off by the sound of a horn blaring in the distance. It belted out a song, then repeated it twice. Aren swore after the first pass, his hand reaching for the large spyglass mounted at the center of the watchtower. He panned the water, unleashing a tirade of curses when he caught sight of whatever it was he was searching for.

"What is it?"

"Raiders." He flung himself at the stairs, then caught himself on the doorframe, halting his progress. "Stay here, Lara. Just . . . don't move. I'll send someone for you."

She started to argue, but he was already gone. Leaning over the edge of the tower, she watched him exit the base, sprint through the clearing, then disappear from sight.

Standing on her tiptoes, Lara peered through the spyglass. It took her a moment, but she finally caught sight of the ship passing under the bridge toward Midwatch, its deck teeming with armed men in uniforms, the Amaridian flag flying from the mast. A naval vessel. And not, if Aren's words were to be believed, one that had come in peace.

A loud crack split the air. Lara watched as a projectile tore through the rigging, a mast splintering and toppling sideways. It fell, sails and ropes catching on the metal spikes set into the base of one of the bridge piers. The ship keeled over, spilling countless men into the water. Another crack echoed up to her position, and a gaping hole appeared in the hull. A hole that swiftly disappeared as the vessel sank lower in the water.

Hands frozen on the spyglass, Lara held her breath as violent barrage of ammunition methodically destroyed the ship while those still aboard clambered higher, or swam toward shore, fins circling them ominously, no safety within reach. As she watched, one of the sailors was jerked under, and her blood ran cold as a cloud of crimson blossomed where he'd been. After that, it was a frenzy, the sharks attacking one after another after another, the water now more red than blue.

Moving the glass to where the island met the sea, she searched for any sign of Ithicanians, keen to see their defenses in action. But the angle was bad, the jungle obscuring her vision of whatever was happening at the water's edge.

This could be her one chance to see how the Ithicanians repelled invaders from the inside, and she was missing it because of a poor vantage point.

Lara found herself running. Down the stairs and into the clearing, her eyes trained on the path Aren had taken, trusting it would lead her to where she needed to go. The jungle was nothing but a blur of green as she ran, the humid air heavy in her lungs as she leapt over rocks, slid in the mud, caught her balance and kept going. The water wasn't far, and it was downhill.

The path burst out into the open, cutting along the edge of a cliff. Far below, the ocean slammed against sheer rock. She veered around a bend, finding herself at the top of a steep slope. Lara paused, taking cover behind a rock.

She spotted a cove that she hadn't been able to see from the watchtower. With a white sand beach and turquoise waters, it was hidden from the ocean by rocky cliffs, the opening to the sea beyond a gap barely wide enough for a small boat. The gap was currently blocked by a heavy chain connected to stone buildings on each side.

The beach was full of soldiers. Lara's gaze went to the strange boats sitting on the sand, which showed no sign of going anywhere, before shifting her attention to the Ithicanians standing atop the cliffs overlooking the sea, Aren's tall form among them.

Frowning, Lara peered around the boulder, trying to determine where the catapult the Ithicanians had used against the ship was located, when she heard loose gravel sliding down the path behind her. Then a voice: ". . . hardly worth the stones we lobbed at them. A brisk wind would put that decrepit piece of shit on the bottom of the sea."

Her heart skipping, Lara searched for a way to escape, but the beach was crawling with soldiers, to her left was a tangle of jungle vines, and to her right was a sheer drop onto the jagged rocks jutting out of the ocean. The only way to keep from being caught spying was forward.

Stepping out from her cover, Lara picked her way down the steep slope and onto the beach, ignoring the startled expressions of the soldiers.

One man put his fingers to his lips and gave a sharp whistle, causing those standing on the cliffs—including Aren—to turn. He was not so distant that she couldn't make out the surprise, and subsequent irritation, that crossed his face.

Before the soldiers could stop her, Lara circled the cove, climbing the steps carved into the rock that allowed access to the cliff overlooking the sea. Aren met her at the top, clearly not inclined to allow her to watch what was going on. "I told you to stay in the tower, Lara."

"I know, I—" She pretended to lose her balance on the narrow step, hiding a smile as he caught hold of her arm, pulling her onto the clifftop and giving her an unencumbered view of the bridge and the ship sinking next to it. "What's going on?"

"It's no concern of yours. Go down to the beach and someone will take you back up to the house." He motioned to one of his soldiers, and Lara's mind raced, grasping for a reason to linger.

"There are drowning men out there!" She waved away the soldier trying to take her arm. "Why aren't you helping them?"

"Those are raiders." Aren shoved the spyglass he was holding into her hand. "See the flag? That's an Amarid vessel. They were trying to find a way into the bridge under the cover of the fog."

"They could be merchants."

"They aren't. Look at the bridge. See the lines hanging from it?"

Through the glass, Lara pretended to look at the men dangling from ropes when really she was examining the structure itself, searching for openings. This was a vantage point no one but the Ithicanians had, and it was possible she might learn something valuable. But Aren plucked the spyglass out of her hand before she could get more than a quick glance.

"This is an act of war against us, Lara. They deserve what they get."

"No one deserves this," she replied, and though her reaction was an act, her stomach still twisted as the waves pummeled the ship, swallowing the wreckage whole. All the Amaridians were in the water now, some trying to reach the dangling ropes, others swimming in the direction of the island on which she stood. "Help them."

"No."

"Then I will." She whirled around, keen to use a dramatic display of empathy to get a closer look at the small craft on the beach, only to find herself face-to-face with three of Aren's soldiers. "Let me pass."

None of them moved, but neither did they reach for their weapons. Lara glanced over her shoulder, taking in the twin stone structures with solid doors and no windows, which guarded the mechanism for lifting the chain. She suspected they were always guarded. Yet her eyes were drawn from her assessment to the handful of sailors who, against all odds, were within reach of the gap leading to the cove. But several of them were floundering, the heavy waves washing over their heads.

"Please." Lara shouldn't care whether the Amaridians lived or died, but she found that she did, the shake in her voice genuine as she said, "This is cruelty."

Aren's face was dark with anger. "Cruelty is what those men would've done to *my* people if they'd managed to get past our defenses. Ithicana never asked for this. We never invade their lands. Never slaughter their children for sport." He pointed his finger at the sailors, and bile rose in Lara's throat as another was jerked beneath the waves, the water frothing red as the shark tore him apart. "They brought war to us."

"If you let them die, are you any better?" There were only three sailors left, and they were close. Except fins trailed in their wake. "Show some mercy."

"You want mercy?" Aren twisted on his heel, reaching into his quiver even as he turned. Three blurs of black fletching, and the remaining sailors sank beneath the waves. He rotated back to face her, knuckles white where they gripped his bow.

Lara dropped to her knees, closing her eyes and feigning distress even as she sought her own inner focus. Ithicana was showing its true colors. Not peaceful courtyards and soothing hot springs, but violence and cruelty. And Aren was its master.

But she would be his doom.

"Wait for the winds to die, then pick off those hanging from the rock," Aren ordered his soldiers. "The last thing we need is one of them finding their way in at low tide." Then boots thudded past her, and he went down the steps to the hidden beach.

Lara stayed where she was, smiling inwardly as the Ithicanians gave her and her moral outrage wide berth even as she considered Aren's words: *a way in at low tide*. A way into where, was the question. Into the cove? Or had he been referring to a far greater prize?

The winds died, the sun retreated behind another bank of clouds, and the rains returned, soaking her to the bone. But she did not move. In stoic silence, she watched the soldiers push the boats out into the water, sail beneath the bridge, and methodically shoot the sailors who'd managed to cling to the ropes through the entire ordeal, their lifeless bodies falling to the ocean below.

She said nothing as they returned, only marked the meandering route they took, which was too purposeful to be without design, the necessity revealed as the tides reversed, the waters trailing away to reveal the deadly traps beneath the surface. Steel spikes and jagged rocks, all intended to destroy any approaching vessel unaware of the correct path.

The tide hit its lowest point, and Lara started to rise, convinced she'd seen all there was to see. Then a shadow at the base of the nearest bridge pier caught her attention. No, not a shadow. An opening.

Her heart sped, and it was a struggle to keep a smile from her face as elation filled her. She'd found a way into the bridge.

"A MARID'S QUEEN MUST TRULY be desperate to be crewing her ships with this sort." Gorrick flipped over the corpse that had been pulled from the ocean, blood seeping into the white sand. It was missing a leg, courtesy of one of Ithicana's sharks. It was also missing its left thumb, but in that, the sharks were blameless. For the missing digit combined with the brand on the back of his hand indicated that this man had spent some time in one of Amarid's prisons for theft.

Kneeling down, Aren examined the dead soldier's threadbare uniform, the elbows worn through on both arms. "All convicts, you say?"

"Those that we could get a look at."

Standing, Aren frowned at the mist-covered waters of the cove. The Amaridian navy was well acquainted with Midwatch's shipbreakers, but the vessel had sailed right into their path, making them easy pickings. Perhaps an ancient ship with a crew of convicts was all the Amarid Queen had been willing to risk on the tail end of storm season, but still . . . What was the point?

Aren turned back to Gorrick. "Write a report and have it sent to the Watch Commanders informing them that raids have come early." Then he strode up the path toward the barracks, having no interest whatsoever in returning to his house.

"Wife chase you out already, Your Grace?" Jor was lounging next to the fire, a book in one hand. "She didn't seem too pleased with the Ithicanian form of mercy."

That she had not.

Lara had sat and brooded on the cliff edge until he'd wondered if he needed to get someone to drag her back to the house. Then abruptly she'd risen, trotted down the steps to the beach, and stormed past him without a word, the guards he'd posted on her looking as though they'd rather be swimming with sharks than watching over their new queen. About an hour later, Eli had arrived with a letter written by Lara to her father, and now, Aster's comments fresh in his ears, Aren was debating whether or not to send it.

"I doubt she's seen much of the way of violence before." Aren headed toward his bunk before thinking better of it and sitting next to the old soldier. "Read this."

Taking Lara's letter, the older man read it, then shrugged. "Looks to me like a proof of life letter."

Aren was inclined to agree. The letter said little more than that she was well, was being treated kindly, along with a lengthy description of his house, with a great emphasis on the hot spring. Even so, he'd read it over several times looking for code, not sure if he was happy or disappointed when he found none.

"Interesting that she doesn't mention you. Me thinks you have a cold bed in your future."

Aren snorted, the blurry remnants of the dream he'd had of Lara in his room, in his bed, in his arms, flashing across his thoughts. "She seems to take issue with being a treaty prize."

"Maybe she was expecting a better-looking husband. Some people handle disappointment poorly."

Aren lifted one eyebrow. "That's probably the only thing that hasn't been disappointing for her."

Jor shook his head. "Maybe she dislikes cocky little bastards."

"I've heard there are kingdoms where the people show a little respect for their monarchs."

"I can respect you and still think your shit stinks just as bad as the next man's."

Rolling his eyes, Aren accepted the mug that Lia, one of his honor guards, passed him, smiling until she said, "You're just pissed that the Rat King of Maridrina sent you a girl with an opinion rather than a brainless twit who'd"—she made a vulgar gesture—"without question."

"Like you, Lia?" Jor said with a wink, laughing as she tossed the contents of her cup at him. Aren snatched the letter out of the man's hand before it could suffer any further damage.

"You don't actually intend to send it, do you?" Jor asked.

"I told her I would. And besides, if Silas is wanting proof she's alive, it's best we satisfy him. The last thing we need is to give him an excuse to come looking for her."

"Lie. We can get a forger to carry on the correspondence."

"No." Aren's eyes drifted across the lines of neat writing. "I'll either send it or tell her that I chose not to. Is there anything on the surface here that we need to be worried about the Magpie seeing?"

Jor took it back, reading it once more, and not for the first time, Aren cursed having been born those few minutes before Ahnna. Those few damning minutes that made him King and her Commander, when he'd have given anything for their roles to be reversed. He was suited to fighting and for hunting and for sitting around the fire making bad jokes with other soldiers. Not for politics and diplomacy and having his whole goddamned kingdom depending on his choices.

"From the description of your fancy house, they might guess she's at Midwatch with you. They'll realize from her details about the jungle that we're granting her some liberty to move about. Speaking of"—Jor lifted his head—"what *was* she doing running around the island? She came from the same direction as you, which wasn't from the house . . ."

Chance would have it that Aren had arrived at the house right before Lara departed on her unsanctioned exploration of the island, and rather than have Lia stop her, he'd decided to see where his wife intended to go. "She was wandering."

Jor's eyebrows rose. "For what purpose?"

"Looking for the bridge."

All eyes in the common room turned to look at them, and Aren scowled. "It was mere curiosity . . ." He didn't know exactly why he was defending Lara, only that the things she'd said to him had struck a chord. It had been so easy to focus on the sacrifices he was making as part of this marriage that he hadn't stopped to think of what it had cost her. Of what it would continue to cost her. The exact same things he wanted to protect Ahnna from, and why he'd pay Harendell a fortune rather than force his sister into a marriage she didn't want. "Nearly got herself bitten by a snake, so I expect she won't go wandering again anytime soon."

"I wouldn't be so confident about that," Lia said. "When we blocked her from the boats, she looked about ready to punch me in the face. She might not be a warrior, but she's no coward."

"I'm inclined to agree," Jor said. "I'll have a couple extra guards stationed to keep an eye on her when you're not around."

Aren nodded slowly. "Send the letter to Southwatch for Ahnna and our codebreakers to look at and get a forger to transcribe it onto fresh paper. Then send it to Maridrina." His people knew every one of the Magpie's codes. If she was using one, they'd crack it.

"You think she's a spy?"

Exhaling a long breath, Aren considered his new wife, who was nothing like how he'd expected. Maridrinian kings used their daughters as bargaining chips, ways to secure alliances and favors within the kingdom and without. Lara and all of her sisters would have been raised knowing an arranged marriage to him—or someone else—was part of their future. They'd have been trained to do their duty as a wife, regardless of the circumstances.

Yet Lara had made it clear that the treaty secured her presence in Ithicana, not her compliance as a wife, and he respected that. Every woman who'd shared his bed had done so because she'd wanted to, and the idea of spending his life with a woman who was there solely out of duty was unappealing. He'd prefer a cold bed. "I'll give her some space. I think if she's been sent here to spy, she's going to come to me in pursuit of information. Maridrinians aren't known for their patience."

"And if she does?" Jor asked.

"I'll cross that bridge when it comes."

"And if she doesn't?"

In a way, if Lara was, in fact, an innocent girl who'd been sent to secure a peace treaty, it made Aren's task harder than if they exposed her as a spy. Because he had his own agenda when it came to his Maridrinian wife, and he wouldn't get very far with it if she hated his guts. "I'll win her over, I suppose."

Lia's drink sprayed out from between her lips. "Good luck with that, Your Grace."

He gave her a lazy smile. "I won you over."

Lia gave him a look that implied he was the stupidest creature to walk the earth. "She and I are *not* the same."

Yet it wasn't until Lara had continued to give him the cold shoulder for one night, then a week, then two, that he started to think that maybe Lia had been right.

THE WEEKS AFTER the shipwreck and the slaughter on the beach passed without incident. Aren rose at dawn and didn't return until late in the evening, but he didn't leave her unattended. Wise to Lara's prior unsanctioned exploration of the island, the servants kept close watch on her, Clara always seeming to be dusting or mopping nearby, the scent of wood polish perpetually thick on the nose. Though in truth, the storms that passed overhead did more than the servants or guards ever could to keep Lara contained. Violent winds, lightning, and a ceaseless deluge of rain were regular occurrences. Moryn, the cook, told her these were the last gasps of the season and nothing in comparison to the typhoons she'd witness when the next began.

Though she was desperate to get another look at the opening into the pier, Lara, by design, did nothing to provoke interest, using the time to discreetly search the home for any clues that might assist in planning Maridrina's invasion of Ithicana. Maps were her primary goal, and the one thing she failed to find. Serin had countless documents detailing the islands that made up the kingdom, on which a long line depicting the bridge was always drawn, but none with any detail. Lara had now seen for herself—the kingdom was nearly impossible to infiltrate due to the lack of beaches, compounded by the defenses in the water, which the Ithicanians seemed capable of shifting and changing at will.

The other mystery was where the islanders themselves resided. No civilizations of size had ever been spotted from the sea, and successful landings and raids only spoke of small villages, leading Serin and her father both to believe the population small, violent, and uncivilized, dedicated to basic needs, vicious defense of their bridge, and little else. But though she'd only been in Ithicana a short time, Lara was not inclined to agree with that assessment.

It was what Aren had said to her in the tower. *The bridge . . . For Ithicana, it's everything. And Ithicana is everything to me.*

The tone in his voice showed genuine sentiment. There were civilians here. Civilians Aren believed needed protection, and all of her training told her they would be Ithicana's greatest weakness. She need only determine where they were and how to exploit that knowledge. Then pass it back to Maridrina.

She'd sent her first letter to her father already, a code-free missive carefully crafted to ensure it gave no reason for the Ithicanians to detain it. A test to see if Aren would allow her to correspond before she attempted the riskier task of trying to get intel past the codebreakers at Southwatch.

Proof that Aren had been true to his word came in a response from her father. And the letter was delivered by none other than King Aren himself.

She'd seen him arriving home through the window, soaking wet from the most recent downpour, and not for the first time, she wondered what it was he did during his days. More often than not he returned wet, muddy, and smelling of sweat, his face shadowed with weariness. Part of her had wanted to approach him—had feared that she'd erred her strategy of gaining his trust and had alienated him entirely. But another part had told her that she'd made the right choice in forcing him to come to her.

"This arrived in Southwatch for you." He dropped the folded pieces of paper in her lap. He was bathed and changed into dry clothes now, but the exhaustion lingered.

"You read it, I assume." She unfolded the letter, noting Serin's spidery imitation of her father's script and feeling the faintest stab of disappointment. Of course it had been him to write it. He knew the codes, not her father. She set it aside, not wanting to read it just yet.

"You know I did. And to save you the trouble, my codebreakers helpfully translated the piss-poor code. Transcription is on the back. I'll let the deception slide this time because it didn't come from you, but there won't be any second chances."

So much for Marylyn's unbreakable code. Flipping over the page, she read aloud, "Relieved that you are well, dearest daughter. Send word if you are mistreated, and we will retaliate."

Aren snorted.

"What did you expect? That he'd marry me off to you and not care what became of me?"

"More or less. He got what he wanted."

"Well, now you know otherwise." And now *she* knew that getting information out of Ithicana would be just as challenging as predicted. "Perhaps you might send him a letter yourself reassuring him of your good intentions."

"I don't have time for carrying on a casual correspondence with your father, or"—he picked up the letter—"the Magpie, judging from the penmanship."

Bloody hell, the Ithicanians were good. Lara averted her gaze. "Your time is clearly precious. Please do carry on with whatever it is you need to do."

He started to turn, then hesitated, and from the corner of her eye, she watched him catch sight of the deck of cards she'd left sitting on the table. "You play?"

A mix of nerves and excitement filled her, the same feeling she got before stepping into the training yard to fight. This was a different kind of battle, but that didn't mean she wouldn't win.

"Of course I play."

He hesitated, then asked, "Do you care for a game?"

Shrugging, she picked up the deck and expertly shuffled, the cards making sharp snapping sounds in her hands. "Do you really wish to gamble with me, Your Majesty? I must warn you, I'm quite good."

"One of your many talents?"

Lara's heart skipped, and she wondered if he remembered more from their intimate encounter than she realized. Yet he only eyed her for a moment, then took the seat across from her, resting one booted foot on his knee. "Do you have any coin to bet, or am I risking my money on both sides of every wager?"

She gave him a cool smile. "Pick a different stake."

"How about truths?"

Lara cocked one eyebrow. "That's a children's game. What are we to do next? Dare each other to run around the house naked?"

Because nudity had been more in line with what she'd thought he'd suggest. The cards were a trick of seduction that Mezat, their Mistress of the Bedroom, had taught the sisters. All men, she had told them, were happy to risk their own clothing for a chance to see naked breasts. Except, it turned out, for the King of Ithicana.

"We can save the naked sprints for storm season. It's far more exciting if there's lightning biting at your ass."

Shaking her head, Lara shuffled the cards again. "Poker?" Best to choose a game in which she would not lose.

"How about Trumps?"

"More luck than skill in that game."

"I know." The way he said it was like a dare. And for better or worse, she never turned down a challenge, so she shrugged. "As you like. To nine?"

"Boring. How about a truth for each trump."

Her mind raced with questions she might ask. With questions that *he* might ask, and the answers she'd give.

Reaching over to the corner table, Aren picked up a bottle of amber liquor, took a mouthful, then set it between them. "To make things more fun."

One of her eyebrows rose. "There are glasses on the sideboard, you know."

"Less work for Eli this way."

Rolling her eyes, she took a mouthful. The brandy, as it turned out to be, burned like fire down her throat. Then she dealt the cards, silently cursing when he had the trump. "Well?"

Taking the bottle, Aren eyed her thoughtfully and Lara's heart began to hammer. There were a thousand things he could ask, for which she had no answer. For which she'd have to lie, and then keep that lie alive for the length of her time here. And the more lies she had to balance, the greater chance of getting caught.

"What is"—he took a mouthful—"your favorite color?"

Lara blinked, her heart stuttering and then settling even as she looked away from his hazel eyes, feeling heat rise to her cheeks. "Green."

"Excellent. Plenty of that about, so I need not ply your favor with emeralds."

Giving a soft snort of amusement, Lara handed over the cards, which he swiftly shuffled and then dealt.

She won the next round.

"I'll not ask you nonsense questions," she warned, taking the bottle from him. Her questions needed to be strategic—not intended to uncover the secrets of the bridge, but to understand the man who held those secrets so close to his heart. "Did you take pleasure in killing those raiders? In watching them die?"

Aren winced. "Still angry about that, then?"

"A fortnight is not sufficient time for me to forget the cold-blooded slaughter of a ship full of men."

"I suppose not." Aren leaned back in the chair, eyes distant. "Pleasure." He said the word as though he were tasting it, trying it out, then shook his head. "No, not pleasure. But there is a certain satisfaction to seeing them die."

Lara said nothing, and her silence was rewarded a moment later.

"I've served at Midwatch since I was fifteen. Commanded it since I was nineteen. Over the past ten years, I've lost track of the number of battles I've fought against raiders. But I remember all thirteen times we were too late. When we reached our people after the raiders had their way with them. Families slaughtered. And for what? Fish? They have nothing worth taking. So instead they take their lives."

Lara pressed the palms of her hands to her skirts, sweat soaking through the silk. "Why do they do it, then?"

"They think they can learn ways into the bridge through them. But the civilians don't use the bridge. They don't know its secrets. You'd think after all these years our enemies would have figured that out. Maybe they have." His face twisted. "Maybe they just kill them for *pleasure*."

His fingers brushed hers as he passed over the deck, warm against her icy skin. Aren won the next hand.

"Since we are asking difficult questions . . ." He tapped one finger against his chin. "What's your worst memory?"

She had a hundred worst memories. A thousand. Of abandoning her sisters to fire and sand. Of Erik, the man who'd been like a father to her, taking his own life in front of her because he believed she'd been driven to murder her own sisters. Of being left alone in a pit in the ground for weeks. Of being starved. Of being beaten. Of having to fight for her life, all while her masters told her that it was to make her strong. To teach her to endure. *We do this to protect you*, they had told her and her sisters. *If you need someone to hate, someone blame, look to Ithicana. To its king. If not for them, if not for him, none of this would be necessary. Bring them down, and no Maridrinian girl will ever suffer like this again.*

The memories triggered something deep within her, an irrational wash of rage and fury and fear. A hatred for this place. An even deeper hatred for the man sitting across from her.

Slowly, she shoved the emotions deep down inside her, but as she lifted her head, Lara could tell Aren had seen all of it play across of her face.

Give him a truth.

"I was born in the harem in Vencia. I lived there with my mother among all the other wives and younger children. After the treaty was signed, my father had all of his female children of appropriate age taken to the compound for their—for *our*—protection from Valcotta and Amarid and anyone else who sought to disrupt the alliance. I was five years old." She swallowed, the vision of the memory fuzzy, but the sounds and smells sharp as though they were yesterday. "There was no warning. I was playing when the soldiers grabbed me, and I remember kicking and screaming as they dragged me away. They smelled awful—like sweat and wine. I remember more men holding my mother against the ground. Her fighting, trying to get to me. Trying to stop them from taking me." Lara's eyes burned, and she chased away the tears with a mouthful of brandy. Then another. "I never saw her again."

"I wasn't fond of your father before," Aren said quietly. "Less so, now."

"The worst part is . . ." She trailed off, staring at the insides of her eyelids, trying to find what she was looking for. "Is that I can't remember her face. If I met her on a street, I'm not sure I'd even know it was her."

"You'd know."

Lara bit the insides of her cheeks, hating that he, of all people, would say something that would bring her comfort. *It's because of him you were taken from your mother. It's his fault. He is the enemy. The enemy. The enemy.*

A knock sounded loudly against the door, and Lara jumped, ripped from her thoughts by the interruption.

"Come in," Aren said, and the door opened to reveal a beautiful young woman dripping with weapons. Her long black hair was shaved on the sides, the rest pulled into a tail on top of her head—a style that seemed to be favored by the female warriors—and her eyes were a pale grey. Half a head taller than Lara, her bare arms were solid with muscle, her skin marked with old scars.

"This is Lia. She's part of my guard. Lia, this is Lara. She's..."

"Queen." The young woman inclined her head. "It is an honor to meet you, Your Grace."

Lara inclined her head, curious about Ithicana's female warriors. Her father had told Lara and her sisters that they'd be underestimated because they were women, but the women here seemed to be as respected as any man.

Lia had turned her attention back to her king and was handing him a folded piece of paper. "Season's been declared over."

"I heard the horns. Two weeks earlier than last year."

Lara picked up her own letter, hoping they'd say more if they believed her distracted. Serin had written about her eldest brother, Rask, who was heir. He'd apparently fought successfully in some tourney, and the Magpie described the events in vivid detail. Not that she cared, having never had anything to do with her brother. The Ithicanian codebreaker had circled the letters that formed the code, but not, she realized, *Marylyn's code*. Rereading the document with an eye for the code her eldest sister had created, Lara contained a smile as she lifted the pattern from the page. Apparently the Ithicanians were fallible, after all.

Her hidden smile vanished as she parsed the code. *Maridrina receiving only rotten produce. Molding grains. Diseased cattle. Valcottan ships departing with holds full of superior goods.*

Serin had explained the new trade terms that had been negotiated as part of the treaty. The elimination of taxes on goods Maridrina purchased in Northwatch, which would then be shipped to Southwatch with no tolls. On the surface, it was a good deal for Maridrina and a large concession for Ithicana. Unless one considered that it placed all the risk of goods deteriorating during transport on Maridrina's shoulders. If the grain purchased in Northwatch rotted before it reached Southwatch, it was Maridrina's loss and not Ithicana's problem. And what wonder Maridrina was receiving the worst of goods when it was Ithicana who coordinated the transport. The pages crumpled slightly under Lara's grip, and she tore her eyes from the writing as she heard Aren say, "No getting around her request, I suppose."

Lia agreed, then inclined her head. "I'll leave you to it."

Lara watched the other woman leave, struggling to master her expression. Serin's message didn't surprise her, but it was still infuriating to know that the man calmly sitting across from her playing cards was consciously making choices to harm her people.

Cards snapped against the table. Another hand. Another truth.

Picking them up, Lara eyed the hand, knowing they were high and that she should think up a question that gained her something. But when she won, the question that came out was something different. "How did your parents die?"

Aren stiffened, then scrubbed a hand through his hair. Reaching over, he jerked the bottle out of her hand, draining it dry.

Lara waited. In her failed searches for maps, she'd found other things. Personal things. Drawings of the prior king and queen, the resemblance between Aren and Ahnna and their beautiful mother striking. She'd also found a box full of treasures that only a mother would keep. Baby teeth in a jar. Portraits. Notes written in a childish script. There had been rough little carvings, too, with Aren's name scratched on the bottom. A much different family than her own.

"They drowned in a storm," he answered flatly. "Or at least, he did. She was probably already dead."

There was more to that story, but it was clear he had no intention of sharing it. And that he was running out of patience for this horrible game of chance. More cards on the table. Lara won again.

You rattled him, she told herself. *He's been drinking. Now is the time to push.*

"What's it like inside the bridge?" Her eyes skipped from the cards, to the empty bottle, to his hands, resting on the arms of his chair. Strong. Capable. The sensation of them running across her body danced across her skin, the taste of his mouth on hers, and she shoved the thoughts away as her cheeks—and other parts of her body—heated.

His eyes sharpened, the haze of brandy wiped away. "You need not concern yourself with what the bridge is or is not like, as you'll never have cause to be in it."

Aren rose to his feet. "My grandmother wishes to meet you, and she is not one to be denied. We'll go tomorrow at dawn. By *boat*." He leaned down, resting his hands on the sides of her chair, the muscles of his arms standing out in stark relief. Invading her space. Attempting to intimidate her the way his damned kingdom intimidated every other.

"Let me make myself abundantly clear, Lara. Ithicana has not held the bridge by spilling its secrets over a bottle of brandy, so if that's your intent, you'll have to get more creative. Better yet, save us all the trouble and forget it even exists."

Lara leaned back in her chair, never breaking eye contact. With both hands, she pulled up the skirt of her dress, higher and higher until her thighs were revealed, seeing the intensity of his gaze shift to a different target. Lifting one leg, she pressed a naked foot against his chest, watching his eyes race from her knee to her thigh to the silken underthings she wore beneath.

"How about you take your bridge," she said sweetly, "and shove it up your ass." His eyes widened right as she straightened her leg, shoving him out of her space. Picking up her book, she tugged her skirt back into place. "I'll see you at dawn. Goodnight, Your Grace."

A faint chuckle filled her ears, but she refused to look up even as he said, "Goodnight, Princess," and disappeared from the room.

VITEX WOVE HIS way in a serpentine pattern between Aren's ankles, purring as he went, seemingly not inclined to desist in his pursuit of attention, despite the fact that Aren had been ignoring him for at least ten minutes.

The nearly blank sheet of paper on the desk taunted him, golden edges glinting in the lamplight. He'd gotten as far as writing out the formal greeting to King Silas Veliant of Maridrina, but not a word further. His intention had been to accede to Lara's request and correspond with her father, to assure the man of his daughter's wellbeing. But now, the pen in his hand on the verge of dripping onto the expensive stationery, Aren found himself at a loss of what to say.

Mostly because Lara remained an enigma. He'd attempted to learn more about her nature during that awful card game, and after hearing how she'd been taken from her mother, it was very clear that if she was a spy, it wasn't out of love for her father. But that didn't mean she was innocent. Loyalty, to a certain extent, could be purchased, and Silas had means.

Irritated with the circular nature of his thoughts, Aren tossed his pen aside. Picking up the box of stationery, he pulled up the false side to reveal the narrow drawer designed to hide documents from prying eyes, and shoved the letter to Lara's father inside. He would complete it once he was more certain that Lara's welfare was something he could assure.

Patting his cat once on the head, he shooed the animal out the door and strode down the hallway. Eli was polishing silverware, but he looked up at Aren's approach. "Going to the barracks, Your Grace?"

It was painfully tempting to escape down to the barracks where he could sit around the fire with his soldiers, drink and properly gamble, but that would raise questions as to why he *wasn't* spending his nights with his new wife. "Just a walk down to the cliffs."

"I'll leave a lamp burning for you, Your Grace." The boy turned back to his work.

Forgoing a lantern, Aren walked down the narrow path to a spot where naked rock overhung the sea. Waves crashed against the black rock of the cliffs below, water rushing as it retreated only to surge forth again, slamming against Midwatch like an implacable, relentless hammer. Ferocious, yet somehow peaceful, the sound lulling Aren's senses as he stared at the blackness over the sea.

Groaning, he laid back, the water pooled on the rocks soaking into his clothes as he stared up into the night, the sky a patchwork of cloud and stars, not a light in any direction to distract from their glimmer. His civilians knew better than that, especially in the shoulder season. The moment in the year when the storms ceased to protect Ithicana, and his kingdom was forced to rely on steel, wits, and secrecy.

Would that ever change? Could it?

Paper crinkled against his chest, the pages tucked inside his tunic what had driven him to seek Lara tonight. They were kill orders.

Two fifteen-year-old girls had stolen a boat in an apparent attempt to escape Ithicana. They'd planned to go north to Harendell, according to the information that had been gleaned from their friends.

The kill order was for them. The charge: treason.

It was forbidden for civilians to leave Ithicana. Only highly trained spies were granted the right to do so, and always on the order that if they were ever caught, they'd die on their own sword before revealing

Ithicana's secrets. Only the career soldiers in his army knew all the ways in and out of the bridge, but it was impossible to keep the island defenses from the civilians who lived on them, and *everyone* knew about Eranahl. Which was why any civilian caught attempting to leave was flogged. And any who succeeded in the attempt were hunted.

And Ithicana's hunters always caught their quarry.

Fifteen. Aren clenched his teeth, feeling sickness rising in his guts. The report didn't give a reason for why the girls had fled. It didn't need to. At fifteen, they'd been assigned to their first garrison. It would be their first War Tides, and they'd have no choice but to fight. And rather than doing so, they risked their lives to flee. To find another path. Another life.

And he was supposed to order their execution for the offense.

His parents had rarely fought, but this law had brought out the shouts and slammed doors, his mother pacing the rooms in such fervor that he and Ahnna had both listened in fear of one of her fits taking her, of her heart stopping, never to beat again. Closing his eyes, he heard the echo of her voice, shouting at his father, "We are in a cage, a prison of our own making. Why can't you see that?"

"It's what keeps our people safe," his father would shout back. "Let down our guard, and Ithicana is *done*. They will tear us apart in their fight to possess the bridge."

"You don't know that. It could be different, if we tried to make it so."

"The raiders who come every year say otherwise, Delia. This is how we keep Ithicana alive."

And always, she would whisper, "Alive isn't living. They deserve more."

Aren shook his head to drive away the memory. Except it only receded, content to haunt him.

Allowing civilians to come and go from Ithicana all but ensured every one of the kingdom's secrets would leak. Aren knew that. But if Ithicana had strong alliances with Harendell and Maridrina, the consequences of those leaks would be far more palatable. With the navies of those two kingdoms supporting the bridge's defense, it would give some of his people a chance to pursue paths other than the sword. To leave and educate themselves. To bring that knowledge home and share it. It would mean he'd no longer have to sign kill orders for children.

But the older generations were adamantly against such a move. A lifetime of war had turned them against outsiders, filled them with hate. And filled them with fear. He needed Lara to help him change that, to make them see Maridrinians as friends, not foes. To convince them to fight for a better future, no matter the risks.

Because how things were . . . It couldn't continue forever.

Pulling the papers from his pocket, Aren shredded them, allowing the breeze to carry them out to sea.

Then there was a commotion in the bushes, and Aren was on his feet, blade in hand in time to see Eli burst into the open. The servant boy skidded to a stop, breathless, and said, "It's the queen, Your Grace. She needs your help."

HANDS HELD HER wrists, pinning them to the table. Cloth covered her eyes. Her nose. Her mouth.

Water poured down, an endless torrent.

Only to cease.

"Why were you sent to Ithicana?" a voice whispered in her ear. "What is your purpose? What do you want?"

"To be a bride. To be queen," she choked, fighting her restraints. "I want peace."

"Liar." The voice sent fear through her. "You're a spy."

"No."

"Admit it!"

"There's nothing to admit."

"Liar!"

The water poured, and she drowned all over again. Unable to voice the truth to save herself. Unable to breathe.

There was sand beneath the fingers, cold and dry. She couldn't move, her wrists and ankles bound and tied to her waist. Trussed up like a pig.

Darkness.

She rolled, colliding with a wall, more sand falling onto her head, dragging at her hair. Backward, the same.

No way out.

Except up.

Fear binding her in place, she lifted her head to see faceless figures staring down at her.

So far away. With her wrists tied so tight the skin sloughed off, there was no way to climb.

"Why have you come to Ithicana? What is your purpose? Are you a spy for your father?"

"To be queen." Her throat burned, so dry. So thirsty. "To be a bride of peace. I am no spy."

"Liar."

"I'm not."

Sand struck her in the face. Not just tiny grains, but chunks of rock that bruised and sliced. Forcing her to cringe. To grovel. Eleven shovels flung sand at her from all sides. Striking her. Hurting her. Filling the hole.

Burying her alive.

"Tell us the truth!"

"I am!" The sand was up to her chin.

"Liar!"

She couldn't breathe.

She was seated on a chair, her wrists bound together. Her nails picked and scratched at the ropes, blood trickling down her palms. Fabric covered her eyes, but she could feel the heat of flames.

"They will do worse to you in Ithicana, Lara," Serin's voice crooned in her ear. "Far worse." He whispered the horrors, and she screamed, needing to get away. Needing to escape.

"Worse things will be done to your sisters," he sang, pulling off her hood.

There was fire in her eyes. Burning. Burning. Burning.

"You will not touch my sisters," she screamed. "You cannot have them. You will not hurt them."

Except it was Marylyn holding the coals to her feet, not Serin. Sarhina, tears running down her face, who tightened the noose.

And it was Lara who was burning. Her hair. Her clothes. Her flesh.

She could not breathe.

A hand was gripping her, shaking her. "Lara? Lara!"

Lara reached up, catching hold of the hilt of her knife, remembering herself just in time to stop from stabbing Aren in the face.

"You were having a nightmare. Eli fetched me when they heard you screaming."

A nightmare. Lara took a deep breath, digging deep into her core for some semblance of calm. Only then did she see the door hanging crooked on its frame, the latch in pieces scattered across the floor. Aren wore the same clothes he had earlier, his hair damp and clinging to his forehead.

Tearing her eyes away, Lara reached for a water glass, her mouth tasting sour from too much brandy. "I can't remember anything." A lie, given the smell of burning hair still filled her nose. Nightmares that weren't dreams, but memories of her training. Had she said anything incriminating? Had he realized she was reaching for the knife under her pillow?

Aren nodded, but his brow furrowed, suggesting that he didn't quite believe her. The sweat-soaked sheets peeled off her skin as she leaned out of the bed to fill her glass with the water pitcher, knowing the nightgown she wore only barely covered her breasts and hoping the flash of skin would distract him.

"Who did that to you?"

Lara froze, certain in an instant that she *had* shouted something damning while caught in her fugue state. Her eyes skipped to the open door, calculating her chances of escape, but then his fingers grazed the skin of her back, following a familiar pattern. Scars, which her sister Sarhina had rubbed oil into every night for years until they'd faded into thin white lines.

"Who did this?" The heat in his voice made her skin prickle.

Serin had ordered it done after she'd snuck out of the compound and into the desert to watch one of the caravans as it passed, countless camels and men laden with goods to sell in Vencia. For her troubles, she'd received a dozen lashes, Serin screaming the entire time that she'd put *everything* at risk. Lara had never entirely understood why he'd been so angry. There'd been no chance of the caravan catching sight of her, and all she'd wanted was to see what goods they carried.

"My teachers were strict," she muttered. "But it was a long time ago. I almost forget they're there."

Rather than appeasing him, Aren only appeared to grow angrier. "Who treats a child this way?"

Lara opened her mouth, then closed it, no good answer coming to mind. All of her sisters had suffered beatings for infractions, though none as often as she. "I was a disobedient child."

"And they thought to beat the trait out of you?" His voice was icy.

Pulling the sheet up to cover her body, Lara didn't answer. Didn't trust herself to.

"For what it's worth, no one will lay a hand on you in Ithicana. You have my word." Rising, he picked up the lamp. "Dawn is only a few hours away. Try to get some sleep." He left the room, pulling the broken door shut behind him.

Lara lay in bed, listening to the soothing patter of rain against the window, still feeling the trace of Aren's fingers on her bare skin. Still hearing the adamancy in his voice that she'd never be hurt in Ithicana, a promise so entirely at odds with everything she knew about him and his kingdom. *His word means shit,* she reminded herself. He gave his word to allow Maridrina free trade, and all her homeland had to show for it was rotten meat.

Her goal was the bridge. Finding a way past Ithicana's defenses and into the structure coveted by all. And today, Aren was taking her on a tour of his kingdom. With luck, she'd see how they traveled, where and how they launched their boats, where their civilians were located. It was the first step toward a successful invasion. The first step toward Maridrina returning to prosperity.

Focus on that, she told herself. *Focus on what this means for your people.*

But no amount of deep breathing steadied the rapid pulse in her throat. Rising from the bed, she went to the doorway to the antechamber. Jumping, she caught hold of the frame, her nails digging into the wood as she pulled herself up and lowered herself down, the muscles in her back and arms flexing and burning as she repeated the motion thirty times. Forty. Fifty. Imagining her sisters doing pull-ups next to her, urging each other on even as they fought for victory.

Dropping to the ground, Lara lay on the floor and moved on to crunches, her abdominals fiery beasts as she passed one hundred. Two hundred. Three hundred. The Red Desert was hotter than Ithicana, but the humidity here was murder. Sweat dripped down her skin as she moved from exercise to exercise, the pain doing more than any meditation to drive away unwanted thoughts.

By the time Clara knocked on the door with a tray full of food and a steaming cup of coffee, Lara was ravenous and beyond caring if the servant noticed her red face and sweaty clothes.

Drinking the coffee, she mechanically shoveled food down her throat, then bathed before donning the same clothes she'd worn during her last trek through the jungle, including the heavy leather boots. She belted her knives at her waist and wove her hair in a tight braid that hung down the center of her back. Light was beginning to glow around the heavy drapes on the window when she left the room.

She found Eli sweeping the hallway. "He's waiting for you out front, my lady."

Aren was indeed waiting, and Lara took a moment to watch him through the glass window before making her presence known. He sat on the steps, elbows resting on the stone behind him, the muscles of his arms bare beneath the short sleeves of his tunic, vambraces buckled onto his forearms. The rising sun, for once not obscured by clouds, glinted off the arsenal of weapons strapped to his person, and Lara scowled at her lone pair of knives, wishing she were similarly armed.

Pushing open the door, Lara took a deep breath of the humid air, tasting the salt of the sea on the soft breeze and smelling the damp earth. A silver mist drifted through the jungle canopy, the air filled with the drone of insects, the call of birds, and the screeches of other creatures for which she had no name.

Aren rose without acknowledging her or her nightmare, and she followed a few steps behind so that she could watch him without scrutiny as they walked down the narrow, muddy trail. He had a predatory grace about him: a hunter, his eyes roving the ground, the canopy, the sky, his bow held loosely in his left hand rather than slung over one shoulder the way her father's soldiers carried them. He would not be caught unaware, and she idly wondered *just* how good a fighter he was. Whether, if it came down to it, she'd be able to best him.

"You always look like you want to kill someone," he remarked. "Possibly me."

Kicking a loose rock, Lara scowled at the muddy pathway. "I hadn't realized the dowager queen still lived." Indeed, she'd been under the impression that all who remained of the royal line were the king and his sister.

"She doesn't. Nana is my father's mother." Aren turned his head as something rustled in the bushes. "My mother, Delia Kertell, was the one born to the royal line. My father's family was common-born, but he rose through the military ranks and was chosen to join her honor guard. Mother took a liking to him and decided to marry him. My grandmother . . . she's a healer, of some renown. Although others might use different words to describe her, my sister included."

"And why does she want to see me, exactly?"

"She's seen you," he said.

Lara narrowed her eyes.

"When you first came and were still asleep. She checked to ensure your health was good. What she wants is to meet you. As to why . . . She's meddlesome and everyone, including me, is too terrified to say no to her."

The idea of a stranger inspecting her body while she was unconscious felt profoundly invasive. Lara's skin crawled, but she covered the reaction with a shrug. "Checking to see if my father had sent a pox-ridden girl to send you to your grave?"

Aren tripped and dropped his bow, swearing as he reached down to retrieve it from the mud.

"Not the swiftest method of assassination, but effective,

nonetheless." She added, "And some might say the repugnance of the victim's final years, hours, days, is worth the wait."

The King of Ithicana's eyes widened, but he recovered quickly. "If that's how you intend to do me in, you'll want to move quickly. The pustules and skin rashes will reduce your appeal, I'm afraid."

"Hmm," Lara hummed, then clicked her tongue against her teeth in mock disappointment. "I'd hoped to wait until the dementia had taken over so as to spare myself the memory. But one must do what one must do."

He laughed, the sound rich and full, and Lara found herself smiling. They rounded a bend and came into a clearing dominated by a large building, a group of Ithicanian soldiers loitering in the sunlight.

"Midwatch barracks," Aren said by way of explanation. "Those twelve are my—our—honor guard."

The stone structure was large enough to house hundreds of men. "How many soldiers are here?"

"Enough." He strode through the clearing toward those waiting for them.

"Majesties," one of them said, bowing deeply, although there was amusement in his tone, as though such honorifics were rarely used. Tall and corded with muscle, he was old enough to be Aren's father, his close-cropped brown hair laced with grey. Lara stared into his dark brown eyes, something about his voice familiar, and after a heartbeat, she recognized it as that of the man who'd conducted the Ithicanian portion of her wedding.

"This is Jor," Aren said. "He's the captain of the guard."

"So nice to see you again," she replied. "Do all Ithicanian soldiers have side jobs, or are you an exception?"

The soldier blinked once, then a smile grew on his face, and he gave her an approving nod. "Good ear, princess."

"Poor memory, soldier. I'm a princess no longer—you yourself ensured that." She walked past them all, heading down the narrow path to the sea.

The older man laughed. "I hope you sleep with one eye open, Aren."

"And a knife under your pillow," Lia added, and the whole group laughed.

Aren laughed along with them, and Lara wondered if they knew that he'd yet to consummate their marriage. That by the laws of both kingdoms, they could walk their separate ways. Casting a backward glance over her shoulder, she met Aren's gaze unblinking and he swiftly looked away, giving a root crossing the trail a violent kick.

It didn't take long to reach the tiny cove where they hid the boats, which were a variety of sizes. They resembled canoes, except they had an outboard frame linking them to either one or two additional hulls, which she supposed balanced them in the waves. Some of them were rigged with masts and sails, including the pair into which the group loaded their weapons and gear. A hint of fear grew in Lara's chest. The boats were *tiny* compared to the ship she had taken for the crossing to Southwatch, and the seas beyond the cliff walls protecting the cove suddenly seemed rougher than they had moments ago, the whitecaps rising high and fierce, certain to swamp the flimsy vessels.

A dozen excuses filled her mind as to why she shouldn't, couldn't, leave the shore. But this was why she was in Ithicana—to find a way past their defenses—and Aren was about to reveal the information without any concession on her part. She'd be a fool to pass up the opportunity.

Aren stepped into the boat, then held out a hand for her, easily keeping his balance as the vessel rose and fell beneath him. Lara held her ground, biting the insides of her cheeks as she felt his scrutiny. He opened his mouth, but she beat him to it. "I can't swim, if that's what you're wondering." She hated admitting the weakness, and from the faint smile on his face, he knew it.

"I'm not sure I've ever met anyone who couldn't swim."

She crossed her arms. "It's hardly a necessary skill in the middle of the Red Desert."

All the soldiers studiously busied themselves with various tasks, every one of them clearly listening.

"Well." Aren turned to squint at the sea. "You've seen what prowls these waters. Drowning might be the easier way to go."

"How comforting." She ignored his hand and stepped into the boat before she could lose her nerve. It swayed beneath the added weight, and Lara dropped to her knees, clinging to the edge.

Laughing softly, Aren knelt next to her, holding up a black piece of fabric. "Sorry for this, but some secrets must be kept." Not waiting for assent, he blindfolded her.

Shit. She should've known it wouldn't be this easy. But sight wasn't the only way to discover information, so she kept her mouth shut.

"Let's go," he ordered, and the boat surged away from the beach.

For a moment, Lara thought it wouldn't be that bad, and then they must have slipped out of the cove, because the boat began to buck and plunge like a wild horse. Lara's heart thundered in her chest, and she clung to the bottom, not caring what Aren or the rest of the Ithicanians thought of her as water splashed her clothes, soaking them through. If they tipped over, or if one of them threw her in, none of her training would help her. She'd be dead.

And then eaten.

On the heels of her terror came a wave of nausea, her mouth filling with sour saliva no matter how many times she swallowed. *You can do this. Get control of yourself.* She clenched her teeth, fighting against the rising contents of her stomach. *Do not throw up,* she ordered herself. *You will not throw up.*

"She's going to puke," Jor said.

As if on cue, Lara's breakfast rose fast and violent, and she leaned blindly toward the edge right as the boat tipped sharply in the same direction. Her grip on the boat slipped even as she vomited, and she fell face first into the water. The cold sea closed over her head, and she flailed, imagining the water filling her lungs, fins circling around her. Teeth rising up to jerk her under.

She'd been here before. Drowned. Smothered. Strangled.

An old terror with a new face.

She could not breathe.

Hands grabbed at her tunic, hauling her back into the boat. She slammed into something solid and warm, then someone peeled up the edge of the fabric covering her face, and she found herself staring into the depths of Aren's hazel eyes.

"I've got you." His grip on her was so fierce it should've hurt, but was instead almost as comforting as being on dry land. Behind him was the bridge pier with the opening at its base, so tantalizingly close that her fear eased. But Aren pulled the blindfold back down, plunging her back into darkness.

The loss of her sight sent a wave of dizziness through her. Sweat mixed with the water dripping down her face, her breath coming in frantic little gasps.

She inhaled a ragged breath, fighting for the calm void she'd been trained to find if tortured when one of the guards said, "We could take the bridge. This seems cruel."

"No," Jor snapped. "Not happening."

But Lara felt Aren still. He was considering the idea. Which he'd only be doing if he, too, believed unnecessarily terrifying her was cruel. So she let her fear take hold.

Once she did, there was no turning back. Her terror was a wild beast of a thing bent on consuming her. Her chest clenched, her lungs paralyzed, and stars danced across her vision.

The waves tossed the boat up and down, the spikes set into the sea scraping along the metal-lined hull. Lara clung to Aren, the strength of his arm holding her against his chest and her fingernails digging into his shoulders the only things keeping her from falling into madness.

Vaguely, she heard the group arguing, but their words were a dull drone of noise, as unclear as a foreign language. But Aren's command, "Just do it!" cut through the fog.

The soldiers around her grumbled and swore. The steel plates on the hull ground against rock, and a second later, the violent buck and swell of the sea ceased. They were inside the bridge pier, but her panic didn't ease, for there was still water everywhere. She could still drown.

A crackle of a torch. The smell of smoke. The boat shifting as the soldiers disembarked. Lara fought to take note of these details, but her focus centered on the water surrounding her, on what was lurking within it.

"There's a ladder." Aren's chin, rough with stubble, brushed against her forehead as he shifted. "Can you reach up and grab it? Can you climb?"

Lara couldn't move. Her chest felt like bands of steel were wrapped around it, every exhalation painful. There was a faint repetitive thumping against the bottom of the boat, and it took her far too long to realize that it was because she was shaking and her boot was hitting the hull. But she couldn't seem to stop it. Couldn't seem to do anything but cling to Aren's neck, her knees clamped around his thighs like a vise.

"I promise I won't let you fall in." His breath was warm against her ear, and very slowly, she mastered enough of her panic to let go of his neck with one hand, reaching up to find the cold metal of the ladder. But it took all the bravery she possessed to let go of him, to pull herself up, blindly reaching for the next rungs.

Aren stood with her, gripping her waist with one arm, his other braced on the steel. He lifted her up, holding her steady until her feet found the ladder.

"How far?" she whispered.

"Sixty more rungs, from where your hands are now. I'll be right beneath you. You won't fall."

Lara's breath was deafening in her ears as she went up, rung by rung, her whole body quivering. She'd never felt like this before. Never been so afraid—not even when she'd stared death in the eye when her father had come to take Marylyn from the compound. She continued up and up, until someone grabbed her by the armpits, hauling her sideways, and set her down on solid stone.

"We'll keep that blindfold on only a little longer, Majesty," Jor said, but Lara hardly cared. There was a solid surface beneath her hands, and the ground wasn't moving. She could breathe.

Rock scraped against rock, boots thudded softly, then strong hands gripped her shoulders. Her blindfold was peeled back, and Lara found herself looking up into the King of Ithicana's worried face. Around them stood the soldiers, three of them holding torches that flickered yellow and orange and red. But beyond them yawned a darkness deeper than a moonless night. A blackness so complete, it was as though the sun itself had ceased to exist.

They were inside the bridge.

"ARE YOU ALL RIGHT, Lara?"

It took several seconds for Aren's question to register, Lara's attention all for the grey stone beneath her, which was stained dark with dirt and lichen. The bridge wasn't made from blocks, as she had thought, but rather a smooth and unblemished material. Like mortar . . . but stronger. She'd never seen anything like it. The air was musty and ripe with the smell of mildew and moisture and manure. Aren's voice echoed off the walls, asking after her well-being over and over before the sound disappeared into the endless corridor of black.

"Lara?"

"I'm fine." And she was, in the sense that her panic had settled with the solidness of the bridge beneath her feet, excitement slowly bubbling up to take its place. She had done it. She'd found a way into the bridge.

Everyone was staring at her, shifting their weapons and supplies with obvious unease. Aren had caved to her fear, and in doing so, had revealed one of Ithicana's secrets. Jor, in particular, did not look pleased.

Aren's face was unreadable. "We need to get moving. I don't want to miss the tide on our return." He frowned. "Not while they're running cattle."

Cattle. Food. According to Serin's letter, the best of it was finding its way into the holds of Valcottan ships, not Maridrinian stomachs.

Jor held up her blindfold. "Best we put this back on."

The group's footfalls reverberated as they walked, Lara's hand resting on Aren's arm for guidance, the wind and sea only faintly audible. The bridge bent and curved, rising on gentle inclines and dipping down on declines as it meandered through the islands of Ithicana. It was a ten-day journey at walking speed between Northwatch and Southwatch islands, and she could scarcely imagine what it would be like to be enclosed within the bridge for so long. With no sense of day or night. With no way to get out other than to run toward the mouths of this great beast.

Though there *were* ways out; she knew that with certainty now. But how many? How were they accessed from the interior of the bridge? Were the openings only to the piers, or were there others? How did the Ithicanians know where they were?

Foreigners from every kingdom, merchants and travelers, traversed the bridge regularly. They were always under Ithicanian escort, but she knew for fact they weren't blindfolded. Serin had told her and her sisters that the only markers in the bridge were those stamped in the floor indicating the distance between the beginning and end. There were, to his knowledge, no other signs or symbols, and the Ithicanians were apparently fastidious in removing any marks anyone attempted to place. Those caught doing so were forever forbidden from entering the bridge, no matter how much money they offered to pay.

Answers would not be easily gained. She needed to earn Aren's trust, and to do that, she needed him to think he was winning her over.

"I'm sorry for my . . . loss of composure," she murmured, hoping the others wouldn't overhear, though the acoustics made it impossible that they would not. "The sea is . . . I'm not . . ."

She struggled to articulate an explanation for her fear, settling with, "Thank you. For not letting me drown. And for not mocking me mercilessly."

With the blindfold in place, Lara had no way to judge his reaction, and the silence stretched before he finally answered. "The sea is dangerous. Only war takes more Ithicanian lives. But it's unavoidable in our world, so we must master our fear of it."

"You don't appear to fear it at all."

"You're wrong." He was silent for a dozen strides. "You asked me how my parents died."

Lara bit her lip, remembering: *They'd drowned.*

"My mother had been sick for years with a bad heart. She was taken by a fit one night. A bad one. One she wouldn't come back from. Though there was a storm blowing in, my father insisted on taking her to my grandmother on the slim hope she could help." Aren's voice shook, and he coughed once. "No one could say for certain, but I was told my mother wasn't even breathing when he loaded her into the boat and set sail. The storm came in fast. Neither of them was seen again."

"Why did he do it?" She was both fascinated and horrified. This hadn't been just any pair, but the king and queen of one of the most powerful kingdoms in the known world. "If she was already gone, why risk it? Or at the very least, why didn't he have someone else take her?"

"Moment of stupidity, I suppose."

"Aren." Jor's voice was chiding from where he walked behind them. "Tell it right or don't tell it all. You owe them that much."

Lara considered the older guard, curious about their relationship. Her father would've had the head of anyone who'd dare speak to him in such a way. Yet Jor seemed to do so without fear; and indeed, she felt nothing more than mild irritation from the king striding on her left.

Aren huffed out a breath, then said, "My father didn't send her with someone else, because he wasn't the sort of man to put his well-being ahead of another. As to why he risked it at all . . . I suppose it was because he loved my mother enough that the hope of saving her was worth his own life."

To risk everything for the slim chance of saving those you loved . . . Lara knew that compulsion because that was how she felt about her sisters. And it might cost her her own life just yet.

"Ill-fated romance aside, my point is, I know what it's like to lose something to the sea. To hate it. To fear it." He kicked a bit of rock, sending it rattling ahead of them. "It knows no master, most certainly not me."

He said nothing more on the issue, or on anything else.

There was no sense of time in the bridge, and it seemed they'd been striding down the path for eternity, when Aren finally came to a halt.

Blind, Lara stood utterly still, relying on her other senses as the soldiers shifted about. Boots scuffed against stone, the echoes making it difficult for her to tell from which direction they were working, but then a breeze brushed against her left hand at the same time it hit her cheek, fresh air filling her nostrils. The opening was in the wall, not the floor.

"The stairs are too steep to navigate blind." Aren flipped her over his shoulder, his hand warm against her thigh as he balanced her weight. Instinct had her grip him by the waist, her fingers digging into the hard muscles of his stomach as he stooped down. Only at the last second did she think to reach out, her hand running the length of a solid slab that must have made up the door. A door that, unless she missed her mark, blended seamlessly into the wall of the bridge.

The sounds of the jungle grew as they went down a curved staircase, then the soft light of the sun filtered through her blindfold.

Aren set her back onto her feet without warning. Lara swayed as the blood rushed from her head, his hand on her back, guiding her forward before she could find her bearings.

"Good enough," Jor announced from somewhere ahead, and the blindfold was tugged from her eyes. Lara blinked, looking around, but there was only jungle, the canopy blocking even the bridge from sight.

"It's not far," Aren said, and Lara silently trailed after him, careful to keep to the narrow path. The guards encircled them, weapons held loosely in their hands, their eyes watchful. Unlike her father, who was constantly surrounded by his cadre of soldiers, this was the first time since their wedding that she'd seen Aren treated like a king. The first time she'd seen them protect him so aggressively. What was different?

Was this island dangerous? Or was it something else? There was a crackle in the trees, and both Jor and Lia stepped closer to her, hands going to their weapons, and Lara realized it wasn't the king they were worried about protecting. It was her.

They skirted the edge of a cliff overlooking the sea, the water thirty feet below crashing violently against the rocks. Lara searched in both directions for a spot where men could land, but there was none. On the assumption it was the same way all around the island, she could see why the builders had chosen it as a pier. It was nearly impenetrable. Yet, given Aren had intended to come by boat, there must be a way.

The house appeared out of nowhere. One minute it was trees and vines and vegetation, the next, a solid stone structure, the windows flanked with the ubiquitous storm shutters that all buildings on Ithicana likely possessed. The stone was coated with green lichen, and as they approached, Lara determined it was made of the same material as the bridge, as were the outbuildings in the distance. Built to withstand the lethal tempests that battered Ithicana ten months of the year.

Coming around the house, she caught sight of a stooped figure working in a garden fenced by stone.

"Brace yourself," Jor muttered.

"Finally deigned to grace me with your presence, Your Majesty?" The old woman didn't rise or turn from her plants, but her voice was clear and strong.

"I only received your note last night, Grandmother. I came as soon as I could."

"Ha!" The woman turned her head and spit, the glob flying clear over the garden wall to smack against a tree trunk. "Dragged your heels all the way here, I suspect. Either that or the weight of your crown is making you sluggish."

Aren crossed his arms. "I don't have a crown, which you well know."

"It was a metaphor, you fool."

Lara lifted a hand to her mouth, trying not to laugh. Somehow, the motion caught the old woman's attention despite her back being turned. "Or is my grandson's tardiness the result of him tarrying to wipe puke off your face, little princess?"

Lara blinked.

"Smelled you from a hundred paces away, girl. All those years in the dunes gave you no stomach for the waves, I take it?"

Flushing, Lara glanced at her clothes, which were still damp from falling out of the boat. When she looked back up, Aren's grandmother was on her feet, an amused smile on her face. "It's your breath," she explained, and Lara struggled not to stomp on Aren's foot when he covered his own mouth to hide a smirk. The old woman noticed.

"A little seasickness wouldn't have killed her, you idiot. You shouldn't have caved."

"We took precautions."

"Next time let her puke." Her gaze shifted back to Lara. "They all call me Nana, so you can, too." Then she pointed a finger at one of the guards. "You, pluck and dress that bird. And you two"—she jerked her chin at another pair—"finish picking these and then wash them up. And you." She leveled a steely gaze at Lia. "There's a basket of laundry that needs scrubbing. See it done before you go."

Lia opened her mouth to protest, but Nana beat her to it. "What? Too good to scrub the skids from an old woman's drawers? And before you say yes, remember that I wiped your shitty ass more times than I care to count when you were a babe. Be grateful that I can at least still do that much for myself."

The tall guardswoman scowled but said nothing, only collected the basket and disappeared down the slope to retrieve water.

"I assume Jor has gone off to bother my students." It took Nana pointing it out for Lara to realize with a start that the man had abandoned them without her noticing. "It still hasn't sunk in that they aren't interested in an old lecher like him."

"Your girls can take care of themselves," Aren replied.

"That wasn't my point, now was it?" Nana pulled the gate to the garden shut, then shuffled in their direction. Her hair was solid silver, and her skin wrinkled, but her eyes were shrewd and discerning as she squinted at her grandson. "Teeth!"

The barked command made Lara jump, but without hesitation, Aren bent over and opened his mouth, allowing his grandmother to inspect his straight white teeth. She grunted with satisfaction and then patted his cheek. "Good boy. Now where's your sister been? Avoiding me?"

"Ahnna's teeth are fine, Grandmother."

"Not her teeth that concern me. Has Harendell asked for her yet?"

"No."

"Send her anyway. It shows good faith."

"No." The word came out of Aren as a growl, which surprised Lara. Surely he didn't intend to break his contract with the northern kingdom? Not when he'd been willing to fulfill his half without argument?

"Ahnna doesn't need your coddling, boy. She can take care of herself."

"That's between me and her."

Nana grunted and spit before turning her attention to Lara. "So this is what Silas sent us, is it?"

"Pleased to make your acquaintance." Lara inclined her head with the same respect she'd have given a Maridrinian matron.

"We'll see how long that pleasure lasts." Faster than Lara would've believed an old woman could move, Nana reached over and gripped her by the hips, twisted her this way and that, before running her hands up Lara's sides, laughing when Lara batted them away. "Built for bedding if not breeding." She leveled a stare at her grandson. "Which I'm certain you've noticed, even if you haven't availed yourself."

"Grandmother, for the love of god—"

Reaching up, Nana flicked his earlobe hard. "Mind your tongue, boy. Now as I was saying"—she turned back to Lara—"you'll labor hard, but you'll deliver. You've the willpower." She ran a quick finger down an old scar on Lara's arm, one she'd earned in a knife fight against a Valcottan warrior. "And you've known pain."

This woman was too shrewd. Too close. Lara snapped, "I'm not a broodmare."

"Thank goodness for that. We've little time for horses here in Ithicana. What we need is a queen who'll produce an heir. Unlike your father, my grandson won't have an entire harem to ensure the royal line continues. Just. You."

Lara crossed her arms, annoyed though she had no right to be. There was zero chance of her producing *anything*. She'd been supplied with a year's worth of contraceptive tonic. There would be no surprises on that front.

"Come with me, I'll give you something for the seasickness. Boy, you go find something else to keep you busy."

Lara followed her inside. She expected the interior of the home to be damp and musty like the bridge, but instead it was dry and warm, the polished wooden panels on the walls reflecting the flames in the fireplace. One wall hosted floor-to-ceiling shelves filled with jars packed with plants, powders, colored tonics, and what appeared to be insects of various sorts. There were also several long glass cages, and Lara shivered as she saw coiled forms move within them.

"Don't like snakes?"

"I have a healthy respect for them." This earned a cackle of approval.

After rooting around in her shelves, Nana produced a twisted root, which she passed to Lara. "Chew this before and while you're on the water. It will help keep the nausea at bay." Lara sniffed it uncertainly, relieved to discover the smell, at least, was not disagreeable.

"I've got nothing for overcoming fear, though. That's your own problem to manage."

"Given I can't swim, I feel my fear of water is as healthy as my respect for snakes."

"Learn." The curtness of the old woman's tone conveyed a lack of tolerance for complaint that reminded Lara briefly, painfully, of Master Erik.

With a jerk, Nana opened the curtains covering one of the windows, allowing the sunlight to spill inside, then beckoned Lara closer. "You've your father's eyes. And your grandfather's."

Lara shrugged. "The color is some small proof that I'm a true princess of Maridrina."

"I wasn't talking about the color." Quick as the snakes in the cages, Nana caught Lara by the chin, fingers pressing painfully against her jaw. "You're a sly little thing, just like them. Always searching for an advantage."

Resisting the urge to pull away, Lara stared back into the woman's eyes, which were hazel. Like Aren's. But what she saw within them was very different from what she saw in his. "You speak as though you know my family."

"I was a spy when I was young. Your grandfather recruited me into his harem. He had the foulest breath of any man I've ever met, but I learned to hold my breath and think of Ithicana."

Lara blinked. This woman had infiltrated the harem as a spy? That it could be done was alarming of itself, but only the loveliest girls were brought into the King's harem, and Nana was . . .

"Ha, ha!" Nana's laugh made her jump. "I didn't always look like the last prune left in the bowl, girl. In my day, I was quite the beauty." Her fingers tightened. "So don't think I don't know firsthand how you use your fair face to achieve your own ends. Or the ends of your country."

"I am here to nurture the peace between Ithicana and Maridrina," Lara replied coolly, considering whether she'd have to find a way to see this woman put down. While she was confident in her ability to manipulate Aren and those close to him, Nana was quite another story.

"This kingdom wasn't built by fools. Your father sent you to make trouble, and if you think we aren't watching you, you're wrong."

Unease flickered in Lara's chest.

"Aren cares a great deal for honor and he'll keep his word to you no matter what it costs him." Nana's eyes narrowed. "But I don't give a squirt of piss for honor. What I care about is family, and if I think you are a true threat to my grandson, don't think for a heartbeat that I won't arrange for an *accident* to occur." The woman's smile was all straight white teeth. "Ithicana is a dangerous place."

And I'm a dangerous woman, Lara thought before answering, "He seems more than capable of taking care of himself, but I appreciate your candor."

"I'm sure." Nana's eyes seemed to delve straight into Lara's soul, and she felt no small amount of relief when the old woman twitched the curtains shut and gestured to the door. "He won't want to miss the tides. Harendell is running cattle and he hates cows in the bridge."

Because they're not making him any money, Lara thought bitterly. But she couldn't help asking, "Why is that?"

"Because he got trampled during one of the annual runs when he was fifteen. Three cracked ribs and a broken arm. Though he'd tell you the worst was having to stay with me while he recovered."

Annual runs? What the hell was the old woman talking about? The only reason there was cattle in the bridge was because her father had arranged to have them purchased at Northwatch. Not for the first time, unease flickered through her at the disconnect between what she knew to be true and what she was seeing and hearing in Ithicana. *They must have been sold to Valcotta or another nation*, she decided. *Loaded onto ships so that Maridrina was bypassed entirely.* Though given Valcotta's enormous herds, she didn't see why they'd be importing them.

Pushing the thought aside, Lara followed Nana outside where she was blinded for a few paces by the brilliant sunlight, but when her vision cleared, it revealed Aren frowning as he haphazardly hung laundry on a line, a glowering Lia crouched next to a washbasin by his feet.

"I see there have been gaps in your education, boy." Nana scowled at a dripping sheet.

"I'm willing to accept certain personal failings." Aren jerked his hand away in horror from a voluminous pair of undergarments that Lia was trying to hand to him.

Nana rolled her eyes. "Useless child." But Lara didn't miss the faint smile that grew on the old woman's face as Aren dried his hands on his trousers.

"You intend to elaborate on why you had me drag Lara all the way here? I assume it wasn't for a five-minute conversation."

"Oh, Lara and I will be talking a great deal over the coming weeks, because you're going to leave her here with me."

Lara's mouth dropped open in horror, no amount of training enough to hide her dismay over this development.

Aren rocked from his heels to his toes, eyes narrowed. "Why would I do that?"

"Because she's the Rat King's spawn, and I'll not have her roaming

Midwatch while you're distracted with more important matters. Here I can keep an eye on her."

And probably arrange an accident within the week.

"No."

Nana planted her wrinkled hands on her hips. "I wasn't giving you the choice, boy. Besides, what need have you of her? Despite all the practice you've had over the years, you haven't had her on her back once, by my reckoning. And you aren't going to have time for it over the next two months, so she might as well be here where I can put her to use."

Aren exhaled a long, slow breath, casting his eyes up to the sky as though searching for patience. Lara bit her tongue, waiting for his response. Knowing she was screwed if he acceded to his grandmother's request.

"No. I didn't bring her to Ithicana to keep her locked up as a prisoner, and I certainly didn't bring her so you could keep her as a servant. She's coming with me."

Nana's jaw hardened, her muddy fingernails digging into the fabric of her tunic. *He's never said no to her before*, Lara thought, amazed.

"You've too much of your mother in you, Aren. Both of you blind, idealistic fools."

Silence.

"We're done here. Lara, come on." Aren twisted on his heel, and Lara scampered after him, half convinced that Nana would stick a knife in her back in a last-ditch effort to keep her from Aren. From behind, she heard the old woman snap, "Jor, you keep that boy safe or I'll cut your balls off and feed them to my snakes."

"Always do, Nana," Jor drawled, then trotted past Lara and Aren. "I'd walk faster. She's not a woman used to being denied."

Aren snorted, but kept to his measured pace. "I should've guessed this is what she wanted. Controlling old bat."

Controlling, yes, but also far too canny for her own good. Lara might be walking away with Aren, but he'd heard Nana's warnings. If Lara wasn't careful, he might begin to take those warnings to heart.

"You can't fault her for trying to protect her grandson. She's fond of you." Lara shied away from a tree hosting an enormous spider.

"Most people are. I'm quite charming, or so I'm told."

Lara shot him a pitying look. "A king should rarely take a compliment at face value. Sycophants, and all that."

"How fortunate that I now have you to give me the unvarnished truth."

"Would you prefer varnished lies?"

"Possibly. I'm not certain my untested ego is ready for so much abuse. My soldiers might not follow me if they're subjected to night after night of me crying in my cup."

"Try sobbing into your pillow—it muffles the noise."

Aren laughed, then glanced backward at the house. "What did she say to you?"

Holding up the root she'd been given, Lara paused, realizing that Nana had suspected Aren would refuse. Which begged the question: Why had he? The reason, she guessed, was more complicated than a desire to get her between the sheets. "Apparently she takes offense to the idea of me puking on your boots."

He rewarded her with a low chuckle that sent an unexpected thrill racing through her. Then he extracted the blindfold from where it had been tucked into his belt, her shoulders tightening reflexively as he wrapped it around her face, his fingers smelling like soap. "Do you want to walk or be carried?"

"Walk." Though she came to regret the decision when she'd tripped for about the dozenth time, relief filling her when they stepped into the cool darkness of the pier, Aren holding her elbows to steady her as she climbed the steps. She counted them, calculating the distance.

Back inside the bridge, the group moved at speed, no one speaking. So it was unmistakable when the faint sound of a horn, long and mournful, pierced the thickness of the stone encasing them. Aren and the rest stopped in their tracks, listening. It sounded again, the same long note, followed by a pattern of short peals that repeated three times in rapid succession before cutting off in the middle of the fourth, as though the horn had been ripped from the blower's lips.

"That's Serrith's call for aid," Jor said.

"Have its civilians departed for War Tides yet?" Aren demanded.

War Tides?

"No." Even with the blindfold on, Lara felt the tension running through the group crackling like an electric storm.

"Who's closest?" There was a shake to Aren's voice. A hint of something Lara had yet to see in him: *fear*.

Jor cleared his throat. "We are."

Silence.

"We can't leave her alone in the bridge," Aren said.

"We can't spare anyone to stay with her, and we don't have time to bring her back to Nana."

Lara bit her tongue, wanting to weigh in but knowing she was best served in saying nothing.

"No helping it. We'll have to bring her with us." Aren's hands brushed against the side of her face as he pulled off the blindfold. "Keep up. Keep silent. And when the fighting starts, stay out of the way."

Praying he'd mistake her excitement for fear, she nodded once. "I will."

The group broke into a run.

L ARA STRUGGLED TO keep pace with the Ithicanians, the stale air
burning in her chest as the group sprinted through the bridge.
Only luck allowed her to notice when Lia planted a foot square
on a mile marker, her mouth moving silently as she began counting
her strides.

Lara picked up Lia's count, storing away the number when the
other woman held up a hand and skidded to stop. Jor boosted her on
his shoulders while the rest prepared their gear. None of them spoke,
and Lara kept to the shadows as she watched Lia reach up to press her
palm against what appeared to be smooth stone. There was a heavy
click, then, with a heave of effort, she lifted up a hinged hatch in the
ceiling of the bridge.

Another way in.

Triumph rushed through Lara even as cool air gusted inside,
catching at the loose strands of her hair as Jor and Aren lifted the other
soldiers into the opening. Then Jor was up, and only she and Aren
remained.

"You ever reveal any of this to anyone, I'll kill you myself."

Without waiting for a response, he grabbed Lara by the waist and raised her up into the opening.

Jor caught hold of her arms, lifting her onto the top of the bridge before leaning down to haul Aren up as well, the two of them flipping the hatch shut. But it was hard for Lara to focus on what the men were doing, because she stood on a bridge through the clouds.

Wet mist had settled back on Ithicana while they'd been inside, and it whirled and gusted, pulling at her clothes before spinning away in violent little eddies. Below, the sea crashed against a pier or an island or maybe both—she couldn't tell. Couldn't see more than a dozen paces in either direction, and it was like being in a totally different world. Like being in a dream that stood on the brink of a nightmare.

"Be careful," Aren warned, taking her hand. "It's slippery, and we're at a high point. You wouldn't survive the fall."

She followed him at a slow run, everyone struggling to keep their balance on the slick surface as the bridge sloped down toward the next pier, which Lara could only faintly see through the mist. But before they reached it, the guards all dropped as though given an invisible cue, Aren hauling her down with him.

As Lara's hands pressed against the wet stone, her eyes landed on a mile marker, the wheels in her mind turning as a strategy for invasion began to form.

Jor had a spyglass out, which panned this way and that before freezing in place. "Amarid naval vessel." He passed the glass to Aren, who looked once, then swore.

"We should wait for reinforcements," Jor continued, taking the glass back and crawling to the opposite side of the bridge, staring out in the same direction as the rest of the soldiers. The mist swirled, revealing an island for a heartbeat before obscuring it again. "Once they get their whole crew on land, we'll be badly outnumbered."

No one spoke, and it was then that the winds shifted direction. With them came the screams.

"We go now," Aren ordered.

None of the guards argued. One of them attached a cable to a thick metal ring embedded in the bridge, the other end fixed to a heavy bolt that was fitted into a weapon designed like a crossbow. Then he handed it to Aren. "You do the honors, Your Grace?"

Aren took the weapon, kneeling on the stone. "Come on," he muttered. "Let me see."

The winds stalled, and no one seemed to breathe. Lara dug her fingers into the stone, watching and waiting, the anticipation making her heart race. Then the air roared against them, sweeping away the clouds, and Aren smiled once.

He released the bolt with a loud twang, grunting against the force of the recoil. The bolt soared toward the island, trailing the slender cable after it, and with a loud crack audible even from the distance, it spiked through one of the trees.

The soldier who'd given him the weapon tightened up the slack on the cable and knotted it off. Then, with seemingly no fear, he pulled on a heavy glove, attached a hook over the cable, and swung out into the open air. Lara watched in amazement as the man shot along the wire over the open sea, going faster and faster until he was over land, and then reached up with the glove and slowed himself, dropping like a cat into the brush beneath the tree.

The rest of the soldiers followed swiftly, but as Lara glanced over her shoulder, she determined Aren wasn't paying them the slightest bit of attention. Instead, he was mixing powders into a small bladder. As she watched, he added water to the mixture, then, very carefully, attached the device to an arrow with a bit of twine. He lifted it to his bow and shot it at the ship anchored below.

Seconds later, an explosion shook the air, the ship visible through the mist as flames climbed the rigging. "That ought to keep them busy."

Slinging his bow over his shoulder, he removed a hook and glove like the others had used. "I'm going to need you to hold onto me."

Wordlessly, Lara wrapped her arms around his neck and her legs around his waist. Heat rushed through her as he pulled her tight against him with his free hand.

"Don't scream." He flipped the hook over the line and jumped.

Lara barely contained her shriek, clinging to him as they dropped, soaring downward at incredible speed. Below, the surf broke against the island cliffs, and she could make out the longboats retreating from a small cove to the burning ship to assist their comrades. Wind roared in her ears, and then they were above green jungle.

"Hold on tight," he said into her ear, then he let go of her, reaching up with a gloved hand to grip the cable, checking their speed until they hung safely above the others.

Lara let go, landing among them, and she purposely wobbled and fell on her ass even as Aren landed with predatory grace next to her. In a practiced move, he extracted a leather mask identical to those all the guards were now wearing and pulled it over his face.

"Stay here," he whispered. "Keep out of sight and watch out for snakes."

Then they were gone.

Lara waited until the count of fifty, then went after them, knives in hand. She moved carefully, trusting that their passage would have sent any snakes racing away. It wasn't difficult to determine the direction they'd gone; she only had to follow the screams.

A battle waged in a village, the interiors of the stone houses ablaze, countless dead and dying lying on the paths running between them. Some had been armed, most had not. Families. Children. All cut down by the Amaridian soldiers fighting Aren and his guards. Keeping behind a tree, Lara watched the King of Ithicana hurl himself against the other men, machete in one hand, dagger in the other, leaving only corpses in his wake. He fought like he'd been born to it, fearless, but clever, and she found herself unable to look away.

Until shouts from the beach caught her attention. Abandoning her position, Lara retreated in that direction, her stomach tightening as she caught sight of the Amaridian soldiers moving up the trail toward the village. The ship was fully engulfed with fire, which meant these were desperate men with no avenue for escape. And Aren and his bodyguard were outnumbered three to one. Unless she wanted Amarid to be the kingdom taking control of the bridge, she needed to even the odds.

Lara picked a point just around the corner from a gap in a towering pair of rocks through which the soldiers would have to pass.

Two soldiers rounded the bend, starting in surprise at the sight of her standing in their path. "It's her. The Maridrinian girl."

She waited for them to rush her, these men as much Maridrina's enemy as they were Ithicana's, but they stood their ground, gaping at her as if uncertain what to do next. "You're not supposed to be here."

Lara shrugged. "Your bad luck, I suppose." Then she threw her knives in rapid succession. The soldiers dropped, blades in their throats. Three more came, and Lara snatched up one of the dead men's swords and launched herself forward, slashing one man's gut even as she dove under the blade of another, hamstringing him as she rolled. His comrade swung at her and she parried, then kicked him in the knee, burying her blade in his chest as he fell.

Taking up his weapon as she rose, Lara attacked the third, driving him back before slicing off his hand at the wrist. The soldier screamed, his blood splattering her in the face even as he collided with the soldiers who'd come up from behind.

It was screaming and chaos. Men tripping over the bodies of their companions as they tried to squeeze through the narrow pass, Lara killing them when convenient, maiming them when it wasn't, her goal to keep them from joining the battle and from overwhelming Aren and his soldiers.

But when a pair of arrows whistled over her head, she threw herself into the jungle, hiding in the underbrush as the rest of the Amaridian soldiers rushed past. Once they were gone, she retrieved her throwing knives and sheathed them in favor of using one of the Amaridians' heavier weapons. Slicing throats as she went, Lara ran up the trail to the village.

There was blood everywhere. Bodies everywhere. Several of the honor guard had fallen, and Lara's stomach plunged as she searched those remaining for Aren.

She found him fighting an enormous man wielding a chain. Aren's clothes were bloody, his once sharp movements now sluggish and sloppy. The Amaridian warrior swung his chain hard, and Lara hissed as it caught Aren in the ribs, doubling him over. She instinctively took several steps in their direction, knife in hand, ready to intervene, but Aren came up swinging, catching the big man in the face with his fist, then plunging a knife into his gut. They both went down in a heap.

Before Aren could get back to his feet, another Amaridian soldier charged toward his exposed back.

Without thinking, Lara threw herself between them, her knife sinking in beneath the sternum, angling up to pierce the soldier's heart.

His momentum knocked her over, the wind rushing out of her lungs as her shoulders hit the ground, the dying soldier falling on top of her. He was flailing and thrashing, the hilt of the knife digging into her stomach, and she couldn't get out from under him.

Couldn't breathe as the meaty bulk of his chest pressed down against her face.

The weight abruptly lifted.

Lara gasped, sucking in air, before rolling onto her hands and knees, watching as Aren unnecessarily slid a knife across the dead soldier's throat. Hands slick with the other man's blood, Aren grabbed hold of her arms, pulling her close. "Are you all right? Are you hurt?" He was pulling at her clothes, the blood of the dead sailor mercifully concealing that from her victims on the pathway.

"I'm fine," she gasped, finally able to breathe. "You're not." He was bleeding heavily from a gash on his forearm, but she suspected that wasn't the worst of it.

"It's nothing. Stay back. Stay out of sight." He tried to push her behind one of the village homes, but she clung to his shoulders, desperate to keep him out of the fray. If he died, *everything* was for naught.

He hesitated, and she buried her face in his shoulder, certain he'd set her aside and reenter the battle. But he was injured and spent, and it would not end well. Panic rose in her throat, and she whispered the only thing she could think of that would get him to stay: "Please. Don't leave me."

His hands were hot against her back, both of them soaked with the blood of their enemies. "Lara . . ." His voice was pained, and she knew he was seeing the bodies of his people. That he was seeing his bodyguards, fighting and faltering against the enemy.

You could fight.

You could fight for him and save these people.

The thought danced across her mind, but she was saved from having to make a decision by the arrival of reinforcements.

Ithicanian soldiers poured into the village, Aren's bodyguards falling back, encircling him and Lara as the others cut down the Amaridian soldiers, ruthlessly dispatching the injured until the only sound was the moans and cries of the villagers.

Aren didn't let go of her until it was over.

Smoke burned Lara's eyes as she looked around. As she saw, for the first time, what war really looked like. Not just dead soldiers, but unarmed civilians lying on the ground. The still forms of children.

Do you think it will be any different when your father comes with his army? Do you think they'll show any more mercy?

Villagers who had fled began to return to the village, mostly older children clutching babies and the hands of small children. Some of them began to sob as they found the still forms of their parents. But far too many just stood frozen, faces lost and hopeless.

"Still believe those Amaridian sailors deserved mercy?" Aren said softly from behind her.

"No," she whispered as she strode toward the nearest injured Ithicanian, ripping strips of fabric from her tunic as she dropped to her knees. "I don't."

AREN STARED INTO the basin of water, its contents slowly turning red as he washed away the blood crusting his fingernails. His blood. The blood of his enemies.

The blood of his people.

The water trembled and he jerked his hands out of the basin, wiping them dry on a piece of toweling that had been left for him. Every inch of him ached, especially his ribs where that big bastard had caught him with the chain. Nana had informed him nothing was broken, but his side was already a livid bruise, and experience told him that tomorrow would be worse. Yet he'd take the pain a thousand times over if it meant arriving at Serrith sooner. Twenty minutes earlier. Ten. Five. Even a heartbeat sooner might have allowed him to save at least one of the villagers who'd been killed today.

"The call to assemble the council in Eranahl has been sent and replies received. Everyone will be there by nightfall."

He turned to find Jor standing behind him, the bandage wrapped around his head concealing the deep gash he'd taken in the fighting. A gash that Lara, of all people, had stitched up. Of their own accord,

Aren's eyes drifted to where his wife knelt among the wounded, silently taking direction from Nana and her students. Her honey-colored hair was crusted dark with blood, as were her clothes, but rather than detracting from her beauty, it only made her seem fierce. Like a warrior. Half a day ago, the notion would've been laughable.

But not anymore.

Jor tracked his gaze, giving a deep sigh when he saw whom Aren was staring at. "She's in possession of a problematic amount of information."

"There was no helping it."

"Doesn't mean it isn't a problem."

"She saved my life."

Jor sucked in a deep breath, then blew it out slowly. "Did she now."

"I was down and one of them came at my back. She got in the way and stuck a knife in him." Every time he blinked, Aren saw Lara beneath that brute of an Amaridian, blood everywhere. Felt the fear of certainty that all the blood was hers. "Sort of ruins the theory that she's here to assassinate me, don't you think?"

"Maybe she wants to do it herself," Jor replied, but his voice was unconvinced.

Lara lifted her head, as though sensing their scrutiny. Aren turned away before their eyes could meet, and the pile of dead Amaridians came into his line of sight. He'd pulled the bastard off her and slit his throat, but the man had been already dead, the knife Lara had picked up somewhere embedded with precision in his heart.

Luck, he told himself. But Aren's instincts were telling him something else.

"If anything, we need to keep a closer eye on her now," Jor said. "If the Maridrinians determine where she is and come for her, that little lass's head is full of enough bridge secrets to cause us some serious trouble."

"What are you suggesting?"

"I'm suggesting that maybe she's more trouble than she's worth. Accidents happen. Snakes find their way into beds. The Maridrinians could hardly hold it against us—"

"No."

"Then keep pretending she's alive." Jor had mistaken the reason for Aren's refusal. "Get a forger to fake her letters to her father. They never have to know."

Aren turned on the man who'd watched over him since he was a child. "I will say this once and never again. If anyone harms her, they lose their head. That goes for you, it goes for Aster, and it goes for my grandmother, too, lest she think me ignorant to her ways. Understood?"

Without waiting for a response, Aren walked to the pyres that had been hastily assembled on the outskirts of the village, the air thick with the smell of the oil drenching the wood. Dozens of bodies, big and small, were laid out in even rows, and the survivors stood around it, some weeping, some staring into nothingness.

Someone passed him a torch and Aren stared at the flickering flames, knowing that he should say something. But any words he might offer these people that he was supposed to protect—that he had *failed* to protect—seemed empty and meaningless. He couldn't promise it wouldn't happen again, because it would. He couldn't promise revenge, because even if raiding Amarid were a possibility for his already strained army, he wouldn't lower himself to harming Amaridian civilians just because their queen was a vindictive bitch. He *could* tell them that he fully intended to send a crate full of heads along with the charred remains of the ship's flag back to their mistress, but what did that even mean? It wouldn't bring back the dead.

So he said nothing, only leaned forward to touch the torch to the oil-soaked wood. Flames tore along the branches, the air growing hot, and it wasn't long until his nose filled with the awful smell of burning hair. Charring blood. Cooking flesh. It made his stomach churn, and he gritted his teeth, wanting to flee but forcing himself to hold his ground.

"The ships are here from Eranahl," Jor said. "We need to start loading the survivors or we'll lose the weather." As if to emphasize the point, a droplet of rain smacked against Aren's forehead. Then another and another.

"Give them a minute." He couldn't tear his gaze from a sobbing mother standing too close to the now hissing flames. This morning she would've woken believing that by nightfall she and her family would be on the way to the safety of Eranahl, and now she'd be making the journey alone.

"Aren . . ."

"Give them a goddamn minute." Heads turned at the sharpness of his tone, and he strode away from the flames. Past the injured whom Nana and her students were preparing for the journey, and down the path to the cove where the ships waited.

Rounding the bend, he frowned at the dozen or so dead enemy soldiers that had been dragged to the side of the path when something caught his eye: a man with an Amaridian blade embedded in his chest. Backtracking, Aren examined the corpses more closely.

Most of his soldiers fought hand-to-hand with knives and the machetes they needed to move through the dense jungle underbrush, and the wide blades made for distinct injuries. But most of these men bore wounds inflicted by the slender swords favored by Amarid, and several of them had the eight-inch knives these soldiers carried embedded in their bodies.

They were killed by their own weapons.

Aren stepped back a few paces to examine the scene, eyes drifting over the pools of blood mixing with rain to create growing puddles. These men had been killed by individuals they'd encountered coming up the path, not from behind by his reinforcements.

But by whom? All of his guard had been with him in the village, as were the civilians who could fight.

A prickle rose on the back of Aren's neck. Hand going to the blade at his waist, he whirled around. Only to find Lara standing in the middle of the path.

Her eyes drifted to where his hand lingered on his weapon and one of her eyebrows rose, but for reasons Aren couldn't articulate, he couldn't let go of the hilt. *She'd killed that soldier with an Amaridian blade . . .*

But her only visible injury was a bruise on her cheek. Never mind that Maridrinian women were forbidden from fighting, the very idea that she could've accomplished this on her own was utter lunacy—his best fighters couldn't have done it alone.

"Where will they go?" Her voice cut through his thoughts.

"There are safer places." He wondered why he was being so cagey when now she knew so much. But it was one thing for her to know about the bridge. Quite another for her to know about Eranahl.

Without the bridge, Eranahl doesn't exist, his father's voice whispered in his ear. *Ithicana doesn't exist. Defend the bridge.*

"If there are safer places, why don't you keep your civilians there?"

There were practical reasons. Keeping every Ithicanian civilian within Eranahl year-round was impossible, but that wasn't the reason he gave. "Because that would be like keeping them in cages. And my people are . . . free." The word caught in his throat, a sudden understanding of what his mother had been fighting for slapping him in the face. For what was Ithicana but a larger prison, those born to it forbidden to ever leave.

Lara went very still, her head cocked and eyes unblinking, as though his answer had dug deep into her thoughts, leaving no space for anything else. "Their freedom seems to come at a significant cost."

"Freedom always has a price." How much larger would the price be to allow his people the freedom of the world?

"Yes." The word seemed to stick in her throat, and she shook her head once, her eyes going to the dead men lining the path. Aren watched her closely, searching her expression for any clue that she was somehow complicit in their deaths, but she only appeared deep in thought.

"You should head down to the cove. The boats are waiting."

Tearing her eyes from the corpses, Lara walked toward him, silent as any Ithicanian as she navigated the slick slope. His heart skipped then accelerated, the steady *thump thump* rhythm it took when he was heading into battle or trying to outrun a storm. The thrill that, despite knowing he should not, Aren had sought all his life.

Lara stopped in front of him. Her hair was wet from the rain, a stray lock plastered against her cheek. It took all his self-control not to brush it away.

"Once the boats are loaded, I'm leaving for a . . . meeting. You'll stay with my grandmother until I return for you."

Lara frowned, but rather than arguing, she reached up and placed her hand on his, her skin feverishly hot. Then, with surprising strength, she pushed down, snapping his blade back into its sheath.

"I'll wait by the water." Without another word, she stepped over a puddle and made her way down the path toward the beach.

W AR TIDES.

That's what the villagers on Serrith Island had called it. The two coldest months of the year when the Tempest Seas were calm enough for Ithicana's enemies to attack.

And this year War Tides had come early.

So early that the villagers had not yet been evacuated to the mysterious location where they spent the season, which was probably why the Amaridian navy had twice risked getting caught in a late storm. For while a well-defended singular location could be protected, countless little civilian outposts were another matter.

It was the best time to attack, the cold, strategic part of Lara thought. When Ithicana's army would be forced to split their efforts between protecting dozens of small villages and protecting the bridge. And if it came to it, she *knew* Aren would put his people's lives first. It had been written on his face when those horns had sounded, the panic and desperation. The willingness to risk *everything* to save them. And the dead look in his eyes as he'd surveyed the massacred village and known that he'd failed.

They aren't your responsibility, she viciously reminded herself. *Your loyalty is to Maridrina. To the civilians of your homeland who suffer under Ithicana's monopoly on trade. To the Maridrinian children who have nothing on their plates but rotting vegetables and rancid meat, if they have anything to eat at all. They are dying as surely as if Ithicana were slitting their throats.*

The thoughts were enough to turn her mind to the matter of smuggling information out of Ithicana. While it might be possible for her to code short messages into her letters to her father, she didn't dare attempt to include any of the details she'd learned about the bridge. If the codebreakers noticed them, she'd be lucky to get out of Ithicana alive, and everything that she'd done would be for naught. Aren knew where she'd been and what she'd learned. It would be easy for them to shore up the defenses, and there would be no catching them by surprise.

No, she had to gather the information she needed, and then smuggle it out all at once. The question was how.

Instinctively, she knew that the way had to be through the King of Ithicana himself. Her thoughts went to her cosmetics box, within which the ink Serin had given her was hidden. Not only did she need to entice Aren to write a message to her father, she needed to steal it for long enough to write her own, never mind the problem of resealing it without anyone noticing that it had been tampered with.

"Quit plotting and help Taryn with the dishes, you lazy tit."

Nana's voice ripped Lara from her thoughts, and she turned to scowl at the old woman. "What?"

"Did you not hear, or did you not understand?" Nana's hands were on her hips, a large snake wrapped around her neck and shoulders. It lifted its head to regard Lara, and she shivered.

"This is my island," Aren's grandmother barked. "And on my island, if you wish to eat, you work. On your feet." She clapped her hands sharply.

Lara rose, instantly annoyed with having obeyed, but to sit back down would be childish.

"Out."

Glowering, she stepped out into the morning air, catching sight of

Taryn, who sat next to a washtub, up to her elbows in soapy water. The young woman was the only one of Aren's guards to remain with her— the one to have drawn the short straw, she'd readily griped to Lara on her blindfolded walk back through the bridge to Nana's island, which was called Gamire. A group of unfamiliar soldiers silently trailed them. Lara had thought it Taryn's reluctance to spend time with her, or perhaps disappointment over not going to wherever Aren had scuttled off to, that had made the role undesirable, but after a night spent in Nana's house, the real reason was apparent.

The old witch was an obnoxious, bullying harridan, and Lara had no idea how she was going to keep from murdering the bloody woman in her sleep.

"You'll get used to her, after a while." Taryn dunked a plate into the steaming basin. "Helps that most of us have been patched back together by her at least once." Letting go of the dish, the woman lifted up her undershirt to reveal an oval-shaped series of scars that covered the better half of her ribs. "I fell into the water during a skirmish and a shark had a go at me. If not for Nana, I'd be dead."

A knife or a sword or an arrow—those were wounds Lara could fathom, but that . . . "Nasty creatures."

"Not really." Taryn dropped her undershirt and returned to the plate. "They've been trained to be man-eaters, but it's not their preference."

Taking the dripping plate and rubbing it with a towel, Lara thought of the Amaridian sailors being dragged beneath the surface. The blooms of blood. "If you say so."

Pushing back her long dark ponytail, Taryn smiled, revealing straight white teeth that must please Nana greatly. "They are brilliant creatures. There are a few who stay with us always, but most of them are only here during War Tides. That, more than the weather, is how Nana knows when storm season is coming or going. The fishermen notice their numbers."

Did her father and Serin know that? Lara chewed the insides of her cheeks, considering the information. One of the risks of attacking at the beginning of the calm season was that there was no way to predict exactly when it would begin.

"They always congregate at the places where raiders attack the most, like at Midwatch." Taryn swirled a rag inside a chipped mug before handing it over. "There are myths that say they are guardians of Ithicana's people, which is why it is forbidden to harm them unless absolutely necessary." She laughed. "It's just a myth, though. They come to be fed, and they don't discern between us or our enemies. Anyone in the water is fair game."

Lara shivered, setting the dry cup in a clean basin with the rest.

"Quit your chattering," Nana barked from a distance. "There's other chores that need doing."

Taryn rolled her eyes. "Want to escape?"

"Is escape from Nana possible?"

A wink. "I've had lots of practice."

True to her word, after the clean dishes were put away, Taryn managed to have them assigned to a task that sent them down into a village Lara hadn't even realized was there. She took in the Ithicanians bustling about between the stone houses or cajoling children who were shirking their chores. "Why isn't it evacuated?"

"They don't need to be. Gamire Island is safe."

Find the civilians. Lara remembered Serin's words, the back of her neck prickling as two children ran past her, sacks of oats in their arms. Her eyes took in the village again. There were groups of men gutting fish, but her nose picked up the scent of baking bread, of red meat on the grill, and the faint tang of lemon, though not once had she seen a fruit tree in this place. Which meant it had all come as an import via the bridge.

"Those living on the other islands . . . where do they go for War Tides?" she asked, because *not* asking would be more suspicious. And because she was deeply curious where this mystery location might be.

"That's for the king to tell you." Taryn gave her a sideways glance. "Or not, as the case may be."

"He's not particularly forthcoming."

Shrugging as a way to silence that line of questioning, Taryn led Lara down a narrow path through the jungle. They walked until the breeze rose and the scent of salt filled the air, waves loud where they crashed against the cliff walls. Lara didn't see the shipbreaker until the older soldier manning it shifted next to it. Pleased recognition gleamed in his eyes at the sight of Taryn, but his gaze hardened as it landed on Lara.

"We're your relief for the next hour," Taryn said. "Use it wisely and get yourself some of that meat I smelled cooking."

After the soldier had departed, she said, "Don't take it personally. Most everyone above a certain age lost a loved one or two to the war with Maridrina. Even after fifteen years of peace, it's hard for them to see you as anything other than the enemy."

I am the enemy, Lara thought. "You don't?"

"I did, at first." Taryn's grey eyes stared off into the distance. "Until you saved my cousin's life."

"Cousin?" Lara blinked, eyeing the muscular brunette in a different light. "Aren is your cousin?"

"I see that surprises you." Huffing out an amused breath, Taryn said, "My father was Aren's father's brother, which makes Nana my grandmother, too, if you're keeping track."

She hadn't been, but perhaps she should. The female guard was not exactly royalty, but very nearly. And there was nothing about her that had even hinted it was so. Taryn wore the same drab gear as the rest of the guards, lived in the spare accommodations of the barracks, cooked and cleaned with the rest of her comrades. Other than her weapons, which were quality, there was nothing about her that suggested wealth or privilege. *Where does all the money go?* Lara wondered, remembering the incredible revenue numbers she'd seen on the pages in Aren's desk. As a child, she'd believed Ithicana must have palaces made of gold filled with everything they took from Maridrina and the other kingdoms, but so far she'd seen only modest luxury.

"You could have stood by and let him be killed, but instead you risked your life to save him. That's not the act of an enemy."

If only you knew. Lara's stomach hollowed, her breakfast no longer sitting quite so well.

Picking up a spyglass, Taryn panned the ocean, allowing Lara the opportunity to examine the shipbreaker. The catapult was large, made of solid wood and steel and mounted to a base that was bolted to the rocky ground beneath it. There were a number of levers and gears, and to either side of it were two identical, yet much smaller devices. A glance over her shoulder revealed a lumpy pile covered with grey-green canvas, which were undoubtedly the projectiles.

Easing up the corner of the tarp, Lara eyed a stone that might've weighed fifty pounds. It didn't seem big enough to have done the damage she'd seen enacted at Midwatch, but combined with enough force . . . She turned back to the shipbreaker to find Taryn watching her.

The other woman grinned. "We launched Aren, once."

"Pardon?"

"Lia and I. Though it was *his* idea, lest you think us total idiots." Taryn patted the machine. "We were maybe twelve or thirteen, and he got the grand notion that it would be fun to see how high we'd fly. Though he was the only one who got to try it out."

"Did it . . . work?"

"Oh, he flew all right. But what he didn't account for was how much the landing would hurt." She cackled merrily. "Thankfully there was a fishing boat nearby to pull him out. Nana had us lugging rock for *weeks* as punishment, and that was after Jor screamed at us up and down the entire island."

"He's lucky not to have gotten himself killed." And how different would Lara's life have been if he had? Or would she even have a life at all? She could easily imagine her father receiving the news of the Prince of Ithicana's untimely death only to turn around and exterminate all those involved in the plot that had depended on the Fifteen Year Treaty.

Taryn grinned. "You could say that about half the things he does." She patted the weapon again. "Want to give it a try?"

Gasping out a laugh, Lara said, "And now I see to the heart of the ploy of bringing me down here."

"Not *you*. A rock."

"Oh." Lara eyed the machine in a whole new light. "Yes. Yes, I would."

It was an incredible piece of machinery, able to be operated by a single individual, but given the weight of the stones, Lara was glad there were two of them. It rotated silently on its base, and various cranks allowed the user to adjust it to change the distance a stone could be thrown. The smaller catapults, she learned, were intended to mark distance, everything finely calibrated.

"We'll try to hit that piece of driftwood." Under Taryn's watchful eye, Lara lobbed small rocks at the floating debris until she struck it.

"Nicely done, Your Majesty. Now we adjust the big one to the same distance like so." The woman turned the cranks and Lara watched intently until she stepped back. "Now you do the honors."

Hands sweating with excitement, Lara took hold of the biggest lever of all and pulled. The catapult released with a tremendous crack, and they both stepped around the machine to watch as the rock sailed through the air and crashed into the driftwood.

Taryn punched her fist into the air. "You sank your first ship!"

There was a commotion behind them, and the soldier they'd relieved raced up next to them. "Raiders?" he demanded.

"Tests." Taryn's voice was cool. "His Majesty ordered that all the shipbreakers be tested again. This one appears to be fine order." Taryn nodded at Lara. "Shall we carry on, Your Grace?"

Lara hid a smile. "By all means."

They spent the day touring the island *testing* the shipbreakers, and then found themselves back at the village for dinner, which they took standing around an open fire with nearly all the villagers in attendance. It was, Taryn told her, to honor those lives lost on the neighboring island of Serrith. Lara ate grilled meat and vegetables from the sticks on which they were skewered, drank the frothy beer from a mug that never seemed to empty, and warmed her hands against the flames when the night breeze turned cool.

The villagers were wary of her at first, and Lara stood somewhat apart, listening as they told stories about the myths of Ithicana, of serpents and storms that defended the emerald isles. Of the ancient bridge itself, which their legends said was not built, but had grown out of the earth like a living thing. Their words rose and fell until children dozed off in their parents' arms and were tucked under woolen blankets. Then instruments were brought out, drums and guitars and pipes, the music accompanying the men and women as they sang and danced, Taryn joining in with a surprisingly lovely soprano voice.

They cajoled Lara to join in the singing, but she begged off, pleading a terrible singing voice, but it was mostly because she wanted to watch. And listen. And learn.

When the gathering began to quiet, couples slipping off into the darkness hand in hand, the older folk forming circles where they gossiped and complained, passing around a smoking pipe from person to person, Taryn finally rested a hand on Lara's shoulder. "We should get back before Nana comes looking for us."

Guided by the faint light of a lantern, they made their way up the narrow path, the sounds of the jungle wild and riotous around them.

"I didn't want to be a soldier, you know."

Lara cast a sideways glance at Taryn. "I'm not surprised. You strike me as more of a fisherwoman."

Taryn spat out a laugh, but her tone turned serious. "I wanted to go to one of the universities in Harendell to study music."

The universities in Harendell were renowned throughout all the kingdoms, north and south, but the idea that an Ithicanian would wish to attend struck Lara as odd, because it was . . . impossible. "But Ithicanians never leave?"

"Because it's forbidden." Taryn waved her hand. "Oh, there are spies who go, of course, but it's not the same. It's a false life where you aren't yourself, and I couldn't abide that. To follow my dream as someone else—" She broke off. "I never told my parents, because I knew they wished for me to train as a warrior and eventually be named to Aren's council. But I told my Aunt Delia."

Aren's mother, Lara thought. *The queen.*

"My aunt believed that the surest way to earn trust was to give it." Taryn pulled on Lara's arm, stopping her to allow something to slither across their path before carrying on. "Everyone supported the treaty to end the war with Maridrina, but no one supported the inclusion of a marriage clause. No one wanted Aren to marry an outsider, especially a Maridrinian. But Aunt Delia believed it was the only way for us to ever have peace with our neighbors. The only way for people to stop seeing an enemy when we sat across the table to trade."

It's a lie, Serin's voice shrieked inside Lara's head. *Using kindness to get you to reveal what you should not.* But Lara silenced the voice.

"If she believed this marriage would stop Maridrinians from viewing Ithicana as an enemy, she was mistaken."

Taryn shook her head. "She didn't want to change your kingdom's beliefs. She wanted to change *ours*."

No more could be said, as they had reached Nana's home, the old woman standing in the doorway, watching them approach. "The wayward children return."

"We kept busy, Nana."

"Busy drinking, from the smell of it."

A somewhat hypocritical comment given Lara could smell alcohol on the woman's breath, a bottle and a half-filled glass sitting on the table behind her.

"I'm off to bed," Lara said, in no mood to be berated, but Nana caught Lara's arm in an iron grip. With the other hand, she held out a bag that twitched and squeaked. "First you feed the snakes."

Lara eyed the bag with distaste. Not because she had any particular aversion to mice, but because she was sick of the old witch ordering her about like a servant. What she wanted to do was sneak out tonight to have a look at the bridge pier, but Nana probably intended to sit up watching her. "No."

Nana's eyebrows rose. "No? Is the little princess too good to feed an old woman's pets?"

Lara's fingers tightened reflexively. Then her eyes lighted upon the shelves above the snake cages, and an idea began to form. "I'm afraid of mice," she lied, flinching away from the bag as Nana swung it her direction.

"Get over it."

Lara was forced to catch the bag or have the mice scatter everywhere. Silently cursing the old woman, Lara plucked a mouse out of the bag by its tail, carefully unlatched one of the cages, and tossed the creature inside before moving onto the next.

The snakes were all poisonous. Taryn had told her that Nana harvested their venom and used it to create antidotes, as well as medicines for various natural afflictions. There were dozens of vials of foggy liquid stored above the cages, and above those, countless more plants and remedies, all clearly labeled. Between each cage, Lara scanned the contents, smiling when she found what she was looking for.

Dropping the still wriggling bag of mice, Lara shrieked, "It bit me!"

"Which snake?" Nana demanded, a hint of panic in her voice.

"Not a snake," she sobbed, sticking one of her fingers into her mouth and biting down to create a realistic injury. "A mouse!"

"Dammit, girl!" Nana snatched up the bag, but it was too late. The remaining mice were running every which way. "Taryn, catch the damn things before they get into my larder."

Lara wailed, climbing onto a chair while the rodents took advantage of their freedom. But the second Nana's back was turned, she snatched a small jar from the shelves.

"Catch them, catch them!"

Taryn was dutifully chasing after the mice, but she'd drank enough that night that her movements were too slow, the rodents dodging easily until she turned to stomping on them with her heavy boots. Lara took the moment to uncork the jar.

"Don't kill them!" Nana had two mice by the tails and was shoving them into the bag. "The snakes won't eat them if they're dead!" She lunged for another mouse, and Lara leaned sideways and dumped a generous splash of the jar's contents into Nana's cup, once again grateful for the Ithicanian preference for strong drink.

"Got one!" Taryn tossed the mouse into Nana's sack. Lara corked the vial and shoved it back in its place on the shelf, then stood on her chair watching, uselessly, as the two women collected the remaining mice.

Muttering under her breath, Nana proceeded to finish feeding the snakes, then she grabbed hold of Lara's hand, examining the tiny bleeding wound. "Idiot. Will serve you right if it festers."

Jerking her hand out of the old woman's grip, Lara glared at her. "I'm going to bed." Her boots thudded imperiously as she made her way over to the cot that had been made up for her, and she curbed a smile as, from the corner of her eye, she watched Nana down the contents of her cup.

Now to wait.

NOT AN HOUR later, the home dark, Nana's groan split the silence. A moment later, the old woman climbed from her bed and staggered out the door. On her feet in a flash, Lara went to the wall of vials, plucking up one she'd noticed earlier. Measuring out a drop, she held it beneath Taryn's nostril, silently apologizing for the headache it would cause in the morning as the gently snoring woman snorted it up.

Lara stepped outside into a pool of lantern light. A gentle breeze tugged at her hair, smelling of jungle and rain, the stars overhead only visible in patches through the growing cloud cover. Lara took the lantern, turned the flame up as high as it would go, then strode toward the small outbuilding where the toilet was located.

Stopping outside, she smirked at the sounds coming from within, then rotated in a circle, peering into the darkness. As predicted, a tall Ithicanian man appeared. "Is there something I can help you with, Your Grace?" He hooked his thumb on his belt as he eyed her.

"Oh!" Lara jumped, then pressed a hand to her mouth as though startled. "Well, I needed to . . . ." She gestured at the building right as a tremendous fart reverberated from within, followed up by a groan of dismay. Lara might be out of her element in Ithicana, but when it came to narcotics, she was right at home. Nana was exactly where she expected her to be.

The guard's eyes widened in the lantern light. "Right." He was obviously trying not to laugh. "I see. Well, perhaps you could . . ."

"A bush will do." Lara giggled, pushing the lantern at him. "Can you hold this for me?"

Relieving herself behind the cover of a tree, Lara returned to the guard and retrieved the lantern. Holding it up, she marked how he squinted and blinked from the brightness. "Do you suppose she'll be all right?" Lara gestured to the outhouse. "Do you think we should . . ?"

"No!" The thought of interrupting Nana in the toilet was clearly not something he cared to risk. "I'm sure she'll be fine."

"I hope so." Lara gave him a winning smile, then retreated to the house. Nana would be shitting for hours, but she'd be fine come morning. Snuffing the lantern, she hung it on the hook and went inside.

But she didn't shut the door all the way.

Counting to five, she eased it back open, greeted by nothing but blackness. Her eyes hadn't adjusted from the brilliant light of the lantern, but that meant neither would have the guard's. Moving blind, Lara edged around the corner of the house where she waited until she could make out the shadows of the trees, then she dropped to the ground, crawling silently next to Nana's garden wall until she was in the jungle.

The trees on this island weren't nearly as thick as they were on Midwatch, faint moon and starlight filtering through the leaves, allowing Lara to move at a slow trot up the path toward the bridge pier. Any sound she made was covered by the ocean breeze, but she paused occasionally to listen for sounds of pursuit. There were none.

The faint scent of wet rock drifted over her nose, strange and yet familiar, and after a heartbeat, Lara recognized it as the unique odor of the bridge stone. Moving more cautiously, lest there be guards, she crept up the path until, through the trees, she made out the large shadow of the pier rising up into the night. A shadow that spread out north and south: the bridge.

Picking her way through the trees, Lara searched for any sign of a guard, but there was none, so she made her way to the base of the pier. It was constructed from the combination of a natural rock outcropping and bridge stone, and it held the bridge perhaps twenty feet above the ground. The terrain around it was rocky, so there was no obvious path leading to the entrance she knew was there. Lara ran her fingernail against the expanse of bridge stone that made up the pier, searching the base for the outline of the door, but she soon gave up. There were too many scratches and marks, and she didn't have that much time. So she resorted to pushing on the surface, throwing her weight against the stone in the hopes it would open.

Nothing.

Swearing, Lara went to the part of the pier that was natural stone. Kicking off her heavy boots and tucking them into a shadow, she started climbing. Higher and higher she rose, back and shoulders burning from the effort. She reached the bottom of the bridge, feeling along the side of it and smiling as she found linear striations in the stone that provided just enough handholds for her to climb. Her fingers screaming at her, Lara scrambled up the side of the bridge, rolling onto the top.

Darkness spread out beneath her in an endless sea of night, only a few pinpricks of light from the island's interior breaking the velvety blackness. Moving slowly, Lara trailed her fingers down the middle of the bridge, knowing that she'd eventually find a mile-marker twin to the one inside.

Sweat dribbled down her back, her internal clock telling her that she needed to get back to Nana's house, but she pressed on until she found it. Then she strode back to the pier, counting her carefully measured paces.

Only to hear voices coming from the opposite direction.

"Goddamn idiots. What were they thinking parking a whole merchant party above Gamire for the night?"

It was Jor. He and who knew how many others were on top of the bridge with her.

Heart thudding, Lara dropped to her stomach, crawling to the edge and peering over. Below, a group exited from the trees, one of them carrying a jar of a faintly glowing substance.

"They don't know they're above Gamire, Jor." Lia's voice. "That's the whole damn point."

"Doesn't make it less of a pain in our asses."

Lara rolled to the opposite edge from the party below, then carefully lowered herself down the side, her sweating fingers quivering from the effort.

"Are you two about finished up there?"

Aren's voice. One of Lara's hands slipped, and she gasped, dangling from one hand until she regained her grip.

"We had a look. There's a merchant party camped for the night right below us, and the topside hatch is too close for us to enter undetected. It's a three-mile walk either direction to the next hatch, and with those winds blowing in, I wouldn't advise it. No one is looking to spend the night tied to the bridge top in the pouring rain."

Aren let out a weary sigh. "By boat it is, then."

"And rough waters. I hope whatever Nana gave your lovely bride will settle her stomach enough for the journey. Though something strong might be in order to deal with her damned panic."

"Leave Lara alone." Aren's voice wasn't amused. "She was raised in the desert, and she can't swim. Falling in the water is a valid fear."

"Yeah, yeah," Jor muttered, and Lara used the sound to clamber down farther. When she was ten feet from the bottom, she jumped, her bare feet making only the faintest slap as she hit the ground and rolled, taking five long steps until she was out of sight in the trees. Mud squished between her toes as she circled around, watching as Aren rested his hands against the pier, one above the other, and pressed twice. A faint click, and a panel of rock swung open. He went inside.

Above, Jor and Lia had looped a rope through one of the many rings embedded in the bridge and were climbing down the pier side by side. Lia was pulling the rope through the loop when Aren reemerged and said, "There's someone sleeping right against the bloody door."

"Like I said," Jor replied. "Idiots."

"It is what it is. Let's go." Aren started down the path toward

Nana's home. To retrieve *her*, she realized.

Shit. Lara waited until the others had followed before creeping up to the pier to retrieve her boots from their hiding place. It was going to be a mad dash to get back to Nana's ahead of them undetected, but she couldn't leave without having a look inside. Pressing her hands twice in the same spot Aren had, Lara grinned as the door swung open.

She'd expected it to be entirely dark inside, but the curved stairs leading upward were illuminated by more glowing jars. Taking the steps three at a time, she reached a smooth stone wall. Knowing there was a risk of being caught, but judging it worth the reward, she pressed her hands against it twice.

Click.

She winced at the sound, then eased the door open a crack, the heavy block moving on silent hinges. There was indeed a man sleeping in front of it, his snores likely all that had kept the masked Ithicanian soldiers sitting guard inside from hearing the noise.

The doorway needed to be marked so her father's soldiers could find it from the inside. Yet she knew the Ithicanians swept the bridge for any signs of tampering, so it had to be something they wouldn't notice.

Her mind raced through the years of Serin's lessons, knowing she needed a solution and that it needed to present itself immediately or Aren was going to reach Nana's before her and find her missing.

An idea sprung into her thoughts. Pulling out her knife, Lara sliced open a shallow wound on her forearm then tucked away the blade. Covering her fingers in blood, she carefully traced the outer rim of the door. Once dry, it wouldn't be noticeable against the stone. But if sprayed with the right compound, it would react.

There was no time to do anything else.

Carefully closing the door, Lara flew down the stairs and pushed the door in the base shut. Then she was running as fast as she dared, her bare feet scraping against roots and rocks. But she couldn't move this swiftly in her heavy Ithicanian boots while maintaining any level of silence.

Ahead, she picked out the faint glow of the jar Aren carried, and she slowed her speed, moving up as close behind them as she dared.

She considered trying to pass them in the trees, but there was no chance of them not hearing her. Not in the dark, at this pace.

Nana's house appeared ahead.

Think of a plan, she silently screamed at herself even as she watched Aren round the house. Open the door. He was back out in a flash shouting, "Where is she?"

Tugging on her boots, Lara cut into the trees, then stepped out into the clearing, walking through it toward Aren. "I'm right here, so quit yelling."

He stared at her, as did his bodyguard and the guard tasked with watching the house. Nana chose that moment to fling open the door to the outhouse clad only in a nightdress and boots.

"What," Aren demanded, "are you doing wandering the woods in the middle of the night?"

Serin's voice echoed through her head: *Most people lie to avoid embarrassment. Very few people lie to embarrass themselves, which inclines others to believe them.*

Lara looked at the ground, knowing that the sweat running down her face and her ruddy complexion would only add truth to the lie. "I wasn't feeling well, and the facilities were"—she gestured at Nana— "occupied."

Aren turned to his grandmother. "Are you ill?"

"The shits. I'll live."

"It must've been something we ate." Lara pressed a hand to her stomach as though it pained her. "Or perhaps some filth on those mice you made me touch."

"Mice? You made her feed your snakes?" Shaking his head, Aren rounded on the guard. "Where the hell were you?"

"Here. I didn't see her leave. I was watching."

"Not very well."

"I was trying to be discreet," Lara snapped, kicking the toe of her boot into the dirt. "Now if you're all finished gaping at me, I'd like to go back to sleep."

Aren exhaled a long breath.

"What?" Lara folded her arms under her breasts and looked

up at him.

"A fleet of thirty Amaridian ships is lurking off Ithicana's coast. There's a squall blowing in that might buy us some time, but Midwatch is under my command, and I need to get back to prepare our defenses."

"They intend to raid?"

"Likely." He exhaled. "You can come back with us or stay here with Nana for War Tides. Your choice."

"I'll go back to Midwatch." There was no bloody way in hell she was spending another day with that awful woman. Never mind that judging from Nana's narrow-eyed expression, the old woman wasn't entirely fooled by her deception. No doubt she'd tie Lara to the bed every night and triple her guard. And because she needed to step forward with her plan to lure Aren in, Lara added, "I want to go with you."

His brow furrowed, and he glanced away. "We can't go through the bridge. There's a merchant party on their way to Southwatch camped above this pier for the night, and we can't get in without them seeing. It will have to be by boat."

Lara swallowed the unease that burned in her stomach, hearing the rising winds. *Control your fear,* she commanded. *There is much to be gained here if you keep your wits about you.*

"I'll manage," she muttered.

Aren turned on Taryn, who was rubbing her temples. "Not your finest hour, soldier. Jor will deal with your punishment once we're home."

"Sorry, Your Grace," Taryn said, and guilt briefly rose in Lara before she swallowed it away.

Aren led Lara by the hand through the darkness, Jor in the lead and the groggy Taryn behind, the other woman carrying something bulky that bumped against her shoulder as she ran.

The winds were rising higher by the second, but over them, the surf slamming against the cliff walls filled Lara's ears, and her heart thundered riotously knowing they intended to sail upon it. Sweat rolled in beads down her back as they reached the cliff tops overlooking the sea, nothing visible in the blackness, the moon and stars obscured by clouds.

It began to rain.

A cold drizzle that soaked her hair and trickled down the back of her tunic as she watched the soldiers stationed on the island strain to lift what appeared to be an enormous wooden ladder up into the air. The end of it was attached to ropes, and it took eight of them to lower it over the edge of the cliff into the darkness below.

"There's a large rock outcropping below," Aren shouted into her ear. "We'll climb down, then wade over to the islet where we have the boats moored. It's low tide, but the water will still be up to your knees."

"Let's go!" Jor was on the ladder and climbing down toward the crashing sea below, Lia following him.

"I'll go first. Then you, then Taryn."

Lara nodded wordlessly, unable to speak around the chatter of her teeth. Aren swung onto the ladder and clambered down, but when Lara gripped the rungs, her fingers felt numb. Her arms and legs trembled, and it took all her willpower to descend. Down and down toward the water.

If they can do it, so can you. She repeated the chant, her lips moving silently, her hands slick with sweat, spray drenching her clothes as wave after wave hammered the outcropping below. Finally, Aren's hands closed around her waist, steadying her as she stepped onto the slimy rocks. Taryn was down a moment later, and when she gave the call, there was a creak as the soldiers lifted the ladder back onto the island.

Lara could see nothing. *Nothing.* But all around her, water roared. One step in the wrong direction and she was done for. The thought had her dropping to her knees, her fingers clutching at the rocks.

"We don't have time for you to crawl," Aren shouted over the noise. "We'll be in a far worse spot if we're stuck out here when the tide turns."

Her knees trembled as she rose, her breath coming in great gasping whooshes as she took one step, then two, allowing Aren to guide her.

"Jor's marked the path." Aren lifted her hand, using it to point, because she couldn't so much as see his outline in the blackness.

There.

Smears of glowing algae were faintly visible every few paces. Her heart steadied, and she pressed forward, her confidence growing with each step.

"There's about a ten foot stretch here that's submerged. You'll be up to your knees, but the current is strong, so hold on to me."

"Damn you for making me do this."

Aren laughed, which pissed her off enough to take the first step.

Lara's boot filled with water, the current shoving against her leg, then dragging her in the opposite direction as it surged. She clung to Aren's belt, feeling Taryn's steadying hand on her shoulder from behind.

Step.

Step.

Her toe caught on a rock, and Lara stumbled, a sob tearing from her throat as she caught her balance.

Step.

Step.

A large wave surged against her, and she slid sideways, her legs washing out from under her. She was up to her waist in water, only her grip on Aren's belt keeping her upright. Her scream cut the night, frantic and desperate and primal, then his hands closed around her arms, dragging her from the water.

"You're out. It's all right. Worst is over."

"The second I'm on dry land, I'm going to gut you like a pig!" She hated being afraid and the only thing strong enough to chase the emotion away was anger. "I am going to smother you in your sleep!"

A dozen voices laughed, Jor's voice the loudest of them all. "And she finally shows her true intentions."

Aren snorted. "You might want to curb your vitriol until you're in a place where I can't pick you up and toss you into the drink." Then Aren stomped to the far side of the islet.

Taryn's hand caught her elbow, helping her up. "It will only take us an hour to get to Midwatch." She pressed a strap into Lara's hand. "I had one of the villagers make this for you. If something happens, it will keep you afloat until one of us can get you back in the boat."

Lara ran her hands along the object, which was a looped strap secured to a cask. A small act, but an enormous kindness. And one Lara didn't deserve. "Thank you."

The Ithicanians deposited her in one of the boats, and she cowered there, clinging with one hand to her cask and the other to the edge as they pushed out into the water. Their voices were unconcerned, despite this being madness that no sane individual would undertake under any circumstances.

The boat rose and fell on waves, and her stomach did the same, but Lara couldn't let go long enough to dig the root Nana had given her out of her pocket. She was busy puking over the edge when the group went silent, their hands still on ropes and rudders and lines.

"There they are." Lia's voice.

Jor cursed under his breath. "I hope this storm turns nasty and puts them at the bottom of the sea."

Lifting her head, Lara stared blearily out over the water. Bobbing in the distance were dozens, no, hundreds of lights. And carrying on the wind toward them was the sound of music and singing voices.

Ships.

The Amaridian fleet.

"We should go light a few of them up," Lia snapped. "That would put a damper on their party."

As one, all heads turned in Aren's direction. Fingernails digging into the edge of the boat, Lara waited to see how he would respond.

"Keep on to Midwatch." His voice was low.

"But we could sink a few of them," Lia argued. "We have the supplies."

"Midwatch," Aren repeated. "They haven't attacked, and we do not instigate."

"But they will! You know as soon as the weather turns, they'll raid!"

"When they do, we'll fight them. Same as always."

There was no emotion in Aren's voice, but Lara could feel frustration and anger coming off him in waves.

"Or we could stop them now." Lia was not giving up.

"They're outside our waters and they've shown no aggression." Aren shifted restlessly, his knee brushing against Lara's back. "If we attack unprovoked, Amarid will have cause to declare war against us. This is a few ships—*a raid.* We can deal with that. The full force of Amarid's navy against us is quite a different matter. Ithicana does not instigate conflict—we can't afford to. Now get us back to Midwatch."

Wordlessly, everyone began to move and the boats regained their speed, skipping across the waves. Yet Lara couldn't tear her gaze from the fading light of the fleet, her father's speech from that fateful dinner shifting and rattling through her head. *For as long as memory, Ithicana has placed a stranglehold on trade, making kingdoms and breaking them like it were some dark god.*

She'd believed that. Believed *him* without question. Yet Aren's words . . . they weren't those of a ruler with god-like power. Quite the opposite. They were the words of a leader of a kingdom fighting to survive.

REN RUBBED HIS eyes, which felt like they'd been filled with sand and then left to bake in the summer sun for a week. His ribs throbbed, his back ached, and his palms were marked with blisters from too many days of overuse. The worst was the tooth he was fairly certain had been knocked loose when Lara accidentally smacked his face after she'd been almost swept into the ocean. He prayed it resolved itself, or Nana would never let him hear the end of it.

"We're as ready as we can be." Jor drank deeply from a silver flask he took from a pocket before passing it across the firepit to his king. "You look like you need this."

He probably did need it, but Aren waved the flask away. His team, the green-faced Lara in tow, had returned to Midwatch just prior to dawn, and the entire day had been spent in preparation for the inevitable Amaridian attack. Now, there was little to do but watch the weather. With the winds still high, the raiders would be unlikely to attempt a landing, but a light squall like this one wouldn't last. And it certainly wouldn't be enough to drive the ships back to the safety of

Amaridian harbors. "I'm going to take the next patrol."

Jor lifted one eyebrow. "You already did your shift."

"I need to move. You know the sitting drives me to madness."

"It's a cold rain. You'll be regretting your decision halfway around the island."

"Regret," Aren said, picking up his cloak, "is currently my middle name."

"You're particularly whiney tonight."

Scratching his cheek with his middle finger, Aren lifted a hand to acknowledge the soldier who'd just come in from walking the perimeter, then started to the door.

"Might as well go with you. Just in case you give up halfway and run to the comfort of the fancy house."

"I wouldn't count on it."

The driving rain was, in fact, freezing, the wind tearing at the hood of Aren's cloak until he gave up on covering his head. They walked in silence for a long time, more focused on keeping their footing on the slick rocks and mud as they traversed the cliffs overlooking the sea. More than a few soldiers had fallen to their deaths, and despite the series of shitty days he'd had, Aren didn't care to join their ranks.

When they reached the first lookout, both of them casting their eyes out over the storm-tossed waters, Jor finally said, "You were right to stand your ground with them yesterday."

"Maybe." Aren's thoughts drifted to the meeting at Eranahl, to the hard faces of his Watch Commanders as they had arrived, weaving their way through the evacuees disembarking from their ships, supplies and crying children everywhere. *Most disorganized evacuation in recent history*, he'd heard muttered more times than he could count. He was inclined to agree with the sentiment.

"It's the council's duty to question you. They pushed your mother constantly, especially about this. She learned to know when they were giving good advice and when it was their fear talking—when to stand her ground and when to concede."

Aren extracted his spyglass, scanning the blackness for any lights on the horizon marking a ship. "You think I was right to stand my ground on this?"

The only sound was the wind howling and the waves slamming against the cliffs below. "I don't know. I'm not sure there is a *right* choice in this, Aren. All paths lead to war." Jor leaned back on his hands. "But what's done is done, at least so far as the battle facing us is concerned. Now if you'll excuse me, I need to take a piss."

The older man silently disappeared into the jungle and then not so silently did his business. Aren remained crouched on the rocks, shoving his hands in his pockets to warm them. With the evacuation mostly complete, his people had answered the annual call to arms, everyone between fifteen and fifty either at or on their way to their assigned garrison, the only exception being families with small children, who only sent one parent. Able bodies fought. Those unable played other roles, whether it be watch duties, dispatching signals, organizing supply drops, or managing the complex task of ensuring every one of the hundreds of outposts were appropriately manned. Ithicana didn't have civilians during War Tides. It had an army.

An army that was furious that Amarid had caught them with their trousers down at Serrith. An island that just happened to be under Aren's watch.

Over and over, he replayed the War Tides council meeting in his head, seeing a hundred things he could've done differently. Said differently.

"I understand you took heavy losses at Serrith, Your Grace." Watch Commander Mara's voice echoed in his head. "That's twice Amarid has sneaked up on you, and War Tides has only just begun. The pretty Maridrinian girl must be *quite* distracting."

Everyone in the room had shifted uneasily, *Lara* the crux of the barb, not the losses. They knew that Serrith was a nightmare to defend, the proximity of the bridge to the beach allowing vessels to hide beneath it while launching landing craft, rendering the shipbreakers useless. It took manpower and preparation to hold off an attack, and even then, with heavy fog, the soldiers stationed there would only have had a few minutes—the time it took for the longboats to reach the beach—to mount their defense. Which would've been enough if the man on watch hadn't fallen asleep at his post. A mistake the soldier had paid for with his life.

"I understand she was with you when the attack happened. In the bridge."

There'd been no hope of keeping that quiet. Not with all the evacuees from Serrith now in Eranahl. Gossip moved faster than a tempest in Ithicana. The only saving grace was that Aster was late to the meeting. If the Watch Commander knew what Lara had seen, the old bastard would burst a blood vessel. "It's never been my intention to keep Lara locked up. You all know that."

Yet neither had it been his intention to bring her into the bridge or for her to see how his military used it to fight their enemies. But watching her panic in the boat, gasping for breath and shaking uncontrollably . . . He hadn't been able to take it. He wasn't about to admit *that* in front of these battle-hardened men and women whose respect he needed to earn.

"Knowing your intentions isn't the same as agreeing with them. The Maridrinians are rats. Let one loose, and soon all of Ithicana will be infested with them."

"The Maridrinians are our allies," Ahnna said from where she stood at the far end of the large replica of Ithicana, her hand resting protectively on Southwatch island.

Mara made a face. "The Maridrinians are our *business partners* at best, Ahnna. We pay them for peace. That's not an alliance."

But it could be, Aren thought before he interjected. "They gave us fifteen years of peace in exchange for nothing, *Mara*. They proved their commitment to the treaty, and now it's time for us to do the same."

"But at what cost?" Mara gestured to the middle of the map, where model Amaridian ships sat to represent the lurking enemy fleet. The Amaridians were always Ithicana's worst raiders, primarily because they were competitors for the same business: trade between the continents. Amaridian merchant vessels took the greatest risks, making the crossing north and south even during storm season, primarily trafficking goods Ithicana wanted no part of in its markets. Maridrina had made heavy use of their services. Until now. And the Amaridian Queen clearly intended to make her displeasure over that fact known.

"Once terms are negotiated with Harendell they'll check Amarid's navy," said Aren. For while Amarid might risk quarrelling with Ithicana, picking battles with their enormous neighbor was another thing entirely.

"Has Harendell sent for Ahnna yet?"

Aren sensed his twin shifting nervously behind him. "No."

"Begun trade negotiations?"

"Not yet." Sweat dribbled down Aren's back, and it was a struggle not to grind his teeth. "Which isn't surprising. They'll be waiting to see how the peace stands in the south before they start making demands."

"Doesn't smell like peace." Everyone turned to watch Commander Aster enter the room. "Smells to me like war."

He handed Aren a folded letter sealed with amethyst-colored wax stamped with the Valcottan emblem of crossed staffs. "Ran into the mail runner in the bridge and thought to bring this to you directly."

You mean you thought to have me read it in front of everyone, Aren thought, cracking the wax with more force than was necessary, reading the few lines and struggling to keep a grimace from his face as he set the page down on the replica of Midwatch. The Empress of Valcotta was a reasonable woman. The Valcottans were reasonable people. But both *hated* Maridrina in a way that bordered on religion. It was a sentiment that the Maridrinians returned.

"Well?" Mara demanded at the same time Aster blurted out, "Has Valcotta declared war on us?"

Eyes on the page, Aren read: "*To His Royal Majesty, King Aren Kertell, King of Ithicana, Ruler of the Tempest Seas and Master of the Bridge.*"

Everyone in the room seemed to hold their breath, and he knew why. Until today, the Empress had always addressed him as Dearest Aren, beloved son of my friend, God keep her soul in peace. The use of his titles was *not* a good sign.

He continued. "Long have Valcotta and Ithicana been friends—"

"Friends who raid when the weather's nice," Jor muttered from where he stood at Aren's left.

"All friends quarrel on occasion," Aster said. "Will you continue,

Your Grace?"

Aren coughed. "Long have Valcotta and Ithicana been friends, and it grieves us terribly to learn that you have chosen to betray that friendship by siding with Maridrina against us."

Someone in the room let out a low whistle, but Aren didn't lift his head from the page. "It breaks our heart to know that our dear friend Ithicana now supplies our mortal enemy in their unjust attacks against our lands. And all our dead we shall lay at your feet."

No one spoke.

"Strong is our desire to maintain our friendship with Ithicana, but this affront cannot go unanswered. Once the calm is upon us, we shall deploy our fleets to blockade our foe, Maridrina, from reaching your markets at Southwatch island until this offensive alliance is broken."

He was prevented from reading the rest, as both Aster and Mara broke into laughter, much of the room echoing them. "Good fortune favors us after all," Aster finally managed to get out. "Silas thought he was so clever. Thought he'd managed to extract the one thing from us that we didn't want to give, but neither he nor Maridrina will see *any* of it."

Aren hadn't laughed then, and he certainly wasn't laughing now. A twig snapped, and he jerked from his thoughts, turning to watch Jor step back out onto the rocks, still in the process of buckling his belt.

"Winds are strengthening," Jor said. "Storm is going to rage harder before it gives its last gasp. Amarid will have to cool its heels for a few days before they come for blood." The old soldier smirked at Aren. "It's an opportune moment for you to go spend some time with that pretty wife of yours. She's starting to take a shine to you, I can tell."

"You came to all those realizations while you were taking a shit?"

"It's when I do my best thinking. Now go. I'll finish the patrol."

Rising to his feet, Aren cast his gaze in the direction of his house, then shook his head. Lara was supposed to be the first step toward a better future for Ithicana. But with Amarid about to wage war and Valcotta doing its best to destroy the treaty, a better future no longer felt like a dream.

It felt like a delusion.

L ARA RESTED HER chin on her forearms, one eye on the faint
glow in the east and the other on the Ithicanians grouped in the
clearing in front of the barracks. Rainwater dripped down the
back of her neck, but after three nights spent spying from the roof of
the large stone structure, she barely noticed the endless damp anymore.

The population of Midwatch had grown by four, if not five,
times in the past few days, men and women arriving by boat to join
the ranks. They were civilians—or at least had been until War Tides
began—but calling them such seemed a misnomer, as they fell into the
efficient routine of Midwatch with practiced ease. Even the youngest,
who couldn't have been more than fifteen, seemed to have arrived
fully trained.

Still, the ranking officers—who were all career soldiers at
Midwatch—ran them through drill after drill, day and night, leaving
nothing to chance.

And anything that happened in the midnight hours, Lara was
witness to.

Sneaking out of the Midwatch house was no great challenge

despite the number of guards Aren now had posted around the home. For one, she'd earned a bit of trust from them by saving Aren's life during the battle on Serrith Island, so they were no longer waiting for her to do something nefarious. Two, the clouds from the rainstorms made for the darkest of nights, giving her perfect cover for escape. And three, the Ithicanians were distracted by what they perceived as a far greater threat than a young woman soaking herself in a hot spring:

The Amaridians.

The fleet remained off the coast of Ithicana, though there had been no attacks since Serrith. Eli, the source of much of Lara's information, had told her that they were unlikely to make a move until the weather cleared. The waters were shallow and full of rocks and shoals, as well as the man-made defenses Ithicana was known for, and unpredictable winds and poor visibility made attacking during foul weather inadvisable.

But the storm wouldn't last forever, and Midwatch seethed with anticipation of the battles to come. Which served Lara's purposes well.

Already her head was full with what she'd learned during her venture off Midwatch with Aren, and the past three nights had yielded even more. From her perch, she'd learned much about how the bridge was patrolled, inside and out, where sentries were stationed on the surrounding islands, and the signals they used to communicate with Midwatch, which seemed to function as a central control point for this area of Ithicana. She'd learned about the explosives they used to destroy enemy ships, shot by arrow or launched by shipbreaker and, if the story she'd overheard was true, occasionally planted by hand under the cover of night.

She'd watched them train, working in the rain with only faint lantern light to avoid the attention of anyone on the water. Hand to hand, with blades, and with bow, the worst of them were at least proficient. The best of them . . . well, she wouldn't want to go up against the best of them unless she had to. Their weapons were all of fine make, every one of them armed to the teeth, the garrison stockpiled with enough to supply them with spares.

Midwatch was only one piece of the puzzle, but if it was the standard that Ithicana held itself to, then what Serin and the rest of her masters had told Lara and her sisters about Ithicana being impenetrable had been alarmingly accurate.

But as to the rest of what she and her sisters had been told about Ithicana . . . that, Lara was questioning. Questioning what was truth and what was lies, because it was impossible that all parties had been honest with her. Not with everyone claiming to be the victim and no one the aggressor.

Someone was deceiving her.

Or everyone was. Pushing back a strand of wet hair from her face, Lara wished, not for the first time, that she'd been allowed to spend time away from the compound. Everything she knew had come from books and from her masters. Outside of combat, she was like a scholar who studies the world but never leaves the library. It was a limitation, and one she'd pointed out to Serin several times, much to his endless irritation.

"It's not worth the risk," he had snapped. "All it would take is one slip on your part, and everything that we've worked for, fought for, would be undone. Is your desire for a sojourn worth losing the only chance Maridrina has at escaping Ithicana's yoke?" He'd never waited for a response, only slapped her cheek and said, "Remember your purpose."

Master Erik had given her a different answer when she'd pressed. "Your father is a man who needs *control*, little cockroach," he said, passing a whetstone up and down a blade. "Here, he can control every variable, but outside"—he used the weapon to gesture to the desert— "true control is beyond even a king's power. Your life is as it is out of necessity, my girl. But it won't be this way forever."

His words had infuriated her at the time—a vague non-answer, in her childish opinion—but now . . . Now she wondered if there was more depth to his response than she'd once realized.

Now she wondered if the variable her father had most wanted to control was her.

The main door to the barracks opened and shut beneath her, and Lara's attention perked as a tall figure exited the building. He had his hood pulled up against the rain, clothing identical to that of every other soldier, but she knew instinctively it was Aren. Something about his stride. The way he held his shoulders. The hint of pride that radiated from him as he surveyed the troops. And something else that she couldn't quite put a finger on . . .

She knew that what her father and Serin had told her about the King of Ithicana had been a lie—though she understood why. It was easier to stab a demon in the back. A much harder thing to betray a man whose actions and choices were driven by a desire to do right by his people. But she also knew that her homeland and Ithicana were at odds, and what would save one would damn the other. The welfare of her people was her priority, her mission to give them the one thing that would ensure their future. And for that reason, Aren could never be anything to her but the enemy.

Aren stepped closer to the training soldiers to say something to the woman leading the exercises, and Lara leaned forward to catch what it was. When she did, a piece of debris slipped off the roof of the barracks, landing with a soft thud on the ground.

Aren turned on his heel, one hand going to the weapon belted at his waist, the other shoving back his hood.

Lara froze. Dressed in black clothes, she was hidden in the darkness atop the roof. *Unless* someone held up a lantern to investigate a noise.

With the toe of his boot, Aren nudged the fallen bit of branch and leaves. Lara silently willed him to look away. *It's nothing. Just foliage knocked loose by the wind. Happens a hundred times a day.* But even as she did, she could relate to the sixth sense that was telling him something wasn't right.

"Someone bring a lantern over here. And a ladder. I think we've got snakes on the roof again."

Pulse roaring in her ears, Lara eased backward, her fingers clutching the slimy stone of her perch. He'd hear even the slightest noise, but if she didn't move fast . . .

A horn sounded in the distance, and the Ithicanians—Aren included—stopped what they were doing and turned in the direction of the water. Another horn sounded, this one closer, and Aren gave a sharp nod. "Amaridians are on the move." He started shouting out orders, but Lara couldn't afford to stay to listen. Dawn was approaching, and she needed the cover of night to get back into the house undetected. And she needed to be inside by the time the sun was up, or her absence would be noted.

Easing around the back of the barracks, she jumped, catching hold of a tree branch that really needed to be cut back. From tree to tree, she climbed, then dropped into the shelter of the jungle. Using the route she'd established on her first night, she cut over to the path leading up to the house, moving as fast as she dared on the muddy earth.

Gorrick and Lia were guarding the exterior, and she silently circled until she found a place out of sight of both of them, then scaled the wall, crawled over the roof, and dropped into the courtyard. Easing inside through her cracked window, she swiftly scrubbed the mud from her boots and clothes, putting everything back in the wardrobe where it could dry undetected.

A knock sounded at the door, the lock rattling. "Your Grace? It's dawn."

Taryn. The woman was like damned clockwork. Since her perceived failure to watch Lara while they were staying at Nana's house, Taryn was intent on redeeming herself by monitoring Lara like a hawk. She slept in the hall outside Lara's door—would've slept right next to her bed if Lara hadn't gently noted that Taryn's snoring rivaled the thunderstorms for volume.

If she didn't answer, Taryn would likely break down the door. "Coming!"

Throwing on a robe and wrapping a towel around her hair, Lara trotted across the floor and opened the door. "Is something wrong? I heard horns?"

"Amarid," Taryn replied vaguely, then her eyes narrowed. "Why is there mud on your face?"

"I was just washing it off. Certain muds are good for the skin. They cleanse the pores."

"Mud?" Taryn gave her a dubious frown, then shook her head, passing a weary hand over her eyes before stepping into the room, giving it a once-over. "I've told you not to leave your window open. You're asking to wake up with a snake under the covers with you."

"I only opened it just now," Lara lied. "It was stuffy in here."

Taryn checked under the bed. "The storm's blown over, so you can go outside if you want fresh air." Then she flipped back the cover and swore, stepping back several paces. "What did I tell you?"

A small snake, black with yellow bands, was coiled in the center of the bed, hissing angrily at them. Muttering under her breath, Taryn stepped in the hallway and shouted for Eli, who appeared moments later, a long stick with a loop of rope at one end. He deftly caught the creature, the loop tightening around its neck, then departed as quickly as he'd come, snake in tow.

Apparently, Lara needed to add *check room for snakes* to her routine when returning from a reconnaissance mission.

Though there wasn't much more to be gained from the roof of the barracks. Or from Midwatch, for that matter. It was a nearly impossible nut to crack unless her father could get someone on the inside. Ideally, that would be her, but she fully intended to be long gone before Maridrina invaded, her life as much in danger from her father's soldiers as it would be from the Ithicanians once they realized she'd betrayed them. Which meant she needed to find an entry point other than Midwatch for her father to exploit.

"I'm going to nail your window shut." Taryn stepped aside so that Eli's aunt could enter with the breakfast tray, which was deposited on the small table. "Or else start locking Vitex in here with you at night."

The thought of sleeping with the enormous cat watching gave Lara the shivers. "I'll keep it shut. I promise."

Sitting at the table, Lara loaded two plates full of food and then gestured at the other woman to join her, both of them drinking deeply from their steaming coffees. They'd grown increasingly familiar in their time together, Taryn easy to be around in a way that reminded Lara of her sisters. "Has Amarid attacked?"

"Not yet. They know they no longer have the element of surprise, so they'll look for points of weakness."

"Is Aren . . ."

"He'll be on the water, making sure we have no points of weakness. Why?" Taryn smirked. "Miss him?"

Lara gave a snort of amusement that could be taken either way, but the wheels were turning in her head. Aren gone meant there was no one on Midwatch to tell her *no*. "I wanted to ask him something . . ."

"Oh?"

"I want to get used to being on the water."

Taryn paused in her chewing of a mouthful of ham, then swallowed. "War Tides isn't exactly the ideal time for sailing aimlessly about, Lara."

Lara gave her a gentle kick under the table. "I *know* that. I was thinking I could sit in a boat in the cove. Then perhaps by the end of War Tides, I'll have adjusted to the water enough that I might venture further without subjecting everyone to my vomiting."

Taryn took another bite of meat, her brow furrowed. "There's a lot of comings and goings right now . . ."

"Is there another location that would work better? I don't want to be in the way." And if there was another landing point on the island— perhaps one with fewer defenses —it might mitigate her need to find another entrance to the bridge.

"Nowhere with a proper beach."

Lara exhaled in disappointment. "It's only that I feel so trapped. I want to see more of Ithicana, but with my seasickness and my . . . fear, it seems impossible."

Trapped the way Taryn felt trapped. Limited in where she might go and what she might do by circumstance and necessity. Lara watched her words strike home, the other woman setting down her fork, eyes distant as she thought. "I suppose we could try it for an hour and see if anyone takes issue."

Lara grinned. "Let me wash the rest of this mud off my face, and then we can go."

Three hours later, the two of them sat in a bobbing canoe, Lara trying to keep track of the goings-on in the cove while periodically leaning over the side to empty her guts.

Taryn had taken her to another building not far from the barracks, which was filled with a variety of vessels that weren't currently in use. She'd selected a small canoe that wouldn't fit more than the two of them, so old it barely appeared seaworthy. No one would miss this particular vessel. As they carried it down to the beach, Lara silently considered how she might secret it away for her eventual escape.

She rested her forearms on the edge of the canoe and watched the chain guarding the mouth to the cove rise so that vessels could ferry goods from the pier to the shore. Crates of food, supplies, and weapons, all hailing from Harendell. There were cages of clucking chickens, three live pigs, and a dozen sides of beef, the Ithicanians' movements concealed by heavy mist.

The signal horns never seemed to cease their blowing. Ripples of sound that conveyed countless different messages, judging from the various reactions they incited, and not something that could be mimicked by an untrained Maridrinian soldier. Lara suspected her father would need to enlist musicians should he wish to turn the form of communication to his advantage. Taking a sip from a canteen of water, Lara rubbed her throbbing temple as she listened to the notes, attempting to memorize patterns and responses, though it would take days, probably weeks of listening and watching for her to make any sense of them.

The canoe had swung around so she was facing away from the cliffs guarding the cove from the sea, but the rattle of the chain caught her attention and she turned to watch a series of vessels enter, her eyes immediately finding Aren in one of them.

And his finding her.

She watched him exchange words with Jor, then the vessel altered its course from the beach to Lara's little canoe. Standing, he held onto the mast as the two boats came alongside. "I suppose there's an interesting explanation for this?"

Taryn rose, the canoe rocking, and Lara's stomach rocked along with it. "Her Grace is of the opinion that exposure will cure her seasickness."

"How's that working out?"

Taryn gestured at the school of tiny fishes circling the boat, and Lara felt her cheeks warm as they both laughed at her expense. Then Aren said, "Go get some rest, Taryn. I'll take over for a bit."

Lara's heart skipped as Aren settled on the seat facing Lara. He waited until the other boat was nearly to the beach before asking, "Why exactly have you volunteered yourself for this particular misery?"

Lara stared at the bottom of the canoe, which was taking on a bit of water through a tiny crack that she'd need patch. "Because. If I don't learn to master the sea, I'll never be able to go anywhere with you."

"Master?" He leaned forward, and her eyes, of their own accord, fixed on his lips, heat rising to her cheeks as she remembered the feel of them against her own.

"Perhaps tolerate is a better word," she murmured, noticing a nasty scrape on the inside of his forearm. "You're hurt."

"It's nothing. I had an altercation with a rock, and the rock came out better in the exchange."

Part of her was afraid to move closer to him, already aware that in his presence, she'd stopped seeing and hearing what was going on around them. But, she told herself, he was also the key to seeing more of Ithicana, and that was a necessary part of her plan. "Let me have a look."

He shifted nearer, unbuckling the greave that protected the backside of his arm. "See? Nothing of consequence."

"It should still be bandaged."

It didn't need to be bandaged. Both of them knew it. But that didn't stop her from taking hold of his wrist. Or him from supplying her with salve and a roll of fabric. The boat rocked on a series of larger waves, and his knee bumped against the side of her thigh, sending a surge of heat the rest of the way up her leg, filling her with a sensation that was decidedly distracting.

Forcing her attention on the injury, Lara picked out a few bits of rock, smeared the raw spots with salve, then carefully wrapped the bandage, but it was impossible not to notice how his breath moved the errant wisps of hair on her forehead. The way the muscles in his forearm flexed when he moved. The way his other hand brushed her hip as he gripped the side of the canoe.

"You're knowledgeable in the healing arts."

"Any idiot can wind a bandage around an arm."

"I meant more what you did on Serrith."

Lara shrugged, tying off the bandage. "All Maridrinian women are expected to be able to put their husbands back together. I received the appropriate training."

"Practicing stitches on a cloth isn't the same as running a needle and thread through a person's bleeding skin. I nearly fainted the first time I had to do it."

A smile rose on her face, and she unfastened the bandage knot, unsatisfied with it. "Women haven't the luxury of such squeamishness, Your Grace."

"You're avoiding the question, *Your Grace*." His voice was light, teasing, but beneath she sensed a seriousness, as though he were searching for a lie.

"My sisters and I practiced on the servants and guards whenever there was an injury. On the horses and camels, too." That was the truth. What she didn't tell him was that her true training came from trying to save the lives of the Valcottan warriors she and her sisters fought on the training yard. It had been a twisted way to learn. In one heartbeat, trying to take a man's life. In the next, trying to save it. Only to take it again.

"It's a useful skill to have around here. That is, if you're willing."

Buckling the greave over the bandage, the back of her hand brushed his palm, and he closed his fingers around hers. Her train of thought vanished. "I'll help as much as I'm able to. They're my people now."

His expression softened. "That they are."

Both of them jumped as something rapped sharply against the hull of the canoe, and Lara looked up to see Jor standing in the boat next to them, paddle in hand. "You ready?"

"For what?"

The older man gave him an incredulous look. "The horns, Aren. Amarid is moving south."

Lara hadn't heard any horns blow. Hadn't seen the other canoe approach. Hadn't noticed a goddamned thing while bandaging that arm. And neither, it appeared, had Aren.

He clambered out of her canoe and into the other vessel, setting them both to rocking, and then they were on the move toward the entrance to the cove. Lara stared after them, finally shouting, "How am I supposed to get back to shore?"

"You have a paddle," he shouted back, a wild grin on his face as the wind caught at his hair. "Use it!"

From that moment, a pattern formed of Lara and Taryn coming down after breakfast to float on the water, rain or shine. At first, it was misery. The incessant bobbing up and down made Lara's head spin and her stomach heave, but gradually the sickness began to ease, as did the surge of fear she felt stepping off dry land and into the boat.

The raids were endless, the music of the horns so constant, it seemed an endless song of war. Aren and his soldiers were continuously on the move, chasing off raiders, reinforcing defenses, and ensuring the countless watch stations and outposts were kept supplied. More often than not, their excursions turned into skirmishes, the boats returning full of wounded men and women, the faces of their comrades drawn and exhausted.

The worst of the injured went to the dozen healers stationed at Midwatch, but those needing only stitches or bandages were left in Lara's boat for her to tend to. More often than not, one of her patients was Aren, which was the *only* time Taryn left her side.

"I'm starting to wonder," she said as she applied a leech to the swelling on his cheek, smirking when he recoiled from the creature, "if you are purposefully trying to get yourself injured or if you are just that inept."

He cringed as she lifted another leech out of the jar. "Is there a third option?"

"Sit still." She applied the leech the way the healers had shown her, marveling at the way the swelling almost instantly reduced on his cheekbone, the engorged creatures dropping into her hands when they'd finished. Along with supplies, the healers had also insisted that she be given a better boat, returning her little canoe to its dry dock. She'd been sneaking out at nights to slowly move the vessel to the hiding place she'd selected near one of the cliffs, along with a number of stolen supplies, ready to facilitate her escape when the time was right.

"You seem to be doing better with the water."

"I don't get sick anymore. Though I suppose it might be different out in the open where the waves are larger."

"Perhaps someday we'll test that theory."

Someday. Which meant no time soon. It was a struggle to keep the frown from her face because she was running out of ideas for winning him over. She had won his lust, that much was clear from the way his eyes skimmed over the unlaced neckline of her tunic. Winning his trust, however, was proving to be far more of a challenge.

She'd thought, for a time, it was because their marriage had yet to be consummated. That maybe he needed that step before he'd hand her the metaphorical keys to the kingdom, but she had since rejected that theory. Aren was not, judging from the offhand comments she'd heard from his soldiers, inexperienced with women, so it would take more than skill in the bedroom to make him fall for her.

And it would take more than him falling for her to make him trust her.

For as much as he might come to care for her, he loved his people more. His trust would only come if he believed she was as loyal to his people as he was.

"I'm not certain that leech deserves so much of your attention." Aren's voice pulled Lara from her thoughts, and she blinked, realizing that she'd been regarding the squirming creature in her hand for far too long.

"They just gave you back your handsome face, so perhaps you should give them the credit they deserve."

Aren smiled and Lara realized what she'd said. With everyone else, she was strategic, but Aren flustered her. Things had a way of slipping out when he was around.

"It's going to rain tonight. I thought I might take the opportunity to have a proper dinner at the house. With you."

Her face was burning, heart a riot in her chest. "Tonight?"

He looked away from her. "My ability to predict the weather has its limits. But yes, tonight looks promising."

Say yes, her inner voice screamed. *Do what you need to do.* Except being alone with him . . . Lara wasn't sure what would happen. Or rather, she *was* sure and wanted to avoid it at all costs.

Not because she didn't want him to kiss her, because she did.

And not because she didn't want him to peel the clothes from her body, because god, she'd envisioned that more than once.

It was because she *did* want him that she needed to avoid this situation, because betraying him was already going to be hard enough.

Horns blasted, and this time the rhythm wasn't music, but an anxious rippling blare that tore at her ears. Aren stiffened, his expression intent. "What is it?" she demanded.

"Aela."

"Who?"

"It's one of the islands under Kestark's watch. It's being attacked."

"Kestark?"

"The garrison south of us." His eyes were distant, listening. "But Aela's outpost is calling for Midwatch's aid."

Already soldiers were pouring down the beach, pushing boats out into the water. More horns sounded, and Aren's face paled.

"What's happening?"

"Their shipbreaker is jammed." He stood, gesturing to his guards, who were paddling hard toward them. "The outpost is going to be slaughtered. Amarid will take the island, and it will be a bloody nightmare to dig them out."

Lara's mind raced, deciding on a plan even as it formed in her mind. She caught his hand. "Take me with you. If there are injured, I can help."

"That's what we have healers for."

"Five of which are elsewhere, two of which are injured themselves. Which leaves you only five to bring with you. It's not enough to deal with slaughter."

"Others will come."

The boat was only yards away. She had seconds to convince him.

"And how many of your people will die in the time it will take for them to arrive?" She tightened her fingers on his. "I can help them."

Indecision ricocheted across his face, then he nodded. "Follow orders. No arguments." The other boat came alongside, and he hauled Lara and her box of supplies in with him. "Go!" he shouted.

Paddles drove them toward the gap, the chain already up, the ocean covered with whitecaps beyond. Wild and unpredictable. A prickle of fear crawled down Lara's spine as she sat in the bottom of the boat.

"Time to put your experiment to the test," Aren said as they passed between the towering cliffs, the vessel bucking and plunging the moment they hit the open sea.

"To Aela!" Jor roared. "Let's give these Amaridians a taste of Midwatch steel!"

"To Aela!" The soldiers on the other vessels echoed the chant, and behind them, horns called over the water. Not the musical ripple of a signal, but a violent blast of rage.

A battle cry.

THE BOATS BARELY seemed to touch the water as they skated across the sea, a strong north wind filling the sails. Lara's heart was in her throat, but with her nausea under control, she was able to study the bridge as they followed its great grey length south, eyes picking out scouts perched on its top and the glints of spyglasses on the islands to either side.

"How long until we reach Aela?" she shouted over the wind.

"Not long," Aren replied. "The closest Midwatch teams will already be there."

Time seemed to both fly and crawl. A thousand details flooded her mind even as her heartbeat moved into the swift but steady thud it always did before battle. *You aren't here to fight,* she reminded herself. *You're here to observe under the cover of helping the healers, nothing more.* The words did nothing to calm her anticipation.

When they rounded an enormous limestone karst tower, all the Ithicanians pulled their masks from their belts and donned them. Weapons loosened. Eyes intent.

Then she saw it.

The ship was larger than any she'd seen before, a great three-masted monstrosity as tall as the bridge itself. She picked out the Amaridian flag, countless soldiers scurrying about its deck. Beyond, a half dozen longboats were moving toward a narrow beach on which a battle was being waged, the sand soaked with blood.

Swiftly she saw the reason the Amaridians had chosen Aela Island beyond the relatively easy landing the beach provided them. There was a pier on the western edge of the island, the bridge curving inland before heading back out to sea. And if the Ithicanians were fighting this hard to defend it, she'd bet that pier had an opening in its base. "How many men are on that ship?"

"Four hundred," Jor replied. "Perhaps a few more."

"And us?"

No one answered.

Aren caught her hand, pulling her close. "See the line of rock and trees?" He pointed. "We'll get you and the other healers past that line. You stay there and the injured will be brought to you, understood?"

"Yes."

His hand tightened. "Keep your hood up so the Amaridians don't recognize you. And if things go badly, go with the other healers. They know how to make a retreat."

And she'd bet that retreat was into the bridge. But gaining that information wasn't worth the cost of Aren's life.

Her heartbeat was no longer steady, but a wild and chaotic beast. "Don't let it go badly," she whispered. "I need you to win this."

But Aren was already shouting orders. "Bring down those longboats. The rest of you, to the beach!"

The boats flanked the enormous ship, the air thick with arrows shot from both sides. Aren knelt in the boat next to her, emptying a quiver into the backs of the Amaridians climbing into longboats, their corpses falling into the water below. Lara's fingers itched to snatch up a weapon, to fight, but she forced herself to cower low in the boat, flinching every time an arrow thudded into the thick wood.

Then they were past the ship.

Four of the Ithicanian vessels veered away from the pack, skipping over the surf to slam into the longboats full of soldiers heading to shore. Wood splintered and cracked, men toppling into the water. The Ithicanians boarded the longboats with lethal grace, blades flashing, the sun glinting off sprays of blood.

The rest of the boats drove toward the carnage on the beach. There were bodies everywhere, the sand more red than white. Maybe two dozen Ithicanians were holding the enemy to the waterline, using the narrow access and higher ground to their advantage, but they were falling back. Dying beneath the Amaridian onslaught.

They had to hurry, or the island would be lost.

The Midwatch boats dropped their sails, riding the waves as they were launched onto the shore. At the last second, Aren snatched up Lara's hand. "Jump!" he shouted.

Lara leapt, her boots sinking into the sand, the momentum nearly sending her sprawling. Then they were running toward the Amaridians, who were now sandwiched between two forces.

Screams shattered the air, bodies and limbs hitting the sand, the stench of blood and opened guts oppressive. Lara held tight to her box of supplies, keeping behind Aren as he pushed up the hill, stepping over his victims as she went. The weapons of the fallen littered the sand, and every instinct demanded she pick one up. That she fight.

You mustn't, she commanded herself. *Not unless you have no choice.*

But the warrior in her railed against the limitation, so when a soldier got past the Ithicanian line, she slammed her supply box into his face, watching with satisfaction as he toppled backward, the point of Aren's blade appearing through his chest.

The King of Ithicana used one booted foot to shove the dead man off his weapon, the leather of his mask coated with gore. Catching her hand, he drew her at a run, dodging around the few remaining Amaridians who were on their knees begging for their lives.

"Show them no mercy!" he shouted, then pulled Lara behind a series of boulders. An older Ithicanian woman, her face drawn, clothes drenched with blood, was closing the lids of a young man, his body marked with several mortal wounds. Three other soldiers lay on the ground, wounds bandaged, their faces tight with pain.

178

The healer's eyes widened at the sight of her king. "Explain to Lara what you need her to do," Aren told her. Then he was back around the rock, shouting, "Taryn, get that shipbreaker working and sink that bitch!"

The Midwatch healers appeared, their escorts already having abandoned them. "What do you want me to do?" Lara asked.

"Wait for them to bring us the injured. What do you have for supplies? I'm short."

Lara handed her the box, then scampered up the back of one of the boulders to watch the battle unfolding below. Her blood ran cold at the sight.

Aren stood on the beach with maybe a hundred Ithicanians, but beyond, the water was full of longboats. Dozens of them, all bursting with heavily armed soldiers, and more still waiting on the ship's deck to be unloaded. There were hundreds of them. And no way to stop them.

The Ithicanians were firing arrows at the front-runners, but it wasn't long until they were spent, leaving nothing for them to do but wait.

The old healer had climbed up next to her, expression grim as she took in the scene.

Lara dug her nails into the rock. "We can't win this. Not against these odds."

"We've won against worse. Though this one will cost us."

Was it still a victory if everyone was dead? Lara thought.

It must've shown on her face, because the older woman sighed. "Have you ever seen a battle before, Your Majesty?"

Lara swallowed hard. "Not like this."

"I'd tell you to prepare yourself, but you can't." The old woman rested her hand on Lara's. "This moment will change you." Then she climbed down the rocks to join the Midwatch healers.

The scene was eerily silent, the only sound the roar of the surf and the occasional cry of pain, the wounded left on the beach until the battle was won. So quiet. Too quiet.

Then the first of the longboats hit the shore, and everything turned to chaos.

The two forces slammed into each other, the air filling with shouts and screams, the clash of metal against metal and weapons against flesh.

Wave after wave of boats hurtled into shore, the heavy vessels crushing and killing Amaridians and Ithicanians alike, the waterline a teeming mass of humanity. The sailors struggled to withdraw, to get back to the ship to retrieve more soldiers, but Aren's men flung themselves at the sailors, cutting them down. Pulling the vessels onto the sand.

Yet still more came.

The Ithicanians fought with vicious efficiency, better trained and better armed, but grossly outnumbered. They fought until they couldn't stand, taking injury after injury until they collapsed on the beach or were pulled under waves that were more blood and bodies than water.

And still the enemy came.

It was the perfect opportunity to sneak away. To go look at the bridge pier and determine whether she could use it in her strategy, but her body remained rooted in place.

You have to do something. The voice rose up from the depths of Lara's mind, incessant and tenacious. *Do something. Do something.*

But what could she do? There were no injured behind these rocks for her to tend, and there wouldn't be until the battle was over. She could take a weapon and fight, but this wasn't the same circumstances as Serrith. In this madness, she couldn't turn the tide.

Do something.

Her eyes flicked back to the wounded bleeding out on the beach. Drowning in the waves. And then she was over the rocks and running.

Lara had been the fastest of her sisters—*built for speed*, Master Erik had always said. Today she ran like she never had before.

Her thighs burned as she sprinted down the beach, arms pumping, eyes fixed on her target. Skidding to a stop next to a young woman who'd taken two arrows in the back and one in the thigh, Lara bent and heaved her over one shoulder, then raced back to the boulders.

Rounding them, Lara carefully deposited the injured soldier on the ground in front of the startled healers. "Help her."

Then she was back on the beach and running.

Necessity compelled her to choose those with injuries they might survive. As it was, most of those farther up the beach were long past saving, eyes staring blankly at the gray sky.

So she edged closer to the battle.

The soldiers able to fight were doing so on top of the bodies of the fallen. Amaridians and Ithicanians, both tangled in the mess of limbs, dead hands seeming to grasp and trip them as the crimson waves pulled and tugged on carnage.

Most everyone on the ground was dead. Either from their original injuries, or from being crushed and drowned, but still Lara prowled the rear of the Ithicanian line, water filling her boots as she searched.

"Get back," someone shouted at her, but she ignored them, catching sight of a man, younger than her, choking as he tried to climb out of the battle, the waves rolling over his head, boots stomping on his back.

Lara dove, catching hold of his hand and holding tight so that the water wouldn't pull him farther out.

Someone kicked her in the side.

Another stomped on the back of her leg, and she cried out.

They were pressing in on her, driving her down into the sand, but the boy was looking at her and she at him, and Lara refused to let go.

Inch by inch, she dragged him back, then a hand closed on her belt and pulled her and the injured soldier the rest of the way free.

"What are you doing?"

Aren's voice. His face hidden behind his mask.

Over his shoulder, she saw an Amaridian raising a cudgel. Snatching up a rock, she threw it hard, shattering the soldier's face. "Fight," she screamed at Aren, then scrambled to her feet.

Holding the injured boy under the armpits, she dragged him up the beach and out of harm's way. Then she threw herself back into the carnage.

The Ithicanians saw what she was doing, and they fought to

give her openings. Called her name when someone fell. Guarded her back while she dragged their comrades out of the water because they couldn't afford to stop fighting.

And the enemy kept coming.

Pushing them farther up the sand.

Step by step, the Ithicanians retreated, and Lara howled in fury, because all those she'd pulled onto the beach were now in danger of being trampled once more. Her body screamed with pain and exhaustion, her sides cramping as her lungs struggled to draw in enough air to fuel her thundering heart.

Then a familiar crack echoed across the island, along with the whistle of something large flying through the air.

Splintering wood and screams filtered up from the deeper water, and Lara lifted her head to see a large hole in the side of the ship. Someone had repaired the shipbreaker.

Another crack split the air, and this time the projectile hit one of the masts. It shattered, falling sideways, the ropes and sails falling to the deck.

Another crack, this time a hole opening in the hull, water pouring in with every wave.

The weapon didn't stop. Boulder after boulder was thrown at the ship, then Taryn turned on the longboats, hitting them with deadly accuracy.

The Amaridians began to panic, lines breaking as they fought to save their own skins. But there was no retreat, and the Ithicanians would show them no mercy.

"For Ithicana!" someone roared, and the chant raced down the beach until it drowned out all other noise as the soldiers rallied around their king, pressing forward.

So there was no one to hear when Lara whispered, "For Maridrina," and dove back into the chaos.

AREN FOUND LARA crouched next to a tide pool washing blood from her hands and arms. Her clothing was soaked in gore, and as she lifted her head to regard him, he noted the red streaks on her cheeks from where she'd pushed aside the strands of hair that had tugged loose from her thick braid.

His soldiers were talking about her; and not, for once, about how she was a useless Maridrinian, good for nothing but bedding. Today had changed that. Time and again, she'd sprinted onto the beach to pull an injured Ithicanian back behind their lines, showing no regard for her own life as the Amaridians had fought their way forward, the battle pitched and desperate.

And once the battle was won, she'd treated the wounded with speed and efficiency, packing wounds and tying tourniquets, buying them time until the healers could reach them. Saving lives, one soldier at a time, her face tight with determination.

Today she'd won Ithicana's respect.

And his own.

"Are you all right?" He crouched down to submerge his own

hands in the water. He'd done it earlier, but his skin still felt sticky and stained.

"Tired." She sat back on her haunches, eyes going to the corpses floating amidst the debris of the shattered ship, the water still crimson. "How many died?"

"Forty-three. Another ten aren't likely to make it through the night."

Lara squeezed her eyes shut, then snapped them open. "So many."

"Would have been more if you hadn't convinced me to bring you. Or if you hadn't ignored my orders." He didn't add that he'd spent a good portion of the battle afraid that the decision would see her dead on the sand, an Amaridian sword in her back.

"It feels like I accomplished nothing in the scheme of things," she murmured.

"The men and women whose lives you saved would beg to differ, I suspect."

"Lives I saved." She shook her head. "I should go back to help."

Aren caught her wrist as she rose, his fingers wrapping around the slender bones, which seemed too delicate to have accomplished what she had. "We need to go."

"Go?" Spots of anger rose on her cheeks. "We can't leave them like this."

He wanted to abandon this beach and his injured people no more than she did, but the defense of his kingdom was a finely oiled machine with a thousand different pieces. Pulling one out of place, even for a matter of hours, put the whole works at risk, and right now, his piece was very much out of place. "I moved significant numbers from the defense of Midwatch and its surrounding islands. We need to return."

"No." She pulled out of his grip. "Fewer than a dozen of the soldiers here are unscathed. We can't leave them undefended. What if the Amaridians attack again?"

Out of the corner of his eye, Aren could see his guard standing by the boats, Jor giving him a pointed glare. Several of the other Midwatch teams were at the ready on the beach, waiting for his order to depart. "There are no Amaridian ships on the horizon, and reinforcements are already on the way. They'll be here within the hour."

"I'm not leaving until they arrive."

She crossed her arms, and it occurred to him that he might have to drag the woman every soldier on this beach was lauding as a hero into a boat if he ever wanted to depart. Which wasn't exactly the visual he wished to present to them.

Huffing out a breath, Aren pulled a knife from his belt and knelt in the sand, drawing a snaking line representing the bridge. "The defense of the bridge is broken into sections led by Watch Commanders, each with a subset of the Ithicanian military under his or her control. The Midwatch garrison is here"—he made a hole in the sand—"and the Kestark garrison is here. Four Amaridian ships were making motions to attack here." He made four holes south of Kestark Island.

"The healers could use my assistance," Lara interrupted. "So perhaps get to the point."

"I *am* getting to the point," he grumbled, hoping a convoluted explanation would convince her to leave rather than provoke questions. "Kestark moved their reserves to reinforce the locations most likely to come under attack, while at the same time, the Amaridians attacked here at Aela Island. Kestark couldn't risk pulling back their reserve, nor could they redeploy the teams making up the net of defense through here"—he drew an oval—"so they called for assistance from Midwatch. But now Midwatch is down the majority of its reserves, so if there are any attacks here"—he drew another oval—"we won't be able to come to their aid in a timely fashion."

Lara stared at the drawing, blinking only once in apparent confusion. Then she pressed her fingers to her temples. "For the love of God, Aren, none of this justifies abandoning these soldiers." She started to pull away, but he tugged her back.

"Listen. The four Amaridian ships that were expected to attack instead withdrew —probably because they saw it wouldn't be an easy fight—and they've moved east and out of sight of our scouts. So now there will be a wave of signals, with teams shifting one position north and west in order to allow the Kestark teams closest to us to move to reinforce. As I said, they'll be here within the hour."

"Fine." Moving out of reach, she started up the sand to where the wounded were laid out in rows.

"Insufferable woman," he muttered, then a whistle caught his attention. Aren turned to see Jor gesturing at a pair of Kestark boats flying across the water on a violent gust of wind that smelled like rain. He turned back to point them out to Lara, but she was already out of earshot.

Growling out a few choice curses, he strode down to the water. "Everyone go. I want you back at Midwatch before this squall hits."

His soldiers immediately pushed off from the beach, but instead of watching them, Aren found his eyes drawn to where Lara walked among the injured, occasionally bending down to speak with one of them. The growing winds caught at the loose strands of her hair, the fading sunlight making it glow like tendrils of honey. His soldiers moved aside for her, inclined their heads to her. Respected her.

The image juxtaposed that of her walking up the road at Southwatch on her father's arm, silk clad and eyes wide: the portrait of a queen he'd worried Ithicana would never accept. Turned out, he'd been wrong.

"And when will we be departing, Your Grace?" Jor asked, coming up to stand next to him. "When your little wife says it's time to go?"

"We'll go when the *Queen of Ithicana* says it's time to go."

The older man chuckled, then clapped him on the shoulder.

The first of the Kestark boats reached shore, and Aren recognized Commander Aster even as the man's eyes lighted upon him, apprehension filling them. "Your Grace. I didn't realize you'd come yourself."

"The benefit of being at the Midwatch garrison. Like I was supposed to be."

Aster's face lost more of its color, and rightfully so. That he was arriving now meant he hadn't been at Kestark garrison, or even with the bulk of his forces warding off the anticipated attack. And Aren was quite certain he knew exactly where the other man had been.

"As you can see, *Commander*, things almost didn't go Ithicana's way today. Aela is a weak point, its outpost was undermanned, and the shipbreaker hadn't been recalibrated after storm season, leaving those who were here sitting ducks for an entire ship full of Amaridians."

"We're behind on inspections, Your Grace," Aster blurted out.

"The season came early . . ."

"Which doesn't explain why you over-deployed to the southeast and left your northern end exposed. Perhaps you'll enlighten me?"

"There were four naval ships. We needed to be ready to defend—"

"To defend a series of islands that wouldn't be assailable if the Amaridians attacked with twenty ships!" Aren snarled. "Which if you'd been paying attention, you would've known. Which suggests to me that you were *distracted* when you gave the order."

"I was *not* distracted, Your Grace. I've been commanding Kestark since you were a child."

"And yet . . ." Aren gestured at the rows and rows of dead faces staring sightlessly at the sky. Then he leaned forward. "Evacuations are complete, so that means your lovely wife and children are safely ensconced in Eranahl, leaving you with all the time in the world to screw your mistress in the house I know you had built for her just west of here."

Aster's jaw tightened, but he didn't deny it. He couldn't, not with his own personal guard listening from where they stood next to their boats. Then his eyes drifted past Aren's shoulder. "What is *she* doing here?"

Turning, Aren saw that Lara stood behind him, a surviving officer—a girl who was only eighteen—at her elbow. He started to defend Lara's presence, but the girl beat him to it.

"Respectfully, Commander, a hell of a lot more of us would be dead if our queen hadn't come."

Lara said nothing, but her blue eyes were cold and eviscerating as she stared Aster down. Then her gaze shifted to Aren and she nodded once.

"No more mistakes, Commander." Aren took her arm and stepped toward the boat where his own guard waited. "And do us all a favor and keep your cock in your trousers and your eyes on the enemy for the rest of War Tides."

"My eyes are on the enemy. She's standing right there."

Temper frayed past repair, Aren turned and slugged the man in the face, knocking him out cold. Then he turned to the girl-soldier. "You've just been promoted to Acting Commander of Kestark until another can be chosen. Do let me know if anyone gives you any trouble."

Lara helped him and the guard push the boat out into the water, then hopped in, sitting in her usual spot, the most out of the way she could be in the small vessel. Aren sat next to her, but there was no space for conversation, all of them forced to row hard to get past the break line, the wind against them.

The squall was coming in hard from the north, lightning dancing across the blackening sky, and the vessel rose and fell on swells that grew with every passing minute. Lara's back was to him, but Aren could feel the fear radiating from her, knuckles white where she gripped the edge of the boat. She kept her composure until a freak gust caught the sail. Lia and Gorrick flinging their weight onto the outrigging was the only thing keeping them from capsizing. That tore a scream from her throat. Lara had thrown herself unarmed into battle, but this . . . this was what terrified her. And Aren found himself unwilling to subject her to it.

"We need to get off the water!" he shouted at Jor, spitting out a mouthful of seawater as a wave washed over them. Jor signaled to the boat carrying the rest of his guard, then he scanned their surroundings and pointed.

Sail lowered, they rowed hard, heading for one of the countless landing points hidden throughout Ithicana.

The rain fell in a deluge, making it almost impossible to see as they wove between two towers of limestone and into a tiny cove with cliffs on all sides. From the top of one of the cliffs two heavy wooden beams reached out over the water, ropes with hooks dangling from each of them. Lia lunged, catching hold of one of the hooks and clipping it to the ring mounted at the stern of the vessel.

Aren passed his paddle to a white-faced Lara. "If we get too close to the walls, push the boat away."

She nodded, holding the wooden paddle like a weapon. Behind him, Taryn waited until the boat swung around to the right angle, then jumped, catching hold of a rope hanging from the cliff, climbing swiftly to the top.

"Aren, get over here and help." Jor and Gorrick had removed the pin holding the mast in place and were struggling to heave it out of its base. Aren stumbled over a seat, then caught hold of the mast and added his strength to the effort. The mast popped out right as a violent swell lifted the boat, sending both mast and Gorrick tumbling into the water.

Aren fell backward on his ass, leaving only Jor standing, the old man shaking his head in disgust. "Why does this never get easier?" He reached down and clipped the other line to the boat, while Aren helped the swimming Gorrick lash the mast to the side.

An exhausting eternity later, they finally lifted the second boat onto shore with the winch, where they tied it down, the lot of them trudging around the bend of rock to where the safe house waited.

The interior of the stone building was mercifully dry and free from gusting wind. After assigning two of the men to first watch, Aren slammed the wooden door shut with more force than was necessary. Without fail, his eyes went immediately to Lara, who stood at the center of the room holding the bag full of supplies.

"Are there many of these places?" She turned in a circle.

There wasn't much to see. Bunks made of wood and rope lined two of the walls. Crates of supplies were piled against the third wall, and the fourth was mostly taken up by the door. His guards were all pulling off their boots and tunics to dry, then turning their attention to their weapons, which all needed to be sharpened and oiled.

"Yes." He tugged off his own tunic and tossed it on a bunk. "But as you noticed, they're a damned pain in the ass to use in the middle of a storm."

"Will the storm sink the rest of the Amaridian fleet?" she asked, and the guard chuckled, reminding him that everyone was listening.

"No. But they'll move out into open water rather than risk being driven up onto a shoal or against any rocks. Will give us a bit of respite."

One of her eyebrows rose. "Not the most comfortable respite."

"Now, now," Jor said. "Don't be so swift to discount the comforts of a safe house. Particularly a *Midwatch* safe house." He went over to one of the crates, prying open the lid and looking inside. "His Grace has fine tastes, so he ensures anywhere he might have to spend a night is stocked with only the best."

Danielle L. Jensen

"Are you complaining?" Aren sat on the bottom bunk and leaned back against the wall.

Jor extracted a dusty bottle. "Amaridian fortified wine." He held it closer to the lantern on the singular table and read the label. "No, Your Grace, I am most certainly *not* complaining."

Popping the cork, Jor poured a measure into the tin cups Lia set out, handing one to Lara. He held one up. "Cheers to the Amarid vintners who make the finest drink of the known world, and to their fallen countrymen, may they rot in the depths of the Tempest Seas." Then the old soldier cleared his throat. "And to our own fallen, may the Great Beyond gift them clear skies and smooth seas and endless women with perfect tits."

"Jor!" Lia jabbed him in the arm. "A goodly number of our fallen were women. I'm sure at least a few of them liked men. At least let them be surrounded by—"

"Perfect cocks?" Nine sets of surprised eyes turned to look at Lara, who shrugged.

"Where mortal life fails, the Great Beyond delivers," Jor intoned, and Aren flung his boot at him.

Lia threw up her hands. "People died. Show respect."

"I *am* respecting them. Disrespecting them would've been toasting their sacrifice with this sludge." Jor plucked a bottle of foggy Maridrinian wine from the crate. It rattled, and he gave it an incredulous glare, eyeing what appeared to be a rock sitting in the bottom of the bottle. "Not bad enough by itself, they need to put bits of rock in it?" His eyes flicked to Lara. "Is this some strange test of the fortitude of Maridrinian stomachs that I haven't heard about?"

Everyone smirked, then Gorrick roared, "To Ithicana!" They all repeated him, lifting their glasses.

As Aren swallowed the wine, which was very good, he heard Lara murmur, "To Ithicana," and take a small sip from her glass.

Refilling the glasses, Aren stood. "To Taryn, who slaughtered our enemy. And to our queen," he pulled Lara forward, "Who saved our comrades."

"To Taryn!" everyone shouted. "To Her Majesty!"

The wine disappeared within minutes, for despite the flippancy,

190

today had left its mark. It was how they managed—by pretending not to care, but Aren knew that Jor would make time for each of them, helping them come to terms with what they'd witnessed. And with what they had done. He was captain of the guard for a reason.

Lara was hugging her arms around her body, shivering despite the wine. The wind and rain had been colder than Ithicana normally saw, and her clothes were soaked through. He watched her eye the other women, who were stripped down to trousers and undershirts, and then her hand went to her belt.

His heart skipped, then raced as she unbuckled it, setting it aside along with the Maridrinian marriage knives she habitually wore. Then she unfastened the laces of her tunic at her throat and pulled the garment over her head.

The safe house went completely silent for a heartbeat, then filled with the over-loud clatter of weapons being cleaned and mindless chatter, everyone looking anywhere but at their queen.

Aren could not seem to do the same. While the other women wore thick standard-issue fabrics, Lara's undergarments were the finest ivory silk, which was soaked, rendering it effectively transparent. The full curves of her breasts pressed against the fabric, her rose-colored nipples peaked from the cold. *There was*, Aren thought, *nothing the Great Beyond could offer that would be more perfect than her.*

Realizing he was staring, Aren jerked his gaze away. Snatching up a thin blanket folded at the end of the bunk, he handed it to Lara, careful to keep his eyes on her face. "It will warm up in here with all the bodies—I mean, people. Soon. It will be warmer soon."

Her smile was coy as she wrapped the blanket around her shoulders, but her mirth at his discomfort fell away as she caught sight of Jor examining one of her knives.

He had the jeweled thing out of its sheath and was testing the edge. "Sharp." He used it to cut the wax off a wheel of Harendellian cheese. "I thought these were supposed to be ceremonial?"

"I thought it wise to render them somewhat useful," Lara replied, expression intent.

"Barely." Jor balanced the weapon, the gem-crusted hilt making it heavy and cumbersome, though the blade itself looked well made.

"We could sell these for a fortune up north and get you something you might actually be able to use."

Lara was shifting and swaying as though she wanted nothing more than to reach over and snatch the knife back, so Aren did it for her, wiping the cheese off the blade with the side of his trousers before returning it to her.

"Thank you," she murmured. "My father gave them to me. They're the only thing he ever gave to me."

Aren wanted to ask why that mattered. Why she cared at all for anything to do with the greedy, sadistic creature who'd sired her. But he didn't. Not with everyone listening.

Jor picked up the bottle of Maridrinian wine. "Desperate times. Desperate times." Then he popped the cork and poured, something landing with a splash in his tin cup. "Now what do we have here?"

"What is it?" Lia asked.

"It appears a smuggler's prize has lost its way." The old soldier held up something that glittered red in the lamplight, then he tossed it Aren's direction. "There's a buyer at Northwatch who's going to be very dissatisfied with his wine purchase."

Aren held up the large ruby. He was no expert on gemstones, but judging from the size and color, it was worth a small fortune. A very unhappy smuggler, indeed. Shoving it in his pocket, he said, "This should cover the taxes the individual was trying to evade."

Everyone laughed then dug into the supplies, all of them battered and half-starved after a day of fighting and rowing and almost dying, more interested in shoveling food down their throats than in conversation. Lara sat next to Aren on the bunk, balancing on her knees a spread of cured meats, cheeses, and a tin cup of water as she ate.

Her slender hands and fingers had an assortment of old scars, nicks and lines, and one knuckle that was slightly larger, suggesting it had been broken at one point. Not the hands one would expect of Maridrinian princess, but whereas before he'd questioned what sort of life she'd been living in the desert to earn those scars, now he was having very different thoughts about those hands.

Of how it would feel to hold them.

Of how it would feel to be touched by them.

Of how it would feel—

"Lights out!" Jor announced. "The wind tells me this storm will break overnight, and we'll want to be back on the water at dawn."

All eyes shifted to the eight bunks, then to the ten people in the room.

"Either double up or draw straws for the floor."

Gorrick climbed to the top of one of the bunks, then pulled Lia up with him, and Aren winced, hoping they'd keep their hands to themselves for once.

"I'll take the floor," he said. "But I'm damn well going up for a nap in my feather bed once we get home tomorrow."

"We appreciate your hardship, Your Majesty." Jor reached over and turned down the lamp, plunging the safe house into near darkness.

Aren lay on the stone floor, one arm folded under his head for a pillow. It was cold and uncomfortable, and despite his exhaustion, sleep wouldn't come as he listened to the deepening breathing of those around him, a thousand thoughts filling his head.

When something cold brushed against his chest, Aren almost jumped out of his skin before realizing it was Lara. She was leaning out of the bunk next to him, her eyes lambent in the faint glow of the lamp. Wordlessly she caught hold of his hand with hers and tugged him upward, drawing him onto the bunk.

Pulse roaring in his ears, Aren climbed over her, his back resting against the cold wall, unsure of what to do with his arms and his hands or any part of himself until she curled against him, her skin icy.

She's just cold, he told himself, *and you need to keep your hands to yourself.*

Which might well have been the hardest thing he'd ever done, with one of her knees between his, her arms tucked against his chest, her head resting on his shoulder, and her breath warm against his throat. He wanted nothing more than to roll onto her, to taste those lips and peel that taunting bit of silk from her chest, but instead he pulled the blanket over her naked shoulder, then rested his hand against her back.

The room was humid with breath and heavy with the smell of

sweat and steel. Taryn was snoring as though her life depended on it, Gorrick was jabbering in his sleep, and someone—probably Jor—was farting at regular intervals. It was very likely the least desirable situation to share a bed with his *wife* for the first time. But even as her hair tickled his nose, his arm fell asleep under her head, and a crick formed in his neck, it occurred to Aren, as he drifted off, that there was nowhere else he'd rather be.

Hours later, Aren awoke to a rhythmic thumping. Frowning, he turned his head and found Lara's eyes open and gleaming in the faint light. Pulling one hand from under the blanket, she pointed upward and cocked her eyebrow with an amused smirk.

Gorrick and Lia. Likely warming themselves up after their turn at watch.

He winced, whispering, "Sorry. It's a soldier's life." Then he mentally ran through the watch, realizing that Jor had skipped him over and that Taryn was gone, which meant it was almost sunrise.

"Want to go outside?" Relief filled him when Lara nodded.

They pulled on boots and clothes and weapons in near silence, Lara taking food from one of the crates and following him out into the night. The storm had blown over, the sky a riot of silver stars, the only sound the crashing of the waves against the island's cliffs.

Taryn was perched on a rock in the shadows, but he heard her murmured thanks when Lara went over and gave her some of the food.

"Aren, take her to the east side."

"Why?"

Even in the darkness, he felt Taryn smile. "Trust me."

"All right." He took Lara's hand. "We'll be back at sunrise."

Aren hadn't been to this particular island many times, so he went slowly. He managed to find his way to the eastern lookout by memory, a flat bit of rock that hung out over the ocean. A sea of blue starlight stretched before them.

Lara stepped ahead, still holding on to his hand. "I've never seen anything so beautiful."

Neither had he, but Aren forced his eyes from her face to the calm water below. "We call it Sea of Stars. It doesn't happen often, and always during War Tides, so it doesn't get much appreciation."

Glowing strands of algae covered the water, the clusters forming brilliant blue spots of light on the sea, making him feel as though he stood between two planes of starlight. It rippled on the gentle waves, casting shadows on the rocks that seemed to dance to the rhythm of the swells. They stood watching for a long time, neither of them speaking, and it occurred to Aren that he should kiss her, but instead he said, "What changed?"

Because something had. Something had shifted, softening her toward him, perhaps to all of Ithicana, and he wasn't sure what it was. For near as he could tell, most of her experiences since she'd arrived hadn't been particularly good. She was the daughter of a man who was more Aren's enemy than his ally, and he shouldn't trust her. Didn't trust her. But with every passing day he spent with her, he found himself *wanting* to trust her. With everything.

Lara swallowed audibly, pulling her hand from his grip and crossing her legs on the ground, waiting until he sat next to her. The blue light from the sea illuminated her face, making her seem otherworldly and untouchable. "When I was growing up, I was told many times the amount of revenue Ithicana was rumored to make in a year off the bridge."

"How much?" He shook his head at the number when she answered. "It's more."

"Are you bragging?"

"Just being truthful."

The corner of her mouth quirked, and she was quiet for a moment before she continued. "To me, the amount was staggering. And I thought . . . I was told that Ithicana played and manipulated the market, gouged travelers afraid to tempt the seas, and exacted heavy taxes and tolls from merchants who wished to transport and market their own goods. That you decided who had the right to buy and sell in your markets, and that you'd take away that privilege if they crossed you in any way. That you controlled nearly all the trade between two continents and eleven different kingdoms."

"Accurate." He didn't bother to add that Ithicana paid in blood for that right, because she'd seen the evidence herself.

"What wasn't accurate . . . was the reason *why*."

"What did they tell you?"

"Greed." Her eyes were unblinking as she stared over the ocean. "When I was young, I believed you must live in enormous palaces filled with all the greatest luxuries the world had to offer. That you sat on a throne of gold."

"Ah, yes. My throne of gold. I keep it on another island and visit it when I need to reaffirm my sense of self-worth and entitlement."

"Don't mock me."

"I'm not." He picked at the top of his boot where the leather had split from too much exposure to salt water. "It must have been quite disappointing to discover the truth."

Lara made a sound that was a half-laugh, half-sob. "Midwatch is just as luxurious as my home in the Red Desert, and my time spent here relaxing by comparison. I was raised hard, Aren."

"Why were they so hard on you?"

"I thought I knew, but now . . ." She lifted her chin from her knees, turning her head to look at him. "You ask me what changed? What changed is that now I know you use that money to feed and protect your people."

There had been a certain inevitability to her learning that truth. Maybe if he'd kept her locked up in the Midwatch house, with no contact with anyone but the staff and his guard, he might have kept it from her. But he'd wanted his marriage to Lara to be a symbol for change in Ithicana, a new direction. And for that to happen, they'd needed to see her, and there had always been consequences to that path, and the revelation of Ithicana's secrets was one of them.

And he so badly wanted to trust her.

"The truth is, Ithicana isn't survivable without the bridge," he said. "Or rather, it is survivable, but only if every minute of every waking day is dedicated to survival." Pivoting on the ground so they were facing each other, he stared into her eyes. The sun was rising, the light shifting from blue to gold, and it was like waking from a dream and being plunged back into reality. If Aren could have stopped it, he would've. "Imagine a life where you had to fight these storms and these waters to feed your family. To clothe your children. To shelter them. Where weeks might pass when you couldn't take a boat on the water. Where a series of days might pass when it would verge on suicide to step outside your home. What else is there but survival in a world like that?"

Aren hadn't realized he'd taken her hands, but she squeezed them tightly then, and he paused, his thumbs trailing lightly over her scars. "The bridge changes that. It allows me to give my people what they need so that some small part of their days might be dedicated to more than just survival, even if it's only an hour. So that my people might have a chance to read, to learn, to make art. To sing or dance or laugh."

He broke off, realizing that he'd never explained this to anyone. Explained what it was like to rule this place. The constant fight to give his people lives worth living. And it wasn't enough. He wanted them to have *more*.

"You could feed every one of them like kings with that kind of money." Lara wasn't questioning his word, but driving him forward, extracting the whole of the truth.

"That's true. But having those things—having the bridge—comes with a cost. Other kingdoms know what sort of revenue the bridge earns, and that makes them want to possess it. Pirates believe we have stockpiles of gold hidden throughout the islands, so they raid us to find it. So we have to fight. My standing army isn't enormous, but during War Tides, nearly two thirds of my people drop their trades and take up arms to defend the bridge. I have to buy them weapons. I have to pay them for their service. And I have to compensate their families when they die."

"So despite everything, Ithicana is only surviving after all."

He tightened his grip on her hands. "But maybe someday it could be something better."

Neither of them spoke, and when a soft breeze blew strands of hair across her face, Aren reached up to brush them away. Lara didn't flinch from his touch. Didn't look away. "You're beautiful." He tangled his fingers in her hair. "I've thought so since the moment I saw you, but I don't think I've ever said it."

Lara lowered her eyes, pink rising to her cheeks, although it might've just been the glow of the sun. She gave the slightest shake of her head.

"I should have." He lowered his head, intent on kissing her, but instead a sharp noise made him jump.

Hand going to his weapon, Aren turned to see Jor coming around the corner, his face filled with amusement. "I hate to break up your picnic, Your Majesties, but dawn is upon us, and we need to be on our way."

As if to punctuate his words, horns sounded out over the water announcing ships on the horizon. "Does this change things for you?" he asked Lara, helping her to her feet.

She closed her eyes, her face clenching for a moment as though she were in pain, then she opened them and nodded. "It changes everything."

Hope, and something else, something uniquely reserved for her, flooded his heart and, taking Lara by the hand, Aren led her back to the boats at a run.

24
LARA

EVERYTHING HAD CHANGED.

And nothing.

It wasn't lust. Lara wasn't so weak as to abandon a lifetime of planning and preparation for the sake of a man too handsome and charming for his own good. If that had been the sum of it, she'd have sated her curiosity, then carried on with as clear a conscience as any spy could have. No, it was her admiration for Aren that was becoming increasingly problematic, as was her grief over what would happen to Ithicana once she was through with it.

Lara and her sisters had been taught to despise Ithicana for a reason. Their purpose had been to infiltrate the defenses of a nation so that it could, at best, be conquered. At worst, be destroyed. An easy thing to envision when the enemy had been nothing more to her than masked demons using their might to keep her people oppressed.

But now they had faces. And names. And families.

All of whom were annually attacked by kingdoms and pirates alike. Perhaps the Ithicanians were cruel and merciless, but now Lara found she couldn't fault them for that. They did what they needed to *survive*, and with every piece of information she stored away about them, her guilt swelled, because she knew Ithicana wouldn't survive *her*. While that knowledge might have once brought her satisfaction, it was now nothing but an inescapable fact that seemed destined to plague her every waking moment with self-loathing.

Her actions on Aela Island had accomplished what she'd feared impossible: earning Aren's trust. And not just his trust, but that of all the soldiers who'd fought in the battle. Their expressions in her presence had gone from distrustful to respectful, and as one, they'd stopped questioning her right to go where she pleased. A right she'd instantly abused. No one had questioned her when she'd stepped away from the healers and the injured after the battle. No one had stopped her or followed her when she'd walked to the base of the bridge pier, where she'd found the nearly invisible entrance, which she marked with a few carefully placed stones that would mean nothing to the Ithicanians and everything to the Maridrinian soldiers when they took Aela Island.

Inside the pier she'd also hidden three of the horns she stolen off corpses on the beach, ready to misdirect Ithicanian reinforcements when the time was right. A strategy that Aren had practically explained to her in his attempts to coax her away from the injured and into a boat. Which he'd only done because he believed she was coming to love them the way he did.

Do not falter, she silently chanted, eyes fixed on the sky as she floated her still aching body in the hot spring. *Do not fail.*

Biting at a hangnail on her thumb, Lara considered what she'd learned. Considered whether it was *enough* for Maridrina to take Ithicana. Enough to conquer the unconquerable, and enough to give Maridrina the bridge that would be its salvation.

It was enough.

All that was left was to get the details of her invasion plan to Serin and her father, then for her to fake her death and escape Midwatch and Ithicana and, hopefully, her father's inevitable assassins. Where she'd go, she didn't know. To Harendell, perhaps. Maybe once the dust had settled, she'd try to find her sisters. Make a life for herself. Though try as she might, she couldn't envision what a life beyond Ithicana might look like. A life without *him*.

Lara's eyes stung, and in a flurry of motion, she climbed out o the spring, reaching for the towel sitting on the rock. Over a week had passed since the attack on Aela, and yet she hadn't taken one step further to putting her plan into motion. She'd told herself it was because the muscle she'd torn in her shoulder during the battle needed time to heal before she would be strong enough to make her escape. But her heart told her that she was delaying for other reasons. Reasons that put her whole mission in jeopardy.

But tonight was the night.

Aren had sent word from the barracks via Eli that there was going to be a storm this evening, and that he planned to dine with her. And if he was with her, that meant Taryn, who still insisted on sleeping outside her door, would take a break from her bodyguard duties. A double dose of a sleeping narcotic in Aren's wine after dinner, and then she'd have the whole night in his bedchamber to work with no fear of interruptions.

Already clouds were rolling in, the wind blowing, for even in the calm season, the Tempest Seas were not without teeth. Lara worked methodically on her appearance, drying her hair, then using a hot iron to create coils that hung down her back. She darkened her eyes with kohl and powders until they smoldered, and stained her lips a pale pink. She chose a dress she hadn't worn before: dark purple, the silk scandalously sheer, her body revealed beneath whenever she passed in front of a light. On her ears, she wore black diamonds, and on her wrist, the clever bracelet that concealed the vials of narcotics.

Stepping out into the hallway, she made her way down to the dining room, her sandals feeling strange after so many weeks of wearing heavy boots. The room was lit with candles, the shutters on the large windows open despite the risk the wind posed to the expensive glass. And a soaking wet Eli stood in close conversation with Taryn, whom Lara was surprised to find still in the house. They both turned to look at her, expressions grim, and Lara's heart skipped. "Where is he?"

"They went on patrol late morning." Taryn scrubbed a hand along the shaved sides of her head. "No one has seen or heard from them since."

rmal?" Lara couldn't control the shake in her voice.

woman exhaled a long breath. "It's not abnormal for
here's somewhere he needs to be other than Midwatch."
eyes gave Lara a once-over. "But I don't think that's the case tonight."

"So where is he?"

"Could've been trouble with one of the boats. Or maybe they decided to wait out the storm. Or—"

Horns sounded, and Lara no longer needed Taryn to tell her what they meant: *raiders*.

"I'm going down to the barracks." Running to her rooms, Lara replaced her sandals with boots and pulled a cloak over her dress.

Outside, the rain was falling steadily, but the wind wasn't high enough to cause the Ithicanians any trouble on the water. Taryn at her arm, and the rest of her bodyguard before and behind her, Lara hurried down the dark path toward the barracks.

Where the tension was higher than she'd ever seen it.

"I'll find out what they know." Taryn left Lara with the other two guards, who followed her as she skirted the cove, climbing the carved stone steps to the cliff tops, where she could see the sea. Several soldiers knelt behind the boulders they used for cover, spyglasses in hand.

"Anything?" But they only shook their heads.

What if he didn't come back?

It would throw her plan to shit. Without Aren to write a letter to her father, she had no way to get a detailed message past Ahnna and her codebreakers at Southwatch. Her only option would be to fake her death and escape, then send the information to her father from outside of Ithicana. But then he and Serin would know she was alive, and that meant a lifetime of assassins chasing at her heels. Yet, as she crouched on the ground to watch the blackness of the ocean, it wasn't solutions to her dilemma that filled her thoughts.

It was fear.

She'd seen so many Ithicanians die in combat, in so many different ways. Run through or gutted. Crushed or strangled. Beaten or drowned. Their corpses danced through her thoughts, all of them now wearing Aren's face.

"They haven't sent any word." Taryn appeared at Lara's elbow. "But that doesn't necessarily mean anything other than that they don't want to announce their presence to the enemy."

Or they were all dead, Lara thought, her chest tightening painfully.

Taryn handed her a folded packet of papers. "This came for you."

Holding the paper next to one of the jars of algae, Lara scanned the contents. Serin, pretending to be her father, discussed his disappointment in her second-eldest brother, Keris, who was demanding to attend university in Harendell rather than take command of Maridrinian forces like her eldest brother. *He wishes to study philosophy! As though there is time to sit around contemplating the meaning of life when our enemies continue to bite at our flanks!*

Some of the soldiers stirred, pulling her attention from the letter, and it was some moments before she could refocus. Marylyn's code felt elusive. Lara's eyes continually dragged out to sea. But eventually her mind pulled Serin's message from the drivel. *Valcotta has blockaded our access to Southwatch. Famine on the rise.*

A wave of nausea passed over Lara, and she shoved the pages into her cloak's pocket. With its shipbreakers, Southwatch was capable of running Valcotta off, but she could understand their reluctance to antagonize the other nation. Understood what it would cost them for Valcotta to join the ranks of kingdoms raiding Ithicana. But it was her people who paid the price.

They sat in the rain for hours, but no horns sounded. No boats appeared below requesting access to the cove. Nothing even moved in the darkness.

Eventually Taryn shifted next to her. "You should go back to the house, Lara. There's no telling when they'll return, and you'll catch a chill sitting in this cold rain."

She should go. She knew she should go. But the idea of having to wait for one of them to bring her news . . . "I can't." Her tongue felt thick.

"The barracks, then?" There was a plea to the other woman's voice.

Reluctantly, Lara nodded, but every few paces up the trail, she cast a backward glance toward the sea, the roar of it beckoning, drawing her back.

"This is Aren's bunk," Taryn said, once they were in the confines of the stone building. "He won't mind if you sleep here."

Shutting the door to the tiny room, Lara set her lamp on the rough wooden table next to the narrow bed, then sat, the mattress rock hard and the blanket rough compared to her soft sheets at the house. It reminded her of the cot she'd shared with him at the safe house. How she'd fallen asleep in his arms, listening to the beat of his heart.

She pulled off her cloak and curled on her side, her head resting on the pillow.

It smelled like him.

Squeezing her eyes shut, Lara drew upon every lesson her Master of Meditation had ever taught her, measuring her breath and clearing her mind, but sleep wouldn't come, so she sat, the blanket wrapped around her legs.

There was nothing in the room to distract her. No books or puzzles. Not even a deck of cards. The sparse quarters of a soldier, not a king. Or at least, not of the sort of king she'd believed existed. The quarters of a leader who did not hold himself above his people. Who wore their hardships like his own. Because they were his own.

Please be alive.

The door swung open, and Lara jerked around to find Taryn standing in the doorway. "They're back."

She followed the other woman at a run down to the cove, her chest tight with fear. It was fear for herself, her mind screamed. Fear for her mission. Fear for the fate of her people.

But her heart told her otherwise.

The sand of the beach shifted beneath her feet, and Lara squinted into the darkness. A faint voice called out, then the chain rattled, clearing the entrance to the cove.

More splashing, waves thudding against hulls and paddles carving through the water. But above all of that, Lara picked out groans of pain. Her heart skipped.

Please let him be alive.

The cove turned into a flurry of activity, boats full of bloodied men and women drifting in, those on shore tying them off and helping the injured onto land. Her eyes skipped over their shadowed faces, searching. Searching.

"Will you goddamned hurry it up?" Jor's voice. Lara wove through the efficient traffic, trying to find the soldier. Finally, she spotted both him and Lia crouched in the bottom of a boat, a slumped figure between them.

"Aren?" Her voice came out as a croak, her feet abruptly rooted on the spot.

The pair reached down, and relief flooded her veins as Aren batted their hands away. "Get off me. I can damn well get out myself."

He stood and the boat wobbled, both Jor and Lia easily catching their balance, but Aren nearly going over the side.

"Enough of your pride, boy," Jor barked, and between him and Lia, they dragged their king onto land.

Lara couldn't see what was wrong with him in the dark, the lanterns casting shadows that appeared like bloodstains, only they shifted and moved. Then Aren turned, and the lantern behind him revealed the outline of an arrow embedded in his upper arm.

"Get out of my way." She shoved two soldiers to the side and ran toward Aren.

"What the hell are you doing down here?" Aren pushed Jor away even as he stumbled. Lara lurched forward and caught his weight, the hot tang of blood filling her nose. "I can walk on my own," he muttered.

"Clearly." Lara's body quivered with the effort of holding him upright as they navigated the sloped beach to the treeline, the path leading to the barracks dimly lit with jars of algae.

Dragging Aren into the barracks, she eased him down on a bench. Throwing aside her sodden cloak, she pulled one of her knives and cut away his tunic, dropping the ruined garment on the floor. Then she knelt next to him, her eyes taking in the injury.

The arrowhead was buried deep in the muscle of his upper arm, the shaft having been broken in half by someone at some point, the wood stained dark with blood.

"Goddamned Amaridians." Jor's voice seemed distant to Lara, every part of her focused on Aren's breath against her neck, hot and ragged.

Lifting her face, she met his pain-hazed gaze. "We can't pull it out—we have to push it all the way through."

"Every moment with you is such a delight." A faint spark returned to Aren's eyes. "Sorry I missed dinner."

"You should be." She struggled to keep her voice even. "It smelled very good."

"Missing the food isn't the part I'm sorry about." He lifted his uninjured arm, fingers brushing against the large diamond still adorning her ear, sending a tremble racing through her.

"Brace yourself on me." She pushed his hand away before her composure was totally shot. "The last thing we need is you squirming and making the injury worse."

Aren huffed out a pained laugh, but took hold of her waist with the hand of his uninjured arm, his fingers digging into the muscles of her back.

"This will hurt," Jor warned, taking a firm grip on the arrow. Swearing, Aren dropped his head against Lara's shoulder and she pulled him against her, knowing she wasn't strong enough to keep him steady if he struggled.

"Relax," Jor said. "You're being a baby."

Lara murmured into Aren's ear, "Breathe." His shoulders trembled as he inhaled and exhaled, and she knew his attention was on her. His fingers flexed, then slid from her waist to her hip. "Breathe," she repeated, her lips grazing the lobe of his ear. "Breathe." As she said the word the third time, she met Jor's gaze.

He pushed.

Aren screamed into her shoulder, shoving against her so hard that Lara almost went over backward, her boots skidding against the barracks floor. Blood splattered her face, but she held on, refusing to let go of him.

"Got it!" Jor said, and a second later, Lara's knees buckled and she fell back, Aren landing on top of her. For a heartbeat, neither of them moved, Aren's breathing labored in her ear, his body pressed against hers. She held him, clung to him, an irrational desire to hunt down and destroy those who'd done this consuming all other thought. Then Jor and Lia were hauling him off her.

Scrambling upright, Lara wiped the blood off her face, her heart hammering as Jor examined the injury. "You'll mend," he said, then moved aside as one of Nana's students arrived.

All around were bloodied soldiers. Some gritted their teeth against the pain. Some screamed as their comrades tried to staunch horrific wounds. Some lay motionless.

Every one of them injured in defense of their home.

Lara's eyes fell on Taryn, tears dribbling down the woman's face as she pressed her hands against a young man's stomach, trying to hold his guts inside. "Don't you die on me." Her whispered voice somehow cut through the din. "Don't you dare die."

But as Lara watched, the young man's chest went still.

How many more hearts would still when her father made his move?

They are your enemy, she chanted. *Your enemy. Your enemy.* But the words were profoundly hollow in her mind.

Lara took one step back. Then two. Three. Until she was out of the barracks and on the empty path.

"Lara!"

She turned. Aren stood a dozen paces behind her on the path, the bandage on his arm half falling off as though he'd pushed away the healer working on him before she could finish.

"Wait."

She couldn't. She shouldn't. Not when every bit of resolve she possessed was crumbling to the ground. Yet her feet remained fixed to the earth as Aren slowly made his way toward her, blood running down his arm and dripping from his fingertips.

"I'm sorry." His voice was shaky. "I'm sorry that all you've seen since you've been here is violence."

All she had ever known was violence. It was nothing to her. And everything.

"I wish it was different. I wish it wasn't like this."

He swayed, dropping to his knees, and Lara didn't realize she'd also knelt until the mud soaked through her dress. Didn't realize she'd reached out to steady him until the hand of his uninjured arm caught hold of her hip for balance. A dance where she led and he followed.

"Eyes just like your damnable father. That's what I thought when I first saw you. We call it Maridrinian bastard blue."

He must have felt her flinch, because his grip on her hip tightened, drawing her closer. She didn't fight him.

"But I was wrong. They're different. They're . . . deeper. Like the color of the sea around Eranahl."

Eranahl? She'd seen that name before, written on one of the pages in his desk . . . Heard it when he'd berated Commander Aster on the beach at Aela Island. Revealing it was a slip on his part, she was sure of it. But she couldn't bring herself to care as his hand slid to the small of her back. It took all the willpower she had to keep from slipping her arms around his neck, to keep from kissing those blasted perfect lips of his, never mind the blood and gore.

Lara withdrew her hand from his shoulder, but he caught it with his own. Folding her fingers into a fist, he kissed her knuckles, eyes burning into hers. "Don't go."

Everything was burning.

Lara's heart beat frantically, her breathing unsteady, her skin so sensitive that the press of her clothes almost hurt.

Stop! The warning shrieked inside her head. *You're losing control.* She tuned the voice out, shoved it away.

Aren's thumb brushed the inside of her wrist, her knuckles still pressed to his lips, and it sent rivers of sensation running over her skin, the desire to have his hands elsewhere making her legs weak. She swayed and he pulled her against him, both of them unsteady.

"You need to go back to the healers," she whispered. "You need to let them stitch that up before you bleed to death."

"I'll be fine." He lowered his head even as she lifted hers, sharing the same air, the same breath, the rapid rise and fall of his chest belying his words. *He was not fine.*

The thought of it filled her with terror. Terror that turned instantly to rage. Why did she care what happened to him beyond the success of her mission? Why did she care whether he lived or died? This was the man who willfully made decisions that caused great harm to the people of her homeland. Perhaps he did so for the sake of his own people, but that did not excuse the complete lack of empathy and guilt he felt in the doing. *He was her enemy, and she needed to get free of him before she made a mistake.*

Then his lips brushed softly against hers, and it undid her entirely. Her fingers tangled in his hair, and she wanted more. More of this and more of him. But instead of giving it to her, he pulled back. "I need you to help me make this stop. I'm tired of fighting against the world, when what I want is to fight to make Ithicana part of it."

And it was as though reality slapped her across the face.

Lara pulled away from him. "It's never going to stop, Aren." Her voice was barren. Dead. Which was strange, because inside her head was a chaos of emotion. "You have what *everyone* wants, and they're never going to stop trying to take it. This *is* Ithicana, and it's all it will ever be. Live with it."

"This isn't living, Lara." He coughed, then winced, pressing his hand against the wound. "And I intend to keep fighting for a better future even if it kills me."

Irrational fury surged through her veins at his words. "Then you might as well lay down and die!" She needed to be away from this situation because it was tearing her apart. Rising in a flurry of motion, Lara turned and ran, up the dark path, slipping on the mud and roots, to the house.

She waited in her rooms until the halls were silent, until there was no chance of anyone disturbing her, then crept through the dark hallways and picked the lock to Aren's room. Vitex sat on the bed, but he only slunk outside, ignoring her as she passed.

Closing the door behind her, Lara brightened her lamp and went to Aren's desk. She extracted the jar of invisible ink Serin had given her, then drew the stationery box of heavy official parchment next to her left hand, flipping open the lid. Taking the top page, she turned it over so the embossed shape of the bridge was facedown, then she dipped a pen into the ink and began to write in tiny script, the liquid drying invisible as she detailed everything she'd learned about Ithicana and a strategy for taking, and breaking, the Bridge Kingdom. Her hand shook as she reached the bottom, but she only set aside the paper to dry and retrieved another, repeating her message. Then another, and another, until all twenty-six pages in the box contained identical damning words.

It took all her strength not to tear them to pieces as she set everything back and retreated to her own room. Exhaustion weighing her limbs, she buried her face in the pillows of her bed, tears soaking the feathers within. *It's the only way,* she told herself. *It's the only way to save Maridrina.*

Even if it meant damning herself.

W AR TIDES ENDED with a typhoon that came in fast and violent, the seas so rough that not even the Ithicanians would venture out on them. Even the bridge was likely empty, Eli told her, the storm too intense for merchant ships to brave the short crossing to Northwatch and Southwatch islands. Midwatch felt profoundly isolated as a result, cut off entirely from the world, and made worse by the fact that Lara was stuck in the house alone with the servants.

Though the fighting was over, Aren was avoiding her. He spent all his days with his soldiers and his nights on the narrow cot in the barracks, not once coming up the path to the Midwatch house.

Even so, she checked the number of pages of stationery in his room nightly, but every last page of the condemning words remained in Ithicana.

As did she.

On the morning after the storm broke, Lara decided it was time. Dressing in her Ithicanian clothes, she filled her pockets with jewels and some of her more favored narcotics, ate as much as she could stuff in her stomach, then told Eli she was going to go outside for some fresh air.

Attempting the seas during a storm would see her dead in truth, so she'd waited for clear skies before enacting her plan to fake her death, knowing that honor would drive Aren to send a formal letter informing Lara's father of her demise. That Serin, ever watchful, would check the page and discover what she'd written. Then she could only hope and pray that, when she hadn't shown up after a time in Vencia, her father and Serin would believe she was dead in truth. Then no assassins would come searching for her in Harendell, which was where she planned to go. She could live her life knowing that she'd given her people a chance for a better future.

At the cost of the futures of everyone living in Ithicana.

With the storms to watch over the island, Taryn and the rest had been given respite from guard duty, and there was no one to evade as she followed a trail to the cliffs overlooking the sea, cutting down the northern side until she came to the spot she'd selected long ago.

It was a high spot, the water forty feet below, but what had drawn her to it was the series of flat rocks jutting out of surf. They were suitable for her to lower her little canoe onto with ropes, and equally suitable for staging what would appear an accidental fall and a tragic death. From there, she intended to hop from island to island, using safe houses as she found them, slowly making her way to Harendell during the breaks in the storm.

It was a plan fraught with peril, yet it wasn't fear that sat heavy in her gut as she stared down at the rocks.

"Don't fall."

Startled, Lara lost her balance, and Aren reached out and caught hold of her arm, hauling her away from the edge.

He made a noise of exasperation, then kept pulling on her arm. "Come with me. You have duties to attend to."

"What duties?"

"A queen's duties."

She dug in her heels, leaving twin trails in the mud until he stopped and gave her a look of disgust. "*That's* not a duty, Lara. Supervising the return of the Midwatch evacuees is. So either start walking, or I'm

THE BRIDGE KINGDOM

going to drag you down to the water and toss you in a boat."

"I'll walk." She was furious that her plan was being disrupted, but also furious at the small kernel of relief that she felt knowing she'd likely have to wait for another storm to pass before leaving Ithicana.

Ensconced in her usual spot in the boat, she waited until they were out of the cove before asking, "Where are we going?"

"Serrith." Aren hunched over, his back to her.

"Just a charming day on the water," Jor said from behind her as he put up the sail. After that, no one said anything more.

The cove at Serrith Island was dominated by two of the large twin-hulled vessels she'd seen during the evacuation, but they were already empty of civilians and supplies, their crews readying to depart. *To depart to Eranahl*, she mused, watching them. Though where exactly that was remained a mystery to her despite all her weeks of spying.

Her skin prickled as she followed Aren up the path through the gap in the rock where she'd killed all those soldiers. They continued on until they reached the village. It was an entirely different sight than the last time they'd been here. Instead of blood and bodies, dead-eyed children and weeping parents, it was bustling with industry. Women opened up the shuttered windows and doors to their homes to air them out, and children ran wild between them.

There was a flood of greetings and well wishes, proud introductions of new babies to their rulers, and children trailing in their wake, desperate for a moment of attention. Aren's tactic was obvious. Trying to pull on her heartstrings by pushing chubby babies into her arms or by giving her sweets to hand out to the children.

And it was effective. She wanted to drop to the ground and weep, because their world was going to be torn asunder. But it was between them and the Maridrinians. Maridrina's starving people *needed* the bridge, needed the revenues, needed the goods that came through it. So she would sacrifice these people for her own and then pray that guilt and grief didn't kill her.

Lara would have given anything to have her sisters here to share the burden, because they would understand. They were the *only* people who would understand. But she was alone, and every minute that passed felt like she was closer to the breaking point of what she could endure.

Only when they returned to the boats did she feel like she could breathe again, sitting with her face in her hands as they sailed back to Midwatch.

"Looks like the guardians have had some visitors," Jor said, breaking the silence.

Lara lifted her head, eyes landing on a small island with gentle white beaches that faded into rock and greenery. Looming above it was the bridge, its length resting on a pier centered on the island. It wasn't that the island itself was unique, only that it appeared remarkably easy to access relative to the others the builders had used as piers.

Because they'd had no choice, she determined, eyeing the distance. The largest bridge span she'd seen was a hundred yards between piers, and to bypass this island would've required a longer stretch than was possible. Her eyes then landed on the three human-shaped forms lying halfway up the beach, bloated and rotting in the sun. "What is this place?"

"Snake Island."

She thought of the countless serpents she'd seen since arriving. "A name that describes most of Ithicana."

"This one in particular." Aren motioned for Jor to lower the sails, allowing the boat to drift over the shallow bottom toward the beach. "Look."

She stared, seeing shifting movement beneath the ledge of rock overhanging the beach, but unable to make out details.

Aren stood up in the boat next to her, a still moving fish that had been caught earlier in one hand, waiting as the waves washed them gently to shore. When they were about a dozen feet out, Jor stuck a paddle in the water, bracing the boat from moving farther. Aren threw the fish.

It landed about midway up the beach, and Lara watched in horror as dozens upon dozens of snakes shot out of the overhang, flying toward the fish with their jaws open. They were big, the average of them longer than Aren was tall, and some much larger than that.

The front-runner snapped its jaws around the fish as the others piled on top of one another, struggling and snapping until the fish disappeared down a gullet, the snake's neck distended to contain its prize.

"Good God." Lara pressed her hand against her mouth.

"One of them gets its teeth into you, you'll find yourself paralyzed within minutes. Then it's a matter of time before one of the big ones comes along to finish the job."

"Big ones . . ." The island became impossibly more forbidding as Lara searched for signs of said snakes. She caught sight of a stone path leading up to the base of the pier. It was overgrown, but compared to all the other piers, it seemed almost welcoming. "Please don't tell me you use this as a route into the bridge?"

Aren shook his head. "Red herring. Does its job well, it's so inviting."

"Too inviting," Jor added. "How many of ours have those blasted serpents fed upon?"

Lara looked askance at Aren.

"It's a game our young people play, though it's forbidden. Two people bait the snakes away from the path, and the runner must make it to the pier, climb up and out onto the bridge, then drop back into the water. A test of bravery."

"More like a proof of idiocy," Jor snapped.

"Certainly a good way to get oneself killed." Lara chewed the inside of her cheeks, debating the usefulness of this particular place. It would be easy to anchor ships and ferry men in, if something could be done about the snakes.

Lara was so caught up in her thoughts she didn't notice Aren had stripped down to his trousers until he hopped over the edge of the boat, standing in the hip-deep water. "Hold this for me." He handed her his bow. "Don't let it get wet."

"What do you think you're doing?"

He cracked his knuckles. "It's been a long time, but I'm sure I can still do it."

"Get back into the boat, Aren," Jor said. "You're not a fourteen-year-old boy anymore."

"No, I'm not. Which should only be to my advantage. Lia and

Taryn, you bait. Do a good job of it unless you want to spend your days watching Ahnna's ass."

"You'll do no such thing," Jor ordered the two women. "Stay put."

Aren twisted round in the water, resting his hands on the boat. "Do I need to remind you who is king here, Jor?"

Lara felt her jaw drop. Never in her time in Ithicana had she seen him pull rank. Give orders, yes, but this was different.

The two men glared at each other, but Jor threw up his free hand in defeat. "Do as *His Majesty* orders."

With grim faces, the two women retrieved a pair of fish each, then jumped into the water. *They've done this before*, Lara thought. *They've done this before for him.*

Lara's heart was pounding in a staccato beat. "Get in the boat. Your arm isn't healed."

"It's healed well enough."

"This is madness, Aren! What are you trying to prove?"

Aren didn't answer, wading until he stood only a few feet back from the water line, then standing utterly still while the two soldiers splashed noisily in opposite directions, drawing the attention of the snakes. The ground beneath the ledge was a twisting mass of bodies, the creatures moving away from the path, watching the women.

This is because of what you said, a voice in her head whispered. *You told him to lay down and die.*

"Aren, get back in the boat." Her voice was unrecognizably shrill. "You don't need to do this."

He ignored her.

Tell him you care. Tell him his life matters to you. Say what you need to say to get him back in the boat.

Except she couldn't. Couldn't tell him a lie like that only to stab him in the back.

But is it a lie?

"Aren, I . . ." Lara's throat strangled the rest of the words.

Jor nodded at the guards in the boat, and those carrying bows silently knocked arrows, but somehow, Aren sensed what they were doing. "If any of you shoots one of those arrows, you're done in my guard."

They lowered their bows. "You can't be serious," Lara snarled. "Aren, get back in the boat, you—"

"Go!"

At his command, the women threw flopping fish onto the beach. Once again, snakes shot out from the under the ledge, dozens upon dozens. More than Lara could count. And just as the frontrunners were about to snap up their prize, Aren broke into a sprint, feet sinking into the deep sand. He only made it halfway up the beach when the snakes saw him, several of them rearing up high to regard the intruder before launching themselves his direction.

He was fast.

But the snakes were faster.

"They're coming!" Lara screamed, watching in horror as the wicked creatures flew across the sand. Aren was on the path, racing toward the towering pier, sweat gleaming on his bare shoulders. He had thirty yards to go.

He wasn't going to make it.

The snakes were throwing themselves through the air, their jaws snapping only paces behind him. And they were closing in.

"Run!"

Lara stood, not even noticing how the boat rocked beneath her. He could not die. Not like this.

Jor was on his feet, too. "Run, you little shit!"

Only a dozen yards. *Please*, she prayed. *Please, please*.

She and Jor saw it before Aren did. An enormous beast of a snake rounding the base of the pier, drawn by the commotion of its smaller brethren. It saw Aren the same time he saw it, the snake rearing even as the king skidded, caught between death on both sides.

Without thinking, Lara lifted Aren's bow and tore an arrow out of the hand of the nearest guard. Nocking the arrow even as she whirled, she let it fly. The black fletching shot through the air, barely missing Aren's shoulder, catching the man-eater square in its open mouth.

Aren reacted instantly, leaping over the fallen snake and jumping to catch handholds in the worn rock, jerking his heels out of reach of the lunging snakes just in time. He climbed to the midway point in a matter of seconds, then turned his head to look at the boat, likely to see who'd disobeyed his orders.

Lara let the bow slip from her fingers, but it didn't matter. He'd seen. They'd all seen. And now she'd have to deal with the consequences.

No one spoke as he climbed, and Lara's heart didn't slow for a moment of it, knowing full well that a fall from that height would kill him. The wound on his arm had broken open, and blood was dripping off him as he climbed, but if it bothered him, he didn't show it. Reaching the top of the bridge, Aren loped down the span until he was back over deep water, then without hesitation, dove into its depths.

Lara held her breath, searching the sea for any sign of him. But there was nothing.

His shoulder was bleeding.

What if there were sharks nearby?

Jor was moving behind her, kicking off his boots, the boat drifting. "Lia, Taryn! Get over here."

Then Aren broke the surface, hauling himself into the boat in one smooth motion. Water glistened on his tanned skin, muscles rippling as he caught his balance, his soldiers half falling out to clear a path as he stepped toward her. "What the hell was that?"

Lara stood her ground, not caring that he loomed over her. "Me saving your childish ass, that's what it was."

"I didn't need saving."

Jor's subsequent cough sounded a great deal like "bullshit." Aren glared at Jor once, before turning back to Lara. "You never said you could use a bow. Would've been a useful thing for you to mention in recent months."

"You never asked." Rising on her toes, she glared at him until he took a step back, the boat rocking as it drifted closer to shore. "And if you *ever* scare me like that again, don't think I won't hesitate to use one on you."

"And here I thought you didn't care."

"I don't! You can walk back onto that beach and bed down with one of those snakes for all the difference it makes to me."

"Is that so?" And quick as the serpents on the island, he picked her up and tossed her into the water.

Lara landed on her ass on the sandbar, the water only up to her waist, but her clothing soaked. "Asshole!" She clambered to her feet, the waves lapping at her knees.

"Says the woman who's been nothing but a thorn in my—" He cut off with a yelp as Jor leaned back in the boat and kicked him solidly in the ass.

Aren landed on his hands and knees with a splash, nearly knocking Lara over. Regaining his footing faster than she had, Aren shouted, "Goddammit, Jor. What the hell was that for?"

But the boat was already sailing away. "We'll be back," Jor shouted, "Once you two work out this little marital spat." Then the vessel rounded the pier and they were out of sight.

Unleashing a string of blistering curses, Aren smacked his hand against the surface of the water. Lara hardly noticed. Instead she watched the snakes making their way down the sand, stopping at the waterline. Several of them reared, swaying back and forth as they watched the two of them. And behind her . . . open ocean. Even if she could swim, Lara damn well knew what lurked within those waters.

She was trapped.

The sun beat down on her head, and her brow prickled as beads of sweat formed, mixing with the seawater drenching her hair.

Her growing panic must have been written all over her face, because Aren said, "The snakes won't come out here. They can swim, but they don't like to. Jor will come back. He's just being an asshole. There's nothing to be afraid of."

"Easy for you to say." Lara's teeth clattered together as though she were cold, but she wasn't. "You can swim away if you want to."

"It's tempting."

"I'm not surprised. Given how little worth you place on Maridrinian lives." The words had crept out, but perhaps it was time they did. Perhaps it was time that she called him out for Ithicana's villainy.

Aren stared at her, jaw open. "Perhaps you might explain to me just what *I* have done to elicit a comment like that from you? I've done nothing but treat you with courtesy, and the same goes for your countrymen."

"Nothing?" Lara knew she was allowing her temper to get the better of her, but anger tasted better than fear. "You think allowing my people to starve because it's good for your coffers is *nothing*?"

Silence.

"You think Ithicana is responsible for Maridrina's troubles?" His voice was incredulous. "We're goddamned allies."

"Ah, yes. *Allies*. Which is why *everyone* knows the majority of the food sold at Southwatch goes to Valcotta."

"Because they buy it!" He threw up his hands. "Southwatch is a free market. Whoever offers the most for the goods gets them. No bias. No favoritism. That's how it works. Ithicana is neutral."

"How easily you wash your hands of all culpability." She was growing furious that he'd spent the day trying to elicit her sympathy for his people, then turned a blind eye on hers. "And how can you claim an alliance in one breath and neutrality in the next?"

Aren swore, shaking his head. "I can't. I can't anymore." He pressed a thumb into his temple. "Why do you think Amarid has been breathing down our necks? It's because they're angry about the concessions we gave Maridrina, and which we will give Harendell if Ahnna ever decides to go marry their prince."

"And what impact have your so-called concessions made? Maridrina is starving, caught between Ithicana and the Red Desert, and I've yet to see you show the slightest bit of empathy."

"You have no idea what you're talking about."

"No? I *heard you* the day I was brought here. Heard you say that concessions you gave to my father were not what you wanted, and that Maridrina would starve before it ever saw the benefit of this treaty!"

He stared at her, face tight with fury. "You're right. I did say that. But if you and the rest of your people want to cast blame for Maridrina's famine, it's best you look to your father."

Lara opened her mouth to retort, but nothing came out.

"Have you read the treaty?" he asked.

"Of course I have. If Maridrina kept the peace with Ithicana for fifteen years, you'd marry a princess of the realm and offer significant concessions to tariffs and tolls on the bridge for as long as the peace between our kingdoms held."

"That's the sum of it. And when it came time to negotiate those concessions, I offered to eliminate all costs associated with a singular imported good, believing that I could force your father toward a choice that would culture peace. Cattle. Wheat. Corn. But you know what he demanded? Harendellian steel."

Her chest tightened. "You're lying. Everything my father has done is for the good of our people."

Aren laughed but there was no humor in it. "Everything your father does is for the good of *his* coffers. And for his pride." He shook his head. "Our taxes on steel and weapons have always been prohibitively exorbitant because the trafficking of weapons has political ramifications we'd prefer to avoid. Never mind that those weapons were often used, in turn, against us."

She couldn't breathe.

"Maridrina has no ore mines, which means the steel for its weapons must be sourced elsewhere. And because your father won't give up his endless war with Valcotta, he has been forced to import his weapons by ship at great cost. Until now."

The sun was too bright, everything a blur.

"I'll continue, since it seems your education in the desert had some gaps." Aren's hazel eyes glinted with anger. They were the only thing she could seem to focus on. "War costs money, believe me, I know. But your father doesn't have the bridge, so he pays for it with heavy taxes that have crippled Maridrina's economy. So even when its merchants dock at Southwatch's *open market*, they are unable to bid competitively. And so they set sail with what no one else will buy."

Diseased meat. Rotten grain. Lara closed her eyes. If he was telling the truth, it meant that everything that had been fueling her desire to capture the bridge had been false. And all that would remain to justify the fall of Ithicana was the very thing she'd railed against her entire life: greed.

"I'm not the one who has been lying to you. Not that I expect you to believe me."

Jor and the others chose that moment to circle back around, and the expression on Aren's face was enough to wipe the amusement off the older man's. The boat drew closer, and Aren grabbed the edge, hauling himself in. Once Lara did the same, Aren ordered, "Put up the other sail."

Jor winced. "That eager to get home?"

"We aren't going home."

"Oh? Where to?"

Aren cast a glance at the darkening skies in the east, then turned back around. But it wasn't Jor his eyes went to.

Lara's stomach flipped as Aren stared her down. Challenged her. "We're going to pay a visit to Maridrina."

THAT HE WAS willing to risk stepping into enemy territory, that he was willing to bring her—who knew so many of Ithicana's secrets—into that territory, should've convinced Lara that Aren's words were true. That her father, Serin, and all her masters at the compound were liars.

But it didn't.

Stories of Ithicana's villainy had been burned into Lara's soul. Whispered in her ears all of her life. Chanted like a mantra through hours, days, *years* of grueling training that had nearly broken her. That had broken many of her half-sisters, sending them, one way or another, to their deaths.

Take the bridge and you will be the savior of Maridrina.

To believe Aren would mean changing that chant to something very different. *Take the bridge and you will be the destroyer of a nation. Take the bridge and you will prove yourself your father's pawn.* For that reason, she, like a coward, immediately argued against going.

"We are in the middle of storm season." Lara pointed at the darkness in the east. "What sort of madman takes to the seas to prove a point?"

"This sort of madman." Aren pulled the line Lia passed him tight. "Besides, the skies are clear in the direction we're going. And if the storm does catch us, we are rumored to be *very* adept sailors."

"We are in a canoe!" Lara despised the shrillness in her voice. "I fail to see how your *skill* will come into play in the middle of a typhoon!"

Aren laughed, sitting down on one of the benches. "We're hardly going to sail into the capital of Maridrina in an Ithicanian vessel."

"How then?" she demanded. "The bridge?"

Jor snorted and gave Aren a meaningful look. "Better to bypass Southwatch, isn't it, Your Majesty?"

Aren ignored him, putting his heels up and leaning back against a pack. "You'll see soon enough."

Soon enough she was clinging to the edge of the vessel as it skipped across the waves, heeled over so far she was certain a strong gust of wind would capsize them, drowning them in the open sea.

Lara reminded herself to pay attention to where they were going. *This is how they infiltrate your homeland, how they spy.* Yet as the bridge and its mist faded into the distance and more islands rose up ahead, all she cared to learn was the depths of Serin and her father's deception.

The Ithicanians dropped one of the sails, the boat easing from its terrifying angle to settle on the sea, and Lara took stock of where Aren had taken her. Columns of rock crusted with green rose out of blue seas so clear that the bottom seemed only an arm's reach away. Birds filled the air in enormous flocks, some diving into the water only to emerge with a fish clutched in their beaks, which they gulped down before one of their fellows could steal it away. Some of the larger islands had white beaches that beckoned invitingly, and nowhere, nowhere, was there any sign of the defenses that turned the waters around Ithicana's bridge red with enemy blood.

Lara rose onto her knees to look up as they passed between two towers of limestone. "Do people live here?"

As if to answer her question, when they rounded another island, several fishing boats appeared, the men and women aboard them stopping what they were doing to lift their hands in greeting, many of them calling out to Aren by name.

"Some live here," he responded slowly, as though the admission cost him something. "But it's dangerous. If they are attacked, we can't come to their aid until it's too late to matter."

"Are they attacked often?"

"Not since the treaty was signed, which is why more people have settled their families here."

"Do they leave during War Tides?"

His jaw tightened. "No."

Lara turned away from the fishing boats to look up at him, a sickening feeling filling her guts. What were the chances that Serin and her father didn't know these people were here? And what were the chances Aren wouldn't do everything in his power to help them if they were attacked?

Even if it meant weakening the bridge's defenses.

They meandered through the islands in silence before sailing beneath a natural stone arch into a hidden cove that dwarfed the one at Midwatch where, to Lara's surprise, several large ships were anchored.

"They're mostly naval vessels that we've captured. We've refit several to pass as merchant ships. This one's mine." Aren pointed at a mid-sized vessel painted with blue and gold.

"Aren't they all yours?" Lara replied sourly, accepting Jor's arm for balance before taking hold of the rope ladder dangling off the side of the ship.

"They all belong to King Aren of Ithicana. But this one is under the command of Captain John, merchant of Harendell. Now come on. That storm's going to chase us into Vencia if we delay much longer."

The hold, as it turned out, was full of the very product that Ithicana had been trying to keep from Maridrina: steel. "Can't keep a hold full of cattle sitting around for these situations," Aren said. "Plus, steel's the only commodity worth the risk of a storm season crossing. Or at least it was."

As they retreated back on deck and into the captain's quarters, Lara broke off a tiny piece of the root Nana had given her, then chewed on it vigorously, hoping it would quell the nausea inflicted by more than just seasickness.

Opening a chest, Aren riffled around and extracted a set of clothes and a floppy cap, which he tossed her way. "Disguises. If you pretend to be a boy, you'll have more liberty once we arrive in the city."

Scowling at him, Lara took the clothes and waited for him to turn his back before shedding her Ithicanian garments. After a bit of thought, she wrapped a scarf tightly around her chest, binding her breasts as well as she could, then donned the baggy shirt and voluminous trousers apparently favored by sailors from Harendell. She twisted her long braid into a coil on top of her head, securing it tightly, then tugged the cap over the whole affair and turned around.

Aren was already dressed in his Harendell attire, a similar floppy hat perched on his head. He frowned. "You still look like a woman."

"Shocking." She crossed her arms.

"Hmm." He turned in a circle, then walked to a corner and rubbed a hand across the floor. "This ship hasn't gone anywhere for over a year, and I don't think anyone's been in to clean." Retreating across the room, he reached for her.

Lara recoiled in alarm. "What are you doing?"

"Finishing your disguise." Holding the back of her head, he rubbed a hand that smelled like dirt and mouse shit across her face, ignoring her protests. Stepping back, Aren eyed her up and down. "Slouch a bit. And keep that frown on your face. It suits that of a thirteen-year-old boy forced into the service of his roguish-yet-charming older cousin."

Lara lifted her hand in a gesture that was universally insulting.

Aren laughed, then shouted out the door. "All hands on deck. We set sail for Maridrina."

With practiced efficiency, the soldiers-turned-Harendellian-sailors were readying the ship, Jor in conversation with a dozen Ithicanians she didn't recognize, but who must have been on the island.

"What's the story, Captain?" Jor called out as Aren and Lara came on deck.

"We saw a break in the storms and risked the crossing for a quick profit. Last chance to make a pretty penny while steel prices are high."

Everyone nodded in agreement, and it dawned on Lara that they'd done this before. That the most sought-after man in Ithicana had waltzed beneath her father's nose with no one, not even Serin, so much the wiser. Aren took hold of the wheel at the helm, shouting orders. The anchor was raised, sails dropped into place, then the ship was drifting out of the cove.

"Do you go to Maridrina often?"

Aren shook his head. "Not anymore. Before my coronation, I spent a great deal of time in other kingdoms furthering my education on trade economics."

"Is that what you were doing?" Jor said as he walked by. "And here I thought all those ventures out of Ithicana were to give you an opportunity to gamble, chase skirts, and piss away money on cheap booze."

"That too." Aren had the decency to look embarrassed. "Regardless, all of it ended when I was crowned, but for *Lara*, I'm going to make an exception."

She rested her elbows on the rail. "How long will it take us to get there?"

"Either ahead of this storm"—he grinned—"or not at all."

"This is unnecessary." She was more worried about what she'd find when they arrived than whether he'd get her there alive.

"That's my call to make. Now, why don't you go find something useful to do?"

Because she knew Aren wouldn't expect her to listen, Lara did just that. Armed with a bucket, a mop, and a filthy brush, she scrubbed the deck before moving into the captain's quarters where she pilfered some gold she found in the drawer of a desk, pausing in her cleaning only to toss the blackened water and haul in fresh. From the corner of her eye, she saw Aren open his mouth each time she passed before snapping it shut and glowering at the sea ahead of them.

Which was satisfying in and of itself, but more than that, the cleaning gave her uninterrupted time to think. As Lara saw it, she had three options once they made port. The first was that she ran. There was no doubt in her mind that she could escape Aren and his guard, and with the jewels she had in her pocket along with the gold she'd already pilfered from the captain's quarters, she'd be able to set up a life for herself wherever she saw fit. She'd have her freedom, and on the assumption that Aren would eventually write to her father on the marked paper, she'd have done her duty to her people.

The second was that she made her way to her father's palace and used the codes Serin had given her to gain admittance. That she'd tell them all that she knew in detail in exchange for her freedom, as had been promised. Though doing so risked her father cutting her throat a heartbeat after she'd given him what he needed. And the third . . .

The third was that everything Aren had told her was true. That her father had been given the opportunity to improve the lives of the Maridrinian people, but had chosen not to. That her father, not Ithicana, was the oppressor of her homeland. Yet Lara's mind balked, unwilling to accept that explanation. Certainly unwilling to accept it without proof.

Clutching a bucket of dirty water in one hand and the railing with the other, she turned to watch Aren sail the ship, her heart lurching despite the ridiculous cap he wore.

What if her life had been dedicated to a lie?

Lara was saved from thinking on it further as a wave washed over the deck, rendering her efforts unnecessary. The seas had grown rough and, lifting her face to the sky, she watched as lightning crackled through the clouds, wind tugging at her foolish hat. Aren was skirting the edge of the storm, which was almost upon them. Squinting, Lara took in the shadow of the continent ahead of them. What were the chances they'd make it?

Dropping her mop and bucket, she staggered across the rocking deck and up the steps to where Aren stood at the helm. "You need to turn west and get ahead of this typhoon, you mad fool," she shouted over the wind, gesturing at the black clouds.

"It's just a little storm," he said. "I'll beat it. But you should hold on."

Clinging to the railing with one hand and her hat with the other, Lara watched as Vencia and its sheltered harbor grew on the horizon, barely visible as the rain began to fall. Unlike the day she'd left, the sky over the city of her birth was black and ominous, the whitewashed buildings rising up from the harbor a dull grey. Lording over it all was the Imperial Palace, its walls washed a brilliant blue, its domes made of bronze. It was where her father kept his harem of wives, one of whom was her mother, if she was still alive.

Dimly, she heard Aren order his crew to drop some of the sails, the ship barely slowing as it raced toward the breakwater protecting the harbor. Lightning flashed, and a heartbeat later, thunder shook the ship. Wave after wave swamped the deck, the Ithicanians holding tight to lines to keep from being washed overboard.

Only Aren appeared unperturbed.

Fighting her growing nausea, Lara dug her fingers into the railing. Surf smashed against the high breakwater like a ceaseless battering ram, froth and spray flying fifty feet in the air. Each time it sounded like an explosion, and sweat poured down her back as she envisioned what would happen to the ship if it ran against the structure.

With a grunt of effort, Aren turned the wheel, his gaze fixed on the seemingly tiny gap through which they would pass.

A wave rose to nearly the height of the breakwater. "This is insanity." Lara barely kept her balance as the vessel swung round and straightened, sliding through the gap with unerring precision. A loud breath of air expelled from her lungs, the wood of the railing digging into Lara's forehead as she rested against it, rain splattering against her forehead.

"I told you we'd make it," Aren said, but she didn't answer, only took in the crowded harbor, the waters smooth relative to those of the open sea they'd left behind.

During storm season, she knew the majority of merchant vessels remained close to the coast, able to duck into a harbor if dark skies threatened, so heads turned at the sight of a Harendellian ship coming in. The likely contents of their hold enticed the harbormaster enough to wave them into the docks ahead of the queue, much to the obvious disgust of those captains and crews.

"It's been a long time, you brave bastard," the man shouted as the ship bumped against the dock, Jor and several of the others leaping over the rail to secure the vessel.

Aren waited until they dropped the gangplank before motioning for Lara to follow him down, the rain growing heavier by the minute. "You say brave, but my grandmother uses quite another word to describe me."

The harbormaster laughed. "Greedy?"

Aren clapped a hand to his chest and staggered sideways. "You wound me!"

They laughed as though they were old friends. Aren extracted a handful of coins and passed them over to the harbormaster, then another golden one, which the man slipped into his pocket while his assistant was recording the details on a piece of paper.

"You're well to have arrived when you did," the harbormaster said. "Steel prices won't hold for long with Ithicana shipping the cursed metal without tax or toll. It's piling up on Southwatch. Not that the Valcottans are giving King Silas much chance to retrieve his prize." He spat into the water.

Aren made a noise of commiseration. "So I've heard."

"Ithicana's new queen has done us no favors. All the gold Silas taxed out of our pockets has been spent on steel, and yet we've seen nothing in return."

"Beautiful women have a way of costing men money," Aren responded.

Lara bristled, and the harbormaster's eyes left Aren to land on her. "Don't much like the way you're looking at me, lad."

Aren clapped Lara on the shoulder hard enough to make her stagger. "Don't mind my cousin. He's only sour as he spent the entire crossing swabbing the deck rather than lazing about, as he's wont to do."

"Family makes for the worst crew."

"Don't it just. Was half tempted to chuck him overboard half a dozen times, but to do so would mean I could never go home."

"More than a few ladies in Vencia would be happy to put you up, I should think."

"Don't tempt me."

A fourth plan, which involved sticking a knife deep into Aren's guts, began to evolve as Lara followed the two men off the docks.

The harbormaster's voice dragged her attention back to the conversation. "I've heard Amarid spent the calm season showing the Bridge Kingdom exactly what they thought of Ithicana stealing away the business of supplying Maridrina with Harendellian weapons."

"Ithicana isn't supplying weapons."

Lara detected the heat in Aren's voice, but the harbormaster didn't seem to notice.

"Same is same. Shipping them for free. Getting them into our hands. Or would be, if Valcotta weren't risking their fleet to keep us from making port." The bitterness in his voice was palpable. "King Silas should've bargained for cattle."

"Cows don't win wars," Aren replied.

"Neither do half-starved soldiers. Or those dead from plague." The harbormaster spat on the ground. "The only good our princess's marriage has done for Maridrina was line the pockets of the beggars the king paid to sit on the street and cheer her name as she passed."

Aren and the man turned to the details of offloading the ship. It was nothing but a drone in Lara's ears as what she'd heard sank deep into her soul. What Serin had told her in his letter about the famine and plague was true, yet . . . Yet if what this man said had any verity to it, she'd been much deceived about who was to blame. Sweat rolled in little beads down her back, making her skin itch.

It couldn't be true. Aren had hired this man to say these things. It was all lies intended to trick her. A band of tension wrapped around Lara's chest, every breath a struggle as she attempted to reconcile a lifetime of teaching with what she was seeing. What she was hearing.

With what she had done.

"Have your crew offload it first thing in the morning. This storm is going to make it next to impossible to do it now."

Lara blinked, focusing on Aren as he shook the harbormaster's hand, waiting until the man was out of earshot before saying, "Proof enough for you?"

Lara didn't answer, pressing a hand to her aching temple, hating how it shook.

"Are we going back to the ship now?" Her tongue was thick in her mouth, her own voice distant.

"No."

There was something in his tone that pulled her from her fugue. Water sluiced down the hard angles of Aren's face, little beads collecting on his dark lashes. His hazel eyes searched hers for a moment, then he scanned the wharf. "We'll need to wait out the storm in Vencia. Best to do it in a bit of comfort."

Her pulse thudded like a drum in her skull as she walked through the market, following on Aren's heels, the Ithicanians casually walking around them. *Run.* The word repeated in her head, her feet flexing in her boots, desperate to take her away from this situation. She didn't want to hear any more. She didn't want to face the fact that she might not be a liberator. She might not be a savior. Not even a martyr.

She wanted to run from these shards of truth telling her she was something else entirely.

Aren climbed the narrow switchback streets, two-story buildings crammed together on both sides, windows shuttered against the storm. He stopped in front of a door with a sign that said *The Songbird* over top of it. Music, the clink of glasses, and the collective murmur of voices seeped onto the street. He hesitated with one hand on the handle, then pulled open the door with a sigh.

The scent of woodsmoke, cooking food, and spilled ale washed over Lara, and she took in the common room filled with low tables, most of them claimed by merchant class patrons. Jor and Aren sat at a table in the corner, the other guards taking places at the bar. Fighting to control the turbulent emotions shifting through her heart, Lara took a seat at Aren's right, slouching in the chair and hoping the rain hadn't washed away the dirt completing her disguise. A female voice caught her attention.

"Well now, look what the cat dragged in."

A young woman, perhaps in her early-twenties, had approached the table. She had long hair, a lighter and more golden shade of blond than Lara's, and a good portion of her generous cleavage was revealed by the low-cut bodice of her dress.

Aren picked up one of the small glasses of amber liquid that a serving girl had brought to the table. "How are you, Marisol?"

"How am I?" The woman—Marisol—planted her hands on her

hips. "It's been over a year since you showed your sorry face in Vencia, John, and you ask how I am?"

"Has it been that long?"

"You damn well know it has been."

Aren lifted his hands in an apology, giving the woman a charming smile that Lara had never seen before on his face. Flirtatious. Familiar. The nature of their relationship dawned on Lara, her skin turning hot.

"Circumstances beyond my control. But it's good to see you."

The woman pushed out her bottom lip and gave him a long look. Then she sat on his knee and wrapped an arm around his neck. Lara's fingers twitched toward the knives hidden in her boots, fury bubbling in her veins. What was he thinking, parading his mistress in front of her? Was this some sort of punishment? Was he making a point?

The woman then greeted Jor and waved at one of the servers to bring another round.

Jor drained his glass, plucking the next from the server before she'd even had a chance to set it down. "Good to see you, Marisol."

The woman's gaze landed on Lara. "Who's the sullen one?"

"My cousin. He's learning the trade."

Marisol tilted her pretty head, eyeing Lara as though she were trying to place her face. "Eyes like that, your mother must've been dallying with King Silas himself."

Aren choked on his drink. "Now wouldn't that be something?"

"You might have more fun if you smiled a bit more, boy. You could learn more from your cousin than how to sail a ship."

Lara gave her a smile that was all teeth, but the woman only laughed, her attention back on Aren. "How long are you here?"

"Only until tomorrow, assuming the storm breaks."

Her jaw tightened in obvious disappointment. "So soon."

"My presence is required back home."

"That's what you always say." Marisol exhaled softly, then shook her head. "You'll be needing rooms for your crew for the night, then? And your cousin?"

Lara's stomach flipped. *But not for him.* Surely he didn't intend

. . .

"For them. And one for me as well."

One of Marisol's eyebrows rose, and Lara fought the urge to punch her in her pretty little nose.

Jor cleared his throat. "He's gotten himself married off, Marisol."

The woman stood so abruptly that she knocked against the table, sending liquid sloshing out of the glasses.

Setting down his drink, Aren gave Jor a black glare, but the older man only shrugged. "No sense belaboring the conversation. Now she's been told, so we can get on with business."

Marisol's eyes glittered, and she blinked rapidly. "Congratulations. I'm sure she's charming."

"She has a temper like wildfire and a sharp tongue to go along with it."

Marisol's gaze shifted to Lara, far too many realizations flashing through her eyes. Rather than staring her down like she wanted to, Lara fixed her attention on a crack in the table. "I'm sure she's very beautiful," the other woman said.

Aren was quiet for a moment. "As beautiful as clear skies over the Tempest Seas. And equally as elusive."

Lara's stomach flipped as his words registered, a compliment wrapped in a dark truth that she couldn't deny.

"Well, that explains why you're in love with her, then," Marisol said softly. "You've always been enthralled by challenges."

Lara snatched up one of the little glasses and downed the contents, her ears buzzing even as she looked anywhere but at Aren.

Jor coughed loudly, then waved his arms in the air. "We need a round of drinks over here."

"Perhaps more than one." Marisol sat at the table, giving the slightest of nods to the musicians. They set aside the stringed instruments, retrieving drums and tambourines, filling the room with rhythm. Young women dressed in bright-colored dresses danced through the tables, the bracelets of bells around their wrists and ankles jingling as their voices accompanied the music. Moments later, the patrons began to clap, the din making it hard for Lara to hear herself think.

Marisol clapped along. "There is no evidence the king is building up his fleet in an effort to fight the Valcottan blockade. Not even any sign that he *intends* to. I have informants up and down the coast, and not a single shipyard boasts a commission from the crown."

Lara blinked. *This woman was a spy?*

"The prices of imports have skyrocketed. Food is limited to what Maridrina can produce itself, which is little given all our farmers have been turned to soldiers, and famine is on the rise in the cities. It's only expected to worsen."

Aren clapped along in time to the music. "Amarid isn't picking up the slack? I would've thought they'd be clamoring for the opportunity."

Marisol shook her head. "Amaridian sailors are crying in every port that the alliance between Ithicana and Maridrina has destroyed their incomes." Her eyes flicked to Aren. "And now that the alliance isn't working out as intended, they seem happy for Maridrina to pay the price."

"Vindictive of them."

Marisol took a sip from her drink, then nodded. "The support of the Maridrinian people for the conflict with Valcotta had been on the wane for years, because no one believed there was anything to be gained from it. But since the wedding and Valcotta's subsequent retaliation, favor for all-out war with Valcotta has grown tenfold. Men and boys both are throwing themselves at army recruiters, fancying themselves the saviors of their people, and—" Marisol broke off, casting a quick glance at Lara.

"And?" Aren prompted.

"And there is a growing number of voices suggesting that the alliance of the Fifteen Year Treaty should be broken. That while Maridrina starves, Ithicana continues to profit off trade with Valcotta. That if the Bridge Kingdom were a true ally, they would deny our enemies port at Southwatch."

Lifting one shoulder, Marisol let it fall. "The concessions Ithicana granted Maridrina haven't benefited our people in the slightest. But rather than blaming King Silas, they blame Ithicana for the hardship. The people are itching for a fight."

Maridrina will starve before they ever see the benefit of this treaty.

Aren's words echoed through Lara's skull. How right he'd been.

The song ended, the dancers faded back to their other posts, and the musicians chose a more subdued song for their next piece. Marisol stood. "I need to get back to work. I'll have food sent over and rooms made up for you and your crew."

Her father, Serin . . . all her masters. They'd lied to Lara and her sisters. That in itself was no great revelation—she'd realized that Ithicana's villainy had been exaggerated and expounded upon in order to turn the girls into fundamentalists with one clear goal: the destruction of Maridrina's oppressor. But until this precise moment, she had believed that while her father's methods had been vile, his motivation had been pure. To save Maridrina's people. To feed them and protect them.

Except Ithicana wasn't the oppressor. Her father was.

Lara and her sisters hadn't been isolated in the desert compound for their safety. They hadn't even been kept there to conceal her father's plans from Ithicana, not really. It had been to keep Lara and her sisters from the truth. Because if they'd known that their mission was driven not by the need to right a wrong, but by their father's endless greed, how willing would any of them have been to betray a husband? To tear apart a nation? To see a people slaughtered? Promises and threats and bribes were paltry motivators compared to the fanaticism that had been burned into her and her sisters' souls.

But for Lara, that fanaticism burned no longer.

"W HY ARE WE HERE?" Jor motioned for one of the girls to bring another round of drinks. "What are we risking wild seas and enemy territory for?"

Pushing his food around on the plate in front of him, Aren didn't answer. Lara had gone upstairs to their room an hour ago, silent, her face pale. He'd told her to remain there until he returned for her own safety. He had no expectations that she'd listen.

He'd known. Standing in the water with her next to Snake Island, he'd known. All the little peculiarities about his Maridrinian wife, the little things that had struck him as odd, had accumulated until there was no denying it.

Lara was a spy.

The woman he'd goddamned fallen in love with was a spy.

In the early days of their marriage, he'd believed Lara's apparent disdain for him was driven by her discomfort of being forced into a marriage that she didn't want. A life she hadn't chosen. But the shock on her face when he told her that her father had been given the chance to feed his starving people and had bought weapons instead signaled she'd been *lied* to on top of everything else.

Aren employed enough spies of his own to know the best of them believed that the work they did was for a greater good. The Rat King would be hard-pressed to find a spy who believed Ithicana was the cause of Maridrina's plight, so he'd created one: a daughter raised in total isolation to implant a false sense of righteousness.

Except now she knew the truth.

"Aren?" Jor's voice was unconcerned, but Aren had never heard the captain of his guard slip on a pseudonym, particularly that of his king. The older man was worried. And rightly so. Ithicana was caught between a rock and a very hard place.

Before Aren had a chance to answer, one of his crew stepped inside the tavern and nodded once. Aren's heart sank. "You're about to find out."

Outside, his guard reported, "She's walking up the main boulevard. Gorrick is tailing her." He handed Aren his bow and quiver.

Aren took the weapons without comment and started up the street, Jor on his heels. Vencia was crowded as always, and it took him a bit of time to find the tall Ithicanian tailing his wife. "Go back," he muttered to Gorrick once he had Lara in his sights. "We'll take it from here."

The man opened his mouth to argue, then saw the expression on Aren's face, and faded into the crowd.

Lara strode up the center of the street, still wearing her disguise, which meant the drunks and rabble-rousers left her alone. Yet as they tailed her, he wondered how the disguise fooled anyone at all. Every time she turned her head to regard something that had caught her interest, torchlight framed the delicate lines of her face, her full lips, the long column of her neck, the rounded curve of her ass. The slight sway to her step. No Harendellian ship boy he'd ever met walked like *that*.

She was so painfully beautiful, and even knowing that she'd used it against him didn't lessen how powerfully he was drawn to her.

He silently pleaded: *Please let me be wrong about what you intend to do.*

But there was no denying the route Lara was taking, up the

switchback streets in the direction of her father's palace, that blue and bronze testament to his hubris and greed.

Jor cursed as he, too, realized which way Lara was going. "We need to stop her."

Aren sidestepped a drunken pair and moved into the shadows closer to the buildings. "Not yet."

The farther they climbed, the fewer people filled the street, but Lara hadn't once looked back. As though it hadn't even occurred to her that he might have her watched.

"What are you doing, Aren?" Jor hissed.

"I need to see if she'll betray me if given the chance."

But what he hoped was that the truth had turned her. That, now awake to her father's deception, she'd turn her back on whatever purpose she'd been set to. If she was the sort of woman he believed, no, *prayed*, her to be.

She kept walking toward the gate, the guards flanking it regarding her with bored interest, a lone youth of no concern to them. Aren stopped in the shadows where the guards wouldn't see him, pulling a single arrow from his quiver. The bow was his own, but the wood felt strange and unfamiliar beneath his sweating fingers.

Jor reached for his weapon. "Let me do this for you."

Aren stepped sideways, nocking the arrow as he shook his head. "No. I brought her into Ithicana. She's my responsibility." Lara wasn't slowing, and the guards at the gate perked up as she approached.

One of the guards called out to her. "What are you about, boy?" Lara didn't answer.

Again, Jor tried to take the weapon. "You're half in love with the girl. You don't need this on your conscience."

"Yes, I do."

She stopped a dozen paces from the heavy iron gates.

"State your purpose or be on your way," the guard shouted.

Aren slowly drew the bow, aiming the arrow at the center of her slender back. At this range, it would punch straight through her heart. She'd be dead before she could damn him, and Ithicana, more than she already had.

Aren's heart was wild and frantic in his chest, hot sweat mixing with the rain running down his back. As he blinked, he saw her fall. Saw her blood spill out in a pool around her. Saw those cursedly beautiful eyes of hers lose their spark. Then he blinked again and she was standing motionless in the darkness. She took a hesitant step forward. His arm quivered.

Another step.

The bowstring dug into his fingers as he slowly began to straighten them, knowing that despite having no choice, he'd never forgive himself for killing her.

Her body rocked and his heart skipped. Then lightning flashed and Lara whirled, sprinting away from the gates. Jor jerked Aren deeper into the shadows as she passed, heading back into the city. He took a step to follow before everything he'd eaten for dinner rose in his throat. Bracing a hand against the wall of the building, Aren puked his guts out onto the street.

"Follow her," he managed to get out. "Make sure she gets back safe."

Only when Jor had disappeared down the street did Aren rest his head against the slimy wet stone. A half a second. That had been the difference between her running into the night and her lying dead on the street. Half a second.

The stench of vomit filled his nose, but that wasn't what made his eyes burn. He scrubbed at them furiously, hating the King of Maridrina to the depths of his soul. The alliance between Maridrina and Ithicana made a mockery of the word, for it felt Aren had no greater enemy than Silas Veliant.

"You," someone shouted. "No loitering. Get on your way!"

Casting one backward glance at the palace where Lara's father slept, Aren melted into the night.

"WHISKEY," LARA MUTTERED AT the barkeep, easing onto a stool back at *The Songbird*, water dripping from her clothing to pool on the floor beneath her.

The barkeep eyed her with amusement. "Can you pay, boy?"

"No," she snapped. "I intend to drink it and then run out the back."

The amusement in his eyes fled, and he leaned over the bar. "Listen, you little—"

"Darling, can you bring up some more wine from the cellar?" Marisol appeared from nowhere. "I'll handle this."

Shrugging, the barkeep strode toward an open door behind the bar. Once he was gone, Marisol pulled a bottle from beneath the bar and poured a generous measure into a glass, which she pushed in front of Lara. "I don't know how they do things in Harendell, but I'm not in the habit of getting children drunk in my establishment."

Lara gave her a cold stare, drained the glass, then pushed it back in front of the other woman. Then she reached into her pocket and retrieved a gold Harendellian coin and slammed it on the bar. "Make an exception."

One eyebrow rose. "You are a charmer, aren't you, Your Majesty."

"Do you bestow titles on all your patrons?"

"Only on women with eyes of Veliant blue who travel in the company of Ithicanian spies."

There seemed little point in trying to dissuade her. "Either pour and talk at the same time, or shut up. I'm in no mood." No mood for anything but to silence the questions that spun wild through her thoughts as she tried to come to terms with a world that seemed turned upside down. And certainly in no mood to make small talk with Aren's former lover.

Marisol poured, then set the bottle down next to the glass. "I saw you when you passed through Vencia on your way to Ithicana." She rested her elbows on the polished wood. "The curtain was pulled back in the carriage, and I caught just a glimpse. You looked like you were going to war, not to be married."

Lara *had* been going to war. Or so she'd thought at the time.

"The king ordered the streets cleared. No one was allowed out of their homes until you'd boarded the ship. For your protection, they said."

It had nothing to do with her protection. It was one last step to ensure that Lara boarded the ship convinced Maridrina was in the direst of straits and that Ithicana was to blame. One last piece of deception.

"Then they loaded you onto the ship, and you were gone. Off to Ithicana and off, unbeknownst to me at the time, to steal away my favorite lover."

Lara gave her a sweet smile. "Given you hadn't seen him in over a year, I'm not sure you had much claim to him at that point. If ever."

"You are quite the little bitch, aren't you?"

Lara plucked the glass Marisol was polishing from her hands, filled it, waited for the other woman to raise it, then clinked hers against it. "Cheers to that."

Swallowing the liquid in one mouthful, Marisol set aside the glass. "We expected things to change. For your father to ease his filthy taxes or at least to use the money for something better than his ceaseless war with Valcotta."

"But nothing changed."

Marisol shook her head. "If anything, it's only gotten worse."

"Makes one wonder why I bothered going." Except Lara knew exactly why she'd gone to Ithicana. To save her sisters. To save her kingdom. To save herself. In this precise moment, she half wondered if she'd damned them all.

"Not your choice, I suppose." Marisol's eyes drifted over Lara's shoulder, taking in the comings and goings of the common room. "What I do know is that you married the best man I've ever had a privilege to meet, so perhaps instead of drowning your sorrows, you ought to consider a better use of your time." She inclined her head. "Either way, I hope you enjoy your evening, Your Majesty."

"Good night," Lara muttered, refilling her glass. She *knew* Aren was a good man. Her instincts, which she should've trusted, had been screaming it at her for longer than she'd cared to admit, but she'd ignored them in favor of what she'd been *told*. She'd been duped. Manipulated. Played.

She'd gone to the palace to kill her father.

Her plan had been to use the codes she'd been given to gain access, then wait for them to bring her to her father—and kill him. With her bare hands, if she needed to. It wasn't as though she hadn't been trained to do it. They'd kill her afterward, but his death would be worth it. Worth that moment when her father realized that she, his prized weapon, had turned on him instead.

But as Lara had stood there in the pouring rain, her father's soldiers watching her with bored interest, Master Erik's voice had filled her ears: *Do not let your temper get the better of you, little cockroach. For when you do, you risk your enemies getting the better of you.*

It would be one thing if her loss of temper only cost *her*. But as she stood there, skin prickling with some sixth sense warning her of danger, it occurred to Lara that it would be Ithicana—and Aren—who would pay the price. The sheets of paper in Aren's rooms at Midwatch still bore all of the bridge's secrets. If even one of them reached Serin's hands . . . that was damage that could never be undone. She needed to ensure they were destroyed. Once that was accomplished, she could turn to vengeance with a clear conscience.

She'd returned, intending to leave Aren a note explaining everything and instructing him to destroy the papers, but the vision of Aren's face when he read it kept spinning across her thoughts. He, who was loyal to his very core, would take her act of disloyalty personally. He'd *hate* her. Lara swallowed the contents of her glass in big gulps, wishing the alcohol would work faster. Wishing it would numb her traitorous heart.

Filling her glass again and again, she ruminated until the bottle was empty, the whiskey doing *nothing* to numb the dull ache in her chest. She would've ordered another and kept on drinking, but there was no one left to serve her, all the bottles and glassware put away for the night, the room silent and still.

Rising to her feet, Lara turned to discover the common room empty of patrons and staff, chairs pushed into tables, floors swept, and door latched. Devoid of life. Except for Aren, who sat at the table behind her.

She stared blearily at him, her heart feeling as though it had been torn into a thousand pieces, then set aflame.

"Waiting for me to go to bed so you can go find Marisol?" The words were slurred. Spiteful. But she almost wished he'd do it if for no other reason than it would give her a valid reason to hate him. A valid reason to leave and never look back.

The corner of his mouth turned up. "Who do you think came to find me to *deal with my shit-mouthed little cousin?*"

Lara made a face. "She knows I'm not your cousin. She knows exactly who I am, and, by extension, who you are."

"Clever Marisol."

"You aren't concerned?"

Aren shook his head, then rose to his feet. His clothes were wet, but whatever rainwater he'd tracked in had long since dried. *How long had he been sitting there?*

"She's been spying for Ithicana for almost a decade—since your father hung hers and then spiked his head on Vencia's gates. She's loyal."

Jealous words danced on Lara's tongue, but she swallowed them. "She's beautiful. And kind."

"Yes." His gaze was intense. "But she's not you."

Her body swayed, the room spinning. Aren closed the distance between them in two strides, hands catching her sides. Steadying her. Lara closed her eyes to try to stop the spinning, but the rotating room was replaced with the memory of his hard, muscled body, his tanned skin beneath her fingers. Heat blossomed low in her belly.

You can't, she told herself. *You're a liar and a traitor. You aren't the woman he believes you to be, and you never can be. You can never be yourself.* Not without risking him discovering the truth. If she couldn't find the courage to tell him the truth, then she needed to get back to Ithicana to destroy all evidence of her betrayal, and then disappear. Fake her death. Return to Maridrina for vengeance.

And never see Aren again.

Her eyes burned, her breath threatening to catch in a sob and betray her.

"Are you all right?"

She clenched her teeth. "I don't feel well."

"Not surprising given the amount you drank. You have a royal's taste, by the way. That's not a cheap bottle."

"Paid for it myself." She said the words slowly in attempt to make them clearer.

"You mean with the coins you stole from *my* ship."

"If you're stupid enough to leave them lying around, you deserve to lose them."

"I'm sorry. I didn't catch that through all the slurring."

"Asshole."

He laughed. "Can you walk?"

"Yes." Untangling herself from his grip, she staggered toward the stairs, when all of a sudden, the bottom step was flying up to meet her. But before Lara's face could slam against the wood, Aren caught hold of her, swinging her up into his arms. "Let's not tempt fate."

"Just need water."

"You need a pillow. Maybe you'll get lucky and the storm will linger long enough for you to sleep this off. But I doubt it."

Lara made an angry sound against his chest, but it was more

for herself. At the ease with which she curled against him. At how appealing a few more nights with him would be, despite knowing that it was only delaying the inevitable.

"Did the whiskey help?"

"No."

"It's never helped me much, either."

A tear leaked onto her cheek, and she turned her face into his chest to hide it. "I'm sorry I've been so terrible. You deserve someone better than me."

Aren exhaled, but said nothing. The methodical movement of him climbing the stairs lulled her, consciousness slowly fading away. She didn't fight it, because against all the odds, she trusted him implicitly. Still, she was aware enough to hear him, his voice hoarse as he said, "Since the moment I set eyes on you in Southwatch, there's been no one but you. Even if I'm a goddamned fool for it, there will never be anyone but you."

You are a fool, she thought as darkness took her.

And that made two of them.

H E'D NEVER BEEN able to sleep past dawn on a clear day.

How his sleeping body knew the winds had died and the rain ceased was a mystery. A sixth sense from a lifetime in Ithicana that warned him when the Tempest Seas lowered their guard, and that it was time to raise his. So when his eyes snapped open with the faintest glow on the horizon, Aren rose from where he'd slept on the floor, dressed silently so as not to disturb Lara, who was still faintly snoring into her pillow, then ventured downstairs for something to eat.

It was as though a burden had lifted from his shoulders. Coming to Vencia was always a risk, but it had been a thousandfold more so with Lara in tow. Yet it had been worth it. Worth having her discover the truth of the circumstances in Maridrina with her own eyes and ears. Having her understand that it was her *father*, not Ithicana, who was the oppressor of her homeland. Having Lara finally see with eyes unclouded by whatever bullshit her mind had been filled with over the years.

Those things had been worth the risk that she'd turn on him and spill every cursed secret she'd learned. Worth those torturous moments when Aren had believed he'd have to stop her.

Worth the moment when Aren became certain that her allegiance had, if not entirely turned to Ithicana, at least abandoned his enemy.

That she'd made that choice had been clear from the time he'd watched her sitting at the bar, drinking whiskey like her life depended on it. Aren knew his wife well enough to tell when she was pissed off. That silent simmering burn that caused any sane individual to give her a wide berth, whether they realized it or not. Last night, she'd been furious. But for the first time, it wasn't at him. No, when she'd turned around and saw him, her anger had been vanquished by another emotion entirely. One that he'd been desperate to see in her eyes for longer than he cared to admit.

Down in the common room, Jor was seated with Gorrick, but Aren only gave them a nod and took a seat in the corner by himself, content to watch the comings and goings while sipping the coffee that Marisol brought him, his friend and former lover too busy with the rush to do more than squeeze his shoulder in passing.

The room was half filled with traveling merchants. Some wore the clear gaze of those keen to make a profit once the markets opened. Others wore the blurry eyes and green faces of those who'd enjoyed a night out in Vencia and were awake only because they feared their masters' wrath.

Aren had far more in common with the latter group. Since he was fifteen, he'd been venturing out of Ithicana. Ostensibly, it was to spy. To learn the ways of his kingdom's pseudo-allies and clear-cut enemies, but there was no denying that he also used the trips to step away from the ceaseless burdens that came with his title. Vencia had always been his favorite, and he'd rode out a dozen or more typhoons drinking and gambling and laughing in one common room or another, more often than not with a local girl to warm his bed, no one believing him to be anything other than a son of a successful merchant.

While the Kingdom of Maridrina was a thorn in Ithicana's backside, the Maridrinian people had long been friends to Aren, which created a certain conflict. He was not supposed to like them, but he did. Liked how they haggled and argued about every damned thing; how they were brash and brave, even the most cowardly of them prone to picking fistfights to defend a friend's honor; how they sang and laughed and lived, every one of them with grand ambitions for *more*.

Vencia itself was a beautiful place, a hillside of whitewashed buildings with blue roofs that always seemed to gleam as he approached from the sea, its streets thrumming with people hailing from every nation, north and south. A metropolis that thrived *despite* its king, who ruled with an iron fist and who used taxes to all but plunder his own people.

No, if Maridrina found itself a new ruler and Aren wasn't the king of his own kingdom, he'd be happy to make a life in Vencia. Sometimes he wondered if that was half of what his council feared about opening up Ithicana's borders and allowing its citizens to leave: that they'd see how bloody *easy* life was in other kingdoms, and never come back. That Ithicana wouldn't be conquered, but rather slowly fade from existence.

Except he didn't think that was how it would go. There was something about the wild thrill of living in Ithicana that spoke to the souls of those born to it, and neither people nor kingdom would ever willingly let each other go.

Aren's thoughts were interrupted by a shadow falling across his table.

"Good morning, Your Grace," a nasally voice said. "I hope you'll forgive me for interrupting your breakfast."

Aren's fork hesitated halfway to his mouth, and it took a great deal of effort to swallow his mouthful of eggs. He lifted his head. "I've been called a great many things in this room, but never that."

The Magpie gave a thin smile and took the seat across from Aren. "I appreciate the game as much as anyone, Your Grace, but perhaps we might forgo the pretense that you are anyone other than the King of Ithicana." His smile grew. "For expedience's sake."

Aren set down his fork and leaned back in his chair. Out of the corner of his eye, he saw Jor and Gorrick lift their heads, Serin's face deeply familiar to them. But they'd only seen Maridrina's spymaster from afar, because never, *never*, had their cover been compromised.

Every Ithicanian spy knew going into enemy territory that if they were caught they should fall on their own sword before giving up their kingdom's secrets, and Aren had no doubt that everyone with him would do just that. Except, perhaps, for the woman upstairs.

"It's the scar on your hand that gave you away." Serin jerked his chin toward Aren's left hand, which rested on the table, the curved white scar from an old knife fight clearly visible. "Along with the mask, you always wore gloves when you met with outsiders. But not at your wedding, which of course I was in attendance for. Such a dramatic ceremony it was."

Gorrick stood, yawning, then strolled over to the bar as though to sweet-talk Marisol. His friend smiled and laughed as she polished the glass she was holding, but a heartbeat later, she'd disappeared from the room. To find Taryn, who'd secure Lara.

If that was even a possibility.

God, he was a fool for lowering his guard. For believing that it had ended last night when Lara hadn't gone into the palace. Perhaps that had only been a ruse, and even now, his Maridrinian wife was spilling out everything she'd learned to her father's lackeys.

"Not like you Ithicanians to make a mistake." Serin lifted his hand to get a servant girl's attention. "We, of course, suspected that you paid our shores visits from time to time, but not until now did you so blatantly announce your arrival."

Aren's eyebrow rose.

"It was the steel, you see. It was marked at Northwatch for transport through the bridge over a year ago, and yet the load somehow arrived in Vencia only yesterday, offloaded only this very morning. And via a ship claiming to have come from Harendell, not from a Southwatch ferry."

Fuck. Ahnna was going to kill him if he managed to survive this.

"I'd suggest that it was an amateur mistake, but this isn't your first visit to Vencia, is it, Your Grace?" Serin accepted a coffee from one of Marisol's girls. "You seem far too comfortable for it to be your first time."

Aren picked up his cup, eyeing the spymaster. "I've always had a fondness for Vencia. Plenty of attractive women."

Serin gave an amused sniff. "I would've thought those days would be behind you now that you're a married man."

"Perhaps they would be if you hadn't sent me such a harridan."

The coffee in Serin's cup quivered, and the tiny man set it down swiftly to hide the reaction. Apparently, Lara had not stuck to the spymaster's plan in her methods of seduction. Which was probably a good thing, because Aren suspected he and Serin had quite different tastes when it came to women.

"We could send you another . . . perhaps one with a kinder, gentler disposition." Serin's eyes flicked to Marisol. "I see you have a fondness for blondes. I can think of just the princess for you. She was my first choice, but fate conspired against me. Against both of us, it would appear."

Aren's curiosity over why Lara had been chosen flared once again before being pushed aside by concern for his friend. Marisol had been linked to him; that meant she was in danger. "Tempting. Unfortunately, such practices are frowned upon by my people. I'll have to content myself with what you sent me."

"Speaking of Lara, how is she? It's been some time since we received word from her, and her father has grown . . . concerned."

Aren's mind raced. If the steel hadn't been unloaded and processed until this morning, it was possible they'd only been under the Magpie's scrutiny for a matter of hours, all of which Lara had spent passed out in a bed upstairs. Alternatively, this could be a ruse to distract Aren while the Maridrinians secured their princess. "She's well enough."

"Her father would like some proof of that."

"When I return home, I'll suggest she put pen to paper. But I must warn you, Lara isn't the most . . . *obedient* of wives. She's more likely to tell me to shove both pen and paper up my ass."

Serin's brow crinkled. "Perhaps remind her of her father's enduring concern for her welfare."

Aren rested his elbows on the table. "Cut the shit, Magpie. We both know your master cares nothing for his daughter. He got what he wanted, which was free trade on steel and weapons. So what else is it you're after?"

Waving his hand as though to dispel the tension, Serin gave him an apologetic smile. "Appearances must be maintained, you understand. Frankly, you can slit the little bitch's throat and my master would care not; what he *does* care about is your commitment to the alliance between our kingdoms."

"He has his steel, as per our agreement. What more does he feel he deserves?"

A sage nod. "It's true you've held to the letter of the agreement, as have we. What I'm referring to is more . . . the *spirit* of the agreement. The treaty was for an alliance of peace between Ithicana and Maridrina, and yet you continue to host and trade with our greatest enemy in your market at Southwatch, allowing *them* to purchase the goods Maridrina so desperately needs. My master asks that you reconsider this practice."

"You want me to cut ties with Valcotta?" Cut ties with the kingdom that provided close to a third of the bridge's revenues every year? Valcotta was no ally, but neither were they Ithicana's sworn enemy the way Maridrina had been in the past. Yet if Aren did what Serin was asking . . . "I've no interest in going to war against Valcotta."

"Nor is my master asking you to." Serin slid an embossed silver cylinder across the table, the lacquered seal Maridrinian blue. "He merely requests that you cease supplying them in their war against us."

"They'll retaliate, and war will be on my doorstep whether I asked for it or not."

"Perhaps." Serin took a mouthful of his coffee. "But if Valcotta attacks your lands, rest assured that Maridrina will retaliate against them tenfold. We do not take kindly to those who interfere with our friends and allies."

Words of support, but Aren heard the threat beneath them. *Do as my master says, or face the consequences.*

"Think on it, Your Grace." Serin rose to his feet. "My master looks forward to your written response detailing your commitment to our friendship." The thin smile returned. "Safe travels back to your homeland, and *please*, do give Lara my regards."

Without another word, the Spymaster of Maridrina left the common room, the door slamming shut in his wake. Picking up the message tube, Aren quickly scanned the contents before shoving it into the bag by his feet, then met Jor's eyes from across the room.

Time to go.

LARA WOKE JUST before dawn, a blanket covering her from toe to chin, a glass of water sitting on the bedside table, and her head throbbing with the worst headache of her life.

Moaning, she rolled over to bury her face in the pillow. The events of the prior night were hazy, but she remembered them well enough for her cheeks to burn as she recalled Aren catching her before she could fall smack on her face. The way she'd curled into his arms as he'd carried her up the stairs. The things she'd said. The things *he's* said.

Sitting upright, Lara eyed her boy's clothes, which she'd slept in, the boots sitting on the floor next to her bed the only garment that Aren had removed from her after she'd passed out.

Her knives.

Looking around frantically, Lara threw the pillows onto the floor, her heart settling and a faint smile rising to her lips as she saw the blades resting there. Apparently Aren had noticed more of her habits than she'd realized.

Picking up the water, she opened the shuttered windows and

looked outside: clear skies and only a light breeze ruffling the laundry hanging from the line across the street. *They could go home today.*

Home. Shaking her head sharply at the slip, Lara drained the glass in several long gulps, and pulled on her boots. The room was decidedly devoid of dirt, so she used a bit of soot from the lamp to complete her disguise before shoving her few belongings into her bag and stepping out into the hallway.

To find herself face-to-face with half of Aren's guard.

"What's going on?" she asked Taryn, who looked strange in the simple dress she wore as disguise.

"Weather's going to turn. Time to go."

She was lying. There were very few things that put fear into the eyes of the Ithicanians, and the promise of a storm certainly wasn't one of them.

Downstairs was already busy with the early-rising merchant class who were breaking their fast, but her eyes immediately found Aren sitting at the bar. Behind it stood Marisol, who, for once, wasn't polishing a glass, her focus entirely on the man in front of her. Lara's jaw tightened, but her jealousy fled as she remembered Aren's words. *There will never be anyone but you.*

Except with all the lies she'd told, all the ways she'd manipulated him, how could she stay with him?

As Lara stood frozen in the entrance to the common room, Aren turned and caught sight of her. What looked like relief spread across his face. With a final word to Marisol, he dumped a handful of coins on the bar. *Something was very wrong.*

He strode across the room. "Finally decided to show yourself, cousin? Barely going to have enough time to make the run to Southwatch as it is without waiting on your primping."

She glowered at him because other patrons were watching, but once he was within arm's reach, he muttered, "We've been compromised. We need to go."

Jor and the rest of the Ithicanians were outside leaning against the wall with false nonchalance. Despite their apparel, no one with half an eye would believe them sailors. They were too alert, and not a one of them appeared hungover. Unlike her.

"Don't want to miss the tide," Aren announced, and immediately they were on the move.

In the harbor, they wove through the crowd at a near run, down to the wharf and onto the dock where their vessel was moored. The Ithicanians who'd remained with the ship were already scurrying about on the deck, readying to set sail. Readying to flee. Lara's focus sharpened, and she scanned the docks and crowds for any sign of pursuit. Aren had said their cover had been compromised, but there were levels to that statement. If the Maridrinians had discovered they were from Ithicana, that was one thing. If they'd discovered Aren's identity—or worse, Lara's—then they were in serious trouble.

"You're mad, John." The harbormaster's paunch shook as he scuttled toward them. "There's a storm brewing."

Aren paused at the base of gangplank, using one hand to push Lara up. "Nothing but a squall. It will keep the Valcottans off my heels."

"Insanity," the man grumbled. "I'll keep a space open for you."

"We'll be back before lunch. You can buy me a drink or two on my return."

"More likely that I'll be toasting your memory."

Aren's laugh cut off abruptly. Her hackles rising, Lara turned from her inspection of the darkness swirling in the east to find Serin standing a dozen paces or so behind the harbormaster, his arms crossed behind his back. Watching.

The ship rocked on a swell, and Lara staggered, her shoulders colliding with Aren's chest, his arm reflexively wrapping around her to catch her balance, holding her against him.

Serin's eyes widened.

"Go," she whispered, seeing the realization dawn on the spymaster's face. Realization that her presence in Maridrina meant she knew the truth. That the gambit fifteen years in the making had played itself out too soon. The realization that if Lara made it out of this harbor, so would any chance of her father ever taking the bridge. "Go!" she screamed.

"Raise the sails!" Aren roared.

The Ithicanians surged into action, and in a heartbeat, the ship was drifting away from the dock, the gangplank landing in the water with a splash. Aren dragged her with him as he raced to the helm, shouting orders even as swarms of soldiers descended upon them.

"Hurry!" The gap between ship and dock was widening, but not swiftly enough. "Aren, I can't let them take me alive." Lara pulled one of her knives from her boot. "They'll make me talk."

He caught sight of her knife, realizing her intentions. "Put it away, Lara! I won't let them take you."

"But—"

He tore the jeweled blade from her hand and threw it, the weapon flipping end over end to land on the dock. Which was filled with sprinting soldiers, the front-runners preparing to leap.

"Come on, wind!" Aren shouted. "Don't let this be the one damned time you refuse to blow."

As if answering the call of its master, the wind howled in from the east, the sails snapping taut. The ship lurched as three of the soldiers jumped, their arms flailing as they fell into the water instead of onto the deck.

The ship collided with another vessel with a loud crunch, the other crew shouting and swearing as they scraped the length of it, slamming into another ship, then another, as Aren used the strength of the wind to force their way through.

Soldiers ran in all directions, leaping onto ships in an attempt to reach their target, but they were too slow. Except in the distance, naval vessels were swarming with sailors making ready for pursuit.

"Can you outrun them?" Lara demanded.

Aren nodded, his eyes fixed on their progress through the crowded harbor.

Bells clanged riotously in the city.

"Shit!" Aren shouted. "We need to get past the breakwater before they lift the chain."

Lara's gaze skipped across the water to the twin towers flanking the gap in the breakwater, to the heavy steel chain that was creaking upward.

"Full sail!"

The deck was organized chaos as the Ithicanians hauled on lines, white canvas streaming skyward. The ship leapt across the waves toward the gap, but the chain was rising just as fast. Even if they managed to get across, it would tear loose the rudder and they'd be easy pickings for the Maridrinian navy.

"We can't hit that gap with full sail," Jor shouted. "We'll be tossed up on the rocks."

"Get them up," Aren ordered. "All of them."

Lara clung to the rail, her hair whipping out behind them with the speed of their progress. Yet the expressions on the crews' faces told her it wasn't enough. That they were headed toward a disaster that would see them all drowned or captured, which would amount to the same thing.

And there was nothing she could do to save them. Even if she jumped overboard, the ship would be trapped. Serin and her father would never let them go free.

Slamming her fists on the rail, Lara snarled in wordless fury, despair carving her insides hollow. Despite *everything*, her father was going to win.

Aren's hand caught hers. "The wind—it gusts around the hill and through the gap in the breakwater. If we time this just right, it might work."

"What might work?" The chain was perilously close.

"You'll see." He shot her a grim smile. "Hold on to the rail, and for the love of god, don't let go!" Then he let go of her hand and heaved on the wheel.

As he did, an enormous gust of wind struck them broadside. The rigging groaned, ropes and wood and canvas straining, on the verge of snapping, and the ship heeled over. Further and further and Lara shrieked, clinging to whatever she could, certain the vessel would capsize.

The ship shuddered, a loud scraping filling Lara's ears as the chain dragged along their port side. The noise was horrific, wood splintering and cracking, their speed flagging even as the wind eased, the ship slowly righting itself.

"Come on!" Aren shouted while Lara stared up at the soldiers manning the breakwater towers, their eyes wide with astonishment.

Then they were through.

Regaining her footing, Lara stumbled to the side of the ship to look back. Arrows rained down on their wake, fired more in desperation than at any chance of hitting a mark. Nor, she thought, would they risk the catapults mounted on the hills. Her father wanted them captured, not dead. The Maridrinian vessels were crowded up behind the now fully raised chain, the captains shouting at those manning the towers.

"It will take them a bit of time to get the chain reversed. They might chase us all the way to Southwatch." Aren's eyes shifted to the black clouds hanging over the dark ocean, promising wild seas. "The race is on."

THE NAVAL VESSELS gave up chase halfway to Southwatch, though whether it was for fear of the storm brewing in the east or the dozen shipbreakers on the fortified island, it was impossible to say.

Docking the ship at the Southwatch wharf was no mean feat, and Lara's whole body ached with tension as Aren eased the battered ship against the stone, Ithicanian crews on land using rigging attached to the wharf to tie the rocking ship down. She, Aren, and the rest of the crew disembarked swiftly, meeting an older Ithicanian man at the guardhouse mounted where the wharf met the island.

"We did not realize you were in Vencia, Your Grace." The man bowed with more formality than anyone at Midwatch ever used. His gaze skipped past his king to land on Lara, his eyes widening as he inclined his head to her.

"Unplanned trip. Where's the commander?"

Aren's voice was crisp and unwavering, but his left hand clenched and then opened in a repetitive motion that betrayed him. He was *not* looking forward to justifying himself to his sister, that much was certain.

"Off island, Your Grace. She left this morning to deal with a conflict on Carin Island, and I expect she'll need to ride out this storm there."

Aren's hand relaxed. "Tell her I'm sorry to have missed her, but we cannot linger. Have the ship stripped, then sink it."

"As you say, Your Grace." Bowing once again, the man continued down toward the ship, shouting orders as he went.

Lara cast a backward glance at the battered vessel. "Why sink it? Can't you just . . . repaint it?"

"No time to return it to safe harbor before this storm hits. The sea will tear it apart and sink it anyway if we leave it here, which could cause problems with other ships trying to make port. Ahnna will cut my balls off if she has to deal with cleaning up that sort of mess."

"I get the impression that she'll be reaching for her knife anyway when she discovers where you've been."

He laughed, his hand falling against her lower back to guide her up the path. "A little luck on our side that we missed her, then."

"Will she let it go?"

"Not a chance, but hopefully she won't feel inclined to follow us all the way to Midwatch to voice her opinion on the matter."

"Your bravery is inspiring."

"We all have our fears. Now let's get inside before the rain hits."

They didn't linger in the Southwatch market, which would've been a disappointment to Lara if she'd hadn't burned with urgency to return to Midwatch. The market was a series of large stone warehouses, plus one smaller building that Taryn told her was where all the trade was conducted. She longed to see what was inside those buildings, what sort of goods had come from Harendell, Amarid, and beyond, and what would depart from her own homeland. Just as she now found herself longing to talk to the Ithicanians who lived and worked here on Southwatch. To *know* them in a way she, out of necessity, hadn't allowed herself to before.

Because now they felt as much her people as the Maridrinians she'd left behind. On the heels of that realization came a deep and unceasing shame that she, who was their queen and whom they believed to be their defender, had nearly put them on the funeral pyre. Men, women, and children. Families and friends. Most who were innocents dedicated to no more than living their lives—those people, as much as Aren, would've been the individuals she'd have betrayed if her words had reached Serin and her father.

With that knowledge burning in her heart, she was glad when Aren and his guards led her into the yawning black mouth of the bridge.

The Bridge. How she hated the cursed thing, which was the source of every bit of despair in her life. With every step she took down its stinking length, she wished it didn't exist. Wished she'd been sent to Ithicana with no agenda beyond being a wife. Wished she was not her wicked, lying, and traitorous self. But wishes were for fools. Which was perhaps fitting, because her foolish self lost all grasp of logic whenever her sleeve brushed against Aren's, every time his gaze fell upon her, every time she remembered the feel of his hands on her body and how much she desired them there again.

There was no day or night in the bridge. Only endless musty darkness. The storm caused a moaning sound within the tunnel, sometimes little more than a whisper, and other times a deafening roar that forced the group to stuff cotton into their ears. It was like a living beast, and by the end of their first day of walking, Lara was half convinced she'd been consumed.

She could not stay in Ithicana, even if she wanted to. And she did want to. More than anything. But her entire relationship with Aren had been built on a lie, and if she told him the truth, what were the chances he'd forgive her? He loved his people too much to allow someone like her to remain his queen. Neither was keeping it a secret an option. Her father would make her pay for her betrayal. There would be no happily-ever-after. Not for her.

Reluctantly, a plan formed in Lara's mind. Her first order would be to destroy the papers with her planned invasion. Then she'd wait for a clear night, and make a run for her hidden canoe and supplies. All that would be left would be to sail toward revenge. Because she fully intended to make her father pay for what he'd done to Maridrina. What he'd intended to do to Ithicana. And what he'd done to her. Plotting the variables distracted her. Took away the tightness that gripped her chest every time she realized she'd never see Aren again.

From time to time they encountered groups transporting goods. Bored donkeys pulled carts filled with steel, fabrics, and grain southward. Men with handcarts transported crates of Valcottan glassworks northward. And once, after following a stream of spilled ale for several miles, they passed a wagon full of barrels headed north. Jor had jokingly put his head under the leaky barrel until Aren kicked his feet out from under him, then informed the man driving to quit making a mess of his bridge.

Sometimes there were merchants in the caravans, but always they were flanked by Ithicanian guards wearing masks. Before encountering any of them, her own group would don identical masks, and Lara idly wondered what the merchants would think if they knew the rulers of Ithicana had passed them in the darkness.

They made camp in the bridge two nights in a row, eating cold rations they'd picked up at Southwatch with only water to drink. The guards took rotating shifts on watch, everyone sleeping with only their pack for a pillow and their cloaks for blankets. Privacy was nonexistent, and by the third day of walking, Lara was almost frantic to be free of the place.

"Home sweet home," Jor said, and the rest of the group stopped, silently watching while the captain rested both hands against pressure points on the bridge wall. A soft click filled the air, and a door-sized block of stone swung inward on silent hinges, revealing a small chamber with an opening in the floor.

Jor stepped inside and looked down. "Tide's still too high. We'll have to wait a bit."

"I'm taking Lara topside," Aren abruptly stated. "The rest of you wait down here."

No one said anything, Taryn and Jor silently opening the hatch in the ceiling. Aren boosted Lara up, then hauled himself outside. Leaving the hatch open, he walked several dozen paces down the length of the bridge. Lara followed, stopping next to one of the thick steel rings embedded in the rock that the Ithicanians used for their zip lines.

The storm had been short, ending on their second day in the bridge, although another was brewing on the horizon. For now, the sky around Midwatch was clear and sunny, the water below a tranquil blue. The fresh air and open space instantly relieved the oppressive pall the bridge had cast.

"We need to talk, Lara."

Her heart skittered, her veins flooding with trepidation.

"I know you're a spy for your father."

Her stomach hollowed. "I *was* a spy for my father. I am no longer."

"I'm going to need more proof than just your word."

"The proof is that I'm here. With you."

Silence.

When Lara's nerve finally frayed, she asked, "Aren't you going to say something?"

Aren turned to face Midwatch, tension radiating off him. "I suppose one question is obvious: Did you pass any information back to him that I should know about?"

"I've given him nothing." Because she hadn't. Not one single thing. Not with all those damnable pieces of paper still sitting in his desk, waiting for her to destroy them.

He exhaled a long breath. "I suppose that's something."

Something.

The need for him to know the reason behind her actions burned in Lara's chest. "Serin and my other teachers, they lied to me. All my life, they lied about the nature of Ithicana, about the relationship between your kingdom and mine. They painted you as a dark oppressor that used its power over trade to suppress my people. To control them. To starve them. All for the sake of profit. They told me that you killed merchants and sailors for no reason other than that they'd come too close to your shores. Not just killed, but maimed and tortured for sport. That you were a demon."

Aren said nothing, so she continued. "They made me believe

that doing this would save my people. That it was righteous. Now I understand that that's why they kept me locked up in the compound—so I might never learn the truth. And they believed you would keep me similarly contained so that I would have no chance to learn the truth until it was too late."

"And what is the truth?"

What was the truth? Lara had no delusions that she was a good person in the way of someone like Marisol. She'd killed Valcottan warriors brought to her compound for no reason other than it was their lives or hers. Learned countless ways to torture, maim, and kill. She'd stood by while the servants who'd cared for her and her sisters since they were children were murdered in cold blood. Had watched while the man who'd been like a father to her slit his own throat out of misplaced guilt. She'd lied and deceived and manipulated, and nearly doomed an entire nation. *Good*, she was not.

Yet neither did she believe that she was evil. She'd condemned herself to this fate in order to save the lives of her sisters, whom she loved above all things. And once here, she'd followed through with her mission on the belief she was saving her people. Noble motivations, perhaps, except she wasn't entirely certain that they absolved her of guilt. Knowing what would happen to Ithicana, she'd still written instructions on how to destroy it. She'd made that choice. All she could do now was try to atone. "The truth is . . . the truth is that *I* am the villain." But she would play that part no longer.

More silence.

"What are you going to do with me?" she asked.

"I don't know, Lara." With his words, the tension between them ratcheted up. "I've . . . suspected for some time now, but hearing you say it . . . I don't know."

A frantic fear fluttered in her chest. A fear that she'd lost him. That he hated her. That he'd never forgive her.

"I didn't give him anything, Aren." She so desperately wanted to salvage what was left between them. "I haven't done anything."

"Haven't done anything?" He whirled around to face her. "How can you claim that? How can you say you've done *nothing* when, from the moment we were married, you've been plotting to stab me in the back? Everything you've said, everything you've done, everything between us has been a damned lie. A way to manipulate me into trusting you so that you could learn Ithicana's secrets, then use them against us. All while I, like a bloody fool, was trying to win you over."

It was the truth, but it wasn't the sum of it. Because during that time, she'd grown to care about him and his kingdom, to understand their plight, and still she'd chosen to destroy them. Had written every detail she'd learned on those pages, a strategy for invading Aren's homeland and stealing away the bridge his people so desperately needed. It had only been sheer *luck* that one of those pages hadn't made it into her father's hands.

"Did you care at all?" he demanded.

"Yes. More than you know. More than I can explain." She shoved the hair that had blown into her face out of her way, grasping for words to make him understand. "But I didn't think there was another way. I believed the only chance my people had was for me to win them the bridge. My whole life has been dedicated to giving them a better future, no matter the cost to me. Surely you of all people can understand that?"

"It's not the same." His voice was cold. "The better future you envisioned was built on the backs of Ithicanian corpses."

Lara closed her eyes. "Then why didn't you just kill me once you knew? Why did you bring me to Vencia, if you suspected? Why did you risk so much?"

Aren scuffed his boot against the bridge, staring at Midwatch. "I realized that you'd been misled. And if the truth gave us a chance, then it was a risk I was willing to take." He let out a ragged breath. "I followed you that night when you walked up to the palace gates. I pointed an arrow at your back, and I . . . I almost did kill you. If you'd taken one more step, I would've." His hands were shaking, the tremor of movement holding her attention like a vice. "But then you turned around and came back. Back to me."

"I couldn't do it." Lara closed her hands over his, needing to stop them from shaking. "And I won't. Not ever. Not even if he tracks me down and kills me for betraying him."

Aren went very still. "Did he threaten you?"

She swallowed hard. "He told me on the ship to Ithicana that if I failed or if I betrayed him, he'd hunt me down."

"If he thinks—"

A scuffle of sound interrupted him, causing them both to jump. Seconds later, with a muttered oath, Ahnna pulled herself out of the hatch, her face a storm cloud.

Aren stepped in front of Lara, walking toward Ahnna even as his sister closed the distance with rapid strides.

"What the hell were you thinking?" Ahnna snapped. "Going into Maridrina yourself? Have you lost your bloody mind?"

"I've been dozens of times before. What of it?"

"Not as king you haven't. You have a responsibility to our people. Plus, you nearly got caught. What the hell would've happened if you had?"

"Then you'd have your chance at the crown."

"You think that's what I want?" Her eyes went past her brother, landing on Lara. "And there stands the worst of it. Bad enough that *you* went, but you took the daughter of our enemy, the woman who, if all the rumors are true, you've been supplying with all of Ithicana's secrets, back to her homeland?"

"I took my *wife* to her homeland for reasons that are none of your goddamned business."

Ahnna's face took on a ghastly pallor, but she balled her hands into fists, and for a heartbeat, Lara thought she'd strike her brother. Strike her king. But all she said was, "There is no reason good enough. She knows enough to allow Maridrina to bring us to our knees, and you practically delivered her to its king. She could've run straight into the Magpie's arms."

"She didn't."

"But what if she had? This wasn't the plan. You were supposed to—"

"I was supposed to what?" Aren lunged forward, looming over his sister. "Keep her locked up here forever? She's my damned wife, not my prisoner."

"Wife? In name only, from what I hear. And don't think that *everyone* doesn't realize that you're risking your entire kingdom just to get between her legs."

No one spoke. Not Aren or Ahnna. Not the soldiers who'd come topside and were now looking anywhere but at their leaders. And not Lara whose heart felt like it was about to burst from her chest. Because Ahnna's fears were valid. Yet Aren was defending her. Despite knowing she'd come to Ithicana with ill intentions, he was defending her right to a life. Her right to a home. Her right to freedom. And she didn't deserve it. Didn't deserve him.

Before Lara could think through the consequences of what she intended to say, she stepped forward, her boots sliding on the slick surface of the bridge. "Ahnna—"

"Stay out of this." Without looking, the other woman swung an arm to block Lara's path.

The blow caught Lara in the chest and she stumbled back, feet scrabbling.

She was falling.

"Lara!" Aren reached for her, but it was too late.

She screamed, arms flailing as the air rushed past her, but there was nothing to grab. Nothing that would stop the inevitable.

She slammed against the water, the force driving the wind out of her in a rush of bubbles even as she plunged down and down.

Panic raced through her, wild and unchecked, and on its heels came the desperate need to *breathe*. She kicked, thrashing her arms, fighting toward the surface that seemed impossibly far away.

You will not die.

You will not die.

You will not . . . The thought faded and the light of the surface began to dim as she sank into the depths.

Until something grabbed her around the waist.

Lara struggled, reaching blindly for her knife until her face broke the surface and Aren was shouting in her ear, "Breathe, Lara!"

She sucked in a desperate mouthful of air. And another. A wave rolled over her head, and fear filled her anew.

Clawing and grasping, she tried to climb. Tried to get above the water.

Then Aren's face was in front of hers. "Quit fighting me. I've got you, but you need to be still."

It was an impossible request. She was drowning. She was dying.

"I need you to trust me!" His voice was desperate, and somehow it cut through her fear. Brought her back to herself. She quit fighting him.

"Good. Now hold on to me and don't move."

Grasping his shoulders, Lara forced her shaking legs to still. They were not quite beneath the bridge, perhaps two dozen yards from the nearest pier: the narrow one with no access to the bridge. And the shore . . .

"Can we make it?" she asked, spitting out a mouthful of water as another wave splashed her in the face.

"No."

"What do we do?" She twisted, looking up at the bridge. She could hear the soldiers shouting, see Jor hanging off the side from a rope, his finger pointing at the water.

"Quit moving, Lara!"

She froze. Because in that moment, she saw what Jor was pointing at. What had Aren's attention—and his fear.

Grey fins cut through the water.

Circling them.

Moving closer.

"We have to last until they can reach us in a boat."

Her eyes jerked to the distant pier, the opening still concealed by the tide. Then to the cove where two boats had been launched. There was no way they'd make it in time.

As if to punctuate her thought, one of the sharks darted toward them before veering off at the last second.

"Shit," Aren snarled.

The creatures were swimming closer, and Lara sobbed as something smacked against her foot.

The soldiers above began firing arrows, the bolts slicing into the water all around them, blood blossoming when they struck true. Then, seemingly as one, the fins disappeared.

"Aren!" Ahnna's scream echoed from above, and a second later, an enormous fin was slicing through the waves toward them.

"Let me go." Lara made the decision because she knew he wouldn't. "Without you, I'll drown. But if you let it have me, you'll have a chance."

"No."

"Don't be a fool. We don't both have to die."

"Quiet."

Aren's eyes were fixed on the circling shark. "I know you, old girl," he muttered at it before glancing up. "You'll come in for a taste before you come from below for the kill."

"Let me go!"

"No."

Lara shoved away from him, tried to swim, but Aren dragged her back, kicking hard. Pulling her with him.

The shark darted toward them. So fast. Too fast to dodge. Infinitely too fast to out-swim. Fear, primal and base, took hold of her, and Lara screamed.

"Now!"

A steel bolt attached to a cable sliced through the air from above, exploding through the shark's side, but the creature kept coming as though the instinct to hunt mattered more than the wound it had been dealt.

Lara screamed again, choking on water, watching it drive toward them, mouth opening to reveal row after row of razor-sharp teeth.

The cable attached to the bolt went taunt.

In one violent motion, the shark was ripped out of the water, its enormous body thrashing through the air before it slammed down against the sea, fighting against the cable leashing it to the bridge.

Water surged over Lara's head, and the shark's tail slammed against her with the force of a battering ram, tearing her from Aren's grasp.

She floundered, not knowing which way was up. Not knowing where the shark was. Where Aren was. Bubbles raced past her face, obscuring her vision while she kicked and fought. Then hands closed on her wrist, pulling her to the surface.

"Swim!" It wasn't Aren's voice, but those from the soldiers above, Ahnna's voice loudest of all. "All the blood is drawing them in! Swim, goddamned you!"

He dragged her through the water, the waves growing more violent with every surge. And above, the skies grew darker. Lightning flashed in the distance.

Aren stopped swimming.

He treaded water, his breathing ragged with the effort of supporting them both.

Lara saw what he was looking at.

The nearest pier, bristling with metal spikes, the ocean slamming against it with the ferocity of the coming storm.

"You need to . . . grab . . . one of the spikes," he gasped. "Don't let go."

And without waiting for her to respond, he hauled her toward the pier.

The waves caught hold of them with irreversible momentum, launching her and Aren at the stone and steel.

There would be one chance. Only one chance.

Lara sucked in a deep breath, marking the spike she'd reach for. The steel that would be her salvation or her damnation.

Aren twisted at the last minute, taking the impact. Lara fumbled blind, knowing she had only a second.

Her hand closed on the spike even as she felt Aren let her go.

Holding on took all her strength as the water dragged at her legs, her arms shaking with the effort. For a moment, her body hung out of the water, then the waves crashed into her again. She clung to the metal, managing to get her legs over and around it, breathing as the water retreated again.

"Aren!" She searched the water for him, terror filling her heart.

"Here!"

He was dangling from the spike where it was embedded in the rock. But he wouldn't last long.

The water pummeled them again, then above the noise, Lara

heard her name. Looking up, she saw Ahnna dangling from a rope above, another line in her hand. She swung it in Lara's direction. "Grab hold!"

The heavy rope whipped past, and Lara reached for it, nearly losing her grip as she did. Again and again the rope swung past her, but she couldn't reach it.

And Aren was running out of time.

So when the rope swung past once more, Lara lunged, knowing that if she missed, she'd fall in the water and that Aren was past the point where he could help her. But that he'd try anyway.

Her balance wavered, her fingers reaching and grasping and catching hold of the rope.

Lara's legs slipped and she was dangling. Silently thanking Erik for every pull-up he'd forced her to do during training, she hauled herself up, hooking the loop under her armpits.

Swinging hard, she caught hold of the spike and crawled hand over hand toward Aren, barely keeping her grip as the water surged against her, drowning her with every pass.

"Grab on to me," she screamed even as a wave knocked her free from her perch.

She swung and slammed against Aren. Instinct had her wrapping her legs around his waist, her arms protesting as his weight dragged against her. Then he was reaching up and gripping the rope.

The sea hurled against them once more, driving them both against rock, and Lara choked and sobbed, knowing she couldn't hold on any longer. Knowing that one more wave would pull her free.

And it was coming, froth flying toward her. Just before it reached them, the rope jerked and they were rising. Faster and faster. They rotated and swung, Aren pulling himself up so that her legs, still wrapped around him, eased the pressure on her arms.

"Do not let go." Blood trickled down a cut on his temple. "You will not let go."

They bumped against the side of the bridge, and Lara whimpered as she was dragged along the rock, but the pain fled in the face of relief as hands grabbed hold of her clothing, hauling her up, laying her down on the solid surface of the bridge. Gasping, she rolled on her side, puking up endless amounts of seawater until all she had the strength for was resting her forehead against the wet stone.

"Lara." Arms pulled her upright, and she turned only to collapse against Aren's chest, clinging to his neck. He was shaking, yet the feel of him against her was more comfort than the solid land beneath her feet.

No one spoke. There were men and women all around them, she knew, but it was as though she were alone with him, the rain from the coming storm pattering against her cheek.

"Aren?" Ahnna's voice broke the silence, the distant boom of thunder echoing his name. "I didn't mean . . . It was . . ."

Lara felt him stiffen, felt his anger even as he said, his voice cold, "Get back to Southwatch, *Commander*. And if I see your face before War Tides, rest assured that I won't hesitate to fulfill Ithicana's contract with Harendell."

Lara turned in his grip in time to see Ahnna jerk as though she'd been slapped. "Yes, Your Majesty." Without another word, she walked away, her soldiers following on her heels.

Rising on shaking legs, Aren pulled Lara with him. "We need to get back to Midwatch. The storm is coming."

But as her heart thudded inside her chest, Lara knew that he was wrong.

The storm was already here.

PULLING OFF THE boots he'd borrowed at the barracks, Aren slowly stripped his sodden and torn clothing, leaving it in a pile on the floor while he eased across the dark room to the wardrobe to retrieve dry trousers. The shutters rattled against the windows as the wind attacked, the rain drumming furiously against the roof, all of it drowned out by bursts of thunder that shook the house to its foundation. The air was full of the sharp, fresh smell of ozone, blending with the ever-present scent of damp earth and greenery that he associated with home.

Boom. The ground beneath his feet reverberated, the pressure changing as the typhoon descended in full force. This was a beast of a storm—the sort that gave the Tempest Seas their name. With winds so wild and feral they seemed almost sentient, this storm would leave swaths of destruction in its wake, and anyone or anything caught out in the water would be wiped from the face of the earth. Ithicana was built to endure the worst the sea and sky could unleash, and indeed it was only during these tempests that Aren ever truly breathed easy, certain that his kingdom was safe from its enemies.

But not tonight.

Exhaling, he rested a hand against the post of his bed, searching for some sense of equilibrium, but it was a lost cause. Like so many other things.

Lara hadn't said a word since they'd been pulled from the sea. He couldn't blame her. She'd been nearly drowned. Nearly eaten. Nearly pummeled against rock. She hadn't broken down entirely, which should've felt like a small miracle except that he would've preferred that to the emotionless silence.

Face blanched so white her lips were gray, Lara had followed numbly where she'd been led, her arms limp in his grasp as she'd been examined for injuries. No sign of her dry humor or the venomous tongue that he simultaneously loved and loathed. Just . . . nothing.

Closing his eyes, Aren rested his forehead against the bedpost because the other option was to rip it free and smash it against the wall. Fury, unbridled and burning, rushed through his veins. At Ahnna. At the bridge. At himself.

A sound more animal than human rose in his throat, and in a flurry of motion, he twisted and slammed his fist against the wall. Pain blossomed in his knuckles, and he dropped into a crouch, wanting to explode, wanting to run. Knowing none of it would do any good.

Boom. The house shuddered, and his thoughts went to the Rat King's letter, shoved into his bag, wherever that was. The ultimatum was clear: ally with Maridrina against Valcotta or face war and blockades like those Maridrina had imposed fifteen years prior, lifted only with the signing of the treaty.

They had been the darkest of times. Maridrina had kept *anyone* from landing at Southwatch for two years, completely shutting down trade. Nothing was shipped through the bridge, and Ithicana's revenues dried up entirely. Without them, there had been no way to feed his people. To keep them provisioned. To keep them alive. Not with violent storms driving fishermen from the seas more days than not. Famine had swept Ithicana. Plague, too. And the idea of going back to that . . .

The alternative was to join with a man who'd been plotting against him in the worst sort of ways. To join a war he wanted no part of. It was profoundly tempting to formally ally with Valcotta for spite. Ithicana's coffers were strong enough to buy what the kingdom needed for a year or more with no additional revenue from the bridge. Between Southwatch's shipbreakers and the strength of Valcotta's fleets, Silas's armies wouldn't have a chance.

Yet such an action would place all the suffering on Maridrina's people. *Lara's* people.

Condemning them to starvation would make him the villain the Magpie had painted. Aren would become the man Lara had been raised to hate. But to cede to her father's request would mean jeopardizing Ithicana when Valcotta came for retribution. There was no solution.

His father's voice danced through Aren's head, words shouted at his mother. *Ithicana makes no alliances. We are neutral—we have to be, or war will come for us.* But like his mother before him, Aren now believed the time for neutrality had come to an end. Except there was a difference between desiring an alliance and allowing its terms to be dictated by another man.

Aren wavered, then in two strides, he was at his desk. Flipping open the hidden compartment, Aren extracted the letter he'd started to Silas those months ago. Staring at the polite greeting and appropriate honorifics, he shoved the page aside, reaching for a clean sheet.

Silas,

Ithicana will not cease trade with Valcotta. Should you wish to see an end to their naval aggression, I suggest you desist in your attacks on Valcotta's northern border. Only with peace between your two nations does Maridrina have the chance to return to health and prosperity. As to your insinuation that Ithicana has not held to the spirit of the agreement between our nations, we feel it necessary to point out your hypocrisy in making such a claim. In the best interests of both our peoples, we will forgive your schemes and allow Maridrina to continue to trade at Southwatch market under the terms agreed upon. Let it be said, however, that should you seek to retaliate against your spy, Ithicana will take it as an act of aggression against its queen, and the alliance between our kingdoms will be irrevocably severed.

Choose wisely.

Aren

He stared at the letter, knowing he could never tell Lara what he had written. Her life had been dedicated to easing the plight of her people, and she wouldn't forgive him threatening those very same people for the sake of protecting her. Yet there could be no other way to ensure Silas wouldn't harm her. God help him if he was forced to follow through.

Rising, Aren stepped out into the hallway, walking until he found Eli.

"Bring this to the barracks when the storm eases. Tell Jor it's to be sent immediately to the King of Maridrina."

Retreating to his rooms, Aren opened the door to the courtyard. And stepped out into the storm.

L ARA LANDED WITH a thump on her knees, knife gripped in one
hand. Darkness surrounded her. Thunder rumbled through
the room, followed by two flashes of lightning that faintly
illuminated the outline of a window. The wood floor beneath her was
polished smooth, and the air was thick with moisture and the earthy
scent of jungle.

Hot tears ran down her face, and she scrubbed them off her cheeks.
The moment she'd returned to Midwatch, she intended to find her way
into Aren's room to destroy the damnable proof of her betrayal before
it could go any further. To do it without him knowing because she
could never let him read those words.

It was one thing for him to know that she'd lied to him. Manipulated
him. Deceived him. Quite another to read the proof of it. For him
to see every moment that he'd believed a connection was growing
between the two of them had been a strategy to gain the information
she needed. That, after all they'd been through, she had still made the
choice to destroy him that fateful night he'd kissed her in the mud.

Not only was it unforgivable, the amount of hurt it would cause him to read it . . . She couldn't let that happen. Not when simply destroying the pages would eliminate all the evidence. Her plan had been to lightly drug Aren at dinner, then to sneak into his room and start a small fire on his desk that could easily be blamed on a candle left too close to a piece of paper. She could then claim to have smelled the smoke, her screams and pounding on the door enough to wake him and alert the staff. Between the flames and the water it would take to douse them, all the stationery bearing her invisible message would be ruined beyond use. It was a dangerous, damaging plan, but she'd rather chance burning the Midwatch house to the ground than risk Aren questioning why all of his stationery had mysteriously gone missing.

But while Lara had waited for the dinner hour, exhaustion had taken over, and she'd fallen asleep on the clean soft sheets of her bed. Now the scents of dinner were wafting under the door, and she wasn't the least bit prepared.

"You can fix this," she muttered, climbing to her feet. Pulling on one of her silken Maridrinian dresses and running a brush through her hair, Lara's mind raced as she shoved a vial of narcotic into her bracelet. Out in the hallway, she hurried toward the shuttered dining room, certain she'd find Aren there. He was not one to neglect his stomach.

But there was only Eli, who started at the sight of her. "We thought you'd want dinner in your room, my lady," he said. "Do you wish to eat in here instead?"

"Thank you, but I'm not hungry. Do you know where he is?" There was only one *he* in this house.

"His rooms, my lady. He didn't want dinner."

Logic and her training whispered that she should wait for another night. Another opportunity. Better to do that than risk being caught. Yet Lara found herself instead hurrying down the opposite hall to Aren's room, her bare feet silent on the cool floor.

She knocked, then waited. No answer.

She tried the handle and, for once, found it unlocked. "Aren?"

Aren was nowhere in sight. *This was her chance. She could pretend she found the fire burning.*

Securing the door, Lara bolted to the heavy desk, immediately spying the open stationery box. And the beginnings of a letter composed to her father.

Her heart in her throat, Lara stared at the few lines of dried ink addressed to her father. How Aren could stomach being so polite to his enemy was beyond her. Though perhaps that he couldn't stomach it was the reason the letter wasn't finished.

A purr caught her attention, and she looked down as Aren's cat began to wind his huge body between her legs, nearly knocking her over. An idea, one better and far less damaging than a fire, jumped into her head. "Sorry for this Vitex. But I need your help."

She staged the scene, placing the box on its side on the floor, then splattering the letter with ink, leaving the well overturned on the rest of the pages so they were soaked through and unusable. But not before counting the stack. Twenty-five blank pages plus the unfinished letter made for twenty-six.

Luring Vitex over, she scratched his ears, gently taking hold of one of his paws and using it to make distinctive prints through the ink. Realizing what she was doing, the cat hissed at her and pulled away, leaving a trail across the room as he went.

Every muscle in her body twitched, and with a ragged gasp, Lara sank to her knees, staring at what had been the culmination of all her efforts. Of all her training. Of her life. Remembering the way she'd felt the last time she held those pages, knowing that the damning words she'd written would save her people. How wrong she'd been.

Yet with them gone so went the weight she'd been carrying since she'd learned the truth of her father's deception. What she'd done before . . . It had been awful. The worst sort of betrayal. But it had been motivated by lies that had filled her ears almost her entire life. Whereas turning on her father now was an act driven by the truth. What she was doing now was her own choice.

And though Lara knew that she'd painted a target on her back, that her father's assassins would never stop hunting her, for the first time in her life, she felt free.

Driven by some strange sixth sense, she drifted into the antechamber and opened the door to the courtyard, the wind buffeting her with the force of a giant. Stepping outside, she found herself in a hell of wind and rain.

The air shrieked as it circled the courtyard, carrying leaves and branches and rain that bit into her bare arms and slapped her cheeks. The tempest was deafening in its fury, multipronged bolts lancing across the sky, the thunder battering her eardrums.

In the midst of it stood Aren.

He was shirtless and barefoot, staring up at the sky, seemingly heedless of the tempest circling around him. Or of the danger he was in.

A branch ripped from one of the trees to hurtle across the yard, exploding against the side of the house. "Aren!" But the storm drowned out her voice.

It was impossible to keep her feet as she struggled down the path, knocked over time and again by gusts of wind that threatened to lift her into the air. Her hair whipped in a wild frenzy, blinding her, but not for a heartbeat did she consider turning back. Regaining her feet on the slick stones, she lunged.

The winds died as her hands closed on Aren's arms, as though the world itself gave a sigh and relaxed, the debris falling softly to the ground and the rain easing into a gentle patter against her skin.

"Lara?"

Releasing a ragged breath, she tilted her face up to find Aren staring down at her, his expression bewildered, as though he couldn't comprehend how she'd come to be standing before him.

"Is it over?" she asked, finding it difficult to breathe. And even more difficult to think. "The storm?"

"No. We're in the eye of it now."

The eye of the storm. Her chest tightened. "What are you doing out here?"

The hard muscles of his forearms flexed beneath her grip. "I needed it."

Instinctively, she understood what he meant. Most people sought solace from danger, but for him, the danger was solace. The rush of adrenaline that cleared his mind, that wiped away the uncertainty that plagued every decision he made as king. The fear of erring. The consequences of doing so. In the storm, he knew his path.

She understood, because she felt the same way. "You could've died today. Doing what you did."

"You would've died if I hadn't."

His hands closed around her arms, and though his palms were feverishly hot, Lara shivered. "You might have been better off if I had."

His grip tightened. "Do you honestly believe that I could have ever forgiven myself if I'd stood there and watched you drown?"

"But what I did—"

"Is in the past. It's behind us now."

Her pulse was a dull roar in her ears as his words sank in. Aren had forgiven her. How he'd found it in his heart to do so, she couldn't understand, but there it was. What she'd wanted more than anything, but hadn't had the hope to wish for.

"Do you want to leave Ithicana? Because if that's what it takes for you to be happy, I'll set you on any shore you wish with everything you need to make a life for yourself."

Lara had planned to leave. Her father's assassins would soon been on her heels, and she hadn't believed there was anything to be gained by staying. A relationship between the two of them would never have a chance—Aren would inevitably discover the truth about her and would never forgive her for it.

But Aren knew the truth. And against all odds, he had forgiven her. Now . . . now the thought of turning her back on this place, of turning her back on *him*, was the worst future she could imagine.

"You can't let me leave Ithicana." Her throat felt tight, and the words came out breathy and strange. "I know too much. You'd be risking too much."

His eyes burned into hers, and never in her life had she felt like someone else saw her so perfectly. "I can let you go, because I trust you."

She couldn't breathe.

"I don't want to leave." The words were a truth dug from the depths of her heart. She did not want to leave Ithicana. She did not want to leave *him*. She wanted to stay, to fight and sweat and bleed for him and his harsh, wild, and beautiful kingdom.

The storm circled, watching but leaving them untouched for this one moment.

Aren's hands loosened on her arms, and for one terrifying heartbeat, she thought he'd let her go. That he wanted her to go.

Instead his fingers traced up the backs of her arms, the light touch leaving rivers of sensation in their wake. Gentle strokes up and down, as though he were calming some wild thing that was apt to bite.

Or testing the waters.

His hands grazed the sides of her breasts, and Lara exhaled a soft breath as his thumbs hooked on the straps of her dress, easing them down as he bent, his lips brushing one naked shoulder. Then the other.

A whimper escaped her as Aren pulled her damp hair away, exposing her neck and kissing her collarbone, her throat, the line of her jaw. Only his grip on her dress kept it from falling away and leaving her naked before him.

Lara wanted to touch him.

Wanted to feel his sleek skin stretched over hard muscles, but she was afraid, because she knew to do so would be her undoing. There would be no turning back.

Aren's lips paused, and she held her breath, waiting for them to descend on her own even as she wondered whether, if she allowed herself to sink into this hot pool of desire, she'd ever surface again. Whether she'd want to.

But he only rested his forehead against hers. "I need you to say that you want this, Lara. That you're allowing this because you choose to, not because it was forced upon you."

Her chest burned, and emotion so intense it hurt surged through her. She pulled back so their eyes locked. "I want this." And because that wasn't the sum of it, she added, "I want you."

The storm returned with a vengeance as their lips collided, but Lara barely felt the winds as Aren lifted her against him, his hands gripping her hips as she wrapped her legs around his waist, her arms sliding around his neck. His mouth was hot, his tongue slick against hers, the rain drenching their skin as he carried her through the tempest and into the shelter of the house.

Inside, his feet slid on the wet tile and they slammed against the wall, knocking what remained on the shelves to the floor. He braced himself, his hands to either side of her, his breath hot against her throat as Lara ground against him. Her heels dug into his back as she pulled him closer, wanting nothing between them, even as the friction of his belt against her dragged a moan from her lips.

Her back arched until only her head touched the wall behind her, and her dress, the skirt already bunched around her waist, was pulled down to expose the top of her breasts. She felt Aren's breath catch.

"God, you're beautiful," he growled. "Insufferable and venom-tongued and the most incredible woman I've set eyes on."

His words made her thighs slick and she gasped. "Door. Shut the damned door."

"Yes, Your Majesty." He slipped his tongue into her mouth, tasting her, before allowing her to slide to the ground, the hardness of him pressing against her stomach before he turned to wrench on the door and shut out the storm.

The heavy bolt in place, Aren stalked toward her, his hazel eyes predatory, ever the hunter. Lara stepped backward into the bedroom, daring him to follow. Luring him in because she was not, and never would be, anyone's prey. Her calves hit the solid wood of his bed, and she stared him down, stopping him in his tracks.

The howl of the wind was muffled now, and over it, she could hear him breathing. Each inhale and exhale ratcheted up her need as her eyes roved over his body, marking the way the muscles in his jaw flexed as he watched her with equal focus.

Reaching blindly for the lantern, Lara turned the flame up high, then set it to one side, her eyes never leaving his. Clasping hold of the sodden bodice of her dress, the neckline clinging to her peaked nipples, she slowly peeled the silk from her body, discarding the garment on the floor. Then she lay back on the bed, resting her weight on her elbows. With deliberate slowness, Lara allowed her knees to fall open.

She watched his control snap, watched as he held his ground only because of the strength of her stare, his desire apparent against the rain-soaked trousers that were all he wore. "Take them off," she commanded, his low laugh making her skin prickle with the need to have his hands on her once more.

He unbuckled his belt, then hooked his thumbs over it and pushed, the weight of the knife fastened to it dragging his trousers to the floor, where he kicked them aside. This time it was Lara's turn to catch her breath as she took in the hard length of him, for while she'd seen him naked before, it had never been like *this*. Her thighs trembled beneath the floodgate of her *need* to have him, and she nodded once.

In three strides, he was across the room, but rather than pinning her to the bed, as she'd thought he would, he fell to his knees before her. Ithicana—and its king—bent to nothing and no one. But he bent for her.

Aren kissed the inside of her left knee. Then her right knee, lingering on an old scar that ran halfway up her inner thigh. His hands, rough with callouses earned defending his kingdom, caught hold of her legs. And with her quivering beneath his grip, he lowered his face and slid his tongue inside of her.

Her hips bucked, but he held her against the bed, licking and sucking at the apex of her thighs until a moan tore from her lips. She fell back against the sheet, hands reaching for him, pulling at him, but he only lifted his head long enough to give her a feral smirk before sliding his fingers into the spot his tongue had just vacated.

Lara's back bowed and she grabbed at the edge of the bed, the world tilting as he caressed the inside of her, his mouth consuming her again, the pressure building deep in her core. Lightning flashed as his teeth grazed her and the world shattered, her vision fracturing as waves of pleasure washed over her until she was left gasping and trembling.

Aren didn't move for a long moment, then with tenderness that broke her heart, he kissed her stomach before resting his cheek against it, her fingers tangling in his hair.

But she wasn't done with him. Nor he with her.

He climbed over her with the grace of a panther on the hunt. Catching hold of her hands, he pinned her arms over her head, his knuckles digging into the mattress. For a heartbeat, she resisted, pushing against his far superior strength. And then her body yielded. Not to him, but to herself. To what she wanted. Her life had been spent as an unwitting pawn in her father's machinations, but no longer. Every victory or mistake, every tender touch or fit of violence . . . They would be hers now. She would own them. She would own this moment.

Lifting her head, she kissed him and felt him shudder as she locked her legs around his waist, drawing him down so their bodies pressed together. The kiss deepened, all tongues and teeth, heavy breaths more felt than heard over the rumble of thunder.

The tip of him brushed against her, and Lara moaned into his mouth, her body knowing what it wanted, desperate for him to fill her. She ground her hips against him, gasping as his cock teased inside of her before pulling away.

"Not everything will be on your terms, love," he growled into her ear. "I will not be rushed."

"You are a demon after all," she whispered, but her ability to speak vanished as he released his grip on her wrists and his face lowered to her breast, mouth sucking and teasing her nipple, his hand back between her legs. Her own hands drifted to his shoulders, fingers trailing over the hard curves of his muscles, tracing the lines of old scars and new, then down his spine, relishing the way he shivered beneath her touch.

But it wasn't enough. She bit at his neck, wanting him closer, wanting their bodies and souls to merge, never again to part.

"Aren. *Please*."

He reared back, taking her with him. On his knees, he held her against him, eyes locked on hers as he slowly lowered her onto his length. Head falling back, Lara shrieked into the storm, clawing at his shoulders as he sank into her and then stilled.

"Look at me."

She did, pressing her cheek against his hand as he reached up to cup the side of her head. "I love you," he said, his lips grazing against hers. "And I *will* love you, no matter what the future brings. No matter how hard I need to fight. I will always love you."

The words undid her, broke her apart completely, then forged her into something new. Something stronger. Something better. She kissed him, long and hard and deep, their bodies rocking together.

Lowering her back to the sheets, he pulled out, then thrust back in with torturous slowness. Then again. And again. With each pounding stroke, their bodies grew slick with sweat. She gripped his hand, her other hand dragging through his hair, down his back, needing to possess every inch of him as her own body tightened, burning, burning toward release.

She would fight for him.

She would bleed for him.

She would die for him.

Because he was her king, and even if it meant assassins hunting her for the rest of her days, she would damned well be Ithicana's queen.

Release washed over her, violent as the tempest battering her kingdom, and she felt her body's pleasure pull Aren over the edge. He buried himself to the hilt, howling her name as the room shuddered beneath the onslaught of the storm, then collapsed, his breath ragged pants in her ear.

They barely moved for what seemed hours. Lara curled into the warmth of his arms, her mind drifting as he stroked her naked back, as he covered her with a sheet when the sweat on their bodies began to cool. It was only when his breathing turned to the soft measure of slumber that she lifted her head.

Brushing the hair back from his forehead, she gently kissed him. And because she needed to say it, but wasn't ready for him to hear, she whispered, "I love you."

With her head resting against his chest and his heartbeat in her ear, she finally allowed sleep to take her.

THE TYPHOON RAGED for four days, most of which Lara and Aren spent in bed. Very little of it did they spend sleeping.

Moments outside the bedroom were spent playing cards and peculiar Ithicanian board games, for which Aren was a terrible cheater. Hours of her reading aloud while his head rested in her lap, his eyes distant as he listened, his fingers interlocked with hers. He told stories of his childhood in Ithicana, which mostly seemed to involve avoiding his tutors in favor of running amok through the jungle until Jor chased him down. He told her about the first time he, Taryn, and Lia had raced for their lives on Snake Island, taking turns while their friends watched from boats on the water.

"What about Ahnna?"

Aren snorted. "She isn't stupid enough for such stunts."

There was an edge to his voice that caused Lara to set her glass of juice down on the table with a loud clink. "You need to apologize to your sister for what you said. It was uncalled for."

Aren turned away, shoving a book back on the shelf and draining his own drink. "She almost got you killed."

"It was an accident. And lest you weren't paying attention, she was also the one to save both our asses."

"Noted."

"Aren."

He refilled his drink. "I've said worse to her, and she to me. She'll get over it."

Lara chewed the insides of her cheeks, understanding that it was not reluctance to apologize, but rather the knowledge that he'd be asked to justify his actions as pertained to *her*. "There is a substantial difference between cruel words exchanged between siblings and threats uttered by a king to the commander of his armies."

He gave her a belabored sigh. "Fine, fine. I'll apologize when I see her next."

"Which will be when?"

"God, but you are persistent."

Lara gave him her sweetest smile.

"The council meeting before the beginning of War Tides when we discuss our strategy. Ahnna represents Southwatch, so she has to be there."

Her mouth opened to ask *where* precisely the meeting would take place, but then she shut it again. These past days Lara had been careful not to pry into any details a spy might be interested in, cautious of giving Aren any reason to doubt her loyalty. Part of her wondered if that would ever change, or if her past would always tarnish their relationship.

"Why don't you ever talk about your sisters?"

Her sisters. Lara closed her eyes, fighting the unexpected burn of tears. It was a conscious effort on her part to think of them as little as possible. In part, it was to avoid the pain in her chest that came with remembrance, the gut-wrenching sense of loss that came every time she realized that she'd likely never see them again. The other part was her fear that if she kept them too close to mind, she might accidentally reveal they were still alive, and that information might get back to her father. And for their sakes, she couldn't even trust Aren with the truth, for if he ever found cause to turn on her, he might do so by turning on them. "They're dead."

The glass slipped from his hand to smash against the floor. "You aren't serious?"

Lara dropped to her knees to pick up the fragments. "Everyone who knew about my father's plot was killed, with the exception of Serin."

"All of them? Are you sure?"

"I left them facedown on the dinner table, surrounded by flames." She remembered the feel of Marylyn's golden blond hair beneath her fingers as she had moved her sister's head out of the soup bowl. The way she, her father, and all of their party had ridden away from the compound, her sisters abandoned to luck and their own wits. A bit of glass pricked her finger and she hissed, sucking the blood from the wound before returning to the task.

Aren's hands closed over hers. "Leave it, love. Someone else will clean it up."

"I don't want Eli doing it." She picked up another fragment of glass. "He tries to do everything too quickly, and he's sure to cut himself."

"Then I'll do it myself."

The shards of glass fell from her hands, and she watched how the bits of amber liquid on them caught the light. There was still so much she hadn't told him.

"My childhood was ugly. They tried to turn us into monsters. It might be that they succeeded."

The only sound was the rain outside.

"That day of the attack on Serrith Island . . . There were a dozen or so dead Amaridians on the path leading up from the cove."

"I killed them, if that's what you're asking."

"All of them?"

"Yes. You were outnumbered, and your death wasn't . . . It wasn't part of my plan."

He exhaled a long breath, then repeated, "Wasn't part of your plan."

Though Aren knew the truth and had forgiven her for it, part of Lara still feared that he'd change his mind. That these past few days were nothing but a trick: a way to show her what might have been if she'd come to this marriage without betrayal in her heart.

He drew Lara to her feet. "No one can know. About any of it. Too many of my people were against this union to begin with. If they learned you were a spy—and a trained assassin—sent to infiltrate our defenses, they'd never forgive it. They'd demand your execution, and if I didn't agree to it . . ."

Lara felt the blood drain from her face. Not because of the threat to her life, but because of the threat to his. "Is it better for you if I go? We can fake my death, and all the troubles my being here present will be solved."

Aren didn't respond, and when she finally found the nerve to lift her head, it was to find him staring off into the distance, eyes unfocused. Then he shook his head sharply. "I swore a vow to you, and I intend to keep it."

Lara's chest tightened. "My father will send assassins for me. Anyone close to me will be in danger."

"Not if they don't know where you are."

"They know I'm at Midwatch, Aren. And it's not as impenetrable as you seem to think. My father won't let my betrayal go easily."

"I'm aware of Midwatch's limitations, which is why we won't be staying here." He pulled her into his arms. "And your father *will* let it go if he believes the cost of revenge more than he wishes to pay."

Revenge was worth any price to her father. "Let me go back to Maridrina. Let me kill him and end this."

"I'm not using you to murder my enemies."

"He's my enemy, too. And the enemy of the Maridrinian people."

"I don't disagree." Aren's hand moved up and down her spine. "But assassinating your father will accomplish the exact opposite of what we're working toward. Even if Serin can't prove it was Ithicana, he'll cast the blame at our feet, and it won't be long until the Maridrinian people forget Silas the tyrant and start demanding vengeance for Silas the martyr. Your eldest brother is cut from the same cloth as your father, and I don't intend to hand him an army set on Ithicanian blood.

"If they attacked," he continued, "we could likely convince

Valcotta to ally with us and crush them, but it would be *your* people who suffered. And at the end of it, we'd be back to the same place as we were fifteen years ago, our peoples hating each other."

"So we do nothing, then?" Everything he said was true, but Lara couldn't keep the bitterness from her voice.

"We watch. We prepare. But . . ." He shrugged one shoulder. "Any action we might take at this point would cause more harm than good."

"With Valcotta attacking Maridrinian merchants attempting to land at Southwatch, my homeland will continue to go hungry."

"It would all resolve if your father would give up the war with Valcotta. Let farmers return to their fields and tradesmen to their trades."

But he wouldn't. Lara knew that for certain because her father would never concede defeat.

"As it is, storm season will help by chasing the Valcottan's back to their harbors. Vencia's harbor is the closest of any to Southwatch, and your people will capitalize on the short breaks in the storms. Impossible as it is to believe, the storm season is better for your countrymen than the calm. Food *will* arrive on Maridrina's shores."

Aren wouldn't lie to her—Lara believed that. She trusted him. Even if it killed her to do nothing.

He was quiet for a long time, then he said, "But there are two sides to this, Lara. Very few Ithicanians have ever left our shores. Very few of them have ever met a Maridrinian. The result is that they believe your father is the sum of your people. I need you to help me change that. I need you to make them see that Maridrinians are not our enemies. To make them want more than just an alliance of paper and words between kings, but an alliance between our people. Because that's the only way we'll ever find peace."

"I don't see how that can happen while he lives."

"He won't live forever."

Lara exhaled a long breath. "But my brother, as you say, is just like him. He'll take advantage of the utopia you envision."

"I don't envision a utopia, Lara. Just something better." He kissed her shoulder, his lips warm. "It's past time we stopped allowing our enemies to dictate our lives and start living them for those we love.

And for ourselves."

"A dream."

"Then make it reality." Reaching into his trouser pockets, he extracted a small silken pouch. "I have something for you."

Lara's head turned, her eyes widening as he extracted the delicate links of gold, emeralds and black diamonds flashing in the light. "You mentioned a fondness for green."

Carefully, he brushed her hair to one side and fastened the necklace around her neck. "It was my mother's. My father had it made for her years ago, and she almost never took it off. The servants found it in their rooms after—" He broke off, shaking his head to clear the emotion. "She always said it was meant to be worn."

Lara trailed one finger down the gold and jewels, then pulled it away, her hand balling into a fist. "I can't take this. Ahnna should have it."

"Ahnna hates jewelry. And besides, you're Queen of Ithicana. You're the one who should wear it."

Taking her hands in his, Aren turned her toward the large mirror on the wall and pressed the fingers of her hand against the large black diamond resting at the center of her collarbone, her pulse throbbing beneath. "Northwatch." Then he moved down the necklace, naming the larger islands as he went.

"Serrith." He paused there, kissing her shoulder, grazing his teeth against her neck, feeling her body hitch, then press against him, her head falling back against his shoulder. "Midwatch." Their fingers trailed over the slope of her right breast, pausing on a large emerald. He made a humming noise of consideration, then continued down the jeweled map, stopping at Southwatch, the emerald nestled in her cleavage.

"It's yours," he murmured into her ear. "Ithicana. Everything that I have is yours. To protect. To make better."

"I will," she whispered. "I promise." Turning, Lara rested her forehead against his chest, focusing on the feel of his hands. On the sound of his heart.

Then he went still. "Listen."

"I don't hear anything."

292

"Exactly. The storm has passed. Which means it will have ended south of here, so the Vencia ferrymen will already be on the water heading to Southwatch."

So strange that she had to put her faith in the Tempest Seas, which she feared more than anything else, to protect both her peoples. Slowly, the tension seeped out of her. "Since it's safe to go outside, I find myself fancying a proper bath."

"Your wish is my command, Your Majesty," he growled into her ear, flipping her over his shoulder and heading to the door. In the hallway, they encountered Eli, who bore a stuffed satchel on one shoulder.

"I'm doing a run to the barracks, Your Graces. Any messages you wish to relay?"

Aren hesitated. "Yes. Tell Jor I want to see him. *After* lunch." He patted Lara meaningfully on the ass, laughing when she kneed him in the chest. "But for now, I need a bath."

Several hours later, they were finishing a meal of grilled fish and citrus sauce when the door to the house slammed open.

Heedless of his mud-splattered boots, Jor tromped into the dining room and took a seat across from them. "Majesties." His twinkling eyes moved back and forth between Lara and Aren as he snaked a cake from the tray. "How nice to see the two of you finally playing nice."

Lara's cheeks warmed, and she took a mouthful of fruit juice, hoping the glass would hide her embarrassment.

"And all it took to earn your affection was the poor boy jumping into shark-infested waters to save your ass." He sighed dramatically. "I'm not sure I'm up for such acts of heroism. I suppose I'll have to put aside the dream of taking you on when Aren gets himself killed with one of his stupid stunts."

"Piss off, Jor."

Lara only smiled. "Fortunately for you, I have a soft spot for elderly men."

"Elderly?" Bits of cake flew from the guard's mouth. "I'll have you know, little miss, that I'm . . ."

"Enough, enough." Aren filled the cup in front of Jor. "That's not why you're here."

"Yes, do tell me why I had to drag my *elderly* ass up the hill to visit you two lovebirds."

Lara turned in her chair to eye Aren, curious.

"How do the skies look?" he asked.

"Stick your head out the door and see for yourself."

"Jor."

"Clear." The guard chewed slowly on another cake, brow furrowed with suspicion. "Why?"

Aren's hand closed over Lara's, his thumb tracing a circle against her palm. "Tell everyone to pack their things and ready the boats. I think it's time we went home."

H OME.
To Lara, Midwatch was home, with its quiet serenity.
But there was no mistaking the excitement on the faces of
the guards as they tied their packs and loads of provision into a trio
of boats, nearly tripping over each other in their haste. Wherever
they were going was home for them, too, and the flurry of activity
only bolstered Lara's curiosity. There were no civilizations of size in
Ithicana, nothing bigger than a fishing village, and the Maridrinian in
her struggled to believe that the King of the Bridge Kingdom would
call one of those home.

"Where are we going?" she asked Aren for the hundredth time.

He only gave her an amused smile and tossed her bag of
possessions into the canoe. "You'll see."

She'd barely been allowed to take anything, only a set of her
Ithicanian clothes, a selection of undergarments, and, at Aren's
request, one of her silk Maridrinian dresses, though of what use that
would be in a fishing village, she didn't know.

Nibbling on a fresh piece of root to help keep her stomach calm,

Lara settled into the boat, staying out of the way as they exited the cove. Though the skies were relatively calm, the sea was full of branches and debris, and through the mist draping Midwatch, Lara noted the jungle had been severely damaged by the storm, trees felled and plants stripped of flowers and leaves.

The boats passed under the bridge, the island fading from sight, and Lara turned her gaze ahead as the sail was lifted, the brisk winds whisking them across the surf. They veered west, away from the snaking bridge, passing innumerable tiny landmasses, all which appeared uninhabited, although well she knew that in Ithicana, appearances could be deceiving.

They sailed for an hour when, rounding a smaller island, Lara's eyes fell upon a veritable mountain rising out of the ocean. *Not a mountain,* she silently corrected herself. *A volcano.* The island itself was several times the size of Midwatch, the slopes of the volcano, which reached up to the sky, thick with verdant jungle. Azure waters slammed against cliff walls fifty feet high, with no signs of a beach or a cove. Impenetrable and, if the smoke rising from the peak was any indication, a dangerous place to inhabit.

Yet as they curved around the monolith, Jor lowered a sail, easing their speed even as Lia rose to her feet, hand balanced against Taryn's shoulder as she scanned their surroundings. "No sails on the horizon," she declared, and Aren nodded. "Run up the flag then."

The bright green flag bisected by a curved black line was unfurled and raised to the top of the mast, the wind catching at it with an eagerness that was reflected on the faces of all the Ithicanians. They drew closer to the island and, shading her eyes with her hand against the glare off the water, Lara picked out a dark opening in the otherwise solid cliff walls.

The entrance to the sea cave grew as the boats approached, barely enough clearance for the masts as they drifted inward, the darkness obscuring whatever lay within.

Lara's heart thundered in her chest, realizing that she was witnessing something that no other outsider had seen. A place that was wholly the domain of Ithicana. A secret greater, perhaps, than even those of its precious bridge.

A deafening rattle made Lara jump. Aren's hand rested against her back to steady her as everyone's eyes adjusted to the dimness. Blinking, she watched in awe as a steel portcullis covered with seaweed and barnacles lifted into a narrow gap in the rock of the ceiling and the three boats were gently washed into a tunnel that bent to the right. Gripping the sides of the boat, Lara held her breath as Taryn and Lia rowed them inward, the tunnel opening into an enormous cavern. Sunlight filtered down through small openings in the ceiling to dance across the smooth water, and the floor of the cave seemed within arm's reach, though Lara suspected it was far deeper.

Moored to the walls were dozens of boats, including the large ones she'd seen evacuating the village on Serrith Island. Half-dressed children swam among them, their shrieks of laughter audible as the rattle of the portcullis descending behind them faded away. There were shouts of recognition as the children caught sight of Aren and his guards, and the lot of them fell in like a school of fish around the boats. Jor laughed, pretending to swat at them with a paddle as they made their way to the far end of the cavern where steps carved into the dark rock led upward.

The children's voices filling her ears, Lara allowed Aren to help her out of the boat, her legs unsteady beneath her. *What was this place?*

Her sweating hand resting on Aren's arm, Lara walked up the stairs toward the sunlit opening, her heart pounding in her chest. Together, they stepped out, and a gust of briny wind caught at Lara's hair, tearing it loose from its braid. The brightness bit at her eyes, and she blinked, half to clear the tears and half because she couldn't believe what she was seeing.

It was a city.

Covering the steep slopes of the volcano crater, the city's streets and houses and gardens all wove seamlessly into the natural vegetation, all of it reflected in an emerald lake which pooled in the basin. Releasing Aren's arm, Lara turned in a circle, struggling to take in the magnitude of this place that shouldn't, that couldn't, possibly exist.

Men and women dressed in tunics and trousers went about their business, and countless children ran amok, likely enjoying the respite from poor weather. There were hundreds of people, and she had no doubt that many more could be found within the structures that were built into the slope, made from the same solid material as the bridge. Trees and vines wrapped around the homes, their roots digging deep into the earth, the greys and greens broken by countless blooms every color of the rainbow. Metal chimes hung from tree branches, and with every breath of wind, their delicate music filled the air.

Every bit a king surveying his kingdom, Aren said, "Welcome to Eranahl."

I T WAS THE worst storm season Aren had ever seen.

Typhoon after typhoon lashed Ithicana, sea and wind and rain battering the fortress that was Eranahl, keeping it even more isolated than normal. The city was forced to dig into its supplies, and it would be a mad dash to restock the vaults before War Tides descended and the city's population tripled, those living on the islands close to the bridge coming to take shelter from the inevitable raiders. They'd bring supplies with them, but with months of only limited clear days to fish and gather, they'd be running lean themselves.

Which meant the bridge would need to provide.

Yet it had been painfully easy not to think about the looming dangers in the intervening months since he'd brought Lara home to Eranahl. Easy to sit around the table with his friends, drinking and eating, laughing and telling stories into the darkness of the night. Easy to lose himself in a book without the anticipation of horns calling warnings of raiders. Easy to sleep late in the morning, his arms wrapped around his wife's slender form. To wake and worship the curves of her body, the taste of her mouth, the feel of her hands on his back, in his hair, on his cock.

There were days it felt like Lara had been with him all his life, for she had wholly immersed herself in every aspect of his being. In every aspect of Eranahl. He'd feared that she'd struggle to integrate herself with his people and them with her. But within a month, she'd learned the name of every citizen and how each of them was related, and Aren often found her working with the people, helping them when they were sick and injured. Most of Lara's time was spent with the youth of Ithicana, partially because they held fewer of the biases against Maridrinians than their parents and grandparents and partially, he thought, because it gave her a sense of purpose. She started a school, for while her asshole of a father might have treated her poorly, he hadn't scrimped on her education, and her efforts to share that knowledge won her more hearts than even her heroics at Aela Island.

Lara made his friends hers, going toe to toe with Jor over who could tell the worst jokes, drinking and eating and laughing as she delved into their lives, her hand tucked in Aren's as they waited out storm after storm. Never did she reveal more than cursory details about her own life, but if anyone noticed, they did not comment. And Aren himself had stopped digging, had stopped asking who had inflicted her scars, inside and out, content that if she wished to tell him, she would.

With much cajoling and prodding, the Ithicanian children had convinced Lara to wade into the cavern harbor, teaching her to float and to paddle about, but she was out in a flash if a fish bumped her and she refused to put her head under the surface. The few times someone had been brave—or foolish—enough to dunk her had been the *only* times Aren had seen her lose her temper at the children, screaming bloody murder. Then she'd stormed half naked and dripping back to the palace, where she refused to speak to anyone, including him, for the balance of the day, only to go right back into the water with them during the next storm break.

Coming to Eranahl had changed his wife. It hadn't softened her, exactly, for she still had the wickedest temper of anyone he'd ever met, but it seemed to Aren that being here had pulled her out of her shell. Out of the fortress she'd constructed to protect herself. She was happier. Brighter. Content.

Except every storm season came to an end, and this one would be no different.

Heaving in a sigh, Aren eyed the sky, the rain pattering gently against his skin. There was only the faintest breeze, the squall barely deserving the name, and he suspected it would only be a matter of days before Nana ruled the season over. Which is why his war council had convened.

For the last hour, Watch Commanders had been arriving by boat: battle-hardened men and women who had seen the worst their enemies had to offer, and had dealt worse in return. Each of the nine, including him at Midwatch, was responsible for the defense of certain portions of the bridge and the islands flanking it, and all of them had arrived ready to discuss what the season would bring. Save one.

Ahnna was late.

Stepping into the shelter of Eranahl's cavern harbor, Aren sat on the steps to wait, annoyed at the anxiety building in his gut. This would be the first time he'd seen his twin since Lara's fall from the bridge. First time they'd spoken since he'd threatened to ship her off to Harendell. Ahnna had been adamantly against Lara being anything more than a glorified prisoner kept at Midwatch, and he couldn't help but wonder how she would react to Lara being in the heart of Ithicana.

The gates began their slow rattle upward, startling Aren from his thoughts. One of the Southwatch boats drifted around the bend, and he squinted into the dim light, trying to make out his twin. Ahnna sat at the stern, rudder in hand, expression unreadable.

The boat bumped against the stone steps, one of the soldiers hopping out and mooring it while the others unloaded supplies. Ahnna flipped her pack over her shoulder, calling to her crew to enjoy their few hours of liberty before taking the steps two at the time.

"Your Majesty," she said, and his heart sank. "I apologize for being late. With the state of relations between the southern kingdoms, Southwatch requires my full attention."

"It's fine." He tried to come to terms with the wedge between them that might never be removed. "We've time."

Ahnna's eyes turned skyward, then she shook her head. "I'm not sure that we do."

The palace was silent as he and Ahnna entered, everyone who wasn't needed having vacated the premises and those who were needed busy with their tasks. It made for a strange quality of sound, as though the absence of people changed the building, causing footsteps to echo and voices to carry.

Not that either of them felt inclined to speak.

Turning down the hall, Aren caught sight of Lara sitting on a padded bench outside the council chambers, shoulders squared, eyes fixed on the solid doors. She wore a silken gown of blues and greens, her hair braided into a coronet that revealed the long column of her neck. High-heeled sandals, the leather inlaid with lapis lazuli, were strapped to her feet, and from here, he could see her cheeks and brow bones shone with golden dust.

"I see she hasn't given up her expensive tastes," Ahnna muttered.

Lara hadn't, and Aren indulged her, but not for the reasons his sister thought. Lara would've forgone the luxuries, would've blended in with his people to the point they forgot she hadn't been born among them, but both of them understood the importance of the people remembering she was Maridrinian. Of them coming to love her as a Maridrinian, which they had.

Lara rose at their approach, and as she turned to face them, Aren heard the soft catch of Ahnna's breath. She was staring at the jewels around Lara's neck, the emerald and black diamond necklace that had been their mother's. "How could you?" Her words came out as a hiss between her teeth. "Of all the things you could have given her, why that?"

"Because Lara is queen. And because I love her."

A thousand retorts flashed through his sister's eyes, but she said none of them. Only bowed to Lara. "I'm glad to see you well, Your Grace." Then she extracted the key marking her as a Watch Commander, unlocked the council chamber, and went inside.

"I told you it would be a mistake not to talk to her sooner." Lara rested her hands on her hips, giving him a slow shake of her perfect head. "You slap her in the face with everything she doesn't want to see and then expect her to grit her teeth and bear it."

Closing the distance between them, Aren pulled Lara against him, her arms slipping around his neck. "Why are you always right?" he asked, closing his eyes and kissing her throat.

"I'm not. It's only that you are so often wrong."

He chuckled, feeling some of his tension dispel only for it to return when she said, "It's too soon, Aren. Let me go get Jor."

"No. You are Queen of Ithicana and that makes you my second in command. That is how it has always been, and for me to take Jor in there with me instead would send a message to the Watch Commanders and the people that I don't see you as capable. That I don't trust you. It would undo everything we've accomplished since you came to Eranahl."

"As far as they know, I *am* incapable."

"I know otherwise." But he was the only one who knew; Lara's past, her training, her deadliness a secret Aren kept from everyone. And would continue to keep in order to protect both his wife and the tenuous peace their marriage symbolized. "Besides, there is more to running a kingdom than martial prowess."

"This is War Tides council meeting," she said between her teeth, eyes shifting down the corridor to ensure they were alone. "The *only* thing that matters is martial prowess. Let me get Jor."

Aren shook his head. "You're the only one who knows all the stakes." He rested his forehead against hers. "I need you at my side."

And before she could argue further, he unlocked the door and tugged Lara inside Ithicana's war room.

ARen dropped her arm the moment they entered, the intimacy that had thickened the air between them moments ago gone. And replaced with something else entirely.

Here, they were not husband and wife. Not King and Queen of Ithicana. In this room, Aren was Commander of Midwatch and she was his second, and Lara instinctively mimicked his squared shoulders and grave expression, following at his heels to the elevated replica of Midwatch, the island one part of an enormous map of Ithicana. The only complete map of Ithicana in existence.

No one was allowed in this room but Watch Commanders and their seconds. Not even servants were admitted to clean, the group taking care of the duty with typical Ithicanian efficiency. That she, a Maridrinian, stood in this room was unprecedented, a fact made clear when every head turned toward her, their eyes wide with shock.

"Where's Jor?" Ahnna's voice cut through the silence from where she stood next to the replica of Southwatch, her hand resting possessively on the large island.

"Downstairs." Aren's voice was curt, though Lara suspected the tone had more to do with nerves than with irritation. He'd known her presence would be questioned.

"Commander, perhaps we might discuss whether Her Majesty's presence is appropriate," Mara said. Which was unsurprising. The woman had made no secret of her distaste for Lara, barely speaking to her whenever she was in Eranahl.

Aren turned cool eyes on the commander of Northwatch. "We choose our seconds. Our choices are not questioned." He jerked his chin toward Aster, whom Mara had taken on as her second after his dismissal from the Kestark command. "Unless you'd care to change that protocol?"

Mara held up her hands in defense. "I only thought you'd wish to have someone with experience as your second, Commander. Emra"— she gestured at the young commander of Kestark—"selected someone with age to compensate for her youth."

Emra had chosen her mother—a battle-hardened warrior whom Lara liked immensely—as her second, and the woman in question rolled her eyes skyward as her daughter replied, "I chose someone I could trust."

A small beacon of solidarity, but what relief Lara felt at the young woman's words was washed away when Ahnna said, "Since when don't you trust Jor?"

Aren shifted next to Lara, his legs brushing her skirts. She knew that not having his sister's support hurt. From what she'd gleaned from Taryn, Jor, and the rest of the guards, the twins had been close, fighting at each other's backs until Ahnna had moved to Southwatch. She'd been the key vote of support in this council chamber in Aren's marriage to Lara, but judging from the princess's expression, she deeply regretted that decision.

"Lara is my wife. She is Queen. I trust her, and she is my second." Lara held her breath as Aren's gaze roved around the room. "Anyone who has a problem with that can get the fuck out now."

Mara snorted, but everyone else held their tongues. "Let's begin, shall we? I want to be on the water before nightfall."

It was a long process of Mara detailing the developments that had taken place over the storm season. What the Northwatch spies had learned about Harendell and Amarid's intentions. Where their armies and navies were located. The number of ships that had been built or destroyed. Lara listened intently; it was not lost on her that every ruler in the world would kill to have a spy in her shoes.

"Amarid is replacing the ships they lost raiding last year," Mara said. "But we've tracked their progress, and none will be ready by the beginning of War Tides, so we may see some respite."

"All of them?" Aren asked. "With what funds? Amarid is nearly bankrupt."

A bankruptcy that Lara knew had been cemented by Ithicana taking the income Amarid usually received for shipping steel across the Tempest Seas. Of all the kingdoms, north and south, her marriage to Aren had cost Amarid the most.

"Straight from the coffers, near as we can tell," Aster answered. "It's not on credit. No one will lend to them anymore." The older man lifted the page in his hand. "There's a rumor the ships were financed with gemstones, but that seems unlikely."

Gemstones. The word plucked at Lara's mind, important somehow, though she couldn't think of why. "What sort of gemstones?"

Every pair of eyes in the room shifted to her before moving to Aren. His jaw tightened with obvious irritation. "Answer the question."

"Rubies," Aster said. "But Amarid has no mines, so it's likely nothing more than a rumor."

Lara's fingers went to the knife belted at her waist, trailing over the crimson stones embedded in the hilt.

"I'm not interested in rumors," Aren said. "I'm interested in facts. Find out how Amarid's paying for the ships. If they're in bed with someone, I want to know who it is. And what their intentions are." He waved a hand at Mara to continue, but Lara's mind stayed with the ships. With the idea that there might be someone outside of Amarid interested in financing further attacks against Ithicana.

". . . a marked increase in Amarid's import of certain Maridrinian goods." Mara's words stole back Lara's attention.

"What manner of goods?"

Mara's expression was unamused. "Cheap wine, mostly."

"Why, given that Amarid makes the best wines and is known the world over for their distilleries, would they import Maridrinian wine?"

"Clearly a few Amaridians have a taste for cloudy swill," Mara snapped. "Now moving on."

"Commander, watch yourself." Aren's voice was cold.

The older woman only threw up her hands in exasperation. "I assume the Maridrinians are selling what they can in order to buy what they need—I only noted them as they were unusual and it might be a market we can exploit in the future."

"It wasn't a large shipment," Ahnna interrupted. "Our tolls would have eaten up half the profit, it was such cheap stuff. I snaked a crate of it and included it with the supplies for Midwatch."

Lara's pulse was roaring in her ears now, the memory of the bottle of Maridrinian wine in the safe house supplies dancing in front of her eyes, along with the smuggler's ruby they'd found in it. A ruby that was sitting in her jewelry box at Midwatch. How better to smuggle gemstones than in cheap wine that the Ithicanians were unlikely to touch, that they wouldn't have even noticed, if Ahnna hadn't played a prank? If Aren had made the connection, Lara couldn't tell—he was guarding his reactions too closely.

"May I continue?" Mara demanded, and at Aren's nod, she gave a swift rundown of Northwatch's defenses, then passed the meeting to the next commander.

The islands both north and south of Midwatch suffered most of the attacks during the past War Tides, and much of the conversation turned to speculation of whether this year would be the same. Lara listened with one ear, but her mind would not let go of the notion that someone in Maridrina was financing the Amaridian navy.

The conversation moved progressively south, the meeting stopping only when someone needed to relieve themselves and resuming immediately upon the individual's return. There was no time. Lara could feel it: the galloping thrum of adrenaline that usually preceded a storm, but this time it whispered *war*. Aren took his turn for Midwatch, barely referring to the notes Lara passed him.

"Midwatch Island itself was only attacked once. On the shoulder season, and obviously by an inexperienced captain, as they sailed directly into the path of our shipbreakers. It was as though they were asking to be sunk. Even still, we had little respite, the other islands under our watch were attacked repeatedly."

They turned to the particulars, but Lara scarcely heard the conversation, her skin ice-cold. Key to her father's plan had been Lara witnessing Ithicana's military tactics from the inside, her training allowing her to understand those tactics and how they could be exploited. All of War Tides, she'd believed every opportunity she had to watch the Ithicanians in action had been luck, but what if it hadn't been? What if it had been by design? What if it had been ordered by the individual financing the rebuilding of those ships?

What if that individual was her father?

"The Amaridian attack on Serrith was the only occasion where we took significant losses . . ."

Serrith. Unbidden, the memory of the attack surfaced in her mind. Of the way the Amaridian sailors had recognized her, but instead of attacking, had backed off until it became clear it was her life or theirs. Which made no sense at all, given that Lara and the treaty she represented were the cause of all of Amarid's woe.

"You're up, Emra," Aren said. "How fares Kestark?"

The paper in the young woman's hands trembled as she spoke, but her voice was clear and steady as she summarized the state of her watch, which had taken heavy losses during War Tides. Reaching the end of her notes, she paused before saying, "An Amaridian merchant vessel passed through Kestark two days past."

"Keep to the important details, girl," Aster said, and Lara curbed the urge to throw the glass in her hand at his head. "We don't have time to discuss every merchant vessel blown into our waters during a storm season crossing."

Emra's eyes flashed with irritation, but she shut her lips in habitual deference to the older man.

Anything to do with Amarid was important now, and Lara opened her mouth to ask Emra to elaborate, but Aren beat her to it. "Why do you mention it?"

"I was on Aela Island doing an inspection of the outpost, Commander. We noticed the vessel anchored on the east side out of the wind, the crew making a show of doing some repairs."

"And?"

"And I noticed it was sitting high in the water. Which, given she'd come in from the north, seemed odd. So we boarded her to see what was what."

"You *boarded* an Amaridian ship?"

"Peacefully boarded. Hold was empty, and when I inquired their business, the captain told me they were transporting a wealthy noblewoman."

"Such an exciting tale this is," Aster said dryly, but Aren waved him silent, which was well timed, as Lara was considering ways to poison the man's drink to get him to shut up. "Did you see the woman?"

"Yes, Commander. A very beautiful woman with golden hair. She had a maid with her, along with some military types for escort."

"Did you speak to them?"

Emra shook her head. "No. But I noticed her dress was the same style as those Her Majesty sometimes wears."

"She was Maridrinian?"

Emra shrugged, her cheeks reddening. "I've not enough experience to say. Her Majesty is the only Maridrinian I've ever met."

"Perhaps you ought to have consulted your mother, *Commander*," Mara interjected. "She, after all, fought in the war against Maridrina and is thus well aware of what they look and sound like. Either way, it matters little. Maridrinians who can't afford bridge passage often risk the voyage on Amaridian vessels. They're cheap."

"And I wouldn't have thought much more of it, Commander," Emra replied, "except we passed through Midwatch territory on our way to Eranahl, and we spotted the same vessel. And a merchant tub like that wouldn't make it to Maridrina and back to Midwatch in less than two days."

Lara's skin pricked with goosebumps as though she were being watched, despite there being no windows in the room. Her father didn't use women in battle or as spies, the only exception being Lara and her sisters. And she'd paid for her sisters' freedom in blood.

"Anyone else notice the same?" Aren asked.

Danielle L. Jensen

Heads shook, but the commander of the garrison north of Midwatch said, "Our scouts caught sight of an Amaridian merchant vessel heading south and east, past Serrith and Gamire Islands, but it looked to be sailing ahead of a squall forming in the west."

"Is there something we should know about?" Mara asked.

The *something* was that Lara's father was hunting for her. Lara knew it and, judging from the tension she felt radiating from Aren, he suspected it as well. But neither of them could say so without raising the question of *why* Silas was so interested in tracking down his wayward daughter.

Aren shook his head. "Carry on."

It was Ahnna's turn at Southwatch.

The princess rubbed her chin, then reached to touch the replica of the island she guarded so fiercely. "All of Southwatch's defenses are in good order. What damage was inflicted during the storm season we were able to repair during the breaks." Referring to the page in her hand, Ahnna detailed the numbers of soldiers stationed, the weapons cache, the food and water supplies.

"You all know"—she set the papers down—"that Valcotta was able to maintain a partial blockade of Maridrina's access to Southwatch, despite the toll it took on their fleet. We'd expected to take a hit to our profits, but the Valcottan Empress is too savvy to give us a reason to complain. We had Valcottan merchant ships lined up ten deep during every storm break, and they bought everything, often at a premium. When the Maridrinian vessels did have the chance to make port, there was little for them to buy. Though, to his credit, King Silas has them prioritizing food, not his precious steel and weapons."

"It's all still at Southwatch?" Aren asked.

"We've a whole warehouse full of weapons," Ahnna replied. "It's all going to turn to rust by the time he ever sees them at the rate things are going. And yet they keep arriving."

"His buyers take all the steel and weaponry the Harendellians offer at Northwatch," Mara said. "And the Valcottan buyers know that."

Ahnna nodded. "But he doesn't dare use his resources to retrieve it. Not with his people rioting in the streets. They're starving. And they're desperate. And they blame Ithicana for all of it."

Lara's heart seemed to come to a standstill as a sudden understanding took hold of her. She'd been a fool, imagining it might be over. Had believed, with delusional hope, that without the efforts of her spying, her father would have no way of infiltrating Ithicana's defenses.

Her father had waited *fifteen years*, invested a fortune and the lives of twenty of his daughters in his bid for the bridge. He'd lied and manipulated and murdered to keep it all a secret. There was no chance that he'd ever let it go.

No matter what it cost Maridrina.

She needed to speak with Aren alone. Needed to warn him that Ithicana was in as much danger as it ever had been. Needed to do it before this meeting ended, so that these individuals who protected Ithicana's shores would go back to their watch prepared to fight.

But she couldn't very well ask to speak to him privately without everyone questioning what she and Aren were keeping from the council.

Picking up Aren's stack of notes, Lara fanned herself vigorously enough that eyes shifted to her. Then she reached for her glass of water, purposefully knocking it to the floor, the glass shattering.

Aren broke off in his argument with Mara, twisting to look at her.

"Sorry," she murmured.

His eyes narrowed as Lara swayed on her feet. "It's very hot in here."

"Are you well?"

"I think I need to sit down," she said, then fell sideways into his arms.

"THIS BETTER BE GOOD," Aren said through his teeth as he carried her down the corridor. "Because I sure as shit don't believe you fainted."

"Get us somewhere we can talk," was her whispered response, confirming his supposition.

Kicking open the door to their rooms, Aren waved away the wide-eyed servants who'd scurried up behind him. "Too long on her feet." Then he elbowed the door shut, Lara sliding nimbly from his arms the moment the latch clicked.

"We only have a few minutes," she said, "so listen carefully. My father's formed an alliance with Amarid."

Silence.

"Ithicana has spies throughout both kingdoms, Lara, and *none* of them have reported even a hint of an alliance between Maridrina and Amarid. Quite the opposite, in fact."

"Yes, no doubt that's what my father wishes you to believe."

Aren listened silently as Lara explained the connections between the focused attacks on the Midwatch area, the Maridrinian wine and the smuggled ruby, and the ships being financed in Amarid with the very same gemstones. A stream of small details and coincidences that he might have passed off as nothing, except for the fact he *knew* why Lara had been sent to Ithicana. Knew Silas was his enemy.

"And there's the ships lurking around Midwatch. The noblewoman—" She broke off, hesitating. "The noblewoman is only an excuse for the soldiers to be aboard. You know they're looking for me."

It was there Aren interrupted. "Of course he's looking for you, Lara, because without you, his plots, his alliance with Amarid—everything—it amounts to nothing."

"But—"

Aren gripped her shoulders. "Without you, he has nothing."

Lara hadn't betrayed him, Aren believed that. Trusted her with his heart, with the bridge, with his people. Yet the frantic gleam in her eye formed a seed of doubt in his chest. "You're certain you didn't give him any clues in your letters?"

Lara met his gaze unblinking. "I am certain. Just as I'm certain that he's creating a situation in which he no longer needs me to take the bridge. He's going to do it by force."

Exhaling a long breath, Aren said, "Lara, he's tried it before. Tried and failed, and took catastrophic losses. The Maridrinians remember what it was like to come against our shipbreakers. To see their comrades drowned in the waves, pummeled into rocks, and torn apart by sharks. Silas can hire out all the Amaridian vessels he wants to—it's not a fight your people will support."

"Why do you think he's starving them?"

His blood abruptly chilled. "To try to get us to break off trade with Valcotta."

Lara slowly shook her head. "That's the last thing he wants. My father doesn't want Ithicana as an ally; he wants you as his enemy." Her eyes were bright with unshed tears. "And he's done it. My father has turned you into Maridrina's villain, and very soon, they'll come for your blood."

Even as the words poured from Lara's throat, Aren knew they were true. That despite everything he'd done, everything he'd dreamed of for Ithicana's future, war would be on his doorstep. Twisting away from Lara, he gripped the foot of the bed he shared with her, the wood groaning under his grip.

"Can you defend Ithicana against both nations?" Lara's voice was soft.

Slowly, he nodded. "This year, yes. But I expect our losses will be catastrophic. Both kingdoms have far more soldiers to throw against us than Ithicana has to lose."

And what were his options? The surest way to stop Silas would be to join forces with Valcotta, but that would be disastrous for Maridrina. Lara's people would die by the thousands, cut down by blades or starved to death. Innocent lives lost—all because of the greed of one man. But to do otherwise would likely mean the end of Ithicana unless Harendell intervened, which past behavior indicated unlikely.

"There is no solution," he said.

Silence.

"Stop trade with Valcotta." Lara's words were so quiet, he barely heard them. "Attempt to undercut support for this war with Maridrina. Make Ithicana the hero."

"If I break trade relations with Valcotta and use my resources to crack their blockade on Maridrina, it will decimate our profits. Ithicana needs the income Valcotta brings in at Southwatch in order to survive. Never mind that they'll likely retaliate. You want me to risk that on speculation? On coincidences?"

"Yes."

Silence.

"Aren, you brought me here because you believed your people needed to know Maridrina in order for there to be peace between our people. In order for them to see Maridrina as an ally, not as the enemy of old." Her voice was choked. "It goes both ways. Maridrina also need to see Ithicana as an ally. As a friend."

Aren's shoulders bowed. "Even if I agree with you, Lara, I'll never get the council to go along with it. They believe we've bought peace with Maridrina—that we gave your father what he wanted, so he has no reason to attack us. They won't jeopardize the Valcottan revenue based on the supposition that your father might want more."

"Then maybe it's time you told them the truth about me. Maybe that will be enough to prove to them the gravity of our situation."

Aren felt the blood drain from his face. "I can't."

"Aren—"

"I can't, Lara. Ithicana's reputation for cruelty isn't entirely undeserved. If they discover you were a spy . . ." His mouth felt dry as sand. "It wouldn't be a merciful execution."

"So be it."

"No." He crossed the space between them in three strides, pulling her into his arms, his lips pressing against her hair. "No. I refuse to turn you over to be slaughtered. I'll damn well let them feed me to the sea before I ever agree to that. I love you too much."

And because Aren knew she was brave enough to sacrifice herself whether he willed it or not, he added, "If they learned the truth about you, the last thing they'd do is help your people. They'll force me to ally formally with Valcotta, and what would happen . . . . I'm not sure Maridrina would survive it."

Her shoulders started to shake, and then sobs tore from her throat. "It's impossible. Impossible to save both. It always has been."

"Maybe not." Aren pushed her toward the bed. "I need you to stay here and keep up your performance."

Lara wiped a hand across her cheek. "What are you going to do?"

Stopping with his hand on the door, Aren turned to look at his wife. "Your father sent you to Ithicana for a purpose. He failed. But I also brought you here for a reason, Lara. And I think it's time to see if my gambit worked."

She didn't stop Aren as he exited, his long strides eating up the corridors of the palace as he formed the words. A speech he'd used countless times, but now turned to a different purpose. Reaching the council chambers, Aren extracted his key, unlocked the door, and entered.

Conversation froze, then Ahnna said, "Nana sent word. Storm season is over. War Tides has begun."

There was a shifting and gathering in the room, every one of the commanders and seconds present now keen to return to their watch. To prepare to repel their enemies, whoever they might be. To be through with this meeting.

But Aren wasn't through with them.

"There's one more matter we need to discuss," he said, the tone of his voice causing all heads to turn. "Or rather, finish discussing. And that is the matter of the plight of the Maridrinian people."

"What's there to say?" Aster said, exchanging a chuckle with Mara. "They made their bed."

"As did we."

The smile fell away from Aster's face.

"Sixteen years ago, Ithicana signed a treaty of peace with Maridrina and Harendell. A treaty that both of those kingdoms have held to, neither of them attacking our borders in the intervening period. Our terms with Maridrina have all been met. They provided me with my lovely wife, and we have eased the costs of using the bridge."

"I assume you're driving to a point, Your Grace," Mara said.

"The terms have been met," Aren interrupted, "but the question of the nature of the agreement between our two nations remains unanswered. Is it, as Commander Mara so eloquently described, a *business contract*, where Ithicana has paid Maridrina for peace? Or is it an alliance, where our two kingdoms use the terms of the treaty to foster a relationship beyond the exchange of services and products and coins?"

No one spoke.

"The people of Maridrina are starving. Little of their land is suited to produce, and of that which is suited, more than half rests fallow for lack of hands to work it. The wealthy are still able to import, but the rest? Hungry. Desperate. All while we, their so-called allies, do business with their enemy, filling Valcottan holds with the goods Maridrina desperately needs because the Valcottans pay the most. Sitting idly by while Valcottan ships deny Maridrina the steel they've rightfully paid for. No wonder they call this treaty a farce."

"What's happening in Maridrina is Silas's doing," Ahnna said. "Not ours."

"It *is* Silas's doing. But are we any better for sitting back and watching while innocent children go to their graves when we have the power to save them? Silas is no more the sum of his kingdom than I am the sum of ours, and neither of us is immortal. There is a larger picture."

"Just what are you suggesting, Aren?" Ahnna asked, her voice toneless.

"I'm suggesting Ithicana demand Valcotta drop its blockade. And should they refuse, that they be denied port at Southwatch. That we prove ourselves allies to Maridrina."

The room broke into a flurry of voices, Aster's the loudest of all. "These sound like your wife's words, Your Grace."

"Do they really?" Aren leveled the man with a glare. "How long have I been pushing for us to form unions with other kingdoms so that our people have opportunities beyond war? For us to turn Ithicana into something more than just an army viciously guarding its bridge? How long did my mother push for it before me? These are not Lara's words."

Though in a way they were, because before, he'd only cared about protecting his own kingdom. About how Ithicana might benefit from an alliance. Now Aren saw both sides, and he believed he was a better man for it.

"But to have an alliance that would allow our people these opportunities, we cannot just *take*. We have to give something in return. Maridrina's plight? It's an opportunity to show Ithicana's worth. Our worth."

"Is this to be a proclamation, then?" Aster spat. "For us to risk our own children and have no say in the risking?"

If Aren could've made it an order, he would've, for no reason other than that he would be the one to bear the guilt if things went wrong. But such was not Ithicana's way. "We vote."

Slow nods, then Emra's mother said, "All right, then. Hands for those in favor."

Hers went up immediately, as did Emra's and four of the other younger commanders. Including Aren's vote, that made seven, and he needed nine. It was one of the reasons he hadn't asked Lara to come back here with him. Odd numbers ensured the vote wouldn't hang. And having her absent meant no one could hold her accountable.

Several of the old guard, including Aster, stepped back, shaking their heads. But Aren almost fell over in surprise when Mara lifted her hand. Seeing his shock, the commander of Northwatch said, "Just because I question you doesn't mean I don't believe in you, boy."

All who remained to cast their vote was his sister.

Ahnna trailed a finger over Southwatch, her brow furrowed. "If we do this, it will mean the destruction of our relationship with Valcotta. It means war for Ithicana."

Aren cast his gaze over the replica of his kingdom. "Ithicana has always been at war, and what do we have to show for it?"

"We're alive. We have the bridge."

"Don't you think it's time we fight for something more?"

Ahnna didn't answer, and sweat trickled down Aren's back as he waited for his twin to cast her vote. Waited to see if she could move past her distrust of Lara and Maridrina. If she'd risk taking a chance, this leap of faith. If she'd fight at his side the way she always had.

Ahnna gave her island one last affectionate pat, and then she nodded once. "I swore long ago to fight by your side, no matter the odds. Now is no different. Count Southwatch in."

EIGHT WEEKS LATER, Lara clunked her mug against Jor's over the fire pit, shrieking with laughter when a log burst, spraying sparks at their hands.

For the first time in living memory, the months of respite from storms hadn't meant war for Ithicana, though it felt as though the entire nation had held its breath until the season was declared over.

After a strongly worded warning from Aren to drop the blockade or risk losing the right to trade at the Southwatch market—which the Valcottan Empress had ignored—Ithicana had driven the Valcottan navy ships lurking around Southwatch back, allowing Maridrinian vessels full access. Aren had then proceeded to load Ithicana's own vessels full of food and supplies, which were delivered into Vencia and distributed to the poor. Again and again, Aren had used Ithicana's coffers and resources to supply the belabored city until the Maridrinian people were cheering his name in the streets.

Whether it was because he'd lost the support of his people for war or because Lara hadn't given him the intelligence he'd needed, her father hadn't lifted a hand against Ithicana. Neither had Amarid, which seemed to still be licking its wounds. And now that the storms were rolling in, both kingdoms had lost the chance for another year. Or perhaps forever, if the strength of the relationship between the Ithicanian and Maridrinian people were any indication.

Not that there hadn't been consequences. The empress had responded with a letter telling Aren he deserved whatever he got for bedding down with snakes, turning her armada entirely to merchant transport in an attempt to further undercut the bridge's revenues, which were already halved by the loss of trade with the southern nation. The coffers were drained. But in Lara's mind, both Maridrinian and Ithicanian civilians were alive. They were safe. Nothing else mattered.

She had done her duty as both princess and queen.

"Your brother should be passing by Midwatch right now," Jor said, handing her another full mug of ale. "Tide's low. We could take a stroll through the bridge and pay him a visit. Have a little family reunion."

Lara rolled her eyes. "I'll pass." Her brother Keris had finally convinced their father to allow him to attend university in Harendell to study philosophy, and he was traveling through the bridge with his entire retinue of courtiers and attendants to start his first semester. One of the mail runners had come ahead of them, and he said the party looked like a flock of birds, everyone bedecked in silks and jewels.

"Let's go," Aren murmured into her ear. "I'm looking forward to a night with you in a real bed."

"You're going to fall asleep the second your head hits the pillow." She relished the rising heat of desire between her legs as his fingers traced along the veins in her arms. She'd stayed with him at the barracks all through War Tides, but the narrow soldier's cot had *not* been conducive to romance. Although they'd made do.

"I'll take that bet. Come on."

He led her out into the gentle rain, the worst of the squall already over. One of Aren's soldiers was outside, and he looked at her with surprise. "Thought you already went up to the house."

"Not yet. Jor kept refilling my mug. I expect they'll be out of ale by the time your shift is up."

"Thought I saw you, was all." The big guard frowned, then

shrugged. "They're signaling for a supply pickup at the pier, so we might have more drink arriving."

"I'll send some down from the house," Aren assured the man, tugging on Lara's arm.

"Thank you, Your Grace." But Aren was already towing her up the path, the chain in the cove rattling upward behind them. Mud squelched beneath their boots as they made their way up the trail to the house they'd barely visited over the prior eight weeks, neither of them able to relax enough to step away from the barracks.

"A bath, first," Lara said, thinking dreamily about the steaming hot springs. "You smell like soldier."

"You're not so fresh yourself, Majesty." Aren swung her up into his arms, the lantern light dancing wildly where it hung from her hand. She twisted in his grip, wrapping her legs around his waist. A soft moan escaped her lips as she pressed against him, his hands gripping her ass.

Lara kissed him hard, sliding her tongue into his mouth, then laughed when he slipped, the lantern falling from her hands and going dark. "Don't you dare drop me."

"Then quit distracting me," he growled. "Or I'll be forced to take you in the mud."

She slid to the ground and took his hand, leading him at a perilous run up the slope until she caught sight of Aren's cat, Vitex, sitting on the front step, tail twitching angrily.

"What are you doing out here?" Aren reached for the cat and it hissed and leapt away, limping slightly as it bolted into the trees.

Lara watched him go. "He's hurt."

"The female he's been chasing probably got a piece of him. He likely deserved it." Catching her by the waist, Aren lifted her up the stairs and shoved open the door to the house.

It was dark.

"Not like Eli not to set out a lamp." Lara's skin prickled as she stared into the yawning blackness. Aren had sent word up to the house that War Tides was over, instructing Eli to select an expensive bottle of wine from the cellar for his mother and aunt. But the Ithicanian boy *never* shirked his duties.

"Maybe he drank the wine instead," Aren murmured, raining kisses onto her throat, his hands finding her breasts. "Will do him good."

"He's fourteen." The house was silent. Which wasn't precisely unusual, but there was something about the *nature* of the silence that rubbed Lara the wrong way. As though no one breathed.

"Exactly. Do you know the sorts of things I was doing at fourteen?"

Lara stepped away, listening. "I should check on him."

An aggrieved sigh exited Aren's throat. "Lara, relax. The storms are here and they will do their duty." Pulling her into his arms, he kissed her. Slowly. Deeply. Driving all thought from her head as he gently pushed her down the dark corridor into their room, where, thankfully, there was a lamp burning. The yellow flame pushing back the darkness eased Lara's agitation, and she let her head fall back as her husband's teeth grazed her neck, feeling the faint breeze from the open window.

"Bathe later," he growled.

"No. You stink. Get outside and I'll be there in a moment."

Grumbling, he shucked off his tunic and vambraces, tossing both on the floor, starting toward the antechamber and the door to the courtyard beyond.

Peeling off her hooded cloak, Lara hung the damp garment on a hook to dry and was unfastening the top lace of her tunic when her heart skittered, her eyes falling on a letter with a familiar seal. Next to it, a knife twin to the one at her waist sat in a small pile of crimson sand, its rubies glittering in the light. The knife Aren had thrown on the docks in Vencia. Dread filled her stomach as she walked over to the table, picking the heavy paper up with numb fingers, and breaking the wax.

Dearest Lara,

Even in Vencia, we have heard talk of the affection between the Ithicanian King and his new queen, and how it fills our heart to know that you have, however improbably, found love in your new home. Please accept our most sincere well-

wishes for your future, however short that future might be.

Father

"Aren." Her voice shook. "Why wasn't this letter delivered at the barracks? Who brought it?"

No answer.

A scuffle of motion.

A muffled curse.

Whirling, she reached for the knife at her waist. Then froze. Aren was on his knees on the far side of the room. A hooded figure dressed in clothing identical to Lara's own held a glittering blade to his throat. And beneath the bed next to them, a young man's hand protruded, fingers covered in drying blood. *Eli* . . .

"Hello, little sister," a familiar voice said, and the woman reached up and pulled back her hood.

"**M**ARYLYN." THE NAME CROAKED out of Lara's throat, her chest a riot of emotion at seeing her sister again, even as she knew what the other woman's presence meant. Beautiful, with golden blond hair.

Marylyn had been the noblewoman on the ship Emra had boarded.

"Lara."

Aren started to struggle, snapping Lara out of her trance. "Don't move," Lara warned him. "Her blade will be poisoned."

"You do know my tricks."

"Let him go."

"We both know that's not likely to happen, little cockroach."

The old nickname burned in her ears, while her eyes searched for a way to disarm Marylyn without getting Aren killed. But there was none.

"Who is this woman?" Aren demanded.

"Lara is my little sister. My lying, thieving, little bitch of a sister."

The words were a slap to the face. "Marylyn, I came here to spare you."

"Liar." Marylyn's voice was pure venom. "You stole what was rightfully mine, then left me to rot in the desert. Do you have any idea how long it took me to get to Vencia to explain to Father what you'd done?"

"I did it to protect you!"

"Lara, the martyr." Marylyn's lip turned up in a sneer. "Only I saw through to your true intentions, you lying whore."

Lara stared at her, dumbfounded. The letter she'd left in Sarhina's pocket had explained everything. Her father's intention to have the rest of them killed. That Lara faking their deaths and then taking Marylyn's place as Queen of Ithicana was the only way to save all their lives, except for perhaps her own. She'd given them their freedom. "He was going to kill our sisters. It was the only way. Why don't you understand?"

"I understand perfectly." Marylyn shifted the blade pressed to Aren's throat, angling the tip upward. "Do you think I didn't know that Father intended to kill the rest of you?" She laughed. "Do you think I cared?"

This wasn't her sister. It couldn't be. Marylyn had always been the sweetest. The kindest. The one who needed to be protected.

The best actress.

"You said your sisters were dead." Aren's voice jerked her back into the moment.

"What now, has she been keeping secrets?" Marylyn stroked his cheek with her free hand, laughing as he recoiled. "Allow me to bring you into the fold, Majesty. No one forced Lara to come to Ithicana to spy, she *chose* to. Except 'chose' isn't even a strong enough word. Lara conspired against us all in order to ensure *she* would be Queen of Ithicana so that *she* would have the glory of throwing your people on Maridrinian blades."

"That's not true," Lara whispered.

"That's the woman you married, Majesty. A liar like none I've ever known. Worse than that, she's a murderer. I've seen her kill. Maim. Torture. All in cold blood. All practice for what she intended to do to your people."

That part was true. Painfully and horribly true. "We all did it, Marylyn. None of us had a choice."

Her older sister rolled her eyes. "There was always a choice." Her eyes turned on Aren. "What do you think he would've done in the same position? Do you think he'd have slaughtered an innocent man just to save himself?"

No.

"Selfish little cockroach, always putting herself first. Although I can see *why* you decided to remain around after you plunged the knife in his back." She trailed a finger down Aren's bare chest. "What a prize he is. They didn't tell us *that* during our lessons at the compound. I might have put him through his paces a few times myself before slitting his throat."

Fury seared through Lara's chest, and she unclipped her knife from its jeweled hilt, though the thought of hurting her sister made her sick. "Don't touch him."

Marylyn pursed her lips. "Why? Because he's yours? For one, he's rightfully mine. Two, even if I intended to leave him alive, which I don't, do you really think he's going to want anything to do with you now that he understands what kind of woman you are? When he finds out what you've *done?*"

"I've done nothing."

Reaching into her pocket, Marylyn extracted a heavy piece of parchment edged with gold.

No.

"Recognize this, Your Majesty?" Marylyn held it in front of Aren's face. "You wrote it last fall in response to my father's request you hold true to the *spirit* of the Fifteen Year Treaty. Not the most charitable of responses, although I suppose you did deliver, in the end." Her whole body shook with laughter.

Not possible.

She'd destroyed all the pages.

"There is a type of ink that is invisible until sprayed with another agent. At that point, it becomes quite visible. If you look in Lara's quarters, I'm certain you'll find a jar of it, somewhat depleted."

Marylyn flipped the letter around, and Lara could do nothing as Aren took in line after line of her neat writing laying out every one of Ithicana's secrets, a strategy to infiltrate the bridge that was damning in its details.

She'd brought Ithicana to its knees.

"Lara?" Aren's eyes burned into hers, and the anguish in them was like having her heart carved out of her chest.

"I didn't . . ." *She had.* "I wrote it before. Before I knew the truth." Before he'd risked his life to save hers. Before he'd taken her into his bed. Before he'd trusted her with *everything.* "I thought I'd destroyed all the copies. This is . . . this is a mistake. I love you."

She'd never said it before. Never told him she loved him. Why had she never said it before?

"You love me." His voice was hollow. "Or were you only pretending to?"

"How tragic this is." The clock chimed, punctuating Marylyn's words. "Though I suspect it is about to get so much worse given that Keris's party of *courtiers* has crossed paths with a weapons shipment from Harendell."

A horn sounded. A call for aid. Then another and another until the notes were nothing more than a garbled mix of noise.

"Those courtiers exited piers on Aela and Gamire Islands and attacked your guard posts from the rear, disabling their shipbreakers so that Amaridian vessels loaded with hundreds of our soldiers could land unmolested. Even now, many of them are moving on to Northwatch and Southwatch to attack them from behind. And we have men using Ithicana's own signal horns to ensure no one will come to their aid. That's only the beginning, of course. Lara's instructions were *quite* detailed. Especially in how we might take Midwatch."

Panic flared in Aren's eyes, and she knew what he was thinking: All his soldiers—all his friends—were sitting in the barracks, their guard down.

Marylyn continued to prattle, but Lara's mind raced. If they could get down to the barracks, maybe they could get the chain closed in time. Send a signal to Southwatch warning them. But that was impossible unless she disarmed Marylyn.

Danielle L. Jensen

"Don't do this. Don't be our father's pawn any longer."

Her sister's face darkened. "I'm no one's pawn."

"Aren't you? You do his bidding, and for what? Everything we were told as children was a lie intended to fuel an irrational hatred of Ithicana. To turn us into fanatics who'd stop at nothing to bring our enemy down. But Father was the villain. He is the oppressor Maridrina needs to rid itself of. We were deceived, Marylyn. Why can't you see that?"

"No, Lara. You were deceived." Marylyn gave a pitying shake of her head, the back of her leg knocking against the bed. "I've always seen clearly. You ask what I have to gain? I bring your heads back to Vencia, and Father has promised to shower me with riches. If I hunt down our other wayward sisters, he will make me heir. I will be Queen of Maridrina and master of the bridge." She smiled. "Ithicana will be no longer."

Rage consumed Lara like a sentient beast, prowling through muscle and tendon, making her fingers flex on the knife in her hand. Master Erik had always warned her that anger would make her sloppy. Cause her to make mistakes. But he was a liar. Rage gave her focus. And it was that focus that caught the faint shifting of the sheets on the bed behind Marylyn. That allowed her to hear the faint hiss over the rapid beat of her heart. Aren, born and bred to this wild kingdom, heard it, too.

"You're deluding yourself." Lara watched the shifting shape. "Father knows that you're a mad dog. And once you've done his dirty work for him, he will have you put down. Or I could do it for him."

She threw the knife.

The blade sliced through the air, missing Marylyn, but sinking deep into the bed, the sheets now a flurry of motion.

"Lost your touch." Her sister cackled even as Aren leaned back, shoving his weight against her. They toppled against the bed and the injured snake struck. Marylyn screamed as its teeth sank into her shoulder. Twisting, she released Aren and stabbed her blade into the snake, pinning its body to the mattress.

Lara was already across the room. She slammed into Marylyn, sending them both rolling. They grappled, fists and feet flying with

328

the intent to injure. Maim. Kill. Blow after blow, both of them equally well trained. Yet when it came to this one thing, to violence, Lara had always been better.

Catching Marylyn's head in a lock, Lara whispered, "You are queen of nothing," then jerked her arms and snapped her sister's neck.

The light went out of the other woman's eyes, and time seemed to stand still.

How had it come to this? It seemed a lifetime ago that she'd made the decision to sacrifice herself in order to save her sisters. To be Maridrina's champion. To break the Bridge Kingdom. Everything had changed since then. Her beliefs. Her allegiance. Her dreams. Yet now one of her sisters lay dead at her hands, and Ithicana was on the brink of falling beneath Maridrina's yoke.

Despite everything, her father had still won.

"What have you done?"

The horror in Aren's voice made her teeth clench. "I didn't intend for this to happen."

He had a machete in his hand, but his arm shook as he leveled it at her. "Who are you? What are you?"

"You know who I am."

His breathing was ragged. Eyes never leaving her, he reached to retrieve the piece of paper that was Ithicana's damnation, rereading the lines, his thoughts scorched across his face. *They couldn't fight this.*

There was a commotion outside. The sounds of men shouting.

"I'm not leaving you behind to damn me further," Aren hissed.

Lara didn't fight as he bound her wrists with the tie for one of the drapes. Or when he pulled a pillowcase over her head and dragged her out of the room, even as soldiers spilled into the house. Ithicanian voices, at first. Then Maridrinian. Then chaos.

Screams cut the air, blades against blades, and she was jerked this way and that. Horns still sounded, filling the air with the call for aid that would never come. Night air filled her nose, and she was falling, knees banging painfully against the steps. Arms pulling her upright, then they were running.

Branches whipping her face, roots tripping her feet, the ground slick with mud.

Hissed voices. "This way, this way."

The shouts of pursuit.

"Down, down. Did you gag her?"

Her face was pressed against the ground, wet earth seeping through the pillowcase. A rock dug into her ribs. Another pressed sharply against her knee. All of it felt distant, as though it were happening to her in a dream. Or to someone else.

They carried on through the night, the heavy rain helping them avoid what seemed like countless Maridrinian soldiers hunting them across Midwatch, though logically she knew it couldn't be so many. By now her father's elite would've discovered Marylyn's body—and the absence of hers and Aren's—and there was no doubt that finding them would be nearly the same priority as taking the bridge itself.

Only as dawn came, filtered grey through clouds and the sodden fabric covering her face, did they take cover. There were familiar voices in the group. Jor and Lia. Others from the honor guard. Her ears strained for Aren's, but not once did she pick it out amongst the whispers.

Still, she was certain he was there. Sensed his presence. Felt the guilt and anger and defeat radiating from him in waves as he came to terms with the fall of his kingdom. Knew, instinctively, when he sent everyone away so that he was alone with her.

Lara waited for a long time for him to speak, braced herself for the blame and accusations. Aren remained silent.

When she could take it no more, Lara pushed upright, lifting her bound wrists to tug the pillowcase from her head, blinking in the dim light.

Aren sat on a rock a few paces away, elbows braced on his knees, head hanging low. He was still shirtless, and the rain ran in torrents down his muscled back, washing away smears of blood and mud. A bow and quiver rested under the shelter of an overhang. A machete was belted at his waist. In his hand he held her knife—the one she'd thrown at the snake—and he was turning it over and over as though it were some artifact he'd never seen before.

"Did anyone get out?" Her voice rasped like sandpaper over rough wood. "To warn Southwatch?"

"No." His hands stilled, the blade's keen edge glittering with rain. "Taryn tried. The Maridrinians used our own shipbreakers with shocking proficiency. She's dead."

Sharp pain dug into Lara's stomach, her mouth tasting sour. *Taryn was dead. The woman who hadn't even wanted to be a soldier was dead, and it was because of her.* "I'm so sorry."

He lifted his head, and Lara recoiled from the fury in his eyes. "Why? You got everything you wanted."

"I didn't want this." Except she had, at one point. Had wanted to shatter Ithicana. That desire had gotten them to this point, no matter how much she regretted it.

"Enough of your lies." He was on his feet in one smooth motion, stalking toward her, knife in hand. "I may not have a full report yet, but I know the bridge has fallen to your father using a plan to infiltrate our defenses that was better than I could've come up with myself. Your plan." As he raised his voice, she couldn't help but flinch, knowing they were still being hunted.

"I thought I'd destroyed all the evidence. I don't know how it got away from me—"

"Shut up!" He lifted the blade. "My people are dead and dying because of you." The knife slipped from his fingers. "Because of *me*."

Wrenching the damning piece of paper out of his pocket, he held it up to her face. Not the side she'd written on, but the one *he'd* written, the script flowing and neat. Words persuading her father to reconsider his war with Valcotta and to put his people before his pride. Her chest hollowed as she read the end.

Let it be said, however, that should you seek to retaliate against your spy, Ithicana will take it as an act of aggression against its queen, and the alliance between our kingdoms will be irrevocably severed.

Aren dropped to his knees in front of her, gripping the sides of her face, his fingers tangling in her hair. Tears glinted in his eyes. "I *loved* you. I trusted you. With myself. With my kingdom."

Loved. Past tense. Because she'd never deserved his love, and now she'd lost it for good.

"And you were only using me. Only pretending. It was all an act. A ploy."

"No!" She wrenched the word from her lips. "At first, yes. But after . . . Aren, I love you. Please believe that, if nothing else."

"I used to wonder why you never said it. Now I know." His grip on her face tightened, then he jerked his hands away. "You say it now only because you're trying to save your own skin."

"That's not true!"

Explanations fought each other to make it out of her mouth first. Ways to make him understand. Ways to make him believe her. They all died on her lips as he fished the knife out of the mud.

"I should kill you."

Her heart fluttered in her chest like a caged bird.

"But despite everything, *everything*, you've done, I don't have the balls to stick this blade in your black Maridrinian heart."

The knife sliced between her wrists, cutting the cord in one clean jerk. He pressed the hilt into the palm of her hand.

"Go. Run. I've no doubt that you'll make it off this island." His jaw tightened. "It's in your nature to survive."

Lara stared at him, her lungs paralyzed. He wasn't letting her go, he was . . . banishing her. "Please don't do this. I can fight. I can help you. I can—"

Aren shoved her shoulders with enough force to send her stumbling back. "Go!" Then he reached down and retrieved his bow, nocking one of the black-fletched arrows.

Holding her ground, she parted her lips, desperate not to lose the chance to undo the damage that she'd done. The chance to fight back against her father. To liberate Ithicana.

To win Aren back.

"Go!" He shouted the word at her, leveling the arrow at her forehead even as tears poured down his cheeks. "I never want to see your face. I never want to hear your name. If there were a way to scour you from my life, I'd do it. But until I find the strength to put you in a goddamned grave, this is all I have. Now run!"

His fingers quivered on the bowstring. *He would do it. And it would kill him.*

Lara twisted in the mud, sprinting up the slope, her arms pumping. Her boots slipped and slid as she jumped over fallen trees and slapped aside ferns.

And stopped. Bracing a hand against a tree, she turned. In time to see his arrow shoot past her face, thudding into the tree next to her.

She pressed a shaking hand against the line scraped against her cheek, a trickle of blood running between her fingers. Eyes fixed on her, Aren pulled another arrow from his quiver, nocked it, and aimed the barbed tip. His lips moved. *Run.*

She ran, never looking back again.

"A NOTHER."

The barkeep raised one eyebrow over the mug he was polishing with a dirty rag, but made no comment as he refilled her glass with the swill this tap house passed off as wine. Not that it mattered; it wasn't as though she intended to savor it.

Downing the contents in three gulps, Lara pushed the glass back across the bar. "Fill it."

"Pretty girl like you could get herself in a bit of trouble drinking the way you do, miss."

"Pretty girl like me will cut the throat of anyone who gives her trouble." She gave him a smile that was all teeth. "So how about you don't tempt fate and you just hand over the bottle." She shoved a few coins stamped with the Harendell King's face in the man's direction. "Here. Saves us having to exchange any more words tonight."

Wiser than he looked, the barkeep only shrugged, took the coins, and handed her a full bottle of swill. But even drunk, she marked his words. Her face was familiar here. It was time to find a new watering hole to drown herself in every night.

Which was a shame. It smelled like spilled beer and vomit, but she'd grown fond of this place.

Drinking directly from the bottle, she blearily scanned the room, tables full of Harendell sailors dressed in baggy trousers and those stupid floppy hats that never ceased to remind her of Aren. A trio of musicians played in the corner. No-nonsense serving women carried trays of steaming roast beef and rich soups to the patrons, the smell making her mouth water. A nod at one of the women had a bowl of soup arriving in front of her moments later.

"Here you are, Lara."

Shit. It was time for her to move on. How long had she been in this town? Two months? Three? In the haze of alcohol, she'd lost track of days, it feeling both like a lifetime and just yesterday that she'd dragged her battered boat onto a Harendell beach, half-starved and her clothes still red with the blood of the Maridrinian soldiers she'd slaughtered to get herself off Midwatch.

The smell of soup tickled her nose, but her stomach soured, and she shoved the bowl away, drinking from the bottle instead.

The smart thing would be to move inland, north and away from all those who knew and cared about Lara, The Traitor Queen of Ithicana. Her father's agents would be looking for her—maybe another one of her sisters, for all she knew—and a drunken wreck like her was an easy mark.

But she kept finding excuses not to go. The weather. The ease of stealing coin. The comfort of this shithole of a tap house. Except she knew the reason she stayed was because here, the news from Ithicana was on everyone's lips. Night after night she sat at the bar, listening to the sailors chatter about this battle and that, hoping and praying that the tides would turn. That, rather than grumbles about the growing dominion of Maridrina, she'd hear that Aren was back in power. That Ithicana held the bridge once more.

Wasted hopes.

With every passing day, the news grew worse. No one in Harendell was particularly pleased that Maridrina now controlled the bridge—already the old men were bemoaning the good old days of Ithicanian efficiency and neutrality—and there was much chatter over the likelihood of the Harendellian King taking action. Except even if he did, Lara knew it wouldn't be until after storm season, six months from now. And by then . . . by then, it would be too late.

". . . battle with the Ithicanians . . . the king . . . prisoner."

Lara's ears perked, unease pushing aside the haze of the wine. Turning to the table behind her, which was filled with a group of heavyset men with equally heavy mustaches, she asked, "What was that you said about the Ithicanian King?"

One of the men grinned lasciviously at her. "Why don't you come over here and I'll tell you everything there is to know about the sorry sot." He patted one knee, which was coated with grease stains.

Picking up her bottle, Lara swayed over to the table and set it down among their mugs. "Here I am. Now, what was it you were saying?"

The man patted his knee. She shook her head. "I'm fine on my feet, sir."

"I'd be better with that fine ass of yours on my lap." His hand swung in a wide arc, cracking against her bottom, where it remained, his meaty fingers digging into her flesh.

Lara reached behind, taking a firm grip on his wrist. The idiot had the nerve to smile. Pulling hard, she twisted, slamming his palm against the table and, a heartbeat later, embedding her dagger in it.

The man squealed and tried to pull away, but the knife blade was stuck in the wood beneath his hand.

One of the others reached for it, but fell back, nose broken.

Another swung his fist at her face, but she dodged easily, the toe of her boot catching him in the groin.

"Now." She rested one hand on the knife and gave it a gentle twist. "What was it you were saying about the King of Ithicana?"

"That he was captured in a skirmish with the Maridrinians." The man was sobbing, squirming on his seat. "He's being held prisoner in Vencia."

"Are you certain?"

"Ask anyone! The news just came in from Northwatch. Now please!"

Lara eyed him thoughtfully, nothing on her face betraying the terror rising in her guts. Jerking the knife free, she leaned down. "You slap another ass, I'll personally track you down and cut that hand off."

Spinning on her heel, she nodded at the barkeep and strode out the door, barely feeling the rain that drove against her face.

Aren had been captured.

Aren was a prisoner.

Aren was her father's *hostage.*

The wind ripped and tore at her hair. The last thought replayed endlessly in her mind as Lara strode toward the boarding house, people leaping out of her way as she passed. There was only *one* reason her father would keep Aren alive: to use him as bait.

Taking the steps two at a time, she unlocked the door to her room, slamming it behind her. Guzzling water straight from a pitcher, she stripped off the simple blue dress she wore and donned her Ithicanian clothes, swiftly packing her meager belongings into a sack. Then, a chip of charcoal in hand, she sat down at the table.

The necklace was warm from resting against her skin, the emeralds and diamonds glittering in the candlelight. She had no right to wear it, but the thought of the necklace being stolen, of it being worn by anyone else, was unbearable, so she never took it off.

She did so now.

Laying the necklace on the paper, Lara traced the jewels with the charcoal, the haze from the wine slowly receding as she worked. When the drawing was complete, she returned the necklace to her throat and held up a complete map of Ithicana, her gaze fixed on the large circle to the west of the rest.

This is madness, the logical part of her mind screamed. *You can barely swim, you're a shit sailor, and it's the middle of storm season.* But her heart, which had been a cold, smoldering thing since she'd run from Aren on Midwatch, now burned with a ferocity that would not be denied.

Tucking the map into her pocket, she belted on her weapons and stepped out into the storm.

It took Lara three weeks to get there, and she nearly died a dozen times or more during the journey. Violent storms chased her onto tiny islands, her screaming into the wind as she dragged her little boat above the storm surge. She fought off snakes who thought to hide under the cover of her boat; freak gusts of wind that tore at her singular sail; and waves that swamped her, stealing away all her supplies.

But she was called the little cockroach for a reason, and here she was.

The skies were crystal clear, which likely meant the worst sort of storm was imminent, and the sun nearly blinded her with the glare off the waves. Her boat, the sail lowered, bobbed just beyond the shadow of the enormous volcano, the only sound the waves crashing against the cliffs.

Lara stood, her knees shaking as she held on to the mast for balance. There was a glint of sunlight hitting glass from the depths of the jungle slopes, but even without it, she knew they were watching.

"Open up," she shouted.

In answer, a loud crack split the air. Lara swore, watching as the boulder flew through the air toward her. It hit the water a few paces away, soaking her, the waves nearly flipping her boat.

Climbing back to her feet from where she'd been cowering in the bottom, she dug her fingers into the mast, fighting to master her fear of the water all around.

"Hear me out, Ahnna!" The other Ithicanians would've hit her on the first shot. Only the princess would bother to terrorize her first. "If you don't like what I have to say, you can throw me back into the sea."

Nothing stirred. There was no sound other than the roar of the ocean.

Then, a rattle split the air, the distinctive sound of the gates to Eranahl opening. Picking up her paddle, Lara maneuvered her way inside.

Familiar faces filled with cold fury met her as the boat knocked against the steps. She didn't fight as Jor jerked her out by the hair, the stone stairs biting into her shins as he dragged her up, snarling, "I'd cut your heart out here and now if not for the fact Ahnna deserves the honor." He pulled a hood over her head, obscuring her vision.

They took her to the palace, the sounds and smells painfully familiar, and as she counted the steps and turns, Lara knew she was being taken to the council room. Someone, probably Jor, kicked the backs of her knees once they entered, and she fell, palms slapping against the ground.

"You have a lot of nerve coming back, I'll give you that."

The hood was ripped from her head. Pushing upright, Lara met Ahnna's gaze, her stomach tightening at the cruel scar that now ran from the midpoint of the woman's forehead down to her cheekbone. That she hadn't lost her eye was a miracle. Surrounding her were some half a dozen soldiers, all who bore the marks of having barely escaped Southwatch with their lives. And behind them, hanging on the wall, was a large map of Maridrina.

"Give me one good reason why I shouldn't slit your throat, you traitorous bitch."

Lara forced a smile onto her face. "It's not very creative."

A boot caught her in the ribs, flipping her over. Pressing a hand against her side, Lara cast a dark look at Nana, whose boot it had been, before returning her attention to the woman in power. "You won't slit my throat because my father has Aren as his prisoner."

Ahnna's jaw tightened. "A fact that does not help your cause."

"We need to get him back."

"We?" The princess's voice was incredulous. "Your father has Aren inside his palace in Vencia, which I'm sure you know is a veritable fortress guarded by the elite of the Maridrinian army. My *best* haven't been able to so much as get inside. Every one of them has died trying. By all means, humor me with why *you* will be any help at all. Will you *seduce* your way in, whore?"

Lara stared her down, the silence hanging in the room stifling.

For fifteen years, she'd been trained how to infiltrate an impenetrable kingdom.

How to discover weaknesses and exploit them.

How to destroy her enemies.

How to be merciless.

She'd been born for this.

Yet Lara said nothing because words would not convince these people who believed—rightly—that she was a liar.

Breathe in. Breathe out.

She moved.

These were battle-hardened warriors, but the element of surprise was hers. And she was what she was. Holding nothing back, she whirled, fists and feet a blur as she disarmed the soldiers around her, knocking them down. Driving them back.

Ahnna launched at her with a scream, but Lara snaked a foot around her leg, and rolled with her, coming up with the tall princess in a chokehold, the other woman's knife in her free hand.

Silence filled the room, the warriors regaining their feet and eyeing her with a new and healthy respect even as they considered how they could disarm her.

Lara cast her eyes around the room, meeting each gaze individually before releasing Ahnna's throat. The other woman rolled away, gasping, eyes full of shock. Lara rose to her feet.

"You need me, because I know our enemy. I was raised by them to be their greatest weapon, and you've seen firsthand what I can do. What they never considered is that their greatest weapon might turn on them." And Lara wasn't the only weapon they'd created: There were ten other young women out there who owed her a life debt, which she fully intended to call due.

"You need me because I am the Queen of Ithicana." Twisting, she threw the knife in her hand, watching as it embedded in the map, marking Vencia—and Aren—with perfect precision. "And it's time my father was brought to his knees."

LOVED THE BRIDGE
KINGDOM?

Then read on for the first chapter of . . .

THE

TRAITOR
QUEEN

H E'D BEEN BLINDFOLDED for thirteen days.

Shackled too, and occasionally gagged, but despite the persistent burn of the ropes sloughing the skin of his wrists and the foul taste of the fabric shoved in his mouth, it was the endless shadow of the blindfold that was driving Aren, the former King of Ithicana, to the brink of madness.

For while pain was an old friend, and discomfort almost a way of life, to be confined to what sights his own mind could conjure was the worst sort of torture. Because despite his most fervent wish it were otherwise, all his mind wanted to show him were visions of *her.*

Lara.

His wife.

The Traitor Queen of Ithicana.

Aren had more pressing matters to consider, the foremost how the *bloody hell* he was going to escape the Maridrinians. Yet the practicalities of that need faded as he examined every moment with *her,* trying and failing to decipher truth from lie, reality from the act—though to what end he could not say. What did knowing if any of it had been real *matter* when the bridge was lost, his people were dead and dying, his kingdom was on the brink of defeat, and all of it the result of him trusting in—*loving*—his enemy.

I love you. Her voice and face filled his thoughts, honey hair tangled, her azure eyes bright with tears that carved their way through the mud smearing her cheeks.

Truth or lie?

Aren wasn't sure which answer would be a balm to the wound and which would tear it wide open again. A wise man would leave it alone, but God knew he had no claim to that particular attribute, so around he circled, her face, her voice, her touch consuming him as the Maridrinians dragged him, kicking and fighting, from his fallen kingdom. Only once he was off the seas and beneath the heat of the Maridrinian skies did he get his wish: the blindfold removed.

Wishes were the dreams of fools.